Sentinel

Trudie Collins

DEDICATION

This book is dedicated to Casey Mallia – an angel who
returned to heaven far too soon

ACKNOWLEDGMENTS

Thank you to Pete, Julie, Terry and Wendy for their feedback.

A special mention to Master Clint and Master John for teaching me an alternative way to shoot arrows.

Chapter summary

Prologue

My name is Adara Marie and I am dead. It's not as bad as it sounds. I still get to see the people I love, but seeing them is all I can do. Also, I can now remember almost everything that happened to me. I can see everything I did, after the age of about five, clearly as if it was only yesterday; every action, every interaction, every conversation.

I have not moved on and will not do so until HE is dead. HE who is responsible for my death. And here he comes now, holding hands with a beautiful young girl. He is as stunning as always, dressed in his black cloak with the gold leaf design on the trim. His handsome face looks up to me, but he cannot see me. Sometimes he can, but not today, though he knows I am here. He can always sense when I am watching him. He looks back at the girl and smiles, but I know the cruelty behind that smile, and the heartache.

I want to say something to her, but I can't. Being a ghost means I can't touch anything or communicate with anyone, no matter how hard I try. Maybe one day I will find a way. For now, all I can do is watch.

My name is Adara Marie and this is my story.

Introduction

Let me introduce myself. When I was born, I became the fifth, and last, child of King Andrast and Queen Cyan, rulers of the kingdom of Amanet.

I would tell you that the first three years of my life were great, that I was loved by my entire family and wanted for nothing, but I have no memory of those years. Everything changed when I was three. At least I assume it did. That's when my mother died.

I have been told that the fever took her fast and that she didn't suffer, though whether that was just something I was told to make me feel better I have no idea.

I have no memories of her. I have no idea what she looked like, whether she sang lullabies to me, whether she cuddled me. My siblings tell me she did and I believe them. Why wouldn't I?

I know I missed her, but I was so young when she left my life that it didn't take long for my feelings to change. I ended up missing having a mother rather than missing her as a person.

I was brought up by my nanny and the servants. Would it have been different had my mother lived? I'm not sure. I tell myself it would have. Sometimes I believe myself, other times I don't.

Father was a busy man; he did have a kingdom to run after all. He loved all of his children and spent as much time with them as he could, but I didn't see him often. He was a good ruler, well-liked by his people. He tried to always do the right thing, but, like any human, he didn't always succeed.

And he loved my mother. A lot. My siblings have told me how happy they seemed to be together and how he mourned her death. Part of me thinks he continued to do so until the day he died.

But enough about my childhood. Skip forward several years to when I was sixteen. That was when I first heard that HE would be living with us; the Sentinel.

I knew what a Sentinel was, of course. Unbeknownst to my father, I attended lessons with my brothers. Their tutor didn't mind and everyone kept it a secret from the king. In Amanet, like most other kingdoms, only males are educated. 'A woman's place is looking after her husband' was one of my eldest sister's favourite sayings. All she ever thought about was who she would marry and when. Neither Rosemerta (we all called her Rose) nor Olwen, my other sister, could understand why I wanted to learn about history, science, mathematics and other kingdoms. They were happy being taught how to read and write and nothing more. They did, however, keep my secret.

My brothers, on the other hand, were both of the belief that if a girl wanted to learn she should be allowed to. Not only did they allow me to attend all of their lessons, they also helped me in their spare time.

They drew the line at combat training. I have never even been allowed to hold a sword, let alone use one. Not that I had any interest in doing so. I watched whenever I was able to though. Archery was different. I received all of the training needed so that I would be able to hunt to feed myself, should the need arise. I would never call myself a marksman, but I became skilled enough to be able to kill a man with just one shot. But that comes later in the story.

Back to the Sentinel. I still remember the day that his imminent arrival was announced as if it was only yesterday.

Announcement

"Why has Father called for a family meeting?" I asked excitedly, grabbing my brother's arm to get his attention.

Etain stopped walking and turned to look at me. At eighteen, he was only two years older than me, but those two years felt like a huge gap. It made him an adult, while I was still classed as a child.

When he smiled at me, his whole face lit up. He was an attractive young man, with broad shoulders, a chiselled face and stunning blue eyes. Ladies flocked to him. His light brown hair, usually tied up, was hanging loose, almost touching his collarbone. This told me that the meeting had taken him as much by surprise as it had me.

"It's not just family," he said. "I have no idea what is going on, but it must be important."

"Maybe Father is marrying you off," a deep voice sounded behind us.

I turned around and saw my other brother approaching. Though a couple of years older than Etain, Tephi was a little shorter. When they were together, it was easy to see the family resemblance.

I, however, looked nothing like them; a fact they regularly teased me about. Of all my siblings, I was the only one to inherit all my features from my mother. Rose had her green eyes and Olwen had her dark brown hair, but only I had both. Father once said that I looked so much like my mother it made him miss her all the more whenever he saw me. Maybe that was why he didn't spend as much time with me as he did the others.

Tephi grinned at me and ruffled my hair. "Come on Squid, we'll never know what the meeting is really about if we stand here talking all day."

He placed his hands on my shoulders and turned me around before giving me a gentle push forward. Unlike Etain, he had taken the time to tie his hair back and make himself more presentable. Then again, he always did make himself look immaculate; as heir to the throne, it was expected of him.

As Etain and Tephi made their way to the throne room, I trailed behind them, listening to their conversation. They were discussing the fact that all of the ladies wanted to dance with Etain at a party they had attended the previous night and only approached Tephi when they were turned down.

This didn't bother Tephi. He knew that Etain was more attractive than him, but Etain never made a comment about it, never bragged or teased his older brother. Tephi was not the jealous type. Enough women wanted his attention to keep him occupied so he was happy to be in his brother's shadow whenever they went out together. He was also aware that his marriage would be arranged; he would have no say in it.

The same applied to all royalty, even my cousins, but if the rest of us ever fell in love and petitioned the king to allow us to marry, he would consider it. Tephi didn't have that option.

Part of me was jealous. I wasn't allowed to attend parties yet, at least not on my own and how much fun can you have with a chaperone watching your every move and never leaving your side?

The doors to the throne room were standing open when we arrived and a number of chairs had been set out. Most were occupied. All of Father's advisers were present, including the commander of the army. This was not a good sign.

Three seats were empty on the front row, next to my sisters, and we quickly sat down.

While waiting for the last few stragglers to arrive, I looked up at the dais. It contained two thrones, but only one was ever occupied. I have been told that my mother often used to sit beside the king as he regularly sought her opinion, but I have no memory of ever seeing her there.

Father was tapping the arm of his throne impatiently. He was usually a calm man and did not anger easily, but he liked punctuality and hated having to wait for others. This time, though, he said nothing. He had called the meeting at short notice so he couldn't expect everyone to arrive on time. This didn't, however, stop him showing his agitation.

If his portraits are to be believed, he used to be a handsome man, but he stopped shaving when my mother died. It was a traditional sign of mourning. Men would remain unshaven for a year; only after twelve months had passed would they remove their facial hair and begin courting once again. Father's beard remained in place, hiding most of his face. He was still mourning my mother. He had not so much as gone on a date with another woman since her death and part of me believed he never would.

I quickly scanned the room, trying to see who was missing. There were a number of visiting dignitaries currently staying in the palace, but none were present. This, too, was not a good sign.

Finally the last person arrived and took his seat. The doors were closed and my father rose.

"Sorry for the short notice," he said, loudly and clearly, "but I wanted you all to hear the news from me before any rumours started."

He took a deep breath before continuing. I was holding mine. I was eager to hear what he was about to announce.

"After many weeks of negotiation, I have secured the employment of a Sentinel."

Gasps filled the room. One of them came from me. A Sentinel! I couldn't help wondering if Father had gone insane. Those people were evil. They tortured for fun. What possible reason could he have for employing one?

Everyone started talking at once, demanding an explanation. Nobody wanted to live under the same roof as one of THEM. The king waited until the noise had died down before continuing.

"He will be here to protect me, my family and this kingdom. Many other rulers employ them and find their skills invaluable. I can assure you he will pose no danger to you or your families, unless, of course, you wish to cause me harm."

That last comment silenced the last few mutterers. "This Sentinel is the first of his kind to be a master in three disciplines of magic."

"Three?" someone called out. "That's not possible."

While it was rare for a magic user to be gifted in two disciplines, it wasn't unknown. Nobody since the written histories began had ever been able to do three.

"Apparently it is," Father said. "This Sentinel is also a Healer and a Shield."

That explained why the king thought he would be of use. As a Sentinel he would be able to detect if anyone speaking to the king was lying, as a Shield he would be able to protect my father and as a Healer he would be able to cure him if he failed to protect him.

That didn't stop me not wanting him in the palace though. Anyone who tortured people should not be allowed in the city let alone the royal residence. I strongly believed that all Sentinels were evil and sadistic, regardless of their other talents, and torture should be a crime punishable by death.

Unable to keep my opinions to myself, I opened my mouth, but Tephi grabbed my arm before I could speak. I turned to glare at him and he shook his head at me, silently telling me that there was a time and a place for my objections to be voiced and that a room full of non-family members was not it.

Father was still speaking, oblivious to my altercation with my brother.

"As you can imagine, the rulers of many different kingdoms were interested in obtaining the services of this particular Sentinel, along with multiple members of the aristocracy. Even some of the richer merchants attended discussions. We are very fortunate that he has decided to work for me. He will be treated with courtesy and respect. Have I made myself clear?"

There were a few mumbled replies of, "Yes, your Majesty," but most people just nodded. Looking around, I saw a lot of worried faces. Though many of those present could understand the king's reasoning, it didn't mean they were pleased with the news.

"The Sentinel will arrive early next week," the king said loudly. "Dismissed."

I had never seen the throne room empty so quickly. Soon only Commander Keel and the king's children remained. Keel waited until all of the guards had left and the doors closed before speaking.

"Are you sure this is a good idea, your Majesty?"

Keel was a well-built man of average height. His grey eyes now matched the colour of his hair. It seemed like only yesterday that it had been black. I had known him all of my life. He was well into his sixties and should have been due for retirement, but his apprentice was still in training and Keel wouldn't leave the kingdom under-defended if it could be avoided.

I was glad he had been the first to speak. He had a good head on his shoulders and my father listened to him.

Father smiled at him and placed his hand on his shoulder, as though he was an equal rather than his subordinate.

"I understand your concern old friend, but you have nothing to worry about. Sentinels have a bad reputation because people do not understand what they do."

I couldn't remain silent any longer. "What is there to understand? They use torture to make people say whatever they want to hear. They are monsters."

King Andrast looked at Keel rather than me when he replied. "See what I mean." There was no anger in his voice. It almost sounded as if he was amused.

He turned to look at me, then glanced at each of my siblings, making sure we were all paying attention.

"As you are well aware, a Sentinel can detect if someone is lying. I have no idea how, but what I do know is that they can't make anyone say anything they want. All they can do is make them tell the truth."

He then looked up, as though he could see the sky instead of the ceiling. "If I said that the sun was blue, a Sentinel would know that I was lying and would be able to force me to admit that it is yellow. Could their methods be classed as torture?" He shrugged his shoulders. "I have no idea. I have never seen one in action."

"But everyone knows that the sun is yellow, Father," Etain said. "I don't understand why you need a Sentinel to tell you that."

Father put his hands together like he was praying and tapped them against his top lip. It was a habit he had when he was thinking.

"Imagine I was blind and had been told that the sun was blue. If I repeated this information, I would have no way of knowing if I was telling the truth or not. A Sentinel would not be able to force to me to say the sun was any colour other than blue."

"So they don't make people tell the truth, the person speaking just has to believe that they are not lying," Olwen said.

"Precisely. If I asked someone a question and they refused to answer, they wouldn't be lying so a Sentinel would be powerless to make them tell me the truthful answer to my question. Am I making any sense?"

"You are," Keel confirmed. "I have no more questions. Unless you have further need of me, I will depart."

Father nodded his head and Keel left the room, though he still looked troubled.

"How much is this Sentinel going to cost Father?" Tephi asked. "As heir to the throne, I think I have the right to know."

The king winced. "A lot. There was a bidding war, which we didn't win. I went as high as I thought was reasonable, but the price kept going up. Nobody was more surprised than me when the Sentinel chose to take up my offer."

"Is he worth it?"

Father shrugged. "I don't know. I have been led to believe so. Only time will tell."

"What do we call him?" Rose asked. "We can't just call him Sentinel. It seems rude."

"You often call Keel 'commander', Rosemerta. What's the difference?"

"Commander is a rank."

"So is Sentinel. It's the highest rank in relation to magic users."

"That's different."

"Why?"

Rose had no answer.

Tephi broke the silence. "Where will he be staying? Far away from the family I hope."

"I am arranging for one of the suites in the guest wing to be prepared for him. He requested that he be positioned close to where any visitors would be put up, just in case he needed to listen in on them."

"Spy on them you mean," I muttered.

Father ignored me. "He has also requested a workroom."

He said workroom, but I heard torture chamber.

I wasn't the only one feeling uneasy about the imminent arrival of the magic user. Olwen had distrusted all magic users ever since she had had her fortune told and it didn't come true. The fact the woman had been a charlatan with no real magical ability was irrelevant, as far as Olwen was concerned.

"How will we be able to sleep at night, knowing he might attack us?" she asked.

Father did not take the question well. "I would expect that sort of thinking to come from a servant," he shouted, "but not from my own daughter. Of course you won't be attacked. The Sentinel will only use his abilities to protect the safety of this family and our realm. What do you think he is? Some sort of sadist who enjoys torturing people and will do it to anyone?"

I wasn't the only one to nod my head.

"Then you have a lot to learn. Sentinels are no different to you and me. They have a talent that they use for the benefit of others. It doesn't mean they enjoy doing so."

"But—" Rose started to say but Father cut her off.

"There are no buts. This is going to happen whether you like it or not. The Sentinel will be coming here and you will treat him properly." He emphasised each 'will'.

Then he smiled and softened his tone. "Besides, once you get to know him, you might like him. He is around your age."

The comment took me by surprise. Tephi, too, looked confused.

"I thought it took many years for a magic user to graduate, especially Sentinels."

"Usually it does. Not only is this one gifted in three disciplines, he is also a fast learner. He is the youngest person to ever leave the academy in Sobek. All of the teachers there taught him everything they know so there was no reason for him to remain."

Father didn't see the calculating look that crossed Rose's face, but I did. I knew what she was thinking, but hoped I was wrong. He was young, talented, earned a lot of money and was, hopefully, available. If he was also attractive, Rose would definitely be making a play for him. I suddenly started to feel a little sorry for him.

Arrival

The day of the Sentinel's arrival came all too quickly for me. Despite Father's assurances, I still couldn't bring myself to trust the man. Yes, I know that I should have had an open mind and given him the benefit of the doubt until I got to know him, but I was sixteen. Need I say anything more?

Unable to get rid of the nervous tension inside me, I sought out my brothers. I had some questions that one of them hopefully could answer. I know I could have asked the Sentinel when he arrived, but that would involve speaking to him and that was something I planned to avoid doing for as long as possible.

I found Etain in his room and he was more than happy to educate me.

"Why do all magic users come from the kingdom of Sobek? Why are none ever born in other kingdoms?"

"They are," Etain said. "And technically it's a queendom not a kingdom."

My confusion must have shown on my face as he continued without me asking him to.

"It's currently ruled by a queen, not a king, therefore it is a queendom."

I had never given the word 'kingdom' much thought before, but what Etain was saying made sense.

"Not that anyone has ever seen her," he continued.

That had me intrigued. "You are going to need to explain that."

"Whenever she is out in public, she wears a thick veil. To the best of my knowledge, nobody other than her personal maids and maybe her bodyguards have ever seen her face. It's tradition there. No member of the royal family must show their face. Don't ask me why, I have no idea. She also uses magic to disguise her voice and is only ever seen seated and wearing bulky clothes. Her real size is a mystery. The person everyone sees may even be a decoy."

"Are you saying that she could visit here pretending to just be a noblewoman and nobody would know any different?"

Etain nodded his head.

"Does she ever do that sort of thing?" I asked.

This time Etain shrugged. "How should I know? I would be surprised though. I doubt her bodyguards would allow it."

"She could order them to."

Etain laughed. "Can you imagine how Keel would react if Father tried that? He would immediately be placed under house arrest until he changed his mind. There are some orders that can be ignored."

I could easily picture Commander Keel doing just as Etain had suggested and had to smile.

"But back to your first question," Etain said. "Magic users are born in every kingdom. A group of people from Sobek spend their entire lives travelling, looking for youngsters with magical ability. They are known as Seekers. Everyone is tested, from the richest noble to the poorest peasant. If magic is detected, once they reach a certain age, they are offered a place at the academy."

"So it's optional?" I asked.

"Yes. Nobody is forced to go. The magic inside them has to be activated for them to use it and that can only be done at the academy. If they choose not to go, the magic inside them never surfaces and they live normal lives."

"So why do all magic users say they are from Sobek instead of the kingdom they were born in?" I wasn't just asking these questions to pass the time and take my mind off the arrival of the Sentinel; I was genuinely interested.

"When someone joins the academy, they have to give up their citizenship and swear their allegiance to the ruler of Sobek. While they can work for other kingdoms after they graduate, their loyalty will remain with Sobek. It means that if war breaks out between two kingdoms, magic users won't become involved. They will act as peace negotiators and healers, but won't fight, not even the Warriors."

"So what's to stop Sobek declaring war on all other kingdoms? If all magic users were on the side of Sobek, no other kingdom would stand a chance."

"Nothing," Etain said. "They just have no interest in doing so."

"If they won't fight, why do they have Warriors?"

"I never said they won't fight, they just won't fight in a war between kingdoms. They are often used to hunt down groups of bandits and in the past have been deployed to restore a ruler to the throne when they have been removed due to an illegal coup. Also, they will defend any kingdom in the alliance against aggression by those outside of it."

"Alliance?" I asked. I had heard it mentioned before but didn't know many details.

"Most realms formed an alliance with Sobek. If we allow our children to move to Sobek and be trained, we are allowed to employ magic users. Not all kingdoms agreed and those few who didn't never let magic users cross their borders."

"So what can you tell me about the disciplines? How do the teachers know which students have which abilities?"

"That I don't know a lot about. I know that there is a ceremony for all new recruits. They have to go and see the Oracle, one at a time, and return with a coloured band to show which discipline they will be trained in, but that's about it. Maybe you should ask the Sentinel when he arrives."

I returned Etain's grin with a glare. He knew how I felt about the Sentinel and I didn't like him teasing me.

"How did I not know any of this?" I asked. I attended most of Etain's lessons but none of what he had just told me had ever been mentioned.

He chuckled. "I learned all of that during the week Father forced you to take needlework lessons."

I grimaced. It had been one of the worst weeks of my life. From day one the woman teaching my sisters had made it clear that I had no ability in that area and never would. She wasn't wrong. I couldn't even thread a needle. I didn't learn how to do that until I was much older, but I will tell you about that later.

Needless to say, I did all I could to make the woman complain to my father that I was unteachable and soon I was back in the classroom with my brothers.

Before I could ask anything more, the sound of a gong being struck reverberated around the palace. The visitor had arrived.

At his request, there would not be an official reception committee, but if he had been hoping to make an unobtrusive arrival, he was going to be sorely disappointed.

Etain and I both ran from his room to the balcony which overlooked the main corridor. My father would meet the new arrival there, along with a number of his advisers. And Tephi, of course. The rest of us had not been ordered to attend, but that wouldn't stop us watching from a distance.

Rose and Olwen were already there when we arrived. As soon as we heard the sound of the main door opening, we leaned over the barrier to try to get a look at the new employee.

A man approached, wrapped in a black cloak with a gold leaf design along the edges. He was of average height and build, at least that is the impression I got at the time. It was impossible to know more with a cloak wrapped around him. The hood was up, obscuring most of his face, other than a clean shaven, nicely shaped chin. He was wearing dark glasses, which he removed as he entered the palace.

When he reached my father, he removed his hood and I wasn't the only one to gasp. He was completely bald, with what looked like scars forming intricate patterns all over his scalp.

He must have heard our sharp intakes of breath, because he looked up in our direction. I gasped again. He was gorgeous, there is no other word I can use. His face was absolutely stunning.

His eyes, however, ruined the effect. They were completely black; there was no white or colour in them at all. I felt repulsed by them, yet I couldn't look away.

"His eyes are dreamy," I heard Rose say. "The sort you can lose yourself in."

I thought they looked hard and cold. I wanted nothing more than to turn my head, but I was unable to even move my eyes until he broke the contact to look at my father and respond to something he had said.

As soon as I was able to move, I ran from the balcony and shut myself in my bedroom. This was not a man I could be friends with and I vowed to have as little to do with him as possible. Yes, I know I was judging the man based on his looks, but I couldn't help it. I always believed that the eyes are the pathways to the soul and this man didn't have one.

My vow, however, didn't include spying on him. When I was very young, I discovered that there are secret passageways running between all of the rooms in the palace and I found a way to get into them from my room. Of course I told nobody and would regularly walk the castle alone, secretly observing the occupants.

I also found that there were spy holes from the passageways into most of the rooms. I couldn't resist seeing what the Sentinel had in his bags, both hoping and dreading seeing torture devices. I quickly lit my small lamp, opened the secret door in the panelling and entered the passageways.

It was dark inside, my lamp providing the only light. I made my way to the guest wing then to the suite which had been allocated to the new houseguest. I arrived just as he was entering.

Before removing the cover from the spyhole, I covered the lamp so it would emit no light. The last thing I wanted was for the Sentinel to see the small hole in the wall and the lamplight would have given it away.

I watched as he unpacked his bag, disappointed that it contained only clothes. Suddenly he straightened up and turned around. If I didn't know better, I would say he was looking directly at me, but he couldn't know I was there and he wouldn't be able to see through the wall.

I shivered, but not from cold. I didn't realise I was holding my breath until he turned his back on me once more, then I exhaled.

I replaced the spyhole's cover and unveiled the lamp. I was shaking as I returned to my room, my tremors making the shadows caused by the lamplight seem eerie.

I stayed in my room until it was time for the evening meal. I didn't want to leave in case I ran into him. I desperately wanted to eat alone in my room, but Father would never allow it. Unless he had important business to discuss with a visitor, he liked to dine with all of his family, now that we were older.

I was the last to arrive in the reception room. Everyone was standing around, sipping on goblets of wine. I would only be allowed fruit juice, much to my annoyance.

"This is my youngest daughter, Adara," Father said as soon as he saw me approaching. I nodded my head at the Sentinel and he held out his hand to me. I had no choice but to shake it. It was surprisingly smooth and warm. Instead of letting my hand go, he drew it to his lips and kissed the back of it. The unexpected gesture had me flustered and I wasn't sure how I should react. He kept his eyes on mine the whole time as though he was studying me.

"I am delighted to meet you." His voice was soft and nothing like what I was expecting. "My name is Tallis."

I have no idea why he told me his name. I had no intention of addressing him as anything other than Sentinel.

He released my hand and returned his attention to my father. Rose grabbed my arm and pulled me away.

"Don't look so smug," she hissed at me once we were far enough away not to be overheard. What she thought I had to look smug about I had no idea. "He kissed me and Olwen as well."

Did she honestly think I had enjoyed that? Her next sentence confirmed that she did.

"He's mine. Keep your hands and eyes to yourself."

"You're more than welcome to him," I truthfully told her. "The less I see of him, the happier I'll be."

"Good," she said then turned her back on me and walked back to where the Sentinel was.

Olwen moved closer to me. "Well he's won one of us over already it seems." I could hear the amusement in her voice. "Maybe we should warn him."

There was no malice in her statement. Olwen is one of the sweetest and most sincere women I have ever met. While, at the time, Rose considered herself the superior sister in looks, Olwen definitely won on the personality front. Not that I ever agreed with Rose's view. While I am willing to admit she was very pretty, in my opinion, Olwen was beautiful. Men end up gathered around Rose, but they always made a beeline for Olwen first, only turning to Rose when Olwen's shyness put them off. Rose, however, never noticed that.

I found the meal tedious. For once I was wearing a formal dress. I hated it and found it uncomfortable. While I am happy to wear light summer dresses, formal gowns I always found unnecessary and avoided them as much as possible. Before you ask, no I did not dress up for the Sentinel. Father made it clear that I had no choice in the matter. He wanted to give a good impression for the new arrival's first night.

I ended up having to sit next to the Sentinel when he chose the seat beside me instead of the only other spare one, which was beside Rose. It wasn't my fault and I didn't want him there, but that didn't stop my sister glaring at me the whole time.

The Sentinel was polite, always replying whenever Rose spoke to him, but he never asked her anything, always turning his attention to someone else as soon as he could without it being considered rude.

My father and brothers were fascinated by him and inundated him with questions. I didn't. I replied, if he spoke to me, but I kept my answers short. The first time I called him Sentinel, he said I could call him Tallis. I ignored him.

The second time I called him Sentinel, my father intervened.

"I apologise for my daughter. She is very strong willed, as you can probably see."

Tephi smirked at me. "Yes, she can be a little prickly," he said and rubbed my head, messing up my hair. I didn't care. He would never have done it if he thought it would bother me. He wouldn't have dared to try it on Rose; she would have probably stabbed his hand with a fork.

"I appreciate her showing her real personality," the Sentinel said. "I hate people pretending to be someone they aren't."

I may have been imagining it, but I'm sure he glanced at Rose when he said that.

As soon as the meal was over, the men retired to one of the formal lounges for brandy. Rose wanted to join them, but it was tradition that the men spent some time alone after the evening meal so she was politely told to find something else to do.

I went to my room and changed into something more comfortable; trousers and a silk shirt I had stolen from Etain. He didn't mind; he said the colour suited me better.

I didn't want to, but I couldn't help thinking about the Sentinel. He wasn't what I imagined. He was polite and friendly; my brothers seemed to have taken to him instantly. And he was so attractive it was hard not to stare at him, as long as you avoided his eyes.

But that didn't change who he was or what he did and I was sure it was something I would never be able to get over.

It wasn't until I went to bed that I realised that not once since his arrival had I seen him smile.

Shield

The Sentinel hadn't been with us long when he used his skills as a Shield for the first time. As I often did when they trained, I went with my brothers to the training arena where they were joined by a number of soldiers. I was never allowed to join in, but I enjoyed watching.

I would never have gone if I had known HE was going to be there. I had no idea why he was there. Later, I asked him about it and he said he felt it was where he needed to be.

It was a day just like any other. There was no indication that an attempt would be made on my brother's life. The men were sparring one-on-one, using real swords and shields. And they weren't holding back. When under the watchful eye of Keel, the soldiers always fully committed, even when fighting the heir to the throne. They would regret it if they didn't.

I enjoyed watching the soldiers work out; all those hot sweaty bodies dressed in very little. They always stripped down to fight, much to my pleasure. I was surprised that Rose never joined me; she would definitely have enjoyed all of those bulging biceps and thigh muscles on display. Maybe she was put off by our brothers being present. I did my best to not watch them too closely.

It was a warm day, with a cool breeze preventing the temperature from becoming uncomfortable. I was entranced watching two tall soldiers fight as the clash of metal hitting metal sounded around the arena. Suddenly a voice sounded beside me, making me jump.

"Do you mind if I join you?"

I didn't have to turn around to see who it was. HE had a distinctive voice. I wanted to say I did mind. I wanted to yell at him to leave me alone, but I had been brought up to behave better than that. Not that I was exactly polite.

I shrugged my shoulders. "Sit where you want, Sentinel."

He sat down beside me, close enough that we could talk without having to raise our voices, but not so close I would feel uncomfortable.

"Thank you, your Highness." He always called me that. Never Adara or princess. Always 'your Highness'. Maybe it was in retaliation to me calling him Sentinel. Or maybe it was just the way he had been told to address me. He did the same when talking to my brothers, but when speaking with them it sounded like a mark of respect, whereas his tone when he called me Highness always made me feel he was mocking me somehow.

Father, of course, was always called 'your Majesty'. Never King Andrast or just Andrast. He called Olwen 'my Lady,' and she seemed to like it. It made her smile. Rose was Princess. Not Princess Rose or Princess Rosemerta, just Princess. The way the Sentinel said the word made me believe he didn't like my sister very much, though she was oblivious to this. I'm sure she flirted with him whenever Father wasn't around.

We sat in silence for a while, watching the men practice their skills. The Sentinel was watching them intently and I momentarily wondered if that was the reason he didn't seem to like the attention Rose paid to him, but then I put the thought from my mind. He gave no indication that he was lusting after any of the men. Instead it was almost as if he was looking for something, but didn't know what.

"Why are your eyes black?" I suddenly blurted out.

He dragged his gaze away from the arena and looked at me. His eyes bore into mine, making me shiver. I forced myself to look away.

"They used to be blue," he said. "All of my family had the same colour eyes, until my assessment by the Oracle."

He turned his attention back to the fighting, but something told me he wasn't really seeing it; his mind was on the past.

It was then I noticed that he was wearing his cloak. I had never seen him without it, even when he was inside the palace.

"Aren't you hot in this thing?" I asked, pulling on the sleeve to get his attention.

He shook his head. "No. It's enchanted. It has inbuilt temperature control. I am probably a lot cooler than you are right now."

I almost asked if I could give it a try, but he continued speaking before I could.

"Now, do you want to hear about my assessment or not?"

I nodded my head and was surprised to realise I wasn't just being polite; I was genuinely interested. In the process, of course, not in the man undergoing it.

"Everyone with magical ability who wishes to train has to see the Oracle. She has her own cottage on the palace estate in Sobek. It's well protected by numerous magic users. Nobody gets to see the Oracle unless she wants them to."

"What is she like?" I asked.

"Young," he said. "Surprisingly young. She looked no more than a teenager. A little younger than you are now. I was expecting a haggard old woman, seeing as my parents both went to see her."

"Your parents are both magic users?" I blurted out, then blushed when I realised how rude I was being.

He didn't seem phased by the interruption. "Yes. Magic runs strong in my family. My brother is also a magic user. He's a Warrior as well as a Cloak."

While I wanted to know more about what skills a Cloak had, I was still confused as to how both of the Sentinel's parents could be magic users.

"I thought magic users couldn't marry other magic users."

"There is no law forbidding it, but it is very rare. In my kingdom you are either a master or a slave, an owner or property. Magic users are always owners and their spouse is always a slave."

It took me a moment to work out what that meant. "Are you saying your father owns your mother?" The thought filled me with revulsion.

He shook his head. "No. My father loved my mother so much he could not bear the thought of owning her, so he put aside his ego and became her slave."

The pride in his voice when he spoke was unmistakable. There was obviously more to being a slave than just being owned and he admired his father for making such a sacrifice for his mother.

But I didn't ask. I wanted to know more about the Oracle. "So the Oracle was young," I said, hoping he would take my hint and continue his story.

"Apparently not, though she looked it. During my training, I did some research. We have had the same Oracle for over a hundred years. There have been others and a new one presents themselves to us within days of one dying, but our current Oracle has been with us for a long time."

"Where do they come from?"

"Nobody knows."

He was looking into the arena once again. Everyone had swapped partners and my two brothers were now fighting each other.

"They're very good, aren't they."

I glanced over at them. It looked like they were trying to kill each other. They were evenly matched. While Etain had the advantage of height, Tephi was the stronger of the two.

I'd seen them fight many times before and was more interested in what the Sentinel had to say.

"So what happened?" I asked, dragging his attention back to our discussion. "How did she find out what fields of magic would be your forte?"

"That I'm still not sure about. She placed her hands on either side of my face and looked me in the eyes. Without saying a word, she let one hand drop to her side while the other took my hand and she led me into her kitchen, where cups of tea were waiting for us. Then we just talked. About me. About my life, what interested me, that sort of thing. When our drinks were finished, she traced her finger around my wrist, twice, and these two coloured bands appeared."

"Only two?" I couldn't help interrupting him to ask as he held his arm out so I could see his wrist.

He nodded his head. "Yes, only two. The green is for a Healer and the blue is for a Shield. I was overjoyed when I saw them. Being given a double band is a huge honour. I didn't know my eyes had turned black until I left her cottage and the crowd who had been waiting for me gasped."

Suddenly he stiffened up. "Something's wrong."

I had no doubt that he was telling the truth. He wasn't panicking, but his voice was full of conviction. He was making a statement, not an assumption.

I looked about me wildly, but could see nothing out of place. Other than my brothers and the soldiers, we were the only ones in sight. The Sentinel, too, was looking for the source of his concern, but his eyes were fixed entirely on the fighting going on in the arena.

My brothers were still trying to kill each other, or at least that's what it looked like, while others were doing the same to their assigned partner. A couple got close to the two princes, but moved away before they got too close.

Keel's eyes were on a pair of young recruits, giving them pointers on how they could improve. Again the other two soldiers moved closer to my brothers, one aggressively attacking, driving the other back toward them.

Suddenly, the one under attack span around, raised his sword and stabbed down at Tephi's unprotected back. It all happened so fast I could do nothing more than scream out Tephi's name, but my warning would arrive too late.

But I wasn't the only one to see the attack. The Sentinel was on his feet, his arms outstretched toward the edge of the arena where my brothers were.

I watched in horror as the soldier's sword descended, but it never made contact. It bounced off as though Tephi was protected by some sort of invisible shield. Only then did I realise that he was, that the Sentinel was protecting him.

Hearing unexpected noise so close behind him, Tephi turned around and he used his shield to protect himself against his brother's attack. He wasn't prepared for a second attack, this one a real one, from another direction. The soldier had recovered from the shock of his sword not penetrating his target's back and slashed at Tephi's unprotected side.

Again the attack failed. Etain immediately saw what was happening and his next sword thrust was not aimed at his brother but at the soldier who was attacking him. By the time anyone else could intervene, my two brothers had the would-be assassin disarmed and lying on the ground on his back.

I was too far away to hear what was said, but when Keel rushed over it was obvious that Tephi was commanding him not to kill the traitor. Surrounded by numerous armed men, all with swords pointing at him, the man could do nothing other than wait for death.

Seeing that his Shield was no longer required, the Sentinel let his arms drop and ran down the steps to the arena floor. I ran after him.

"Thank you," Tephi said as soon as he noticed him. "You saved my life."

The Sentinel merely shrugged his shoulders. "It's what I am here to do."

"This piece of garbage," Keel said, unable to keep the anger out of his voice as he pointed to the prone man on the ground, "is refusing to speak. I want to know what his plans were and who sent him. Can you make him talk?"

I already knew that a Sentinel could make someone tell the truth, but only if they had told a lie; if they were refusing to speak, there was nothing he could do, so you can imagine my surprise when the Sentinel said, "Take him to my workroom."

Then the soldier began to cry out. "No, please, I beg you, don't do this. I'll talk. I'll tell you everything you want to know."

A shiver went down my spine when the Sentinel said, "I know you will."

With a nod of the head from Keel, two of the soldiers took hold of the man's arms and pulled him roughly to his feet, then dragged him away. His screams continued until he was far enough away for us to no longer hear him.

Tephi and Etain both handed their swords and shields to a young trainee who had rushed over then instructed Keel to accompany them to the Sentinel's workroom. One of the other soldiers was sent to find the king.

The Sentinel turned to me. "Do not come with us. You might not like what you see."

I was about to tell him that he had no right to order me around when I caught Tephi's warning shake of his head. "Listen to him," he said.

I felt like storming off. I didn't like being told what to do. But they were right; I really didn't want to witness the Sentinel interrogating the man. I hated him for trying to kill my brother, but I could never condone torture, no matter what the reason.

Later that evening, Tephi came to see me in my room. He didn't have to tell me what he had found out, but he knew that I would be interested. The man had told him everything he knew.

Many generations ago, my ancestors won the throne in battle. It was the last civil war to affect my kingdom. Since then, the crown has been passed down from eldest son to eldest son. The relatives of the man who lost that fight were allowed to remain on their lands in the north of the realm, though many said the entire family should have been slaughtered.

A few hundred years later, the resentment against my family came to a boil when the new head of the family decided to get revenge. He knew that he didn't have enough men or money to launch an uprising, so decided instead to hire an assassin. The chosen man joined the army, becoming a trusted member of the unit, biding his time until the opportunity arose for him to kill one of my brothers or my father.

He wasn't the only assassin hired and two other men stood beside him when my father had them executed.

By the time Tephi had finished speaking, I was hugging myself and I couldn't stop shivering. Tephi put his arm around me, but he misunderstood the cause of my distress.

"Everyone is safe now," he said gently. "We are sure there are no more of them waiting in the shadows to kill us."

"How did he do it?" I asked. "How did he make the man talk?"

Part of me didn't want the details, but another part of me had to know.

Tephi smiled. I wanted to hit him. He was about to describe what method of torture was used and he was smiling at me.

"He didn't," he said. "Just the threat of using his powers on the man was enough to make him talk. All the Sentinel did was confirm that nothing he said was a lie."

I'm not sure why, but I felt a little disappointed.

"I have to go," Tephi said. "Father has decided to pay the man's employer a little visit. I'm going with him, along with two companies of soldiers. And Tallis."

He didn't need to say any more. I suddenly felt a little sorry for the man who had arranged to have my brother assassinated.

Poison

It wasn't many months later that the Sentinel saved the life of another member of my family.

A trader from a different kingdom had requested an audience with my father. He had a new type of drink he wished him to be the patron of. As he always was when my father had official visitors, the Sentinel was close by. I, on the other hand, was not permitted to be in attendance. Had I been male, it wouldn't have been an issue, but seeing as I was female, I had to make do with watching from the secret passageways.

The tradesman was short with a rat like face. He didn't look like someone I would want to do business with, but then again, you can't always judge someone by what they look like. Yes, before you say anything, I do see the irony in that statement. After all, isn't that what I was doing with the Sentinel, judging him based on what he looked like and the reputation of Sentinels?

After bowing low and introducing himself, the man produced a bottle from his bag. It was dark green and filled with liquid.

"As my letter of introduction explained," the man said, "I have found a way to extract the juice from a karmel plant and ferment it." He had a nasally voice which I was sure would soon begin to grate on my nerves.

My father did not look impressed. "Based on the smell the flowers on that plant emit, why would I want to drink the juice?"

The man smiled, revealing yellow teeth. "The juice is extracted from the leaves, not the flowers and I can assure you the aroma is pleasant. The taste, however, is divine."

My father glanced at the Sentinel, who nodded. The man wasn't lying. It didn't mean his drink really did taste good, just that the man believed it did.

As he always did when meeting petitioners or visitors who wished to see the king, the Sentinel was wearing dark glasses to hide the colour of his eyes. Father didn't want anyone to know what the Sentinel was until he needed to use his skills.

"My new beverage is already for sale in a number of kingdoms," the man continued, "but I have not yet set up distribution here. I am offering you first refusal to be my patron in your wonderful realm."

Again the Sentinel nodded when my father flicked his eyes toward him. As he was standing behind the man, on the side of the room, the trader didn't see how he was reacting. He may not have even known he was there, seeing as he had kept his eyes on my father since entering the room.

"Why not try a glass before you make your decision," the man suggested. The word smarmy sprang into my mind. It wasn't a polite way to describe someone, but for this man it seemed fitting.

Father nodded his head then indicated with his arm that the tradesman should use one of the glasses put on a nearby table.

The liquid that poured out of the bottle was a shade of red that made me think of blood, though it was much thinner. The man would have to do something about the colour if he wanted it to sell well.

He filled a glass and walked up to the throne, stopping when he was close enough to offer the glass to my father.

As he always did when on duty, the Sentinel was wearing his cloak with the hood up, hiding the scarred symbols on his head, but from my position I could still clearly see him frown. Suddenly I became worried. If something was troubling the Sentinel then it was something to be concerned about.

I watched as my father lifted the glass up to his nose and sniffed the contents. "You weren't wrong about the smell," he said. He then lifted up the glass and looked at the contents. The natural light in the room allowed us all to see that the liquid was clear, not cloudy. This was a good sign in wine. I have no idea about any other type of beverage.

He moved it to his mouth, but before he could take a sip, the Sentinel spoke. "This looks more like a woman's drink to me. Maybe one of the princesses should try it first."

It must have been my imagination, but I was sure he looked directly at me when he spoke. But he couldn't have known I was there; I was hidden by a wall.

I turned my attention to the trader and was sure I saw a look of panic momentarily cross his face, but he quickly recovered.

"Of course," he said, though his smile didn't meet his eyes. "If that is what his Majesty wishes."

Before Father could respond, the Sentinel did. "Unfortunately none are available currently. Why not leave the drink with us and we will have the king's daughters try it when they return? You may come back to the palace in the morning for his Majesty's decision."

Father didn't react to the Sentinel taking control of the meeting. He only ever spoke if there was something he needed to say. There was a reason for him wanting to delay the tasting of the drink and my father would not question him in public.

"That will not be possible," the man said quickly. "I have appointments in another city tomorrow so must depart tonight."

The man's manner had changed. He had gone from being confident to the point of cockiness to someone who seemed as though they desperately wanted to get out of the throne room as quickly as possible.

"In that case," the Sentinel said, "the king will be more than happy to sample your wares." A look of relief crossed the trader's face. He didn't see the Sentinel hold up his hand to my father, indicating that he should not yet drink. "After you have taken a sip."

Whatever the man had been about to say froze in his throat as all colour drained from his face. "I think I have already taken up too much of your time," he stammered.

"Nonsense," the Sentinel said and moved away from the wall and removed his glasses. As he approached the trader, the man began to shake. He knew exactly what he was without having to be introduced.

"Would you care to explain why you don't want to drink your own beverage?" the Sentinel asked. His voice was so smooth and calm it was almost frightening to listen to. The man shook his head frantically. "I really recommend you do. You don't want to take a visit to my workroom."

Tears began to flow down the man's face and when a dark stain appeared at the front of his trousers I had to put my hand over my mouth to prevent myself laughing out loud. Whatever secret this man was hiding had him terrified and he believed the Sentinel would be able to extract the information from him in some painful and sadistic way.

"Guards," Father called out loudly. Those stationed near the door stood to attention, as did those on either side of the throne. The men stationed behind the throne would not show themselves unless instructed to. "Take this man to the dungeons and have this drink analysed. Keel can interrogate him when we find out what is in the drink."

Father waited for the blubbering man to be dragged from the room before speaking to the Sentinel.

"You suspect poison?" He nodded. "Why?"

"I don't know. I sensed that he was hiding something, even though he hadn't lied. When I suggested giving the drink to your daughters, it concerned him. He tried to hide it, but didn't do a very good job of it. If it had been harmless, drinking it himself wouldn't have worried him so much. The man's a fool."

"Why? For trying to kill me?"

"No, for not doing a very good job of it. Personally, if I was going to poison someone, I would keep drinking it myself, slowly increasing the dosage until I developed an immunity to it. That way, I would be able to drink the tainted liquid to prove it was harmless."

I couldn't believe what I was hearing. By the look on my father's face, neither could he. "Are you serious?" he asked, his voice demonstrating his incredulity.

"Yes. There are a number of different poisons that I can now safely ingest and I am currently working on building up my resistance to another."

My father just stared at him.

I quickly returned to my room. I had no idea if the Sentinel was telling the truth or not, but I had been told that they never lied. Suddenly I was even more frightened of him.

But that didn't stop me going to see him later in the day. I wanted to know if he really would have let me or one of my sisters drink the poison. I didn't believe he would, but I needed to hear him say it.

I was nervous when I knocked on the door. I had never visited his suite before and wasn't sure I should be doing so. He didn't seem pleased to see me when he opened the door.

"How can I help you, your Highness?" he asked. Again it felt like he was mocking me, though I could not fault his politeness in any way.

My nerves got the better of me. "Never mind," I stammered as I turned away.

He grabbed my arm, pulled me into his room and closed the door. I would have screamed had he not stepped away from me.

"You obviously have something on your mind."

To say I was scared is an understatement. It was the first time I had ever been alone in a room with the Sentinel and I'm sure I was physically shaking.

He sat down in a chair and indicated with his hand that I should take the one opposite him. The only reason I didn't run from the room is that I didn't think my legs would hold out that long. I collapsed into the chair instead of calmly sitting down. If my reaction amused him, he didn't show it.

"I will ask again. How can I help you?"

"Would you really have let me or one of my sisters drink the poison?" I blurted out. Only then did I realise what I had said. I wasn't in the room when the trader tried to poison my father so I shouldn't have known what went on.

The Sentinel, however, did not seem surprised by the question. He wasn't even offended. He simply answered it, without changing expression, though he did lean closer to me and looked at me intently.

"Part of my job is to protect the king and his family. That includes you, Olwen and Rosemerta." I was sure I heard a pause before he said the last name. "I will never allow any harm to come to you if I can prevent it."

"Like you did when Tephi was attacked," I said quietly.

"Yes," he replied, just as quietly.

"It is true you can't lie?" I needed to know he was telling me the truth.

To answer me, he pulled back his sleeve, revealing the scars on his arm. "These scars are all over my body. They give me the ability to make people tell the truth. Unfortunately they have the same effect on me. I can tell a lie, I just don't like the consequences when I do."

I didn't ask what he meant. I really did not want to hear any details.

"Thank you," I said and stood up. I felt uncomfortable being so close to him and wanted to get out of his suite as soon as I could, but he had other ideas.

"Are you planning on telling me how you knew what I said?"

I turned around and looked at him. "No."

He almost smiled. I had never seen him smile and was a little disappointed when he didn't quite manage it.

"I scare you, don't I."

It was a statement not a question, but I found myself nodding.

"I can understand why," he continued. "Sentinels have a reputation for being something they're not. Is that why you never use my name?"

"Maybe."

His brow creased as though he was confused. "You're not lying, but you're not being completely honest, though I think you believe you are. You really are fascinating."

I wasn't sure how to react to that, so I said nothing.

"I'll make a deal with you," he said when it became obvious I wasn't going to speak. "You call me Tallis and I won't tell anyone you have found a way into the secret passageways."

I knew I would be wasting my time, but I tried anyway. "I have no idea what you are talking about," I lied.

"Try again. There is absolutely no point in lying to me."

"I don't use them often," I said. He grunted but didn't contradict me. "How long have you known?"

"Since the day I arrived. I felt someone watching me when I was supposedly alone in my rooms. I could sense it was you. To be honest, I was relieved it wasn't Rosemerta."

I burst out laughing. "You really don't like her, do you?" He said nothing. The look he gave me told me all I needed to know. "If you have known about my access to the passageways all this time, why have you not told anyone?"

"Because it's not my business to do so."

"And now you can use the information to blackmail me."

"If that's what you want to call it."

I should have been angry, but I wasn't. "Fine," I said. I could have argued with him, but what would have been the point? "I will obey your wishes. In this matter anyway."

He said nothing until I had opened the door and was about to leave. "Adara. Be careful. Those passageways are dark. Make sure you don't fall and break your ankle. Nobody would know where to find you."

"I'll be fine Tallis," I said then closed the door.

Visitors

So that is how I started to call him Tallis instead of Sentinel. But only when there was nobody else around. And it didn't mean I was beginning to like him. He still scared me. He said he wouldn't let anyone harm me, but I wasn't convinced that included himself.

It wasn't many weeks later when Rose found me reading in the library. "I have been looking everywhere for you," she said. She was almost bouncing up and down in excitement. "You will never guess what I saw."

I marked my page in the book then turned my attention to my sister. She wouldn't leave me in peace until I heard her out. "I'm not in the mood for guessing games."

"I saw Tallis leave the palace dressed in a blue cloak instead of his usual black one." She always called him Tallis, though it seemed to annoy him. "He looked like he was trying to disguise himself so I decided to follow him."

"You did what?"

"I followed him."

"You sneaked out of the palace without an escort?"

"Ssshhh," Rose said, frantically looking around her. "Someone may overhear."

"Do you know how dangerous that is?" I tried it once, but Tephi caught me. I can still remember the lecture he gave me. Thankfully he didn't tell Father.

"Never mind that. Don't you want to know where he went?"

I shrugged my shoulders. "Not really." I wasn't lying. I had no interest in what the Sentinel did in his spare time.

"He went to a brothel."

If Rose had been expecting me to react, she was disappointed. "And?" I said. "Many single men visit brothels. So do many women, or so I've heard. Even some of my friends have. I don't see the big deal."

Personally I had never gone to one. I never had the need. Forn, Tephi's close friend, visited the palace so regularly he had been given his own room, not that he always used it; he was often in mine. We had been sleeping together for nearly a year by then, ever since my sixteenth birthday, but neither of us ever let anyone know. There was nothing in it, other than two people having a bit of fun. Neither of us saw the other as marriage material.

Rose was pouting at me. "I would have thought you would have taken more of an interest."

The comment genuinely surprised me. "Why?"

"You like him. A lot. I've seen you talking together when you thought nobody was watching."

I couldn't prevent myself laughing. "Like him? I can't stand the man. Okay, I admit he isn't as bad as I thought he would be, but he is still a Sentinel, still a torturer. And he still frightens me. If you have ever seen us talking it's because he instigated it and I couldn't find a polite way of getting out of the conversation."

That wasn't entirely true, but it was close enough. I no longer actively avoided him, but I didn't seek him out either. Other than that one time I have already mentioned. I may have found myself going to his suite whenever I was in the secret passageways, but that was only to make sure he wasn't doing anything he shouldn't be.

Not that I always got to see what he was doing. He had purchased a thick velvet curtain and hung it on the wall. He enchanted it so it would close at his command, covering the spyhole. It also prevented any sounds from penetrating into the passageways. He only seemed to close it when he had visitors though.

"I don't believe you," Rose snapped at me. "He's mine so keep your hands off him."

With that, she stormed out of the library, leaving me to stare after her. When she was out of sight, I put her from my mind and returned to my book.

It was a few months later that I got to see a different side of the Sentinel.

We were having an evening meal, with me seated as far away from Tallis as possible, as I usually was, when I saw him suddenly tense. I wasn't the only one.

"What's wrong?" Tephi asked.

"Someone has just materialised in front of the palace. More than one someone."

He didn't sound concerned, but his face betrayed that he was. It was common knowledge that magic users could transport themselves to anywhere they wished, providing they had been there before or had a marker, but usually they let people know in advance. It was the reason that most buildings had warding enchantments placed on them. Nobody wanted a magic user appearing in their bedroom unexpectedly.

Just as suddenly as he had tensed, the Sentinel relaxed and a smile appeared on his face. It was the first time I had ever seen him smile. I had begun to wonder if he was capable of doing so.

"It appears I have visitors," he announced. "Do I have your permission to depart, your Majesty?"

My father nodded his head. "Of course. May I ask who your visitors are?"

"My parents."

There was no way any of us were going to remain seated in the dining room. The food was abandoned and we all left the room with Tallis, much to his disgust. He could not, however, order the royal family around, so he had to put up with it.

The front door was just being opened when we got there, revealing a middle aged couple. The first thing I noticed was the woman's blue eyes. If Tallis's had been the same shade before they turned black, he would have been even more stunning to look at.

The woman, who I assumed was his mother, was of average height and build, being not too fat or too thin. Her long blonde hair contained a trace of grey. She was wearing an elegant sleeveless dress which reached to just below her knees. I found myself looking at her wrist, trying to see what colour band she had. Her bracelet moved when she hugged her son and I glimpsed some green underneath. So she was a Healer, like her son.

Then my eyes sought out Tallis's father and I had to stop myself from gasping. He was a handsome man, for his age, and towered over his wife. What shocked me, however, was the fact that he was completely naked and a chain ran from a collar around his neck to his owner's bracelet. I was already aware that Tallis's mother owned his father, but I never imagined that meant he had to be naked and shackled.

Tallis greeted his father warmly. "Please allow me to introduce you to the king," he said when he stepped back.

The man didn't let his nakedness, nor the fact that he was collared and chained, bother him in any way. He held out his arm, which his wife took, and escorted her down the corridor to where my father was waiting for them.

It was then that I noticed a yellow band on his wrist. I made a mental note to ask Tallis about it later.

"Your Majesty," Tallis said as soon as he reached my father, "this is Macha and Balor, my parents. Ma, pa, this is King Andrast, ruler of Amanet."

Macha and Balor both bowed. As soon as they had finished, Father held out his hand for them to shake. "Delighted to meet you. To what do we owe the pleasure?"

Balor glanced at Macha, who gave the tiniest nod of her head that I almost missed it. "We are in the city on business and decided to take the opportunity to visit our son. I hope you don't mind."

"Not at all." Father smiled at them. "The parents of the man who has already saved my life, and that of my son, are welcome any time." Macha beamed at her son, but said nothing. "We were just in the middle of a meal. Would you care to join us?"

"It will be our pleasure," Macha said. "But we are waiting for one more of our party to arrive."

Tallis had tensed while my father was speaking, but his mother's words made him relax.

"Whoever you have brought with you has just arrived." He then tensed again. "What is she doing here?" he asked. He emphasised the 'she'.

"When Mel heard we were coming here she asked to come along and I saw no reason to say no," Balor said. "Is there a problem?" Again he had glanced at his wife before speaking.

"No," Tallis said tersely then turned around to greet the new arrival.

The young lady who was approaching was stunning. Her long black hair, which flowed down her back, shone in the sunlight which streamed through the windows. She was tall and slim and her hips swayed as she elegantly walked down the corridor. Her cloak was pulled back over her shoulders, revealing a tight fitting green dress which emphasised all of her curves. She made me feel inadequate in every way.

Her eyes were black, just like Tallis's. Whoever this young woman was, she was a Sentinel. I didn't like being under the same roof as one, now there were two.

I glanced at Rose, who was seething with jealousy.

"Melantha," Tallis said, his voice devoid of all emotion. He nodded his head at her in welcome.

"Why so formal?" she said. Even her voice was beautiful, with a melodic quality to it. I heard Rose hiss when she flung her arms around Tallis and kissed him on the lips. He did not return the kiss, nor the hug. Instead he pulled her arms off him and turned to address my father.

"Your Majesty, this is Melantha, a friend from the academy." There was an odd tone when he said the word friend. It was almost as if he was unsure if it was the right word to use.

"Most people call me Mel, your Majesty," she said as she gracefully bowed.

"Welcome," Father said. "Any friend of Tallis's is a friend of ours." He didn't hear Rose grunt, but I did. "Come, join us for dinner."

As each of the rest of us were introduced, I couldn't help noticing that Balor glanced at his son as he shook our hands. His handshake was firm and his smile was filled with warmth, but something about him made me feel a little uncomfortable. It was almost as though he was seeing down into my soul.

When we returned to the dining room, it appeared that Tallis had had the foresight to place a warming spell on all of the food. Having heard the king invite the new guests to join us for the meal, the servants had hurriedly set three new places at the table.

The meal was a tedious affair for me. Conversation flowed and most people seemed to be having a good time, but I had the misfortune of being seated next to Melantha and the looks Rose was giving her were making me feel uncomfortable. Not that Melantha noticed; her eyes never left Tallis. Though he responded when she spoke to him, not once did he initiate the conversation. He seemed almost as uncomfortable as I was feeling.

Except when he was speaking with his parents. He couldn't hide the joy he was obviously feeling at having them there. He acted so much like a normal person that I could almost forget what he was for a while. Until I saw his eyes. Then the feelings of dread he always filled me with returned.

As I was seated next to his father, I kept my attention on him as much as possible; anything to avoid looking at Tallis. I finally plucked up the courage to ask him some questions which I hoped he wouldn't think were rude.

"Why do you look at your wife before speaking most of the time?"

He smiled at me, obviously not offended by the question. "She is my owner." I have never heard the word 'owner' spoken with such affection. When he looked over at her, his eyes were full of love. Her eyes were no different when she returned the gaze.

"I know, but I don't understand what exactly that entails."

"Then let me enlighten you, my dear." I liked the fact that he didn't call me 'your Highness' or 'Lady'. He was treating me as though I was part of his family and it made me feel good.

"I will answer your question first," he continued. "As a slave, I have to seek permission to speak, unless I'm responding to someone who is speaking to me directly, as you are."

"But what if your owner isn't with you?"

"My owner is always with me. I am not permitted to leave the house without her, unless she temporarily hands me over to someone else."

I was horrified. He wasn't just a slave, he was a prisoner. "How can you bear it?" I asked.

Again he smiled at me. "We would constantly be together with or without the shackles, so what difference do they make?"

'All the difference in the world,' I thought to myself, but I remained silent.

Uninvited, Melantha joined in our conversation. "Balor is a bit of a legend back home. Never before has a magic user allowed himself to become a slave. Most women are jealous of Macha. Having a man adore you so much that he gives up everything for you is something most women can only dream about."

She looked across at Tallis as she spoke and I could almost read her mind. She was hoping he would do the same for her. Something told me she was going to be disappointed.

"Mel is exaggerating," Balor said. "Something she is prone to. She is the daughter of my wife's best friend so I have known her all of her life. She has been like this since she was a child."

He was affectionately teasing her, which caused her to smile. "It doesn't mean I am wrong," she said then turned her attention back to Tallis.

"Are you ever permitted to wear clothes?" I asked. "Don't you get cold?" While the weather was pleasant in the spring, it could get bitterly cold in the winter.

Balor shook his head. "The collar I wear is not a normal collar. It is magically enhanced to put a shield over me, which protects me from the sun and rain and regulates my temperature. I am probably more comfortable most of the time than you are."

"Like built in central heating."

"Something like that."

That made me a little bit jealous. It must be great to be able to go outside when it was colder without having to wear layers of heavy clothing. Then I remembered that he was naked and my jealousy evaporated.

"What about shoes?" I asked. "Does the shield also protect your feet?"

"It does. There is, however, a downside to wearing the collar. It can also be used to kill me."

I had just taken a mouthful of water and began to choke.

"What!" I spluttered.

My reaction amused him. "All collars are programmed so that the slave's owner can, with just one command, make them tighten, breaking the slave's neck. It stops slaves from attacking their owners."

"What stops the owner abusing the situation to make the slave do whatever they want, no matter how horrible or undignified?"

"Our laws. If slaves aren't treated properly, they can request an investigation and will be taken away from their owners if it turns out they are being treated unfairly. Sentinels are used in the investigation so the truth always comes out. Anyone can report an abuse of a slave if they suspect it is happening and whenever a slave is killed, there is always an investigation to make sure it was justified. The owner is charged with murder if it turns out it wasn't."

Balor was a fascinating man and I could easily have spoken to him for hours, if it wasn't for the fact that I could see Rose out of the corner of my eye.

"What discipline of magic does your yellow band represent?" I asked him.

He looked at his wrist as he replied, as though he had forgotten it was there. "I'm an Empath," he said.

That explained a lot. When he glanced at his son as we were being introduced to him, he was probably reading Tallis's feelings about each of us. Then a horrible thought occurred to me; it was likely he was doing the same to us. Did he know how much Tallis frightened me still?

The thought made me feel ill and the meal couldn't be over soon enough for me

After we had finished eating, we left Tallis alone with his visitors; after all, they were there to see him not us. They were given rooms in the guest wing and we would see them again in the morning for breakfast.

"That bitch is not going to take my man," Rose said the moment we entered the drawing room which we often used for family discussions. Other than my father, all of my family were there.

"Rose," Etain said in shock. "You shouldn't speak that way about a guest in our house."

"Why not? She can't hear me. The way she kept looking at him it's obvious why she's here."

"She's a family friend. Tallis has known her for years. Maybe they have a little history," I said. Was I purposely adding fuel to the fire? Maybe a little.

"History is in the past and that's where she should stay," Rose hissed.

"Tallis didn't seem overly pleased to see her," Olwen said. She always was the peacemaker.

Rose changed the subject. "I'll tell you one thing. I hope that Tallis is as well-endowed as his father."

The comment made Tephi choke on his drink. "You shouldn't have been looking."

"If there was a naked woman in the house, you would be looking."

"That's different."

"Why?"

Tephi had no answer for that.

Sex

When I went to my room, I tried to read a book, but I couldn't settle. Eventually I gave up, got changed into my scruffiest clothes, lit a lamp and entered the secret passageways.

I didn't have a destination in mind, but I soon found myself spying on Tallis. He and his parents were catching up, the way family does. Melantha was sitting next to him and kept placing her hand on his thigh or his hand. Each time he moved her hand away. This was taking flirting to the next level and I was disgusted that she would do it in front of his parents. The look on his face suggested he felt the same.

I know it was rude to eavesdrop, but I couldn't stop myself. I'm not proud of my actions.

They spoke of his brother. It sounded like he had built himself a reputation for being a ladies man.

Melantha hardly spoke. She was still at the academy and didn't seem pleased that Tallis had already left. Her entire demeanour screamed that she wanted to be alone with Tallis, but nobody was taking the hint.

When Tallis said he needed sleep, I moved along the passageways until I reached the spyhole into his suite. He had only just arrived when there was a knock on the door.

Half expecting it to be Melantha, I was surprised to see Rose there. She was dressed in just her nightgown and had redone her makeup.

"Princess," Tallis said, nothing more. No 'nice to see you' or 'how can I help?'. With just one word he let her know how unwelcome she was. She was oblivious to how he felt.

"I just wanted to say how sorry I am that we all had to see your father so demeaned. It must have been embarrassing for you. I can understand you being ashamed of him."

I couldn't believe she had said something so awful. I couldn't see Tallis's face, but I could almost feel the anger rolling off him. "Do not speak of things you do not understand," he hissed. "I am proud of my father and have no reason to be ashamed of him."

Without saying another word, he slammed the door in her face. He then paced the room, clenching and unclenching his fists. I could understand how he felt. What Rose had said was horrible and I couldn't understand what she thought it would achieve. Did she really believe he was ashamed of his father and would welcome her sympathy? I had no idea. What I did know was that anyone observing him during the meal would have known his true feelings about his father.

He still hadn't calmed down when there was another knock at the door. I felt sorry for whoever was on the other side. Part of me hoped that it was Rose again.

Tallis yanked the door open and Melantha waltzed in, and I do mean waltzed. She walked so gracefully it was almost like dancing. Tallis didn't seem impressed. "Why are you here?" he asked.

She smiled at him. "I think we both know the answer to that." She placed her palm against his cheek. "I've missed you." He knocked it away.

"I made it perfectly clear at the academy that whatever we had is over." I was right, they did have a history together and it seemed they were more than just friends.

"You don't mean that."

"I'm a Sentinel. I can't lie."

She swayed her hips as she walked over to a sofa and sat down. She obviously thought it was enticing, but it had no effect on Tallis. "You still want me." She sounded so sure of herself, so confident.

"No, I don't."

Melantha laughed. "You may have yourself convinced, but not me."

"What is it you want from me? You know we can't be together."

"That's not what you said at the academy."

Tallis sat down, as far from Melantha as he could get.

"Don't twist my words, Mel. The academy was just about sex and you know it. It was safe to experiment with each other."

"So you used me." The sorrow she put into her voice was so fake I almost laughed.

"We used each other. Stop trying to pretend it was anything more."

"Why can't it be more?"

"You know why. Are you saying you would be prepared to make yourself my slave?"

"Why would I have to be the slave? Your father seems happy with his choice. Or is the high and mighty Sentinel Tallis too egotistical to follow in his father's footsteps?"

If she was trying to push his buttons, she succeeded.

"Leave my parents out of this," he snapped. "And for your information, for the right woman, I would willingly surrender myself."

Melantha frowned. "You're lying. How are you doing that?" I had been wondering the same thing myself.

"I'm not. I would give up everything for the woman I love, but I won't be allowed to."

"Why not? What's so special about you?" Melantha sneered.

Tallis held out his arm, revealing his coloured bands. "I'm a triple. The first one ever to have existed. Do you really think the Council will allow me to surrender myself to anyone?"

Melantha suddenly looked unsure of herself. Then a calculating look crossed her face. "Then why don't I just give you what you need."

He raised a quizzical eyebrow at her.

"Sex." She purred the word rather than spoke it. I was shocked that a woman could be so direct.

"I don't need sex, Mel," Tallis stated.

It was Melantha's turn to raise an eyebrow. "Really. Now why don't I believe you? You may have convinced yourself that you're speaking the truth, but you won't convince me. It's not as if you are getting any here. You wouldn't take the risk and we both know it."

I had no idea what risk she was talking about. I added that to the list of questions I wanted to ask the Sentinel, though I was sure I would never pluck up the courage to do so.

"You're right," Tallis said. "But that means nothing. I don't need to have sex with someone. I don't crave physical contact with another human being the way you obviously do."

I didn't understand how she could be right. Rose had seen him visiting a brothel so he must have had sex. He had to be lying, but he said he couldn't lie. Or had he been lying when he told me that? Melantha seemed to think he couldn't. Had he found a way? I was so confused.

"I don't need or want sex, Mel," he said.

The smile dropped from her face. "Well I do," she more or less shouted at him. "I haven't been with a man since you left. It's been months, Tal, months."

I watched Tallis cross his arms as though he was putting up a barrier between them. "So this is about you, not me. Why am I not surprised? It's not my fault you haven't had sex, Mel. There are plenty of men at the academy who know how to block their minds and I know from experience that you are more than capable of seducing someone to get what you want."

Melantha pouted. It was not a good look for her. It made her go from being a beautiful young woman to a spoilt child. "I don't trust anyone else."

Tallis glanced across at me. Yes, I know he couldn't have done as I was the other side of the wall and he didn't know I was there, but that's what it felt like. He looked like he was trying to make up his mind about something.

He sighed, then looked back at Melantha. "Alright," he said in a resigned tone. "But this means absolutely nothing. We are not getting back together. And this will be the last time, do you understand?"

A look of glee filled Melantha's face and she threw her arms around him. Then she kissed him, passionately. It took him a moment to respond. I know I should have looked away, but I couldn't.

With one hand, Tallis drew down the zip of her dress. Then he waved his arm in my direction. The next thing I knew his enchanted curtain had fallen into place. I could see and hear absolutely nothing.

There was nothing I could do except return to my room. I went to bed and fell asleep pondering whether I would tell Rose what I saw or not.

Hair

Needless to say, I said nothing to Rose about what I had seen. The next morning, Melantha looked like the cat who had gotten the cream, while Tallis appeared to be avoiding her. Neither of them spoke about what had happened between them, though I suspected that Tallis knew that I knew. I wasn't the only one to breathe a sigh of relief when she departed.

It was many months later that I got to witness for myself the Sentinel's skills. It is not something I will ever forget.

I was called in to see my father one morning. Lord Penbroke, who lived in one of the northern provinces, would be arriving that day, along with his son, Akar. There were rumours that the northern provinces were thinking about claiming independence and my father wanted to form an alliance with this lord through marriage.

"You will be dining with us tonight and you will, for once, wear a dress. And I don't mean one of your summer dresses you put on when it's too hot to wear trousers."

"Why?" I asked. "It's not as if Akar would be interested in me once he has met my sisters."

"He is to have the choice." His tone of voice suggested that he was not going to back down about this. I tried to make him anyway.

"So he gets a choice and we don't? How is that fair? Are your children just commodities that you can trade?"

His answer shocked me. "Yes," he spat at me. "Now make sure you obey me on this. You won't like the consequences."

I stormed out of the room, seething. How dare he say that we are just commodities. We are people, people who deserve a say in what happens to us. I always knew that I would have an arranged marriage, but I didn't like being treated like livestock a potential buyer might be interested in.

Would I obey him and wear a dress? Of course I would; not only was he my father, but he was also the king and, despite the way he came across sometimes, he always had the best interests of his kingdom at heart. But I was going to go down fighting.

I went to my room and slammed the door behind me. Then I rummaged through my drawers until I found what I was looking for. For one of my father's failed attempts at getting me interested in dressmaking, he had bought me a pair of scissors. They had only ever been used once. I made such an appalling attempt at making a dress that the poor seamstress who was trying to teach me walked out and never returned.

I walked over to my mirror, took a bunch of hair in one hand and cut.

It didn't take long to cut it all so short I could be mistaken for a boy. It was haphazard and looked a mess, but I didn't care. My father wanted to put me on display like a painting and I was determined that I was not going to be the one to be purchased.

Tephi was the first member of my family to see what I had done and took me into an empty room. I thought he was going to shout at me, but instead he burst out laughing.

"You look terrible," he said.

"That is the general idea."

"Father is not going to be pleased."

"I know. That's the point."

He folded his arms and looked at me, scrutinising me as though he was trying to work out what to do with me.

"Come on," he eventually said. "You should at least get it tidied up a bit."

He took me out into the city to visit a hair stylist. The poor woman almost fainted when she saw what I had done. It took a long to time to convince her I wasn't there to buy a wig.

Eventually she trimmed my hair so it laid neatly against my head instead of sticking out all over the place. Father still wasn't going to be happy though.

I hadn't been back in the palace long when he spotted me.

"What have you done?" he roared so loudly that I'm sure the walls shook. "Tallis, get here now."

Uncertainty flowed through me. Why was he calling for Tallis?

Tallis arrived and we went to my father's study, Tallis willingly, me not so much. My father had to physically drag me there. I did my best to ignore the amused look on Tallis's face.

Father sat down in his chair and pointed at me. "Can you fix it?"

Tallis looked me up and down. "Probably," he said.

I stared at him in horror. I couldn't believe he was even considering violating my body in such a way.

"Then do it."

I glared at my father. I loved him, but right then I hated him as well. I couldn't believe he would let the Sentinel work his dark arts on me.

"No."

I'm not sure who was more surprised, me or my father.

"What?" Father asked incredulously.

"I said no." There was no emotion in Tallis's voice. "I was employed to protect you, your family and your realm, not to get involved with your internal family issues. If you are having trouble keeping your children in line, that's your problem, not mine."

I stared at him, open mouthed. I had never heard anyone speak to my father like that.

"You are here to do my bidding," Father snarled at him.

"Actually, I'm not. Our agreement clearly states that if you try to force me to do anything I deem to be outside the scope of my role as protector, the agreement becomes null and void. Shall I pack my bags now?"

Father opened and closed his mouth, but no words came out. I couldn't believe what I was hearing. The Sentinel was threatening to leave! I wasn't sure if I was pleased or worried.

Tallis stood rigid, waiting for a response.

Eventually Father backed down. "No," he said quietly. He slumped down in defeat. "You may go. I will deal with this on my own."

Tallis inclined his head barely a fraction, then left the room. It was a while before Father spoke again.

"You will not be dining with us. You will not meet the lord or his son. As far as I am concerned, until our guests leave, I have only two daughters. You are an embarrassment to this family. Now get out of here before I decide to banish you."

I ran from the room before he had chance to change his mind. To this day I don't think he realised how happy he had made me. A few days without having to pretend to be a Lady. Time to myself to dress however I wanted, do whatever I wanted. No sitting around, bored out of my mind while others talked about politics and war and other equally uninteresting things. While my sisters were stuck having to pretend to listen to every word the lord and his son said while remaining silent, I would be off having fun.

It also meant I got to eat with the servants, which I did whenever my father was not at home. They didn't mind and it made mealtimes much more enjoyable.

I literally skipped down the corridor.

I decided to seek out Tallis. I knew he hadn't stood up to my father for me, but I wanted to thank him anyway.

Nerves ran through me. It was the first time I had gone to his suite since I accused him of being prepared to allow me or one of my sisters to drink poison.

My hand was shaking as I knocked on the door and I was praying that he wouldn't be there. My prayers weren't answered.

"Princess Adara," he said as he opened it. "I have been expecting you."

"W…W…What?" I stammered. "Why?"

"You want to know why I didn't force grow your hair." He stepped back out of the doorway and gestured with his arm that I should enter.

I didn't want to, but it would have been rude to refuse. I couldn't help shuddering when he closed the door. I know he noticed, but he didn't react.

He took a seat and waited for me to do the same. I was physically shaking as I did so. He waited patiently for me to speak.

"Actually I came to thank you."

I saw his lips twitch as though he was trying to smile, but he failed.

"There is no need to thank me. I didn't do it for you. What your father was asking me to do was outside the terms of my agreement."

"You could have done it anyway."

He leaned forward, making sure I had his full attention. "Adara, there are many aspects of my job that I don't like, but I will always perform my duty regardless of my feelings. If I started to do things outside of the scope of my employment, where would I be able to draw the line? I don't get to choose what I will agree to do and what I won't, which is why I made the contract so explicit. I will do what is right, regardless of whether I want to or not. Do you understand?"

I nodded my head, even though I wasn't sure what he was trying to say. "So your actions were nothing personal," I said.

"Correct. Unless it was for their protection or for the good of the kingdom, I would have refused your father regardless of whether it was you, Olwen or Rosemerta who he wanted me to use my magic on."

He paused before saying Rose's name. It was only a slight pause, but I noticed it. It wasn't the first time he had done that. Something told me he really didn't like her.

"Can you do it?" I asked. "Can you force my hair to regrow?"

Tallis thought about it for a moment. "I think so, though I have never tired. Why? Do you want me to?"

"No," I said hastily.

He almost smiled again. "Now is there anything else you want or can I have some peace for a while?" It was a dismissal and I hastened from the room.

Before I shut the door however, he called after me. "Your new hair style suits you by the way."

I have no idea why, but the comment made me grin.

The smile fell from my face when I was accosted by Rose.

"Been flirting with Tallis again I see," she sneered at me.

I rolled my eyes. "No Rose, I just had to see him about something. He is all yours. I have no interest in him, as I keep telling you. Never have, never will."

I walked away before she could reply.

I managed to avoid everyone for the rest of the day. I had no interest in seeing the lord and his son arrive so I made sure I spent most of my time in the palace grounds. After a good meal in the kitchens, I decided to get an early night, little knowing that I wouldn't be getting much sleep or that, before the sun rose, I would be sharing Tallis's bed.

Attack

I was woken in the early hours by someone knocking on my door. Dressed in just my pyjamas (I never wore a nightdress), I rubbed my eyes as I opened the door.

"Is anything wrong?" Tallis asked as he pushed his way into my room. He was looking around as if he expected to find someone else there.

"What do you want?" I said sternly. I didn't appreciate being woken.

"I needed to check that you were alright," he said as though barging into my room in the middle of the night was a perfectly acceptable thing to do.

I noticed that he was fully dressed and wearing his cloak and wondered if he ever slept.

"I sensed something," he continued. Then he tensed. "Olwen," he said and headed to the chair I had slung my dressing gown over. He picked it up and passed it to me. "Put this on then come with me." It was an order, but the tenseness with which it was delivered made me obey.

There was no answer when I knocked on my sister's door. I glanced at Tallis, who indicated that I should enter anyway. There was a lamp still lit beside her bed and the sight it illuminated shocked me.

Olwen lay on the bed, curled up in the foetal position. She was completely naked and I could clearly see blood around her most private area. Her entire body was shaking as she sobbed.

I don't think she heard me as I ran over to her. The moment I touched her head to get her attention, she jumped, then cringed away from me. She was cradling her hands, but I could still clearly see the marks on her wrists. They looked like friction burns. My eyes travelled down her body. She was covered in bruises. And bite marks.

Her legs were curled up tightly as though she was trying to hide as much of her body as possible. She made no attempt to cover herself up though. Maybe she didn't even know Tallis and I were there. I couldn't help noticing that her ankles had the same marks on them as her wrists.

Tears filled my eyes. "Oh Olwen, who did this to you?"

She didn't react. I don't think she even heard me.

Tallis grabbed a blanket which had fallen onto the floor beside the bed and placed it over her. When he wrapped it around her, covering her completely, and picked her up, she cried out, but didn't try to stop him.

"We have to get her to my workroom," he said to me.

Anger surged through me. My sister needed help not an interrogation.

"Put her down you bastard," I yelled. "I'm not letting you hurt her."

"I'm going to help her, not hurt her." I expected him to be angry at my outburst, but he wasn't. His voice didn't contain any emotion at all. "I need you to open the door for me. Now."

I was obeying him before I even realised I had moved. Had he used magic on me? I don't think so, but I couldn't be sure.

I led him down the corridor, then down the stairs. We saw nobody as we made our way through the palace. Eventually we reached the lower level where Tallis's workroom was. I had never entered it before and I wasn't sure I wanted to. I pushed on the door, but it didn't move. As soon as Tallis walked up to it, it opened on its own.

Lamps came to life the moment he entered the room and I gasped. Inside was a worktable, covered by a blanket, and the walls were lined with shelves, all full to overflowing with jars full of different coloured ingredients. There was no sign of implements of torture anywhere.

"What did you expect?" Tallis asked. "A torture chamber?"

Worried that he had just read my mind, I decided to remain silent.

"This room is for my work as a Healer, not a Sentinel."

He gently laid Olwen on the table and pulled back the blanket which was wrapped around her. She tried to curl up once more, but he stopped her.

"I need you to be courageous, my Lady. I am going to help you, but it may hurt. Can you be brave for me?" I had never heard him speak so gently to anyone before. His words were almost like a caress and I momentarily wished he had been speaking to me.

Tears continued to flow down Olwen's face, but she nodded.

He then started issuing instructions. He had me make a poultice for the burn marks on her wrists and ankles while he made a potion which would calm her down. I did everything he told me, making sure I took the correct amount from each pot. Despite the drink he gave Olwen also being a pain killer, she winced when the poultice was applied.

I was directed to wrap her wrists and ankles in bandages while Tallis felt her all over, making sure she had no broken bones. She cried out when he had to press on areas which were covered in bruises, but I knew that what he was doing was necessary without him having to tell me.

Once he had ascertained that there were no breaks, the areas on Olwen's torso, arms and legs which she had reacted to being touched the most had the poultice applied to them then we bandaged most of her body.

Olwen remained passive and said nothing while we worked on her battered body. That changed the moment Tallis told her he would have to look between her legs.

She screamed and tried to get off the table, but he held her tight. He said soothing words to her and stroked her hair until she had stopped shaking.

"I'm sorry," he said gently, "but I have to see what damage has been done. I need to know if you need stitches."

Reluctantly she laid back down onto the table. I took hold of her hand and looked away as Tallis parted her legs. As quickly as he could, he performed his examination then closed them again.

"It could be worse," he said. "I will create a cream that will numb the area and will speed up healing. Do you want Adara to apply it instead of me?"

Olwen gripped my hand even tighter and nodded her head. I didn't let go of her until Tallis said the cream was ready.

As he handed the pot to me, he whispered in my ear. "You are going to need to put some in her anus as well."

It was the worst thing I had ever had to do, not only because I was having to touch my sister in places I shouldn't even be seeing, but also because it hurt her. She screamed again and again and tears were flowing down my face by the time I had finished.

While I worked, Tallis created what looked like a nappy using a towel. As soon as I was finished, he put it on Olwen. She looked ridiculous, but it did offer her some level of modesty.

We had done all we could to help mend her body. Now it was time to find out who had hurt her. I helped her off the table and into a chair then covered her up with a blanket. I moved another chair so I could sit next to her and hold her hand. Tallis sat opposite her.

"I need you to tell me who did this to you." His voice was soft and gentle, but I could feel power washing over me. Somehow he was putting magic into his words.

Olwen shook her head. "I can't. He said nobody would believe me and that he would attack me again or go after Rose if I told anyone anything."

I felt like swearing, but Olwen didn't need to see my anger. Despite Tallis's eyes being black, I could see the fury in them. I have no idea how he kept it out of his voice.

"Olwen, look at me." Again I could feel the magic and it made me wonder if he was using some sort of compulsion spell. Whether he was or not, Olwen obeyed.

"I promise you," he continued, "that the man who hurt you will never be able to hurt you or anyone else again. My job is to protect you. I have failed to do that, but I will not fail again. Tell me who it is and I will make him wish he had never been born. Please, tell me who did this."

I shivered, but not with cold. I had no idea what Tallis would do to the man when he found out his name, but I did know that I didn't want to be around to witness it.

"I can't," Olwen said, her voice shaking.

"Please don't make me make you."

I was shocked. He was threatening to torture her to make her talk. I glared at him. He returned my stare, but shook his head ever so slightly, letting me know he would not hurt her.

Then I remembered that he couldn't make people talk, just tell the truth if they did decide to speak. Olwen either didn't know this or was too scared to remember.

"Akar," she blurted out, then started shaking.

I placed my arms around her. "It's alright Olwen. Tallis is going to take care of everything." I hoped I was telling the truth.

I looked up at Tallis. From the look of fury on his face, he knew who Akar was. He forced his feelings aside and his face became neutral once more before he addressed Olwen again.

"I know you don't want to do this, but I have to know what happened. Do you want Adara to leave?"

She shook her head and squeezed my hand. "No. I want her to stay."

Tallis nodded, then waited for Olwen to tell her story.

Olwen moved her head to stare at the corner of the room. There was nothing there to see, so I assumed that it was just a way to avoid looking at anyone. Only later did I realise that she was seeing everything that happened, reliving it in a way she probably would for weeks, or even months. I hated Tallis for making her go through this, but I understood why it was necessary.

Olwen's voice was steady as she spoke, but the way she gripped my hand told me just how hard it was for her.

"I hadn't been in bed long when someone knocked on my door. When I opened it, Akar forced his way in and closed it behind him. Before I could say or do anything, he grabbed me, placing his hand over my mouth so I couldn't call out for help. He told me that if he had to choose a bride, he was entitled to sample the merchandise first."

"Bastard." I said the word quietly but forcefully. It was enough to interrupt Olwen, though that had not been my intention. I expected Tallis to reprimand me, but he didn't. Maybe he understood what I was feeling.

"Go on," he said gently to Olwen.

"He forced me onto the bed then gagged me with some cloth he had in his pocket. He had also brought rope with him and he tied me to the bed. I tried to pull free, but I was bound too tight."

I don't think she realised she was using her free hand to rub the wrist of the hand I was holding. I couldn't help wincing when I remembered what her wounds looked like under her bandages.

"He ripped my nightdress off then started to touch me, everywhere, but not in gentle loving way. It hurt when he grabbed me and squeezed me hard. I cried out when he bit me, but the gag in my mouth muffled the sound. He took all of his clothes off and then he...then he..."

Olwen began to sob. "It's alright," Tallis told her. "You don't have to say the word."

"It hurt, Adara, it hurt a lot."

I put my arm around her and pulled her closer to me. "I know, Olwen, I know."

My first time hadn't been comfortable, but I had been willing. I couldn't even begin to imagine how much it must have hurt Olwen.

"When he had finished, he untied me and told me if I told anyone he would make sure that they didn't believe me and then he would be free to hurt me again or do the same to Rose."

"Do you know why he chose you instead of Rose?" Tallis asked. I had no idea why that was relevant, but he obviously seemed to think it was important.

"He said I had been flirting with him all night and made it obvious what I wanted from him. It's my fault he attacked me."

Tallis spoke before I could put into words what I thought of Akar.

"No," he said forcefully. "None of this is your fault."

He got out of his chair and knelt down in front of her. He took hold of her free hand. "Look at me Olwen." It took a while, but eventually she did. "I was there with you last night, at dinner and afterward. You did nothing other than be polite. Nothing you did could ever be construed as flirting. Even if you had been, it wouldn't justify what he did, but I can assure you, you weren't.

Rose was, but you weren't. I think he chose you because he thought you would be easier prey. Don't let him be right."

I had no idea what he meant by that last comment, but I didn't ask.

Tallis stood up. "You need to get some sleep," he said to Olwen. "You can have my bed. Adara will stay with you. I will sleep on the couch. Nobody is going to get anywhere near you without my permission."

Olwen nodded her head and when Tallis looked at me, I did the same, confirming that I would stay with Olwen.

Then he picked her up and carried her to his room. Once she was settled in his bed, he indicated with his head that he wanted to talk to me outside. I kissed her forehead and told her I would soon be back.

"I've done all I can for her for now," he told me once I had shut the bedroom door. "The potion I gave her will help her sleep, but she will probably have nightmares. I don't think you are going to get much sleep tonight, but I need you to try. I need you awake and alert in the morning."

"Why? What's going to happen in the morning?"

"Akar is going to be made to pay."

Interrogation

Tallis had been right about Olwen having nightmares. Her screams kept waking me up and I felt like I hadn't slept at all by the time the sun came up.

Tallis was already dressed when I left his bedroom. A blanket on the couch suggested that he had slept, but I wasn't convinced. He didn't ask how I had slept, though I'm sure he could see how tired I was. And he probably heard Olwen's screams.

"Please can you find something for Olwen to wear," he said. No 'hello' or 'good morning', straight down to business. "It needs to be light and loose. It doesn't matter whether it covers all of her bandages or not."

I nodded my head. I would go to her room and search through her wardrobe for something suitable.

"I don't want to leave her alone, so please hurry. As soon as you return, I'm going to see your father."

"Do you want me to come with you?"

"No. You need to stay with Olwen."

Nothing more needed to be said, so I left the room.

Despite the early hour, I wasn't the only person out of bed and I almost walked straight into Rose. What she was doing loitering outside Tallis's suite I had no idea.

She looked me up and down, taking in the fact that I was wearing just my sleepwear and dressing gown and jumped to the wrong conclusion.

"You utter bitch," she shouted at me. "How could you? Father is going to hear about this."

"This isn't what it looks like Rose and I don't have time to explain now. And you needn't worry about running off to speak to Father; Tallis is going to be doing that soon."

I didn't wait for her reply. I ran to my room and quickly got dressed. Then I went to Olwen's room to select a suitable dress. Tallis was pacing by the time I got back to his suite.

"Please wake Olwen and get her dressed," he said. "The sooner we get this over and done with the better it will be for her."

Then he left the room. By the time he returned, Olwen was dressed and sitting on the couch. She looked terrible. There were bags under her eyes and bruising caused by the gag was beginning to form around her mouth.

"We have to go. Your father has called a meeting in the throne room."

He picked up his dark glasses and put them on. When he picked Olwen up, she buried her face in his shoulder. "I understand how you feel," he said sympathetically, "but you are going to want to be there for what is about to happen. You need to see with your own eyes that Akar is punished."

By the time we arrived at the throne room, all of my family were there, along with Lord Penbroke and his son. It was the first time I had seen them. Lord Penbroke was an attractive man, for his age. He had kept himself in shape and hadn't let the weight gain that seemed to affect most men his age set in.

Unfortunately for him, Akar didn't take after his father. He wasn't an unattractive man; he was plain and rather boring to look at. Going by appearance alone, he wasn't someone you would remember the next day. He didn't have his father's trim figure and was a little portly around the middle. I couldn't help thinking that some exercise would do him good.

Then I remembered how he had exercised the previous night and had to resist the temptation to attack him. Had I been holding a knife, I would probably have thrown it at him.

Father was sitting on his throne. He was there as ruler of Amanet not as Olwen's father. Rose glared at me. None of my family asked why Olwen was being carried, which told me they had already been informed as to what had happened.

Tallis placed Olwen on a chair then waited for the proceedings to begin.

"Who is this?" Akar asked, gesturing toward me. Of those in the room, I was the only one he hadn't already been introduced to.

Father seemed reluctant to answer, though whether this was because of what Akar was being accused of or whether he just didn't want to admit I was his daughter, I wasn't certain.

"I am embarrassed to admit that this is Adara, my youngest daughter," he eventually said.

"So that is the reason for this meeting," Akar said. "It's a formal introduction."

"No it is not," Father snapped at him. "Tallis, get on with it. The sooner we know the truth of the matter, the sooner I can take action."

Tallis tilted his head slightly in acknowledgement then told me to tell everyone what had happened. Father already knew all of the details and looked like he wanted to kill someone. He sat on his throne, drumming his fingers on the arm.

I told them everything, from Tallis first waking me to sleeping in Tallis's bed. I kept getting interrupted.

"Why did he go to your room instead of anyone else's?" Rose asked. What she really wanted to know was why he didn't go to her room first. Tallis answered her.

"It is the closest room to my suite." While this was a true statement, I wasn't sure that was the real reason. He knew that there was trouble and for some reason he thought I was to blame. At least that's what I assumed.

I described what I saw when I entered Olwen's room and Rose went pale. I noticed Tephi was clenching and unclenching his fists as though that was the only thing stopping him hitting someone. Etain appeared unmoved by my words, but I knew my brother well and he couldn't hide from me the fury he was struggling to contain.

I described how Tallis treated my sister's injuries and then spoke about how he forced her to tell him who had attacked her.

"This is preposterous," Lord Penbroke shouted as soon as I mentioned his son's name. "How do we know she was even attacked? Those three could be making the whole story up."

Tallis did not react to the accusation and signalled for me to remain silent. I looked over at Olwen and could see tears trickling down her face. I wished I could have spared her from having to listen to my account, but she had to be there to back up what I was saying.

"Come here my Lord," Tallis said. Lord Penbroke obeyed and Tallis asked Olwen's permission to undo one of her bandages. She placed her arm in his outstretched hand then looked away when he began to unwind the white material.

"Good grief," Lord Penbroke exclaimed when his eyes saw the burn marks on Olwen's wrist.

"These are rope burns and I can assure you they look a lot better now than they did last night before I put the poultice on them. Do you want to see the bruises and bite marks?"

Lord Penbroke shook his head as he backed away. "I still don't believe my son is responsible," he said. "And I won't unless you have proof. I need more than just the word of this young girl here."

Father stood up. "You will address my daughter by her correct title," he yelled. "Princess Olwen is not just some 'young girl'." He emphasised the Princess.

"I don't care who she is," the lord bellowed. "I am not going to take her word over my son's."

Akar placed a placating hand on his father's arm. "It's alright Father. Let me deal with this." He then turned to face the throne. "Princess Olwen is telling the truth, well partially anyway."

I'm sure my jaw wasn't the only one to hit the floor. Was he admitting to committing rape?

Apparently not. "I did go to her room last night," he continued, "but it was at her request."

Olwen frantically shook her head, but remained silent. Akar kept his attention on my father. "She said she wanted me and she liked it rough. It was her idea to be tied up and she insisted that I rip her nightgown off her."

"Are you trying to tell me," my father snarled, "that all of her injuries were at her request?"

"Yes," Akar said. "And you can't prove otherwise. She cried out so loudly in pleasure when I bit her that I had to gag her. I was afraid someone might hear. I got her agreement first."

Tephi moved forward, his fists raised. Etain had to hold him back. Akar stepped away, putting more distance between them.

"Not only was Olwen a willing participant in what happened, she instigated it."

Akar sounded so sure of himself he almost had me believing him. Had I not known Olwen and that she would never agree to doing such vile acts, elements of doubt would have filled my mind.

"You have heard what my son has to say," Lord Penbroke said. "This is a case of 'he said, she said' with no way of knowing who is speaking the truth. Now if you have nothing more to say, I am leaving and any chance you had of uniting our families has just been blown."

He turned and started moving toward the door when he was stopped by my father's voice echoing around the room. "I think not." Then in a quieter tone he said simply, "Tallis?"

"He's lying, your Majesty."

"What!" Akar cried out. "You're going to take the word of a Healer over that of a nobleman?"

I'm sure Tallis smiled when he replied.

"His Majesty lied to you yesterday. I don't wear these glasses because I have injured my eyes and the light affects them. And I am not just a Healer."

Then he removed his glasses, revealing his eyes, and a feeling of satisfaction flowed through me when I saw Akar go pale.

"You're a Sentinel!" he exclaimed. "Oh shit." The last part was spoken so quietly that I don't think many people heard it.

"I am going to give you one chance to tell the truth before I make you." Tallis spoke as though he was making a statement instead of a threat. It sent a shiver down my spine.

"I am telling the truth," Akar sneered.

Tallis just looked at him. He didn't speak, he didn't make a gesture, he didn't move in any way, but suddenly Akar started to scream.

The sounds he was making were terrible. I had to cover my ears. Tallis just continued to stare at him.

Akar fell to the floor and curled up into a ball. He held his head as he rocked back and forth. I had no idea what Tallis was doing to him, but it was effective. And horrible.

"Make it stop. Please make it stop," Akar begged. Tears were streaming down his face.

"I can't," Tallis said. "Only you can do that. All you have to do is tell the truth."

"I am telling the truth," Akar screamed out.

"The evidence tells me otherwise. My magic would have no effect on you if you hadn't lied."

Between the screams, he swore at Tallis and called him some revolting names. They had no effect on Tallis at all.

Akar turned to his father. "Please, you have to believe me," he sobbed.

"It doesn't matter what your father believes," Tallis said coldly. "All that matters is what you believe."

"Tell me what to say, just tell me what to say."

"I can't tell you what to say. Only you know what the truth is. All you have to do is speak it."

Akar, who had seemed such a proud and arrogant man only a few minutes before, was now nothing more than a crying baby, begging for help. I looked at Tallis and wondered what sort of man could do that to someone. Then I remembered his reasons and turned my hate back to the man who deserved it.

"Alright, I admit it," Akar moaned. The words were so quiet I could hardly hear them. "I attacked Olwen. I did everything that she said I did."

He uncurled and rolled onto his back, panting hard. Whatever Tallis had been doing to him had stopped.

Lord Penbroke was furious when he moved forward. But he didn't approach Tallis; he walked up to his son instead and kicked him viciously in the side. "You are not my son. I disown you." He then turned to address my father. "Please accept my humblest apologies, your Majesty. And my assurances that this piece of filth will be dealt with."

"I will deal with him." The tone of Tallis's voice was daring anyone to argue with him. He did, however, look at my father for permission, which was given by a slight nod of the head.

"Stand up," he said to Akar, who obeyed as quickly as he could.

Tallis then took a knife out of his pocket and turned to look at Olwen. "Would you like to do the honours?" he asked her, holding the knife toward her.

She shook her head, but her eyes never left Tallis as he punished Akar.

He showed no emotion as he slowed walked up to his victim. Akar tried to move away, but was unable to.

"What have you done to me?' he asked. He was panicking, and I couldn't blame him. I had a feeling that what he had already been put through was nothing compared to what was to come. I wanted to look away, but I was too curious to do so.

"I am also a Shield," Tallis said. "I have placed a Shield around you which prevents you from moving."

Akar stared in horror as Tallis undid his trousers and took hold of his manhood. It looked tiny in Tallis's hand, but I was sure it felt a lot larger to Olwen when it was being used as a weapon against her.

Tallis placed his knife under it then, in one swift movement, he cut it off. Blood flowed everywhere and Akar screamed once more.

Tephi and Etain both winced, but my father and Lord Penbroke just watched the proceedings, their faces unreadable.

Tallis then placed the severed piece of flesh in Akar's mouth and closed it.

Rose turned green and ran out of the room. My stomach churned, but I refused to vomit in public. As soon as I was alone, however, I was sure I would be seeking out a bathroom or a chamber pot. What Tallis had just done was barbaric. I couldn't understand why nobody had tried to stop him.

Akar tried to open his mouth, but was unable to do so. He was gagging but couldn't remove his manhood from his mouth.

Tallis had come prepared. He removed a small tube from his pocket and inserted it into the stump which was all that remained of Akar's appendage. Then he withdrew a needle and thread and proceeded to stitch up the wound. He gave Akar no pain relief and I couldn't even begin to imagine how much pain he was in. His face had turned scarlet, the veins in his forehead were clearly visible and sweat was pouring down his face. He was shaking all over.

As soon as he had finished sewing Akar up, Tallis took a small jar out of his pocket, rubbed some of the contents into the stitched up wound, then bandaged the stump.

"I have stopped the bleeding," he said to Akar, "and the cream I have put on it will prevent infection. The tube will allow you to still piss. I don't suggest you ever try to remove it."

Akar tried to speak, but couldn't open his mouth.

"When are you going to release him?" Father asked. He sounded mildly curious, nothing more.

"When I am ready."

With that, Tallis turned his back on everyone and left the throne room. I wasn't the only one staring at his retreating back. I couldn't believe what I had just witnessed.

A few moments later, Akar collapsed onto the ground. He spat out his severed penis then vomited all over the floor.

Forn

"Don't you think he went a little far?" I asked. All of the family were in Father's study, discussing what had happened. Lord Penbroke and his son had left, but not before the lord had promised to try to talk the other northern lords out of claiming independence and had sworn his loyalty to my father. After what Akar had admitted doing to Olwen, my father could have had him executed and, though Lord Penbroke was ashamed of him, he was glad that his son was still alive.

"I don't think he went far enough," Etain said. "I can't believe you allowed Akar to live, Father. Tallis deserves a medal for this."

"If I had executed him, I risked him becoming some sort of martyr and it might have spurred the north into rebellion. Now I can use him as a symbol of what happens to people who break my laws."

"Did you know what Tallis was going to do?" Tephi asked.

Father shook his head. "No. And even if I had known, I would still have given my permission."

"That man, if you can even call him a man, made Akar scream in agony until he confessed then cut off his manhood and put it in his mouth. Am I the only one who can see anything wrong with that?"

I looked at each member of my family. None of them spoke. None of them agreed with me. Of those present, I was the only one to see exactly what Akar had done to Olwen, so I should have been the one defending what Tallis did, but I couldn't. He had gone too far.

Tephi had the audacity to smile at me. "You have no idea what Tallis did to make Akar confess. How do you know he caused him agony?"

"The screams were a good indication. I knew he was a torturer, but I expected him to use implements, not just his mind. He can do that to anyone, whenever he wants and you are all okay with him living with us?"

"So pain is the only thing that causes you to scream is it?"

Tephi was trying to tell me something, but I was too wound up to listen. "That man is evil and should not be living under our roof," I insisted. While I could understand the need to make Akar confess to his crimes, I didn't like the method used and the punishment was cruel and brutal.

"If you ask me," Etain said, "what Tallis did was completely justified. Akar got a taste of his own medicine. Now he knows how it feels for his penis to enter a part of his body against his will."

Then Olwen spoke. "That man, as you put it, helped me. He eased my pain, he treated my wounds, he gave up his bed for me so I would feel protected. He treated me with respect and dignity. He then gave me the opportunity to exact my revenge. I didn't take it, but he made the offer. How can you not see the good in him?"

I said nothing. Olwen's words made me feel ashamed.

"This meeting is over," Father said. "Tallis will continue living here and has my full support for all of his actions. Now can someone let him know that I want to see him."

"I'll find him," Rose said gleefully.

I went straight to my room, but didn't stay there. I went into the secret passageways and made my way back to my father's study. Publicly he had agreed with what Tallis had done, but I wanted to hear what he said behind closed doors.

Tallis arrived just after me. He knocked on the door and was given permission to enter.

"Take a seat," my father said. "Can I offer you a drink of anything?" Tallis shook his head so my father continued. "How is Olwen? Will she recover?"

"Physically, yes. Emotionally?" He shrugged. "I have no idea. What I do know is that it is going to take a long time and she will need the support of people who love her."

"She will get all of the support she needs." Father then paused. He had something he wanted to say but seemed like he was unsure about saying it. "She needs a husband," he finally said.

"You're probably right, but it has to be the right man, someone who will be patient with her and help her recover. Have you got anyone in mind?"

I didn't like the way my father looked at Tallis. Whatever he was about to say was making him feel uncomfortable.

"Would you consider doing it?"

I couldn't believe what he had just said. He knew the sort of man Tallis was, what he was capable of. How could he hand Olwen over to him?

"I've seen the way you treat her," Father continued. "She's comfortable around you. And I know you would protect her with your life. You would give her everything she needs right now."

I, too, had seen the way Tallis was with Olwen, even before the attack. Did he have feelings for her? Would he agree to do as my father was asking? For Olwen's sake, I began praying that he wouldn't.

Tallis didn't seem surprised by what Father was suggesting. "You honour me, your Majesty. Nothing would make me happier than being married to one of your daughters, but regretfully I must decline. Being the spouse of a Sentinel is not easy. It's not something I would wish on someone, especially not Olwen."

I must have been imagining things, but I was sure he turned to look at me as he spoke. But he couldn't have known I was there.

I had heard enough. I closed the spyhole and returned to my room.

It was much later that evening when I saw Rose sneaking down the corridor toward the guest wing. I had just left Olwen's room, having checked that she didn't want me to stay with her, and was heading to my own when I saw her furtively checking around her. Her actions roused my curiosity and, as she hadn't spotted me, I decided to follow her.

I hid around a corner when I saw her stop outside Tallis's suite and knock on the door. As soon as he opened it, she let her dressing gown drop to the ground, revealing a sheer nightdress that didn't leave much to the imagination.

"What can I do for you, Princess?" Tallis asked. He sounded bored.

"After what you did for my sister, I thought you deserved a prize," Rose said in what I can only assume she thought was a seductive manner. I rolled my eyes. She was trying too hard and coming on too strong.

"And what might that be?" he asked. Was he really that naive or did he just want to force her to spell it out for him, I wondered.

"Me, of course."

She tried to enter his suite, but he moved to block the doorway. "I'm not interested."

Rose looked shocked. "What do you mean you're not interested? This may be the only chance you get to have me."

"I don't want you now and I won't want you in the future, now go away."

Tallis didn't say the words in a spiteful way, but they were spoken forcefully, leaving no doubt in my mind that he meant what he said.

"You bastard," Rose hissed at him. "I know what you are. I know why you don't want me. You like men too much. I've seen you going into the male whorehouse. If you don't start being nicer to me, I'm going to tell Father just what sort of man you are."

Tallis was unfazed. "Do whatever you want," he said and shut the door in her face.

I quickly retreated to my own room before Rose saw me. Had she been telling the truth about Tallis visiting a male whorehouse? It would explain why he refused to marry Olwen. But Rose's accusation hadn't appeared to bother him at all. If there was any truth to it, it should have done. My father was a complete bigot as far as homosexuality was concerned. If he found out that Tallis was gay, he would immediately ban him from the house. I contemplated speaking to Rose and trying to convince her to tell Father of her suspicions.

Indecision filled me and it took me ages to fall asleep.

All thoughts about Tallis's sexuality left my mind the next morning when Tephi announced that Forn would be arriving later in the day and that he would be staying for a few weeks.

I didn't love Forn, far from it, but he was fun to be around and I enjoyed his company. As far as I was aware, none of my family even suspected that there was anything going on between us. He was always given his own room, though he rarely slept in it. As soon as he was sure nobody else was awake, he would slip into mine and make sure that he was back in his own room before the rest of the family awoke. Not every night, of course, but most.

I didn't get much sleep whenever Forn visited.

It was hard to stop myself from bouncing up and down when he arrived. It had been a number of months since he had last visited and I had missed the sex. I knew he slept with other women, but it didn't bother me. I, on the other hand, didn't have the opportunity. Nor the inclination.

My enthusiasm was dampened by the fact that Tallis was also there to greet him. The two got on well, a little too well for my liking. But maybe it was a good thing; I didn't want anyone questioning why I was so excited to see my brother's friend.

Forn was a handsome man. Not stunning, like Tallis, but still very nice to look at. Like my brothers, he kept himself in shape by training with the soldiers who worked for his father. His family were rich, so he always dressed well. I knew what a good body those clothes hid.

He kept his hair longer than I liked so it almost touched his shoulders, though I did enjoy running my hands through it. His best features were his eyes. They were a deep brown and I could happily lose myself looking into them. I was glad he kept them open during sex.

He greeted me politely, as always, though there was a twinkle in his eyes that I hoped nobody else noticed. Tallis gave me a strange look, as if he knew something was going on, but he wasn't sure what. I momentarily wondered if he was going to ask me, and what I would say if he did, but Forn greeted him warmly before he had chance to speak. I made my excuses and left.

I saw no more of Forn that day, but he came to my room during the night and I made sure I welcomed him properly.

The first few days were great. I didn't see much of Forn during the days, but we certainly made up for it each night. When he joined my brothers in a training exercise in the arena, I couldn't take my eyes off him. I was well aware of how well he could use his body, but seeing him with a weapon in his hand was strangely exciting.

The week got even better when Tallis's father paid an unexpected visit. I liked him, a lot, and was more than happy to spend some time with him, giving him an official tour of the palace and its grounds. He was alone, which I questioned, and he told me that only in Sobek did he have to be with his owner whenever he left his house. He had teleported to the palace and would teleport back. It wasn't until after he had left that I remembered what he was and began to wonder if he had an ulterior motive for the time he spent with me. Was he reading my feelings? If so, about what and why?

He also seemed to spend a lot of time with Tephi. It wasn't until a few days later that I worked out that Forn was the reason.

As usual, Forn came to my room that night, but he didn't seem his usual happy self. Instead of joining me in my bed, he paced the room.

"What's wrong?" I asked.

When he turned to look at me, he couldn't hide the pain. "We need to talk."

He sat on the bed beside me and took my hand. His eyes never left mine as he said, "This has to be our last night together."

I didn't ask him why; he would tell me when he was ready.

He gripped my hand so tightly it was almost painful. "Tomorrow your father is going to announce that I am going to marry Olwen."

Dream

We spoke no more of Forn's upcoming wedding until after we had made love. For once that's what it felt like. Usually it was just sex, both of us looking for gratification, nothing more. That night, it was tender, as though we were sharing more than just our bodies.

When we were both spent, we talked. I didn't want to marry Forn, and he knew that, but I was still hurt. We knew that both of us would have arranged marriages, but I never thought that his would be to my sister.

Forn confessed his feelings for me. It wasn't love, but he did care for me and he hated the fact he was hurting me. When my father had first broached the subject of marriage to him, he initially thought that he was talking about me and that he had found out about us. Then he was told about what had happened to Olwen.

Forn had always treated Olwen well. He genuinely liked her and I knew, deep down, that he would be good for her. But I couldn't bring myself to feel happy for her.

"I agreed because it was the right thing to do," Forn said gently as he stroked my cheek. I nodded my head. I knew he was right, but it was still hard to accept. I felt warm and protected in his arms and I was sad that it would be the last time.

We had sex once more before going to sleep and when I awoke in the morning, he was gone. I didn't feel sad, I was angry. Angry at Tallis. Forn had told me that it was Tallis who suggested the betrothment to my father. It explained why Tallis's father had visited; my father wanted to confirm that Forn was the right choice for Olwen.

I got dressed, ready for a confrontation with Tallis, but the man in question beat me to it. There was a knock on my door and when I opened it, there he stood, dressed, as usual, in his black cloak with the gold trim.

"Can we talk?" he asked.

My room was just as good as his for what I wanted to say to him, so I moved aside and let him enter. Something was wrong. He wasn't acting like his usual confident self. If I didn't know better, I would have said he seemed unsure of himself.

"I know about you and Forn," he stated before I had chance to speak. "It's one of the reasons I suggested him as a possible suitor for Olwen."

I'm sure my jaw hit the floor. I hadn't been expecting him to just admit it. He couldn't lie, but that didn't mean he had to admit anything.

"Why?" I finally managed to say.

I did nothing to stop him when he placed his hand on the side of my face. "I couldn't bear the thought of anyone else touching you."

I should have shouted at him, told him that my sex life was none of his business and he should stay out of it, but I found I was unable to do so.

I took hold of his wrist and moved his hand away from me. I should have pushed him away; I should have ordered him to leave, but I didn't. The next thing I knew, I had thrown my arms around him and was kissing him passionately.

His tongue never left my mouth as he picked me up and carried me over to my bed. As soon as I was lying down, he moved his mouth onto my neck and planted kisses along my collar bone, making me moan in pleasure.

He was lying on top of me, so I moved my leg across his body and pulled him in tighter. This caused my nightdress to ride up and he took advantage, running his hand up my exposed thigh.

Want and need were coursing through me and I almost cried out in frustration when he pulled away.

I watched in fascination as he untied his cloak and let it drop to the floor. He undressed quickly, revealing a remarkable body, then quickly returned to my side.

I sat up, allowing him to remove my nightdress, which landed on the floor beside his clothes.

His hand moved upward from my waist, making me shiver with excitement and anticipation. His touch was firm, yet gentle. It was everything I wanted it to be.

The way he used his fingers, his lips and his tongue made me want to beg for more. Never before had my body felt so alive.

When he positioned himself between my legs, I was more than ready for him.

He entered me so forcefully I cried out. And woke myself up.

I sat up, shaking all over. I had had erotic dreams before, of course I had, but never about HIM. And this one stuck in my mind. Even now I can still remember all of the details.

I lay back down and placed my arm across my face, trying to hide it, even though there was nobody there to see me. I thanked my lucky stars that Forn had already left.

I felt ashamed and embarrassed. I should not have been having that sort of dream, especially about someone I had no intention of ever letting touch me.

I was hot and sweaty. There was no way I was going to get back to sleep, so I took off my pyjamas and threw them into the wash basket. I never slept in a nightdress so I had no idea why I did in my dream.

The shower I took did nothing to still my racing heart. I turned the hot water off, allowing the cold to cascade down my body, but all that did was make me shiver.

This was all Tallis's fault; it had to be.

As soon as I got dressed, I did my best to put my dream from my mind. I thought about Forn being with Olwen instead of me and my anger returned. I made my way to Tallis's suite and banged on the door.

"I've been expecting you," he said mildly as he opened the door and let me in.

I didn't hold my anger in. "You bastard, how could you? You knew about me and Forn, didn't you?"

Despite what had happened in my dream, I expected him to deny it, but he didn't. "Please, take a seat." He indicated a chair with his arm.

"I prefer to stand." I wasn't willing to do anything he wanted me to.

He shrugged his shoulders. "Whatever you wish." He sat down and watched me stomp around the room. I may have been wrong, but I'm sure he seemed amused.

"You really should sit down," he said. "You're going to wear yourself out."

"Screw you," I spat at him.

He leaned forward. "Yes, I knew about you and Forn, or should I say I suspected. One of the reasons I asked my father here was to confirm my suspicions."

"And as soon as he did that, you spoke to my father." I then called him a few things I shouldn't have known the meaning of. He just sat there and took it. Only once I had finished my little tirade did he speak.

"Actually I spoke to your father before my father arrived. It was my suggestion that my father visit, to find out what Forn really thought of Olwen. Your father agreed. I didn't mention to him that I also wanted to find out your real feelings for Forn."

"Why?" I yelled. "Why are you doing this to me? Do you really hate me that much?"

I'm not sure exactly why my words affected him, but I must have hit a nerve. For the first time ever since he arrived, I witnessed him losing his temper.

He stood up, knocking his chair over. "Grow up, Adara," he shouted at me. "Not everything is about you."

His words stunned me into silence.

He took a deep breath and calmed himself down. He spoke in a much softer voice when he continued. "Forn is just what Olwen needs. He will support her, protect her. He won't put any pressure on her. I made my suggestion to your father for her sake."

He straightened his chair then sat down again. "I had my father talk to you to find out how strong your feelings for Forn were. I would have told your father that Forn wasn't suitable for Olwen if either of you had genuine feelings for each other."

He made everything sound so reasonable, as though there was nothing wrong with what he had done. I shook my head. I didn't trust him and did not believe what he was telling me. He may not have been lying, but he certainly wasn't telling the full truth.

I forced myself to turn away from him. I wasn't going to fall for his words and I was afraid that if I continued to look at him, they would begin to have an effect on me.

I stomped over to the door and yanked it open before turning to address him. "Stay away from me, stay out of my life and stay out of my dreams," I hissed.

He was either a good actor or he was genuinely confused. "What are you talking about?"

"You know full well what I'm talking about. Making me dream of you will not make me change my mind about you. I don't like you and I never will. I don't like you living here and if I had my way, you would be kicked out the palace and, preferably, the kingdom."

Did I realise I was acting like a spoilt brat? Of course I did. He was so convincing when saying he didn't know about my dream that it had me rattled.

"Adara," he said softly. "Sentinels can't invade someone's dreams. We don't have that power."

That was the last thing I wanted to hear. If he hadn't caused me to have a sex dream about him, what had?

"I don't know what your dream was about," he continued. "and I don't want to know, but I can assure you that it had nothing to do with me. I can also assure you that it meant nothing. From the way you have acted toward me this morning, I can only assume that you were thinking about me last night and whatever else was on your mind just combined in your sleep. Don't read anything into it."

He was probably right, but I wasn't going to give him the satisfaction of telling him. "Just stay out of my head," I snarled at him before leaving.

I was sure I heard him mutter, "I've never been in your head," before I closed the door. I didn't slam it. I had already overreacted and slamming the door just felt a little too dramatic.

Breakfast was tedious. Father told the family of his plans for Forn and Olwen. The look on her face suggested it had not been discussed with her. Rose couldn't keep the smile off her face.

"That will keep Tallis away from her," she whispered to me. "He's been spending too much time with her for my liking."

He had been spending a lot of time with Olwen, but he was doing so in his role of Healer. I didn't bother to let Rose know that; I would have been wasting my breath.

Etain was pleased with the announcement, stating that it would be good for the kingdom, as well as Olwen, and Tephi offered his congratulations to his friend, though he did look at me in concern first. I did my best to look pleased, but I couldn't get away from the table soon enough.

Tephi followed me to my room. "Are you alright?" he asked as soon as he closed the door.

"Of course," I said. "Why wouldn't I be? I'm pleased for them both."

"Squid," he said, "I know about you and Forn. You're not as discreet as you think you are."

"Oh."

"So I will ask again. Are you alright?"

"I'm fine," I lied. "Forn and I were just friends having a little fun, nothing more."

Tephi put his arms around me and hugged me tight. "Father wouldn't have done this if he knew about the two of you," he said gently.

I pulled away from him. "Yes he would, and you know it."

"Not if you had real feelings for Forn."

I wasn't sure I believed him, but I nodded my head anyway.

Tephi ruffled my hair. "Come on Squid. I know just what will cheer you up. Feel like another archery lesson?"

That's one of the reasons I love my oldest brother so much; he always knew the right thing to do for me.

Simion

Early one morning, a few weeks later, I couldn't sleep so I went through the secret passageways to Tallis's suite. I didn't know why I went there so often, probably because he was the only person in the palace awake at that hour. I was sure he rarely slept.

He was seated cross legged on the floor with his hands resting on his knees and his eyes closed. It looked like he was meditating.

He was interrupted by a knock on the door. The butler was on the other side and looked at Tallis with distaste. Usually he treated him with respect so I was curious as to what the issue was.

"There is a person of female persuasion at the door," he said. "She asked me to let you know that you are needed at the Red Dragon. She said you would know why."

That explained the butler's attitude. The Red Dragon was the most expensive whorehouse in the city. Before you ask, the reason I know that is because I overheard Tephi and Etain discussing it once.

"Thank you," Tallis said. "Please let her know I will be there as soon as I can. I just need to collect a few things from my workroom."

The butler stiffened. Having never been in Tallis's workroom, I could imagine what was going through his mind. Probably the same things that would have been going through mine had I not known that the workroom only contained things needed for healing.

I ran back to my room and opened my door in time to see Tallis knock on the door to Tephi's suite. Was I jealous that I only had a room but Tephi had a complete suite? Maybe a little, but I wasn't heir to the throne so I couldn't complain.

I did complain to my father when Tallis was given a suite, even if it was in the guest wing not the family wing, but I was told that, as a Healer, he needed somewhere private to see people so a suite was necessary. While the argument was valid, it didn't stop me sulking. After all, he did have his workroom.

But I digress. I was curious as to why Tallis would need healing supplies to go to a whorehouse. His visit to Tephi before heading there had me intrigued.

"It's time," was all Tallis said. Tephi nodded his head.

"I just need to get dressed," he said then Tallis left, heading in the direction his workroom lay. He wasn't wearing his normal cloak, I noticed. It would be easily recognisable whereas dressed as he was, especially if he put on his dark glasses, he would be able to walk through the streets without anyone knowing he was a Sentinel. He was visiting the whorehouse not exactly in disguise, but he certainly didn't want to be recognised.

My suspicions were confirmed when Tephi left his room. I had never seen him wear such plain clothes. I didn't even know he had any.

The two men were gone for most of the day and both of them looked exhausted when they returned. I didn't ask what they had been up to all day; from the state of them it was pretty obvious and I was disgusted with them.

I avoided speaking to both of them for a couple of days. Eventually Tephi took me aside and asked me what was wrong.

"I can understand men going to whorehouses," I said, "when there is no other option, but you have plenty of women throwing themselves at you. And you spent all day there! You disgust me."

To my surprise, Tephi grabbed me by the arm and dragged me into the nearest room. Thankfully it was empty.

"Don't ever speak of this to anyone," he ordered. There was no doubt in my mind that he was giving me a command. "Do you understand?"

He was gripping my arm so tightly it was hurting. "Yes," I said and struggled to get away from him.

"I mean it, Adara."

"You're hurting me," I said.

He seemed surprised when he looked at his hand, as though he hadn't realised he was still holding me. Or so tightly. He let me go. "Sorry," he said, though his tone suggested he wasn't or that his mind was on other things.

"Don't you think you're over-reacting just a little?" I asked as I rubbed my sore arm. A bruise was already beginning to form.

"You have no idea what you are talking about, Adara."

"Then why don't you tell me what's going on?"

"It's none of your business. For your own good, stay out of it." I opened my mouth to speak, but he interrupted me. "And don't even think about speaking to Tallis about this. Just because he can't lie doesn't mean he will tell you anything."

I grunted. "Yeah right. He can lie. I heard him do so."

Tephi frowned. "No he can't."

"Yes, he can," I stated. "I heard him tell his friend Melantha that he hadn't had sex since arriving here, but we both know he has been visiting the whorehouses."

Tephi shook his head. "Oh Adara. How little you know."

He then did something he had never done before; he turned around and left the room without explaining what he meant. I ran after him, but he had disappeared from sight.

On the way to my room, I spotted Etain walking with his friend, Simion. They had been friends for a long time and he stayed at the palace regularly. I was pleased he was visiting again as Etain always seemed more relaxed and happy when he was around.

I liked Simion; he was refreshingly different. He didn't care what people thought of him. He changed his appearance on a regular basis and was currently sporting bright blue hair which he had grown longer since the last time I had seen him. He had put something in it to stiffen it and it stood up in all directions. I struggled but failed to remember what the real colour of it was.

He had somehow managed to change his eye colour to match and the green outfit he was wearing clashed terribly. But that was Simion all over. He liked how he looked and felt comfortable and that was all that mattered.

All thoughts of what Tephi and Tallis had been up to left my mind when he greeted me warmly. I couldn't help smiling. He wasn't the most attractive man I had ever met, but what he lacked in good looks he certainly made up for in personality. He was infectious and was always making me laugh.

"We're going fishing," Etain said. "Care to join us?"

I shook my head. "I remember what happened last time. I still haven't told Father how I really ended up in the river."

"That wasn't my fault," Simion said. Then he grinned. "Well not totally."

I had nothing better to do, so I decided to join them. As usual, Simion was entertaining. I hadn't laughed so much in a long time.

The evening meal that night was the most fun meal I had had since Tallis had arrived. He didn't join in the joking around, but he did nothing to stop us. Father had a visitor so the rest of the family, along with Tallis and Simion, ate in the informal dining room. It was good to totally relax during a meal, for once.

"You're a brave man coming here, Sim," Etain said. "The last time one of the king's offspring had a friend visit, Father arranged for him to marry one of my sisters. You might be next."

Simion knew that Etain was just teasing him and joined in. "Why do you think I look the way I do?" he asked as he pointed at his hair. "I can guarantee this is enough to put anyone off wanting me to marry their daughter."

"I wouldn't be so sure," Rose said. "Some of us look beyond what can be seen."

"Your luck's out there as well Rose," Etain said. I think he was a little drunk. He wasn't the only one, I thought as I looked over at Simion. "I've seen him naked and he's definitely nothing to write home about."

Simion hit him, but in a friendly way. "That's fine coming from you. You're so small I'm surprised you weren't mistaken for a girl."

While I found the comment amusing, Olwen apparently didn't and excused herself from the table.

"That is not what I meant," Rose said indignantly.

Etain grinned. "No, she is more interested in how rich a man is."

"I'm afraid I must let you down there as well sweet Rose," Simion slurred. "My father has promised to disown me unless I 'sort myself out', as he puts it."

"I think you two may have had enough," Tephi said as he took a bottle of wine from Etain's hand, but he was smiling as he said it. He was giving advice, not a reprimand.

"You're right," Simion said. "No more wine. Brandy time I think."

"Good idea," Etain said. Then he looked over at me and Rose. "Would you ladies care to join us?"

Traditionally, women weren't allowed to join the men for after dinner drinks, so of course we both jumped at the chance. Neither Tephi nor Tallis objected, though the latter did decline the invitation.

It was the first time I had ever drunk brandy and I vowed it would be the last. It burned my throat, making me choke. I received no sympathy. All I got was Simion telling me I should sip it. I was too embarrassed to let him know I had been.

We all stayed up late, though I declined any more alcohol. I was the first one to call it a night. The little alcohol I had drunk had gone to my head and I thought sleeping it off would be a good idea.

I went to bed thinking how much fun the next few days were going to be. How wrong I was.

Accusation

The next morning, most of the family, along with Simion, went to the informal dining room for breakfast. Only Rose, my father and Tallis were missing. Simion and Etain hardly ate anything. Both looked like they wanted to be sick and were holding their heads, though they denied being hungover.

"Why did you bother joining us for breakfast if you're not going to eat anything?" Tephi asked, doing little to hide his amusement at their discomfort.

"Coffee," Etain replied and took another tentative sip from his cup.

We had just finished eating, well those of us who weren't avoiding food that is, when Father burst into the room, Tallis on his heels. Father's face was red with rage and Tallis's entire bearing showed he wasn't pleased about something.

Father took one look at the condition Etain and Simion were in then turned to Tallis. "You have one hour to sober them up then I want everyone in the throne room."

Tallis nodded his head and Father turned and strode out of the room.

"What's going on?" I asked, but Tallis ignored me.

He pointed at Etain and Simion. "You two, my workroom, now."

Both of them paled. I tried, but failed to hide my grin. I knew that there was nothing for them to worry about in his workroom, but they obviously didn't. I was pleased that I wasn't the only one jumping to the wrong conclusions about what Tallis had stored there.

Tallis turned and left the room without looking behind to see if he was being followed. Of course both Etain and Simion obeyed his order. And there was no doubt in anyone's mind that it had been an order.

"Tephi, do you have any idea what that was all about?" Olwen asked.

Tephi shook his head. "No. But those two have obviously done something pretty bad. It's been a long time since I saw Father that mad. Tallis doesn't seem too pleased either. I wonder why we are all being ordered to the throne room. To act as witnesses maybe."

A horrible thought occurred to me. "Father wouldn't use Tallis against his own family, would he?"

"Of course not," Tephi replied. "But Sim isn't family, is he."

Nothing more needed to be said. I looked at my brother and sister. Both were clearly as worried as I was.

We immediately went to our rooms to get washed and clean our teeth. By the time I arrived at the throne room, Etain and Simion were both there, looking much better than they had earlier in the morning. I don't know what Tallis did to them, but it certainly worked.

Simion was seated, watching Etain pace. Both seemed nervous and I could hardly blame them. They knew they had done something wrong.

When Tephi and Olwen arrived, I sat down next to them and the waiting began.

"Will you please sit down," Tephi snapped at Etain, whose pacing was becoming annoying. "Do you know what this is about?"

"No," he said so quickly I suspected he was lying.

Then the doors opened and Father walked into the room, closely followed by Tallis and, more worryingly, half a dozen guards. Rose was also with them and took a seat near us, though she wouldn't look at anyone.

Father sat down on his throne then glared at Simion. "Having a daughter attacked by a visitor was despicable, but another one being attacked by someone this whole family classed as a friend is even worse."

Other than Rose, we all looked at each other, none of us knowing what he was talking about. Rose turned her head to stare at a wall. Simion appeared as confused as the rest of us.

"You are going to confess to your crime," Father continued, "or Tallis is going to make you."

Simion went pale, but managed to stammer, "I haven't done anything to confess to."

"So you deny attacking Rosemerta last night," Father spat at him.

"Of course I deny it."

Father looked over at Tallis. "Well?"

"He's hiding something, but he isn't lying. Or at least he believes he isn't lying."

"Interrogate him," Father commanded.

"You can't do this," I cried out. "Simion is a friend and we don't treat friends like this."

"He's a criminal and will be treated as such." I couldn't believe my father had just said that.

"Did you see Rosemerta at all last night?" Tallis asked Simion, who was visibly shaking. Etain, too, looked scared. After all, it was his close friend who was about to be tortured.

"Yes, we all ate dinner together. You know we did. You were there."

"And after dinner?"

"Some of us retreated to one of the lounges for brandy, Rose included."

"And after that?"

Simion swallowed before continuing. He glanced nervously at Etain, then spoke. "I went to my room. Rose followed me and made some inappropriate suggestions."

"This is preposterous," my father roared. "My daughter would never throw herself at a man."

"She did, I swear it."

Tallis nodded his head. As far as he was concerned, Simion was telling the truth.

"Are you claiming everything that happened between you two was not only consensual, but it was her idea?" my father asked.

"No, your Majesty. I am saying that nothing happened. I turned her down."

"He's lying," Rose cried out.

Everyone ignored her.

"So you are saying that you spent the rest of the night alone, with no witnesses to prove that you are telling the truth?"

Again Simion glanced at Etain, who gave a slight nod of the head.

"No, your Majesty. I was with Etain the entire night."

"And what exactly were you doing with my son all night?"

Tallis spoke before Simion could. "What does it matter, your Majesty? Whether they went out partying, visiting a whorehouse or were in the library reading romance novels makes no difference."

I was watching Etain as Tallis spoke and saw him visibly relax. I had grown suspicious about what secret he and Simion were hiding and his reaction to Tallis preventing Simion from speaking more or less confirmed it, in my eyes anyway.

"Very well," my father said. "Simion, it appears that you have been falsely accused. Please accept my apologies."

"What!" Rose cried out. "You are going to just take his word for it? He attacked me and you are going to let him get away with it just because he says he didn't do it?"

"No," Father said as he glared at her. "I am not taking Simion's word. I am taking Tallis's."

"But everyone knows he hates me," Rose wailed.

"I don't hate you, Princess," Tallis said. "Hate is a feeling and I have no feelings toward you at all. I don't like you, but that doesn't mean I dislike you. But I would have believed Simion's story about you coming on to him even if I hadn't been testing him as he spoke because you have been doing the same to me ever since I moved here."

He ignored my father's indignant splutter and continued. "I was hired to do a job and I will always do what I am hired to do. I get no enjoyment out if it and sometimes I even hate it, but it needs to be done. I don't care whether you, as a person, were attacked or not, but I do care if a man attacks a woman. That is a crime and I will see that the truth comes out so the culprit can be punished."

"Simion attacked me," Rose yelled. "And you are lying about him telling the truth."

"I am not able to lie and I am not doing so when I state that Simion is telling the truth." With that he turned his back on Rose as though she was of no consequence to him.

Father looked almost embarrassed when he said, "It looks like the proceedings are over."

Tallis then surprised us all by saying, "Not yet, your Majesty. Two conflicting stories have been told. The truth needs to come out. Rosemerta must confess that she is lying."

"No," I cried out. "Father, you can't let him do that."

"I have heard enough to know that Simion is not guilty of the crime he has been accused of," Father said. "That is good enough for me."

"Well it isn't good enough for me," Tallis said. "I had many offers of employment, even before I graduated. Why do you think I accepted yours instead of one of the others?"

"Because I am paying you a vast amount of money."

Tallis shook his head. "Trust me, I was offered a lot more than you are paying. I agreed to work for you because I believe that you are a just and fair king who doesn't put his family's needs above his people's, that he treats everyone the same. Am I wrong?"

Father collapsed back into his throne. He seemed deflated, somehow. "No, you are not wrong."

"What would you do if Rosemerta wasn't your daughter? If she was just one of your subjects?"

"I would make her confess then punish her for making a false accusation."

"Then I have your permission to proceed?"

I stood up to protest when Father nodded his head, but Tephi grabbed hold of my arm. "Stay out of it," he whispered to me.

How could I stay out of it? Tallis was about to publicly torture my sister.

"Don't make things worse," Tephi continued. "Tallis is right; this has to happen. If not, Father is no better than a tyrant or a dictator. How can he run a kingdom if he doesn't make the laws apply to his own children?"

Tephi was right, but that didn't mean I wanted to witness what was about to happen.

Tallis approached Rose and she stared at him defiantly. His voice was almost gentle when he spoke to her.

"I don't want to do this, Princess. Please tell the truth so I don't have to."

"I am telling the truth," she snarled at him.

Tallis shook his head. Something about his demeanour told me he was looking forward to what he was about to do about as much as I was.

"Did Simion hurt you?" The gentle tone was gone.

"Yes," Rose replied.

Tallis raised an eyebrow. "Now that's interesting. She isn't lying." He thought for a moment, then asked another question. "Did Simion hurt you physically?"

"Yes," Rose said again and then began to scream. I had to look away and cover my ears. I wasn't the only one, but Tallis showed no reaction.

"Tell the truth and it will stop," he said. The gentle tone was back.

I forced myself to look at my sister and I could see tears streaming down her face. She put her head in her hands and began to shake it violently.

I couldn't take any more. "Make him stop Father," I cried out. "Please make him stop."

My words had no effect on either my father or Tallis. Rose continued to scream and Tallis continued to stare at her.

Suddenly the screaming stopped. Rose had said something, but it was too quiet for me to make out what.

"Would you care to say that a little louder?" Tallis asked.

Rose shook her head. "Don't make me, please don't make me." All of her defiance had left her. Within the space of just a few minutes she had gone from someone who always seemed so able to take care of herself to a pitiful excuse for a human who would do almost anything Tallis asked her to do. It scared me that someone could have that much power over someone else.

And there was nothing stopping him using it against anyone he chose.

"Your family needs to hear it. And so does Simion. Why did you lie about him attacking you?"

Tears continued to flow down her face and she was wringing her hands in her lap. She looked down at them as she spoke. "He turned me down. He hurt me so I wanted to hurt him."

"You bitch," Olwen cried out, making me jump. "After all I went through, you trivialise it by pretending it happened to you just because someone rejected your advances?"

She stood up and causally walked up to Rose. She drew back her hand to slap her face, but Tallis caught her arm as it descended.

"Don't do anything you will later regret," he said gently as he lowered her arm to her side.

Olwen didn't argue with him. "I'm ashamed to call you my sister," she said to Rose. "From now on you are nothing to me."

Then she left the room. I wasn't sure if I should go after her or not. Tephi made the decision for me.

"She needs to be alone right now. And you need to stay here."

Tallis turned his attention to Simion. "Have you heard enough?" Simion nodded so Tallis looked at my father. "I will leave the punishment to you."

I breathed a sigh of relief. Whatever Father decided to do to Rose would be nowhere near as bad as what Tallis was capable of doing.

I changed my mind when my father addressed one of the guards.

"Go to Rosemerta's room and bring me her cat."

Punishment

A feeling of dread ran through me. Rose loved that cat more than anything in the world. She had raised it from a kitten. As the runt of the litter it hadn't been expected to survive, but Rose made sure it did. I had no idea what possible reason Father could have for sending a guard to collect it.

I began praying that all he would do was remove it from her care and hand it over to someone else. My prayers weren't answered. Instead he sent another of the guards to collect two hunting dogs from the kennels.

When Rose heard Father's orders, all of the blood drained from her already pale face.

"No," she said, her voice barely above a whisper. "Not my cat. Please, not my cat."

I didn't know what Father was going to do, but I could take a guess and I really did not want to stay and watch. I stood up, but Father noticed before I could even take a step.

"Stay where you are, Adara," he called out. "This is for your benefit as well as Rose's."

I cast a pleading look to Tephi, but he shook his head at me; he wouldn't intervene.

All eyes turned to the door when we heard it open. A guard walked in, cradling Rose's cat. It was curled up in his arms, purring loudly.

He was instructed to place it in the middle of the floor then move away.

The cat was black and white and fluffy. Rose stood and started to move toward it, but a glare from our father froze her in place. The cat looked around, spotted nothing of interest and began to wash itself as though it didn't have a care in the world.

Rose's legs were shaking as she walked back to her seat. Tears were streaming down her face once more, indicating she knew what was coming. She must have felt so helpless.

The door opened again and the other guard walked in, a lead in each hand. On the end of each lead was a hunting dog. These animals were not beloved pets like Rose's cat; they were efficient killers. One on its own could bring down a stag. A pack had been known to track and kill a mountain lion.

They were not growling or snarling or pulling to get to the cat; they were too well trained for that. They calmly sat beside the guard, eyeing the cat, waiting to be given instructions.

The cat, hearing noise behind it, turned around. The moment it spotted the dogs, it arched its back and started to hiss. The dogs did not react.

I pulled my gaze away from the feline to my father, silently begging him not to give the order, to say that he only wanted to scare Rose. But deep down I knew that wasn't the case.

"Release the dogs," he finally said.

The guard unhooked the leads from the collars, but still the dogs remained stationary.

Until the guard said, "Kill." Then they sprang forward. The cat, seeing two dogs full of muscle and teeth bearing down on it, gave up its show of bravery and turned and ran. But there was nowhere to hide.

Unable to stop herself, Rose moved toward her beloved pet, intent on picking it up and running away with it, but Etain grabbed hold of her.

"You can't," he said. "If you get in their way, they will rip you to pieces." He pulled her into his chest so she didn't have to watch what happened, but he couldn't stop her hearing it.

The sound of terror the petrified animal made as it ran is something I thought I would never forget. But the noises once the dogs caught up with it were worse. The scream of agony followed by the sound of ripping flesh made my stomach curdle. I looked at Tallis, expecting him to be his usual stoic self, but even he looked ill.

Thankfully it was over quickly. All that remained of the cat was a lump of bloody fur.

"Take her away," Father said, pointing at Rose. "And someone clean up this mess." He sounded like what he had just witnessed hadn't bothered him at all.

I loved my father greatly, but at that moment I hated him as well.

"I'll take her," I said and Etain released Rose into my care. She was weeping uncontrollably.

I took her to my room; I didn't think she would be able to bear going to her own and seeing all of the cat's toys lying about. I planned to remove them before she stepped foot in there again.

She laid down on my bed and couldn't stop shaking. I placed a blanket over her, but it didn't help. I should have said something to her, some words of comfort, but I had no idea what would help, so I remained silent.

A short while later there was a knock on the door.

"I thought I might find Rosemerta here," Tallis said when I let him in. He had a cup in his hand filled with a green liquid. He carried it over to my bed and placed it on the bedside table. He then gently shook Rose to get her attention. "I have made you a potion to help you sleep. Right now, it's the best thing for you. It's up to you whether you drink it or not."

That was it. No apology for his part in what had happened, no enquiry as to her wellbeing. He was just a Healer, delivering medicine, as was his job.

But I said nothing. After all, he didn't have to brew the sleeping draught for her.

I helped her to sit up and handed her the cup. She drank it all then laid down again. She was asleep almost instantly. I made sure she was covered over then left the room with Tallis.

"Why didn't you stop my father?" I asked as soon as the door was closed behind us. I couldn't keep the accusatorial tone out of my voice. I wanted someone to blame for what had happened and Tallis was an easy target.

"I have no authority over your father," he told me. "There was nothing I could do."

"You could still have tried," I said and ran off. I went straight to Tephi's suite. Tallis may not have had the authority to argue against my father, but Tephi certainly did.

Unfortunately he didn't agree with my assessment that Rose's punishment was unjust.

"Personally, I think Father let her off easy," he told me. "Do you know what the standard punishment for making a false accusation is?" I shook my head. "Having your tongue cut out."

I winced.

"Do you still think Rose's punishment was unjust or too harsh?"

"Yes," I replied. "An innocent animal was made to suffer."

While Tephi conceded that I had a good point, he did ask me a question I couldn't answer. "Would you have preferred she received the usual punishment?"

I didn't want to think about it anymore so I went in search of Etain. I found him in the room Simion always stayed in. Simion was sitting on the bed, clearly shaken by what had happened.

"How's Rose?" he asked as soon as he saw me.

"Sleeping. Tallis gave her a drink which knocked her out."

"I never wanted this to happen. What she did was wrong, but I never asked for her to be punished for it."

I sat down beside him and took his hand. "I know," I said. "This is not your fault. You shouldn't be blaming yourself."

"Of course it's my fault," he said. "If I hadn't turned Rose down, none of this would have happened."

I noticed the pained look on Etain's face before he managed to hide it. He hated that his friend was suffering.

"You have the right to choose who you sleep with, just like Rose does. Nobody should be punished for saying no."

His response was interrupted by a knock on the door.

"You asked to see me, your Highness," Tallis said when Etain let him into the room, closing the door behind him. Tallis didn't seem surprised to see me there.

Etain looked at me. "Adara, would you mind leaving us alone?"

I stood up but Tallis waved me back down. "She knows. Or at least she suspects. You can speak in front of her."

I didn't realise how tense Etain had been until I saw him relax.

"I just wanted to thank you," he said to Tallis. "For not making Sim reveal what he was doing last night."

"There is no need to thank me. The information wasn't relevant to the proceedings."

"You weren't to know that."

"Yes, I was. I could tell that Simion was hiding something and the way you looked at each other made it obvious. The interrogation I had to perform was about Rosemerta, nothing else."

"Now you know the truth, are you going to tell my father?"

"Of course not. It's none of his business."

"So you and Sim are more than just friends then," I said. I was still holding Simion's hand and squeezed it affectionately.

The look Etain gave him almost made me blush. "We're in love."

"What are you going to do?" Tallis asked. "We all know how the king will react if he finds out."

My father was a kind and loving man, but he was also a bigot. Men married women and women married men. Full stop. End of story. Anything that didn't fit that equation was a sin and would not be tolerated. If Etain confessed his feelings for Sim to our father, banishment would be the minimum punishment he would receive.

"We've been making plans to leave together, start a new life in a new kingdom. We have some money saved up, but not yet enough. We need to buy some sort of business, as well as purchase somewhere to live."

"Which kingdom?" I asked. I would be sad to see my brother leave, but I understood that there was no other option.

Etain shrugged his shoulders. "How about Sobek? Your people tolerate my kind, don't they?" he asked Tallis.

Tallis's lips almost formed a smile. "We do more than tolerate people who are attracted to their own sex. We don't judge or discriminate against them in any way. You do realise, however, that one of you will have to become a slave to the other."

"We know," Simion said. "We've decided to toss a coin."

This time Tallis did smile. I couldn't help wishing he would do it more often. Then his face turned serious.

"If you do decide to move to Sobek, come and see me first. I have a house there that is currently empty, well most of the time. I'm sure my brother is using it now and then to take a girl to, but I can easily put a stop to that. It's yours for as long as you need it."

Etain was at a loss for words. Simion wasn't. "Thank you," he said. Those two words expressed so much gratitude. Not only for the offer of a roof over their heads, but also for Tallis's acceptance of their love for each other and his agreement to keep it secret.

I walked up to Etain and hugged him. "Promise me you will see me before you leave, you won't just suddenly disappear," I said.

"I promise."

I kissed him on the cheek then left the three men alone. If they were going to be making arrangements for Etain and Simion's departure, I would just be in the way.

A while later, I was in the library when Tallis came to see me. "I'm here to offer my services," he said. I raised a questioning eyebrow at him. I had no idea what he was talking about. "Can I come in?" It was a public room, but he asked permission anyway.

He entered the room when I nodded my head, then he explained what he meant. "I can take away your memories of what happened. You will still know it happened, but you won't remember exactly what you saw or heard."

I know I should have been grateful that he was making the offer, but I wasn't. I was horrified.

"You tortured Rose, you did nothing to stop her cat being slaughtered, you were going to torture Sim if he didn't tell you the truth and now you come here offering to do me a favour? What sort of monster are you?"

He said nothing.

"So you claim you can alter my memory. If you can do that, why didn't you do it for Olwen when she was attacked?"

His voice was so cold when he replied that it made me shiver. "I did."

Rejection

The vehemence with which he spoke had me temporarily paralysed so all I could do was watch him leave the room, slamming the door behind him.

It was a long while before I managed to stop shaking. I had never heard him use that tone before, not even on Rose. When I finally managed to pull myself together, I went searching for him. I tried his suite first, but there was no response to my knock. He could have been ignoring me, but I didn't think so. I might have wanted something important and he took his roles too seriously to take that risk.

I searched everywhere and eventually arrived at the conclusion that if he was still in the palace, he was in his workroom. Having been in there, it no longer terrified me, but I was still filled with apprehension when I knocked on the door.

"Go away Adara," his voice sounded from the other side. "I'm busy." I hadn't spoken, so I had no idea how he knew it was me.

"What if I want something important?" I called out, hoping my voice would travel through the wooden door.

"You don't," came the reply.

I could have argued, but what would have been the point? Instead I went to my room and checked on Rose. She was still sleeping peacefully.

Not sure what to do with myself, I went to her room, intending to remove anything that would remind her of her cat. I wouldn't throw them out, just in case she wanted them later; I just wanted to remove them from her sight until she was recovered enough to see them.

It didn't go as well as I had planned. Seeing the cat's toys and its basket made images of its death flash in my mind and I ended up curled up on the floor, sobbing like a baby.

When I had cried myself dry, I washed my face in Rose's bathroom then did what I had gone there to do. I had no idea where to store the things, so I found the housekeeper, who promised to keep them safe until Rose asked about them. If she ever asked about them.

I decided to try Tallis again. I had no idea what he had been doing in his workroom, so I couldn't know if he had finished, but there was no harm in trying.

There was no response to my knock. At least I hadn't been told to go away again. I went to his suite once more. I hadn't expected to find him there so I was surprised when he said I could enter.

"I've been expecting you," he said. Was I that predictable? Before I could ask how he knew I would look for him again, he ordered me to approach him. He placed his hand on my head and said, "Open your mind. If you are capable, that is," he added, muttering so quietly I might have misheard him.

I felt something pushing inside my head and instinctively fought against it. "Let me in," Tallis said and when I relaxed the pushing sensation disappeared. "Now think about what happened earlier. I know you don't want to, but it's necessary."

I did as instructed. Without meaning to, I recalled the noises the cat emitted, the smell of the blood and the urine it had expelled from its body when it realised there was no escape, the sight of its destroyed body. One by one, they were removed from my mind. When Tallis took his hand from my head I was still aware of what had happened, but not the exact details. I knew that I hated the smell and the sounds, but couldn't recall exactly what they were like.

"Thank you," I said. "And I'm sorry for what I said earlier."

"Too little, too late, Princess." He said the last word the same as he did when addressing Rose.

"What does that mean?" I asked.

"It means that is the last time I will help you in any way that doesn't fall under my role as Sentinel, Healer or Shield. It means I am done with you. I'm done trying to persuade you that I'm not the monster you have convinced yourself that I am. Before you even met me you decided what I was and closed your mind to any possibility that I could be something else. You have judged me based solely on the fact that I'm a Sentinel, someone who tortures people to get to the truth. And you haven't even bothered to find out the true facts."

A lump formed in my throat and my eyes began to burn with tears, but I blinked them away; I would not let him see me cry. What he was saying upset me, not because of the words or the harshness with which they were delivered, but because they were true. Ever since he had arrived I had behaved like a brat. The tears weren't tears of sadness, they were tears of shame.

I thought about what he had done for Olwen, and for Etain, and even for Rose. I touched my hair, which I still kept short. And for me, I had to admit. He hadn't needed to do any of those things, but all I could ever see was the harm he could do. I wanted to say something, to beg his forgiveness, but he hadn't finished.

"Rosemerta has her faults, and there are many of them, but at least she doesn't judge people by what they are. I have gone out of my way to show you the sort of man I really am, but you have turned a blind eye to everything I've done and everything I've told you has fallen on deaf ears. I'm done trying. You're not worth the effort."

I opened my mouth, but no words came out.

"I am proud to be a Sentinel," Tallis continued. "Others like me have done great things, even prevented wars. We are peacekeepers, not protagonists, but I guess that's just something else that you refuse to see."

He turned his back on me. "Get out," he said. "And don't come back."

I ran from his suite, fighting back tears until I reached the seclusion of my room. Only then did I let them fall. I had behaved so badly toward him and he would never forgive me. I was nearly eighteen, yet I had been acting like a child. I felt so ashamed that as soon as I dried my eyes, I went to Tephi for advice. It didn't go quite how I had imagined.

"You said what!" he roared at me when I told him everything, making me shrink back in fright. I had never been scared of my brother, but right then I was. I had never seen him so angry.

"Are you trying to tell me that Tallis sought you out to help you and your reaction was to verbally abuse him?"

I nodded my head, too scared to speak.

"Grab you cloak," he said. "You are coming with me."

I didn't want to go anywhere with him in that mood, but I didn't dare say no. Rose was still sound asleep when I went to my room to retrieve my cloak, so I couldn't use her as an excuse.

"Where are we going?" I asked when he took me out of the palace grounds.

"You'll find out when we get there."

He led me along streets I had never been down before, eventually stopping outside a large building. The sign hanging in the middle of the front wall stated it was 'The Red Dragon'. I recognised the name.

"Why have you brought me to a brothel?"

Tephi ignored me and knocked on the door. A tall slim lady answered, wearing so little she may as well have been naked.

"Tephi," she said in delight when she saw my brother. They hugged affectionately.

"Hello, Bertha," he said. "Is Cara in?"

I was going from one shock to another. First Tephi lost his temper at me, which was completely out of character for him, then he dragged me to a whorehouse, now he was greeting one of the workers like she was a friend. I was aware that he visited brothels, with Tallis as well as on his own, but I hadn't realised he did it so often that he was on first name terms with the 'ladies of the night'.

"She's in her room," Bertha said and invited us both in. I didn't want to enter the establishment, but I wasn't given much choice. Tephi grabbed my arm and pulled me after him.

He led me down the corridor and up a set of stairs. He knew where he was going. He stopped outside a door and knocked, smiling when he was given permission to enter.

The room was surprisingly nice. It was tastefully decorated and light and airy. The curtains were open, as were a set of doors which led to a balcony. It could easily have been the bedroom of any young lady in any house. It wasn't what I expected at all.

There was a young woman sitting on the bed. She was petite, with short dark hair, which framed her heart-shaped face. She was pretty and had an air of innocence about her. I could imagine her being popular with the clients.

The moment her eyes fell on Tephi, her entire face lit up. She ran from the bed and threw herself into his arms. They kissed so passionately I had to look away.

"I wasn't expecting to see you today," she said when Tephi finally let her go.

"I've brought someone to meet you."

She turned to look at me and I realised I knew her. She used to be a servant at the palace, until she suddenly disappeared one day.

"I think you remember my sister, Adara," Tephi said. "Adara, this is Cara, the woman I love."

The comment made Cara blush. "I am pleased to see you again, your Highness," she said shyly.

"I don't think there is really any need for that, do you?" I have no idea why, but instinctively I reached out to her and hugged her. If Tephi loved this woman, then she was practically family.

Then the sound of a baby crying filled the room and my eyes were drawn to something I hadn't noticed before; a cradle by the bed.

Tephi walked over to it and picked up a wrapped up bundle. The crying instantly stopped.

"He heard your voice," Cara said with a smile.

Tephi positioned the baby so it was cradled in his arms and looked down on it with a look of such adoration it brought a tear to my eye.

"Come and meet my son," Tephi said.

"Y…y…your son," I stammered. "What? How? Where? When?" I didn't know that I was asking.

I was so stunned I have no idea how I managed to walk over to the bed and sit down next to my brother.

"This is Kiran," he said. "It means 'ray of light'. Kiran, meet your aunt Adara."

Tephi pulled back the material covering the baby to reveal a head of dark hair and blue eyes that looked so much like Tephi's I would have guessed he was his father without being told.

"Do you want to hold him?"

I nodded my head, unable to speak. Tephi placed my nephew in my arms and I swear he smiled at me. Tephi later told me it was just wind, but I didn't believe him.

"Cara and I fell in love while she worked at the palace," Tephi said. "We managed to keep our meetings secret and nobody caught us out, despite her spending most nights in my bed. Everything was going well until she found out she was pregnant. I've never been so happy and so scared at the same time."

I forced myself to look away from the cutest little face I had ever seen. "Why?"

"Think about it. Right now, you are holding the heir to the throne. What do you think Father would do if he ever found out?"

I didn't need to think about it. While Cara might just be banished, Kiran would be killed. There was no way my father would allow a bastard to ascend the throne and, had Tephi gone to him to ask permission to marry Cara, Father would have laughed in his face. Tephi would marry whoever my father decided, for the good of the kingdom.

"So why did you bring her here?" I asked as I looked about the room.

"A number of reasons. I went to Tallis for help and he made all of this possible. I get to visit my family without arising suspicion and they are well cared for. There are enough women here to look after them both. The woman who runs this place is like a mother to Cara. You know I've been coming here. Did you ever suspect the reason was anything other than the obvious?"

I shook my head. I had just assumed that both Tephi and Tallis were going to the whorehouse for sex.

"But you were coming here before Cara was pregnant."

"When I found out Tallis was visiting here I knew it couldn't be for the obvious reason so I asked him about it. He took me along with him the next time and it was a real eye opener."

I wondered why it couldn't be for the obvious reason, but I didn't ask because Tephi hadn't finished talking.

"You have to remember, Tallis isn't just a Sentinel, he's also a Healer and, as you can imagine, getting any sort of medical help is difficult for these people. He comes here once a week to treat any sort of medical problem anyone has. He does the same to all of the brothels, even the male ones. I continued to visit here with him sometimes, to help out."

Well that explained a lot. Rose's suspicions about Tallis's sexuality were wrong.

"If there's ever an emergency," Tephi continued, "Tallis is sent for and he always drops what he is doing to attend. Unless he's on official business, that is. Like when Cara went into labour. It was Tallis who delivered my son."

I thought back and could remember that night. It had never occurred to me what was really going on.

"So what are you going to do?" I asked. "Cara can't stay here forever."

"I know. And I have no idea what we are going to do. Tallis is giving it some thought and will let me know if he comes up with anything. I could turn my back on the throne and run away with Cara and Kiran and I know of some kingdoms outside the alliance which will grant me asylum, but I couldn't do that to Etain."

I looked at him sharply and he smiled at me. "You're not the only one to know about Etain's sexual preferences. He confided in me after Rose made her accusation against Simion. I know he is looking to leave and I plan on helping him."

At that moment, Kiran began to cry again.

"He's hungry," Cara said so I held him out to her. She sat down on the bed with him and started to loosen her clothing.

"We should leave you in peace," I said. I had no desire to watch her feed her baby. "May I come back sometime?"

"Of course," Cara said and smiled at me warmly.

"Though we will have to find a way to disguise you," Tephi said. "Unless you want to face some awkward questions."

He had a good point. He kissed Cara goodbye and promised to be back as soon as he could.

"So are you now beginning to understand how wrong you are about Tallis?" Tephi asked as he escorted me out of the building.

"It doesn't change what he is," I said. "No matter what good he does, it doesn't eradicate the fact that he tortures people. And he gets paid a lot of money to do so."

Tephi shook his head at me. "You really are stubborn aren't you." He took my arm. "Come with me, I have one more thing to show you."

He led me down more backstreets to a large building in a quiet area. There was a park in front of it in which a number of children were playing.

"This is an orphanage," Tephi explained. "Tallis's orphanage. Tallis was given an initial payment when he signed on with Father. A lot of that money he used to open this place. Between us, me, Tallis and Etain cover the cost of keeping it open. Tallis set up a similar one in his own kingdom, which his family all contribute to. You wanted to know why he demanded so much money for his services, well now you know."

Tephi had given me a lot to think about and the walk back to the palace was made in silence.

As soon as I got back, I went to see Tallis. I wanted to hear his side of what Tephi had told me. There was no answer when I knocked on his door.

I wasn't sure if he wasn't in or if he was just ignoring me, so I went into the secret passageways and headed straight to his suite to check. I removed the cover of the spyhole and placed my eye against it, but I could see and hear nothing. He had pulled his magical curtain across, preventing me from spying on him. I went back to his suite many times after that, but not once was the curtain pulled open.

Wedding

Life continued on for the next few months. While Tallis didn't actively avoid me, he no longer acted as though I was someone he wanted anything to do with. He treated me the same as he did Rose, and I could hardly blame him.

One day I managed to corner him in the corridor and I said how sorry I was for my behaviour toward him and almost begged him to forgive me. It wasn't that I missed the conversations he used to initiate with me, but it had been nice knowing that he could help out if I needed him. Yes, I do know how selfish that sounds.

I said I was aware of all of the kind things he did and that he wasn't the man I thought him to be. His response was to tell me to look him in the eye and say I no longer saw him as an evil monster. I couldn't do it. No matter what good he did, I still couldn't get over the fact that he was a Sentinel and I didn't think I ever would.

The day of Olwen's wedding to Forn arrived and I think I was the only member of the family to not be looking forward to it. For Olwen's sake I put on a brave face and pretended to be happy for her, but I cried when I was alone in my room.

Forn had visited a few times, to sort out arrangements, but he didn't come to my room at night. My bed felt strangely empty, but only when I knew he was sleeping close by; when he wasn't visiting I never missed him or even thought about him. I really was a terrible person back then and it took me a while to realise that I didn't deserve Forn and Olwen did.

Tallis still treated Olwen with the same level of respect he had always shown her and when I went to see him on the morning of the wedding, telling him that I was there on Olwen's behalf made him open the door to his workroom for me.

"I'm worried about Olwen," I said as I entered. I wasn't lying. The only reason I was there was because of my sister.

"What's wrong with her?"

"I don't know," I admitted. "I know that brides are often nervous on their wedding day, but she seems absolutely terrified. She's not eating or drinking anything and I'm worried she's going to make herself seriously ill."

At Olwen's request, it wasn't going to be a big state wedding; just family and friends would be attending. Father had tried to argue against her, but when Tallis had pointed out that putting all of that public attention on her would do her a lot of harm, he relented.

"Let's go see her," Tallis said, surprising me by taking me at my word.

When we got to Olwen's room, we found her pacing the room instead of getting dressed. She had sent away the maid who was supposed to have been helping her. She was still wearing her sleepwear.

"Well you can't get married dressed like that," Tallis said, a hint of amusement in his voice.

I wanted to hit him. The last thing Olwen needed right then was to be teased. Or so I thought.

Instead of reacting badly to the comment, the beginnings of a smile formed on her face. As usual, Tallis knew just the right thing to say to her.

"So what's the problem?" he asked. He looked at the uneaten breakfast sitting on a tray on her table, then back at her.

"I can't get married," she said. "I can't have a wedding night."

As far as I was aware, Olwen hadn't been with a man since she had been attacked. I wasn't even sure she had been with one before it. I should have known that was what was bothering her.

"Sit down," Tallis said. When she obeyed, he sat down next to her and took her hand. "There is nothing for you to worry about. I have spoken with Forn and he has no expectations about tonight. I wouldn't allow him to marry you if he did."

I raised a questioning eyebrow at him, but said nothing. Did he really believe he had the power to stop the wedding? I then realised that he probably did.

"Forn knows what has happened to you and will not try to rush you, he will let you set the pace," he continued.

I then did something I had hardly ever done before; I put my sister's needs above my own.

I sat beside her and took her other hand. "Forn is a gentle, tender and caring lover." Olwen looked at me in surprise. "We were sleeping together before he became betrothed to you," I explained, "but that is of no relevance right now. What is, is that I know him. I know him intimately. He won't ever do anything to hurt you. When you are ready, and you will be eventually, he will treat you the way a woman should be treated. He will patiently wait until that time."

"Are you sure?" Olwen asked. "I thought men had to have regular, you know, relations."

I rolled my eyes. "You can say the word 'sex' you know."

Olwen blushed.

"Whoever told you that about men," Tallis said, "lied to you. Men don't need sex any more than women do. They like having it, but that is all. Forn is going to be making a commitment to you today. He won't betray you by sleeping with someone else if you are not willing to share his bed for a while."

"Try kissing him," I advised. "He's a very good kisser. As you slowly become more relaxed with him, you can go further, but only as far as you want to go. When you feel up to it, get him to give you oral sex. Trust me, you are really going to enjoy that."

Olwen's jaw dropped and she just stared at me, her mouth open. I grinned at her. "If you don't close that I'm going to put food in it."

I stood up. "I'm going to get changed. By the time I come back I expect to see your breakfast tray empty. Then we will see about getting you dressed."

Olwen smiled at me. "Thank you," she said. "Thank you both."

Tallis left when I did. "You did a good thing just now," he said. "I was afraid I was going to have to give her a potion to calm her down."

"See," I said. "I'm not a total bitch."

119

"Not all the time," he replied and walked away, heading back to his workroom. But not before I had seen the smirk on his face.

The wedding went off without a hitch and Olwen left with Forn when he returned to his father's estate. A few weeks later I received a letter from my sister. All it said was 'you were right'. I didn't write back, asking about what precisely, just in case she told me.

I showed it to Tallis and I could tell he was doing his best to keep a straight face.

It wasn't many days later that I had to visit his workroom again. I missed Olwen. Tephi, seeing that her absence was depressing me, decided to give me some self-defence lessons. He purchased a knife and set about teaching me how to use it. It was a very nice knife, with an ornate ivory handle and a blade small enough to conceal, but large enough to do damage. While I enjoyed myself immensely, I didn't do very well and managed to cut my arm, badly.

Tephi rushed me to Tallis's workroom, yelling at a servant to find him while he ran, with me cradled in his arms. Blood was pouring down my arm and dripping onto the floor and I was doing my best not to scream. It hurt. It hurt a lot.

Tallis was waiting outside his workroom for us by the time we got there.

"What happened?" he asked, all business, as usual.

"Knife wound to the arm," Tephi said. I was in too much pain to speak. "It's deep."

"You know, if you want to kill her, you should go for the throat next time."

I couldn't believe it. Tallis, who was always serious, rarely smiled and never laughed, was making a joke at my expense. At least I thought he was.

He ushered us into the workroom and Tephi sat me down on the table. Tallis had already prepared a potion of some sort and ordered me to drink it.

"It will dull the pain," he said when I appeared reluctant.

I took a gulp, bracing myself for the horrible taste. Then I took another. It was great. I finished the cup then asked for a refill, but Tallis refused. I could understand why. I was already feeling light headed.

I watched in amazement as he stitched up my arm. I was feeling absolutely nothing.

When he was done, he prepared a salve and spread it thickly over my wound before bandaging me up.

"It will take a few days to heal, but there won't be a scar," he said. He glanced at Tephi, who looked as white as a ghost. "There's also no chance of infection," he added. "There's a reason some magic users become Healers. We are able to cause wounds to heal faster than other healers, as well as cure things they can't."

"Thank you," Tephi said.

I tried to speak but I couldn't. My tongue felt thick and swollen and my head was still spinning. I had no idea what Tallis had given me to drink, but I knew I wanted to try it again, though I wouldn't be stupid enough to cut my arm first.

Tallis looked at me then at Tephi. "I should give her that stuff more often. It appears to shut her up."

Tephi was still laughing when there was a knock on the door. A servant was on the other side, patiently waiting. He bowed when he saw my brother.

"His Majesty requests your presence in his study when you are finished here," he said. "All three of you."

That didn't sound good, but I was in no state to worry about it.

"Please tell him we will be right there," Tallis said. Then he turned to me. "Can you walk?"

"Yes," I said, stood up, then fell straight onto the floor when my legs buckled.

"I think you gave her too much," Tephi said as he picked me up.

"I had to. It would be too hard to concentrate on my stitching if she was screaming."

Tephi carried me to Father's study, with Tallis trailing us. Father was fuming when we got there, but he waited until I had been placed in a chair before yelling.

"What happened?" His voice was so loud I'm sure the walls shook, but that might just have been the effect of the potion.

Tephi stood up straight. "I was giving her self-defence lessons. They didn't go well."

"Self-defence lessons?" Father shouted. "With a knife? Women do not use weapons. There will be no more lessons. Understand?"

Tephi nodded his head. He did occasionally argue against our father, but it appeared that this was not going to be one of those times.

Tallis cleared his throat. "What?" Father yelled at him.

"Actually, your Majesty, it might be a good idea for the princess to know how to defend herself. While it is highly unlikely that her life will ever be in danger, it's not beyond the realms of possibility. Knowing how to use a knife might save her life."

Father thought about his words for a moment. "Alright," he eventually said. "But if there are any more injuries, to anyone, the lessons stop."

"Thank you, Father," Tephi said and bent down to pick me up. We were out of the room before Father had chance to change his mind.

"Thank you," Tephi said to Tallis as he carried me to my room.

"It was the right thing to do," was all he replied.

Tephi laid me down on my bed then removed my shoes. "You should train Rosemerta as well," Tallis said as my brother pulled the covers over me. I was having trouble keeping my eyes open.

Tephi grunted. "I tried. She told me that knives are for cooks or soldiers and she is neither and if she needs protection it's a man's job to provide it. I sometimes wish it was she who had been married off instead of Olwen."

"Don't we all," I'm sure I heard Tallis say before sleep claimed me and I heard no more.

Fever

Needless to say, my arm healed, as Tallis said it would. Part of me was disappointed that there was no scar. My lessons with Tephi continued and I became quite good. Not only did he teach me how to use a knife if I was attacked, but he also showed me how to wear it without revealing it. I began to always carry it on me.

A few months later, Olwen and Forn came to visit. They both appeared happy and at ease with each other and I realised that them being together no longer bothered me.

We all thought they had just come for a visit, but it turned out there was another reason. During dinner, Olwen announced she was pregnant. I couldn't be happier for her. Not only because she was going to be a mother, but it showed that Forn was helping her get over her ordeal.

When Tallis took her away to his workroom so he could examine her, I took Forn aside. I wanted to make sure he was taking good care of her. It looked like he was, but looks could be deceiving. I also needed to hear that he was genuinely happy with the marriage.

"I miss you," he said. "I miss you a lot, but Olwen is everything I could have asked for in a wife. You and I were good together, but it would never have worked out."

"I know," I said and kissed him on the cheek. "Do you love her?"

I didn't doubt his honesty when he said, "Not yet. I have strong feelings for her and they are developing each day, but I would be a liar if I said it was love. But it will be. And I'm sure she feels the same about me."

"Good." They were the words I needed to hear. I couldn't bear the thought of either of them being in a loveless marriage.

A while later I found myself alone with Olwen. Tallis had confirmed that the pregnancy was progressing well and he didn't believe there would be any complications.

We chatted and giggled together for a while, like women do when they haven't seen each other for a while. Then Olwen turned serious.

"Thank you for what you said on my wedding day. Your words really helped. I had no idea that there was anything between you and Forn and would never have agreed to the marriage had I known."

I took her hands in mine. "I know. It was never anything serious, just two friends having a bit of fun."

For some reason, my words made her blush.

"He really is good with his tongue, isn't he."

I burst out laughing.

Olwen and Forn didn't stay for long. They had only visited to make their announcement and he had to get back home. His father was teaching him everything about running his numerous businesses and he couldn't afford to be away too long.

For some reason the palace seemed emptier after they had gone than it had the first time they left. My mood soured again. It got even worse when I was eavesdropping on my father's study one day and did not like what I heard.

Tallis and Father were in the room. Father had summoned him and curiosity got the better of me. I didn't usually spy on my father, but I learned some interesting things the few times I did. This wasn't one of them.

"Take a seat," Father said as soon as Tallis entered the room. Tallis did so and waited patiently for my father to explain what he wanted.

"It's about time I arranged for Adara to be married."

I couldn't believe my ears. I was only eighteen. I was too young to be married. Rose was older than me. Why wasn't he talking about marrying her off?

"I have someone in mind for Rosemerta," Father continued, "but the man in question is studying so nothing can be arranged until next year, but I have no idea who would be suitable for Adara. Any ideas?"

I was horrified. My father and Tallis were going to discuss who I was going to be betrothed to. I knew I would have an arranged marriage, but I couldn't understand why Tallis got a say in it.

"That's a tough one," Tallis said. He glanced over at the wall as if he was looking at me, making me wonder if he knew I was there somehow. "You can't use her to strengthen an alliance with one of your allies as they won't be happy with their side of the bargain, unless they have a son that is causing them problems. But if that was the case, would you really want to agree to the arrangement?"

Anger burned through me as I tried to work out what he had meant by that. It got worse when I saw my father nodding as though he was agreeing.

"On the other hand," Tallis continued, "you can't use her to form an alliance with someone you class as a potential enemy as they may take it as a declaration of war, once they get to know her."

By that point I was seething. I don't think I had ever been so insulted.

"I see your point," my father said. "She's not your typical wife material, is she. A lot of men still believe a wife should be seen and not heard. I can't see Adara agreeing to that. And what would happen if her husband insisted on her wearing a dress?"

I have to give Tallis credit, he managed to keep a straight face.

"Do you really want my advice?" Tallis asked.

"It's why I sent for you."

"Leave it a couple of years. She's young enough. You never know, she may become more agreeable as she ages."

He turned and looked at me again. There was no way he could see me through the wall, but something told me he knew I was there, leaving me wondering how much of what he had said was for my benefit rather than my father's.

"Maybe you're right," I heard Father say. "I'll give it some thought."

I breathed a sigh of relief. I was being given a few years reprieve, hopefully. Then I realised that I had Tallis to thank for it and I was filled with indecision as to what to do. If I said anything, he would know I had been eavesdropping. Then again, I suspected he knew that anyway.

I decided to look for him as soon as he left Father's study. I found him in his workroom. For once, the door was open.

"I've been expecting you," he said when I asked permission to enter. The door may have been open, but that didn't necessarily mean I was allowed to go in.

"I've come to thank you. For persuading my father not to marry me off."

Tallis put down the pestle and mortar he had been crushing some leaves in and gave me his full attention.

"I didn't do it for you."

The words were spoken calmly, with no undertone or hidden meaning, but never had six words hurt me so much. They made me feel insignificant. I turned and ran from the room, vowing to avoid Tallis from then on.

Unfortunately, the decision was taken out of my hands. A couple of days later, I became seriously ill with a fever. It wasn't until I had fully recovered that I found out how close to death I was.

I don't remember a lot about the first few days. I have been told that I drifted in and out of consciousness and was delirious. Luckily nobody could make out what I was saying.

Tallis hardly left my side. He ate all of his meals in my room and slept in a chair by my bed; if he slept at all, that is.

Whenever I woke, he forced me to drink water or whatever concoction he happened to have made for me and was continually applying and reapplying salves designed to draw the fever to the surface of the skin and away from the centre of the body.

As I said, I can remember nothing of this. I only have the words of my father, brothers and sister to go by. It got to the point where Tallis said that if my fever didn't break that day, I would not live. He wasn't getting enough sustenance in me for me to fight any longer.

Thankfully, before the end of the day, my temperature began to drop.

I woke to find Tallis beside me, wiping sweat from my head with a damp cloth. I had never felt so physically drained in my life. All of my muscles hurt. I tried to speak, but my mouth was too dry.

Noticing I was awake, Tallis raised my head and put a cup to my lips. He tipped it and water trickled into my mouth. I wanted to gulp it down, but he wouldn't let me.

"You had us all worried," he said when I collapsed back onto the bed.

I was too tired to respond. I closed my eyes and went back to sleep. When I awoke once more, Tephi was there.

"Tallis certainly earned his keep this time," he said. "Nobody expected you to make it. Even he wasn't certain."

"What happened?" I managed to gasp. Tephi helped me to sit, gave me a cup of water, instructed me to sip it, then told me everything.

Tallis had saved my life. I wasn't sure I liked being that indebted to him.

It was many more days before I was finally allowed out of bed. Tallis insisted on making all of my meals until he announced that I was well enough to leave my room. I didn't enjoy any of them. I was sure he was making them horrible on purpose, though he insisted he wasn't. I longed to eat meat, but he told me my body needed to recover and I could only eat light meals. He said light, I heard liquid. What I wouldn't have given to sink my teeth into something solid.

Rose was an absolute angel. The first few days that I was awake but bedridden, she washed me, helped me to the toilet, read to me until a long time after I had fallen asleep. She could have got a servant to do it, but she didn't. She spent as much time with me as she could, leaving me alone only when I wished it or she had to eat or sleep. Her actions didn't absolve her, in my eyes, of what she had tried to do to Simion, but they did go a long way toward fixing our broken relationship.

One morning, when Tallis brought me my broth for breakfast, I decided I was feeling brave enough to ask him a question.

"Why is your curtain always closed these days?" He would know exactly what I was talking about.

He placed the tray on my lap, but didn't sit on the seat beside the bed.

"I kept it open to show you that I have nothing to hide. Now I'm through trying to prove things to you and I appreciate my privacy."

He left before I could ask anything more and sent a servant to collect the tray. I didn't see him again until my evening meal; if you could call it a meal.

"Thank you," I said as he handed me a bread roll to go with the soup. I held it up. "For this, as well as for saving my life. Words cannot express my gratitude."

He shrugged, as though my words meant nothing to him. "I was just doing my job."

That's when it struck me. That was all I had become to him and all I would ever be. Nothing I could say or do would ever change that. And I had nobody to blame but myself.

Elopement

It took a while, but eventually I realised that I didn't care. I didn't like Tallis and, truth be told, I was still terrified of him, so why should it bother me how he treated me as long as he performed his duties?

As soon as I was well enough, Tephi and Etain took it upon themselves to get my fitness back to where it was before I became ill. The fever had taken a lot out of me and I had to take it easy to begin with.

They also continued to teach me bow and knife skills, whenever Father wasn't around to witness my lessons. I was becoming quite a proficient archer, even beating Tephi occasionally when we competed against each other. Etain was a different matter. While Tephi could beat him with a sword, he was by far the best archer I had ever seen.

Tephi was so impressed with my progress that he started calling me Toxo, short for toxophilite, but not in front of our Father, of course.

Life in the palace settled down and everyone seemed to be reasonably happy, though each had their secrets to keep. Tephi continued to go to the brothel to see his girlfriend and son, Etain carried on being more than just friends with Simion and Rose continued to flirt with every eligible bachelor who visited. I had no idea what Tallis got up to and I didn't care.

That all ended when we had a visitor from another kingdom. I had never met someone from outside of the alliance before. He was shown immediately into the throne room and I headed to the secret passageways so I could spy on them.

By the time I got there, they were discussing the possibility of a trade agreement between the two kingdoms. Tephi was there, as was Tallis. He had the hood of his cloak raised and was wearing his dark glasses, hiding what he was, though something told me the visitor had his suspicions. He kept glancing at him nervously.

The discussions were boring, so I concentrated on the man instead. He was of average height and was a little rotund. His short dark hair was neatly trimmed, as was his matching beard. I didn't find him appealing in any way. In some respects I was a little disappointed; he looked no different to men from any other kingdom. I don't know what I had been expecting. Three arms, maybe.

His voice droned on monotonously. I have no idea how the men in the room managed to keep awake.

Father did him the courtesy of allowing him to finish what sounded like a prepared speech before informing him that, as he should have been aware, his kingdom was not part of the alliance and, therefore, Amanet was unable to make any sort of trade agreement with him.

His reaction showed that this was not news to him and he did his best to persuade my father that an agreement would be good for both kingdoms and no other realm within the alliance needed to know about it.

The comment made my father very angry and I could see a vein pulsing in his neck when he shouted that he would never, under any circumstances, consider such an outrageous act.

The visitor offered his apologies for misunderstanding the sort of man my father was and bowed deeply before requesting permission to stay the night, promising he would leave first thing in the morning.

My father seemed reluctant, but agreed. He rang for a servant and gave him instructions to escort the man to one of the guest rooms. I noticed that the one he chose was right next to Tallis's suite. Coincidence? I think not.

After he had left, Tallis pulled back his hood and removed his glasses.

"Well?" Father asked.

"He didn't lie about anything, but there was something off about him. It was almost as if he was concealing his real purpose for being here and a trade agreement was only a secondary reason. I can't tell you more than that I'm afraid."

Father nodded his head. "Tephi?" he said, turning to my brother.

"I agree with Tallis. The man is up to something. I wouldn't trust him."

"I don't," Father said. "The only reason I agreed to meet him was that I was hoping we would be able to figure out why he is here."

"I will keep an eye on him," Tallis said, then bowed and left the room.

Knowing that nothing more of interest would be said, I returned to my room.

I decided to go to the library and was not pleased to find our visitor there. He was lounging in a chair, reading a book, and immediately stood up when I entered the room.

"I will leave if you wish to be alone," were the first words he spoke to me.

I waved away his suggestion. "I'm just here to get a book. I'm not staying."

"Allow me to introduce myself. I am Count Gillain from Draygar. I am delighted to meet you."

He held out his hand to me and, not wishing to be impolite, I did the same. He didn't, however, shake my hand. Instead he gently took hold of my fingertips, raised my hand up to his lips and kissed the back of it, making me blush.

"Princess Adara," I said. I didn't really want to tell him who I was but it would have been rude not to.

He bowed his head. "Please forgive me, your Highness," he said. "I did not realise you were of royal blood."

Looking down at what I was wearing, I could hardly blame him. Dark trousers and a light blue blouse hardly called out 'princess'.

"I try to pretend I'm not," I admitted. The man may not have been attractive, but he was certainly charming.

Despite his charm, I didn't feel comfortable in his presence, so I quickly retrieved a book from one of the shelves and was going to leave the room when Rose walked in.

"I've been looking for you everywhere," she said, then stopped short when she saw I was not alone. "Oh. I didn't realise you had a guest."

Count Gillain gasped when he saw Rose. "You must be Princess Rosemerta," he said and walked up to her. He held out his hand. Like he did with me, he kissed the back of hers when she held it out to him, making me feel less important than I had.

"I had heard rumours about your beauty. I am so pleased to see that they are true."

I couldn't believe what I was hearing. While Rose was pretty, she was far from beautiful. This man was sucking up to her for some reason and had instantly transformed from an intriguing stranger from another realm to a bit of a creep.

Rose looked him up and down, taking in his figure, his face and the fact that he was at least fifteen years older than her, probably a bit more.

"Please accept my apologies," Rose said, a little disdainfully, "but I really must speak with my sister urgently."

At the time, I had no idea whether she was telling the truth, but I didn't question her. Instead I just followed her out of the room. As soon as we were far enough away to not be overheard, she went onto her tiptoes so she could whisper to me. I'm not much taller than Rose, but enough to make her feel short when she stood next to me.

"I have heard that Father has a visitor from one of the kingdoms outside the alliance."

She sounded so excited, I almost didn't want to tell her the bad news.

"I know. You just met him. Count something or other from Draygar, I think he said."

"Oh." The look of disappointment on her face made me laugh.

"Don't worry," I said, putting my arm around her shoulders. "I'm sure others from his realm are much more attractive."

We spent an enjoyable afternoon together, neither of us mentioning the visitor again. I thought I would see no more of him, but unfortunately I was wrong. When we returned from our day out riding, I spotted him leaving my father's study. He was grinning so broadly it made me shiver. He had obviously got what he wanted from my father, but I had no idea what. The king was an honourable man and wouldn't enter into a trade agreement with a kingdom outside of the alliance, not without permission from all realms within it. It made me wonder what the count was really in the kingdom for.

I put it from my mind and went for a shower. It's a decision I still regret. If I had trusted my instincts more and spoke with my father, would it have made a difference to what happened? I have no idea, but it's something I will always wonder.

When it was announced the next morning that the visitor had left, I wasn't the only one who was pleased.

"I didn't trust that man," Tephi said. "He was after something other than what he said he was here for. Thankfully it appears as if he didn't get it."

I thought back to how he had looked when he exited Father's study and I wondered if Tephi's comment was correct, but I didn't say anything. What would have been the point? Tephi would have brushed my concerns away. Tallis, however, didn't seem as relaxed as everyone else around the breakfast table, as though he, too, wasn't sure that the count had left empty handed.

Rose didn't show up for breakfast, but that was nothing new. She often stayed in bed later than the rest of us. Etain had promised to give me another archery lesson, so as soon as we had finished eating, we both left the room.

I didn't see the rest of my family again until the evening meal. When Rose didn't show up to that one either, I began to worry.

"She's probably out for the evening," Etain said when I voiced my concern. "Stop fretting. She'll be back in the morning." Then he paused and thought for a moment. "Actually, knowing Rose, it will be the afternoon."

But by the next evening, there was still no sign of her. I hunted everywhere and questioned all of the servants, but nobody had seen her since the evening meal we shared after we went riding together.

As I felt I had no other option, I tried to open her door, but it was locked. Each of us could lock our rooms, but we rarely did so. People always knocked before entering and didn't do so unless they had permission. The only exception was the cleaners. The only times I ever locked my door was when Forn was with me, for obvious reasons.

I went to find Tallis. I assumed it would be a waste of time, but there was no harm in asking.

"You're worried about Rosemerta," he said the moment he saw me. I nodded my head. "I am as well. It's not like her to disappear for this long."

"Her bedroom door is locked," I told him. "Can you still get in?"

Tallis looked at me for a while, his face expressionless. "Tell nobody about this," he finally said and we went to Rose's door.

Checking that nobody was around to see him, Tallis placed his hand over the lock and closed his eyes. A moment later, I heard a click. He turned the handle, opened the door and walked in.

Nothing appeared to be out of place. The room was messy, but then again, it always was. Then I spied a piece of paper on her dressing table and rushed over to it. I read it through quickly, then once more, slowly. I couldn't believe what it said.

I handed it over to Tallis. "We have to show this to your father," he said as soon as he had finished reading it.

Father was in his study, but gave us permission to enter when we knocked.

"We found this in Rosemerta's room, your Majesty," Tallis said as he handed over the note.

Father frowned as he read it. "She's eloped?" he said, unable to believe it any more than I did.

"That's what the note says." I noted the wording Tallis used. He didn't say 'that's what happened' or 'so it seems'. It gave me the impression that I was not the only one having doubts.

Father sighed. "Well there's nothing we can do about it now. Rosemerta and Count Gillain will be half way to Draygar by now.

Even if I sent my fastest messenger bird to the garrisons near the border, they will have crossed before the bird arrives."

"So you are going to do nothing?" I asked. I didn't even try to keep the incredulity out of my voice.

"What can I do? Rosemerta has made up her mind that this is what she wants and it's too late for me to stop her. I can petition the King of Draygar for her return, but she left willingly so he won't interfere."

I stormed out of the study. Tallis ran after me and grabbed my arm, spinning me around. "Where are you going?"

"To see Tephi. Maybe he will do something if Father won't."

"You will be wasting your time. Politically, there's nothing he can do. When a citizen of Amanet goes into another kingdom, unless they are part of the alliance, there is nothing anyone can do."

"What if she didn't go willingly?" I was certain she had not eloped. The note wasn't written in her handwriting and she had shown no interest in the count. Even Rose wouldn't go from disinterest to running away with him so quickly, especially as she hadn't had the opportunity to spend any time with him. Something was wrong, very wrong and I was the only one who could see it.

"It makes no difference. As your father stated, all he can do is ask the king to find her and return her, which it is highly unlikely he will do. The only other option is declaring war. Do you really think Rosemerta is worth going to war over?"

I wanted to say yes, but I couldn't. War would mean a lot of death and not only for citizens of Amanet. Other kingdoms in the alliance would become involved. No one person would be worth that.

Knowing that Tallis was right, I didn't go to see Tephi; I couldn't bear to hear him say that there was nothing I could do. There was also no point in sharing my suspicions with him. All it would do was make him worry, the way I was.

I waited until it was dark and I was sure that everyone was in bed before grabbing the bag that I had packed and sneaking down to the kitchen. I put enough food inside to last a couple of days, and a water bottle, all the time looking around me to make sure that nobody was around. It was still too early for any of the servants to be up, but I couldn't guarantee nobody would sneak into the kitchen for a quick snack.

I then went to the back door and unlocked it. I had only just put my hand on the handle when a stern voice behind me said, "Where do you think you are going?"

Journey

I turned around slowly. Tallis was standing there, his arms crossed, his face unreadable, as always.

"That is none of your business," I snapped at him.

"It is if you want to get through that door."

I turned to face the door once more and tried to open it. I couldn't move it. I knew I had unlocked it so there was only one explanation.

"You put a Shield on it?" I asked. I couldn't believe he would do such a thing. He didn't give a damn about me so I couldn't understand why he would stop me leaving.

He nodded his head. "And it will remain there until you tell me where you are going and why?"

"Why do you care?" I know it would have been easier just to answer his question, but he had annoyed me. It wouldn't be long before someone would come into the kitchen and I wanted to be long gone before that happened.

"My job is to protect this family and that includes you. How can I do that if I have no idea where you are?"

He didn't sound angry. There was no emotion in his voice whatsoever. He was doing what my father had employed him to do, nothing more. He wasn't personally committed in any other way.

I wanted to lie to him, but what would have been the point? He would have known and not removed his Shield until I told him the truth. I had no choice. I either told him where I was going, and why, or he would make sure I couldn't go anywhere.

"I'm going after Rose. She's my sister and she's in trouble. I have to help her. I don't believe for one moment that she left willingly."

He then surprised me by saying, "Nor do I."

I felt a faint glimmer of hope that he was going to let me leave after all, but he soon dashed it.

"How, may I ask, are you planning on finding out where she is?"

I just looked at him. I had no answer. He hadn't finished.

"And if, by some miracle, you do find out, how are you planning on getting there? And if you do miraculously make it there alive, how are you going to rescue her?"

My shoulders slumped. I hadn't thought about anything other than going after her. I had absolutely no idea what I was going to do once I got out of the palace. I wasn't even sure how I was going to accomplish that if the guards refused to open the gates for me.

"You are going to need help," Tallis said.

Seeing as he was stating the obvious, I almost made a sarcastic reply, but it wouldn't have been a good idea. "Tephi won't help," I said, "and nor will Etain. Who else is there I can turn to?"

"You could have asked me."

I couldn't hold back my laugh. "And why would I ask you? You hate Rose and are probably glad that she's gone. You don't seem to like me very much anymore either. Why would you help me?"

"Because it's the right thing to do." He grabbed my arm and pulled me away from the door. "Come on, we have more things to pack."

He took me to his workroom, threw a bag at me and told me what to put in it. He then said he was going to grab some things from his room and I wasn't to leave his workroom until he returned. I was too stunned to do anything other than nod my head.

He could have been going to see my father, or one of my brothers, to tell them of my plans, but I didn't think he was. He wasn't that underhanded. If that was his intent, he would have dragged me there himself instead of leaving me in his workroom, which he had probably Shielded to make sure I couldn't leave. I didn't try to find out.

He wasn't gone long and when he returned he had a backpack on. He checked the bag I had been filling with his

139

healing supplies and nodded his head. He put a few more items in then closed it.

Without saying a word, he left the room, expecting me to follow like an obedient puppy. Which, of course, I did. Under the circumstances, what choice did I have?

The door closed itself behind me.

We left via the back door, which opened when I turned the handle, and went directly to the stables. Despite having stable hands to do it for me, I had been taught how to saddle a horse and quickly had my horse ready to go. Tallis strapped his bag to the back of his saddle then signalled that he was ready to leave.

"Ride slowly and say nothing," he said quietly to me as we approached the main gate.

Two guards came to attention as soon as they saw us. Both looked tired. I think they had been napping and the sound of our horses' hooves woke them.

"Good morning," Tallis said to them. Then he looked into the sky. "Or is it still night? I'm taking the princess with me to find some plants I use for healing. It might be a good thing for her to learn."

To my surprise, the guards didn't doubt his word. They opened the gate and let us through.

"How did you lie?" I asked as soon as we were out of earshot.

"I didn't. It's going to be a long journey. I may as well teach you something along the way."

I felt like hitting him. I had been dreading travelling with him as it was and now he had just announced that he was going to be taking on the role of teacher as well as bodyguard. I was not amused. Part of me wanted to find a way to escape him, but the rest of me was telling me that I needed him, that I wouldn't even manage to get out of the city without him, let alone the kingdom.

"So where are we going?" I hoped he had some idea because I certainly didn't. I had no clue as to how to track down the count.

"First we have to go to Sobek."

I couldn't hide my surprise. "Sobek? Why?"

"A number of reasons. Firstly, Draygar isn't in the alliance so, as a magic user, I need permission from my queen to enter the kingdom. Secondly, I want to pick up my brother. He's a Warrior as well as a Cloak so may be of great use to us."

"Cloak?" I asked, interrupting him. "What's a Cloak?" He had mentioned it before but I had never heard the details of what exactly a Cloak was.

"He has the ability to make himself, and anyone he is in physical contact with, invisible so others can't see or hear them."

I raised my eyebrows. "Now that's interesting. If he can make himself invisible, what's to stop him using his ability to spy on women while they are undressing, for example?"

"Integrity. Plus, if the authorities ever found out, and somehow they find out about everything, they would strip him of his powers. No woman is worth that. Now, where was I? Oh yes, the third reason. I have a friend whose mother is a great source of knowledge. If anyone knows anything about Count Gillain, it will be her. I'll contact my friend when we take our first break. I'll need him to arrange access to her for me."

"Arrange access? Where is she? Prison?"

"No. She just has a lot of people seeking an audience with her, for obvious reasons, and I don't want to wait in line. It could take weeks. Daranis will be able to get us in a lot quicker."

"How are you going to contact him?" I asked. I didn't really want to be talking to Tallis, but he had me curious. "Do we need to go into the city to find a courier?"

"You'll see." He didn't wink at me, but I envisioned him doing so. I was sure he said that just to annoy me.

A few hours later, once we were far from the city, Tallis slowed his horse down and drew to a halt. "We should take a break," he said once I was close enough to hear him.

I nodded my head and he steered his horse off the road and across the meadow, aiming for a small copse of blossom-filled trees. The air as we rode past them was filled with a lovely fragrance. I breathed deeply, enjoying the aroma and the sunshine on my face, momentarily putting from my mind where we were going and why.

Once we had rounded the trees so they were hiding us from the road, Tallis dismounted. He sat down on a patch of grass, crossed his legs, put his hands on his knees and closed his eyes. I had seen him do that in his room and was curious as to what he was up to.

"What are you doing?" I asked as I slid off my horse's back.

He opened one eye and looked at me. "Contacting my friend. Now be quiet, I need to concentrate."

Knowing I wouldn't get anything more out of him, at least not for a while, I led both horses to a nearby stream so they could take a drink. I also took the opportunity to do the same then refilled both mine and Tallis's water bottles. The water was cold and refreshing; Tallis had put a spell on both containers so the water would stay cool. It seemed he was handy to have around, but not enough to make me glad I was travelling with him.

A short while later he joined me by the stream. I had kept glancing back at him, but he didn't appear to even be breathing. I was watching the slow flowing water, wondering what I would do if he was actually dead, when he placed his hand on my shoulder, making me jump; I hadn't heard him approach.

"Daranis will meet up with us before we reach Sobek. He isn't happy about returning home, but is willing to help out, given the situation."

I said nothing. What could I say? I hadn't been expecting to make the journey with one companion, let alone two. It wasn't as if I was going to get a say in it. My only hope was that Daranis was less frightening than Tallis.

"We should head off again soon," Tallis continued. "But before we go, I might as well give you your first lesson."

I rolled my eyes, but didn't complain when he told me to stand up and follow him over to the trees. I had been hoping he had been joking about teaching me a little about healing, but I wasn't certain if he even had a sense of humour.

He reached up and picked one of the blossoms, held it up to his nose and breathed in deeply, taking in the scent. Then he passed it to me. I did the same. It smelled great.

"Don't let first impressions be deceiving. This flower is pretty and smells enticing. But don't let that fool you. While it can be used to make a great perfume, it's also the main ingredient in a deadly poison. Don't ever try to use it as medicine."

I dropped the blossom flower on the ground. "Are you serious?"

"When it comes to medicine, I'm always serious. But don't worry, it's harmless unless mixed with the right other ingredients. The deadly chemicals aren't released just by holding it. I wouldn't have let you touch it if it was dangerous."

"So what you are trying to tell me is don't trust anything on looks alone. Does that go for humans as well?"

I was trying to tease him a little, to get a smile out of him. It didn't work.

"Some," he said. Then he looked at the sky. "We should head off. I want to reach the next city before nightfall. I'd rather not camp out overnight unless we have to."

It had never occurred to me that we might not be staying in inns on our journey. My first reaction to his statement was absolute horror. Then I realised that I had never slept out in the open and thought it might be kind of fun. When I told Tallis, I didn't get the reaction I was expecting.

"It wouldn't be safe. With there being just two of us, we would be too much of a temptation for robbers."

"Oh. I thought you would be able to put a Shield over us or something."

"I can, but it wouldn't be able to withstand a continued assault and it would drain me too much."

"What do you mean drain you?"

"Mount up," he said. "We can talk while we ride."

True to his word, he went on to explain that all magic takes physical energy. That not only includes creating a Shield, but also maintaining it. If he was to keep us both Shielded all night, he would be too exhausted in the morning to even climb onto his horse. Finding out he wasn't completely invincible was a little disappointing.

"So can all magic users contact each other telepathically?" I asked. Curiosity had taken a firm hold of me and I was eager to learn more.

"No. Only those you have blood bonded with. It's a ceremony that links you together. Not many magic users do it as it involves completely opening your mind to the other person. During the ceremony they can see everything that is inside your head, all of your memories, all of your feelings. It's quite overwhelming."

"So your friend has access to everything you see and hear?" I asked. "Isn't that a bit of a security risk? Does my father know?"

Tallis shook his head. "It doesn't work like that. It's only during the ceremony. A permanent link is put in place, which enables us to contact each other, but nothing else. Daranis knows nothing about me since the ceremony except what I choose to tell him."

So Daranis probably didn't know about my childish behaviour toward Tallis. I have no idea why I was pleased to hear that, but I was.

"Not many magic users," Tallis continued, "find someone they trust enough to go through the ceremony with. Daranis and I grew up together and we already knew so much about each other that we weren't worried about revealing something we wanted to keep private. When Daranis was told he should find a mind-partner, I was the first person he asked. How could I say no?"

"Why did he have to have a mind-partner?"

"Like my brother, he's a Warrior. The Council likes all Warriors to be able to contact someone in case they get into trouble and need to get an urgent message to someone."

"So are you also the mind-partner for your brother?"

"No. It can't be a blood relative. For some reason, the magic used in the ceremony doesn't work if you share the same blood. Osin chose Daranis's brother."

Tallis talked more about magic and his time at the academy as we rode. As he had three disciplines to learn, he had expected to be there a lot longer than was usual, especially as one of those disciplines was a Sentinel. That usually took many years to perfect, which was why Melantha was still studying. Everyone had been shocked at the speed at which he learned everything he needed to know. Even himself.

We made it to the next city before night fell and he booked us a room in one of the inns, making sure it had two beds. He didn't want me sleeping in my own room. It would probably have been safe enough, but he didn't want to take the risk.

He gave me my privacy while I got changed and didn't enter the room until I told him I was in my nightwear and under my covers. He didn't ask me to give him the same courtesy and I couldn't take my eyes off him as he undressed. I had seen a lot of his scars before, but never at such close range. I found them fascinating.

Tallis stripped down to his underwear and I couldn't help admiring his body. The muscle definition was just enough to be appealing.

He must have felt my eyes on him because when he turned around he had a raised eyebrow. He didn't need to voice his question.

"I was looking at your scars," I lied. The look on his face told me he knew I was lying, but he said nothing. Instead he sat down on the bed beside me, allowing me to inspect him more closely.

I raised my hand and waited for him to nod his permission before I touched him. His scars made his skin rough, but not unpleasant to touch.

"Did it hurt?" I asked as I caressed his arm.

"Yes. A lot. I had to be fully conscious and had no pain relief. It took a number of sessions over a few days before they were all complete. They were the worst days of my life. There were times when I begged them to stop."

I reached up and touched his scalp. "Were you forced to shave your head?"

"No. I was given the option. The additional symbols make me a better Sentinel."

Realising I was running my hand over his head as though I was stroking a dog, I quickly withdrew it. "Why does Melantha not have any visible scars? Is it because she's a woman?"

"She hasn't reached that stage of her training yet. When the time comes, which it will soon, she will have to endure everything that I did. The fact she is female will make no difference."

I winced. "What about her hair?"

"She will have the same options I had. Knowing Mel, she will choose not to shave her hair off. She likes it too much. Now, it's late, we should get some sleep."

As soon as he said that I had to stifle a yawn. I hadn't realised I was so tired. Then a suspicious thought entered my mind. Had he just put a sleeping spell on me? I was asleep before I had time to think about it further and was too scared to ask him when I woke.

We left early, after eating a hasty breakfast, and continued to head north. During our first break, Tallis contacted his friend once more. He was heading to Sobek from the east and, as it wasn't much of a detour for him, would catch up with us later in the day.

Later turned out to be just before nightfall. We had stopped earlier than the day before in a small village. Tallis had stayed there before, as had his friend, so it was a good place to meet. The inn was small and clean and the food simple yet tasty so I had no complaints.

We had just finished our meal when the door to the inn opened, letting in a cold breeze. It had started to rain outside, dropping the temperature considerably.

Tallis looked up and a rare smile formed on his face. "Nis," he called out. "Over here."

I turned around to look at the new arrival and I'm sure my jaw hit the floor. He was the most gorgeous man I had ever laid my eyes on.

Daranis

Tallis stood up to greet his friend. As he passed me, he leaned over and whispered, "Stop drooling."

I closed my mouth but couldn't take my eyes off the new arrival. He was absolutely stunning. He had darker hair than I had ever seen before, his hazel eyes were captivating and when he smiled, they lit up. His face structure was perfect and his tanned skin made him even more appealing.

I knew that Rose would be smitten the moment she saw him. If she saw him, I corrected myself. I wasn't an idiot. I was well aware that the chances of us finding her were slim. The thought sobered me up and dragged me from the trance that had taken hold of me.

Tallis threw his arms around Daranis, greeting him warmly. Tallis wasn't a short man, but his friend made him seem so. And this man was fit. Everything about his body told me he was a Warrior. I would have known it even if I hadn't been told and couldn't see the black band on his wrist. The way his clothes clung to him made me want to see what they were hiding.

"Nis," Tallis said to him, "let me introduce you to Adara." He didn't mention my title; we were, after all, travelling incognito. Tallis didn't think that anyone would be looking for us, but he didn't want to take the risk. He had told me that he had left a note in his room for my father, explaining why we had left, but he was hoping it would be a few days before anyone entered his room and found it. He was planning on being out of the kingdom before a search party was raised, not that he believed my father would do so. He was not bothering to disguise himself in any way; there would be no point as his scars would reveal what, if not who, he was so if my father did try to track us down, it wouldn't be difficult.

Daranis knew exactly who I was. Tallis had to tell him to persuade him to help us. He was leaving behind not only his employer, but his wife and young child as well.

Instead of shaking my hand, or kissing the back of it, as I had been expecting, he turned it over and kissed the palm.

"A traditional ancestral greeting," he explained. "I am delighted to meet you."

"Nis's father's family moved to Sobek when he was found to have magic," Tallis said as both men took seats at the table. "Nis was born there and grew up there, but still likes to keep as many family traditions as possible."

"So where do you live now?" I found myself asking.

"Banyan," he said. "Near the border with Amanet."

That explained why he had met us where he had. As our roads were better maintained than most other kingdoms', travelling east through Amanet then heading north would have been the quickest way for him to reach Sobek.

Tallis signalled for the barmaid to bring over a tankard of ale for Daranis before asking him, "What did you tell your employer?"

"Family emergency. It's almost the only thing in my contract that allows me a long period of time away at such short notice."

"Nis has agreed to help us find and retrieve your sister and will be coming with us as soon as we know our destination."

"Thank you," I said. "I know I will feel safer having a Warrior protecting me."

Tallis frowned, but said nothing.

The barmaid made eyes at Daranis as she placed his tankard of ale on the table. I was sure she had loosened her bodice as well so it displayed more of her ample cleavage. Daranis didn't even look at her when he thanked her.

Tallis must have noticed the look I was giving her. "Get used to it," he said. "Women always throw themselves at Nis. He never takes any of them up on their offers though. He fell in love with his wife when they were still in their early teens and hasn't so much as looked at another woman since."

I wasn't sure why he told me that. Was it just a friendly way of preparing me for what journeying with his friend would be like or was he warning me not to bother trying anything with Daranis? I didn't ask; I didn't want to know the answer.

It turned out to be a pleasant evening. Daranis was fun to be around. He soon had me laughing as he recounted some of the tales of his past. I wasn't sure I believed half of the things he was saying, but they were entertaining so I didn't care if they were true or not.

He had been hired by a baron to help keep control of his province. There had been rumours that the neighbouring baron was planning on trying to claim his lands. As soon as the man had found out that Daranis's employer had hired a Warrior, he stopped all plans to invade. There had been a few skirmishes on the border initially, but nothing more.

"I'm getting quite bored," Daranis said. "There's no sign that there is going to be a war between the two barons now, but my employer wants to keep me around as discouragement if nothing else."

"So that's the real reason you agreed to join us," Tallis said. "You want some excitement."

"That's part of the reason, yes. The other part is that I should really go home and visit my mother. I've been away for a long time and this will give me an excuse not to stay long."

While I longed to stay up and spend more time with Daranis, I was so tired I could hardly keep my eyes open. Also, Tallis probably wanted to spend some time alone with him, so I bid them a good night.

"Lock the door," Tallis instructed. "I'll be able to open it."

I didn't need to ask how; I had seen him do it when we needed to get into Rose's room. Something told me, however, that he would end up staying in Daranis's room, if there was a spare bed, so that he didn't disturb me. I also wondered if either of them would be fit to travel the next morning or if their heads would be hurting too much.

Imagine my surprise when I was barely under the covers when there was a knock at the door and Tallis requested permission to enter.

"I thought you would want to stay up late, catching up with your friend," I said as soon as he walked into the room.

He shrugged. "We keep in regular contact. We don't need to see each other to know everything important that is happening in each other's lives."

I watched him undress down to his underwear and waited until he was in his bed before rolling over so my back was to him and closing my eyes.

I expected to dream of Daranis all night, but I certainly hadn't been expecting Tallis to appear as well. I didn't mention my dreams to either of them; I had a feeling it wouldn't be a good idea.

We departed early the next morning and continued our journey north. We would probably hit the border with Sobek before nightfall and I was both looking forward to it and dreading it. I had never been out of Amanet so I had no idea what to expect.

To keep my mind off it, I asked Daranis how magic helped him be a better Warrior.

He was happy to explain that Warriors could control the magic flowing through their bodies and assign it wherever it was needed most. If they concentrated it on their ears, for example, they would be able to hear better while moving it to their eyes made them see much further and clearer than normal humans. They could use it to make them stronger, faster, or more skilled with a weapon. While Tallis used his magic to open a locked door, a Warrior would be able to smash through it.

I found the subject fascinating, or was it the narrator, and wanted to hear more when we stopped for lunch beside a river. Daranis's voice was as nice as his face and I could gladly have listened to it for hours.

While we ate, and Daranis talked, I looked around me. We had stopped near some trees once again and one of them caught my eye.

"What has you so fascinated?" Tallis asked, making me jump. I had been so fixated on the trunk of the tree that I hadn't heard him move closer to me. I hadn't even noticed that Daranis had stopped talking.

"That tree," I said, indicating toward it with my head. "The shape in the trunk looks so much like a human face that I can't take my eyes off it."

"That's because it is a human face," Daranis said.

That got my attention, even though I was sure he was lying. "What?"

His face looked serious. Either he was a very good liar or he was telling the truth.

"It's a venus tree." I had absolutely no idea what he was talking about. Luckily he explained without me having to ask. "It's carnivorous. It grabs hold of anything that goes near it with its branches then absorbs them."

"That's not funny," I said and looked back at the tree. The thought of the face being some poor man made me feel sick.

"He's not joking," Tallis said. "Venus trees are deadly. And very hard to kill. Magic users try whenever they find one. Lucky for us that one has already been taken care of. I wouldn't have stopped here if it had still been alive."

I shivered. "I would rather you hadn't despite the fact it's dead."

"Necessity I'm afraid. The tree may be deadly, but its leaves aren't. It's rare to find a venus tree these days so whenever I see one, I collect its leaves. They are used in many potions and poultices. It's thanks to the healing powers of the venus tree that you are still alive. The fever would have killed you without it."

"If the leaves have such useful healing properties, why do magic users kill the trees? What will you do when there are no more left?"

"We kill wild ones," Daranis said. "We have a fair number in a secure location and there are a group of magic users who tend them. They are never going to go extinct."

"What do you feed them on?"

"Rats, mice, convicted criminals."

"What!" I exclaimed and Daranis winked at me.

"This time I am lying."

I wanted to hit him. I didn't find his comment funny at all.

151

"Can we get out of here?" I asked. I felt uncomfortable being so close to a tree that could kill people, despite the fact that Tallis had told me it was dead.

"As soon as I have gathered what I need," Tallis said.

Daranis helped him remove leaves from the tree and place them in his bag. He asked if I wanted to join in, but there was no way I was going any closer to that thing. I trusted Tallis when he said it was no longer a danger, but that didn't mean I wanted to get close enough that it could grab me if it was faking being dead.

When we next took a break, Tallis decided to give me another lesson. He showed me how to use a pestle and mortar to grind the leaves down into a powder. They were dry so it wasn't difficult, but there were a lot to get through so it was time consuming. Part of me wondered if he was giving me the 'lesson' just so he didn't have to do them all himself.

My hands were aching by the time we finished grinding all the leaves. Tallis said he would teach me how to turn them into a potion when we reached his parents' house. I wasn't sure if it was a threat or not.

"If it's so easy to make potions, why are magic users who are Healers so sought after?" I asked.

"Because we put a little magic into all of our mixtures that makes them more effective. An ordinary healer wouldn't have been able to cure your fever."

He wasn't bragging, he was merely stating a fact.

We travelled for the rest of the day before reaching the border to Sobek. I had been expecting Tallis to take us straight into his homeland, but instead he stopped at an inn and booked us rooms for the night. It was not yet dark so I was curious about why we were stopping so early. When I asked, the only reply I got was, "We have to talk."

"What's the problem?" I asked as soon as we were in the room I would be sharing with Tallis.

"You'd better sit down."

I don't know why, but that made me nervous. "What's going on?"

"We have to stay here for a few days," Tallis said. "One of us needs to go into Sobek to collect someone to stay here with you while Nis and I go and see his mother."

"Why do I have to stay here?" The entire journey, it felt like there was something I had forgotten about and suddenly I had a feeling I was about to find out what it was.

"In Sobek, women are not allowed out without a male chaperone. This can be her father, her owner or a slave."

I thought about that for a moment. "Is there a reason one of you can't act as my slave?"

It was Daranis who answered. He held up his arm, displaying his wrist. It was impossible to miss his black band. For some reason my eyes were drawn to it. "Magic users are only ever slaves to other magic users."

"Okay. How long will it take you to find whoever it is you need?"

"I'm hoping my brother is home," Tallis said. "It will take a couple of days to get to his place. If he isn't, I will have to continue on to my parents' house. That will take another day, maybe a day and a half."

That was not what I wanted to hear. "Are you telling me I might have to stay here for nearly a week? The longer I'm here, the longer Rose is with that man. Who knows what is happening to her. I can't agree to that sort of delay."

"I won't leave you here unprotected," Tallis said, "and I need Nis with me to get me in to see Claudette, his mother." His tone of voice told me there would be no point in arguing.

"There is an alternative," Daranis said.

"Don't even think about suggesting it," Tallis told him.

"It's worth thinking about."

"No, it's not. It is not a valid option. End of story."

"But—"

"But nothing. Have you forgotten Adara is a princess? If her father found out we even mentioned it, he could have us both executed."

That comment had me intrigued. I wanted to know what they were talking about. "Surely I should be the one making the decision."

Tallis turned away from his friend to look at me. "No. I won't agree to it."

"Agree to what?"

"I'm suggesting," Daranis said before Tallis could stop him, "that you act as Tallis's slave."

"Oh." I didn't know what else to say. I didn't need reminding what that would entail. I remembered everything he had ever told me about being a slave in Sobek.

I didn't want to do it. I really didn't want to do it. But I did want to rescue Rose as soon as possible.

"I'll do it," I found myself saying. Rose would have done the same for me. At least I think she would.

"Adara," Tallis said, his voice filled with an emotion I had never heard before. "You won't be allowed to speak without my permission unless you are spoken to directly. You will have to publicly obey me, always. And you will have to be naked."

"I know." He wasn't telling me anything I didn't already know. I clearly remembered everything he had ever told me about his homeland and himself.

"Don't agree to this Adara. Please don't agree to this."

"I have to." There was something I had to ask, though. "Why you? Why would I have to be your slave not Daranis's?"

"I'm fairly well known in Sobek," Daranis said. "I'm not as much of a celebrity as Tal here, but I'm not far off, thanks to my mother. And everyone who knows me knows that I'm married and would never take a slave."

"And Tallis would?" I couldn't believe he would ever really do such a thing.

"No," he said. "I wouldn't. But most people don't know me that well. Plus I have been away for a couple of years. Nobody would question seeing me with a slave."

"So it's decided then?" Daranis asked.

I reluctantly nodded my head. Tallis looked resigned when he also gave his agreement.

"Then I guess I'm going shopping." Tallis and I looked at Daranis, both wondering what he was talking about.

"Well I don't know about you," he said to Tallis, "but I don't own a set of shackles."

Slave

"It's not too late to change your mind," Tallis said. He had the shackles in his hand and was delaying the moment when he had to put them on me. I was wearing nothing but his cloak and was dreading having to remove it.

"I have to do this. You know I have to do this." A week ago I would have given almost anything to get him exiled from my father's kingdom, now I was dressed in only his cloak, waiting for him to shackle me.

"They're just for show, right?" I asked, nervously eying the metal object he was holding.

"No, unfortunately not. As soon as I put these on you, I control you, literally not metaphorically. With these I can make you obey me."

I swallowed. I remembered what I had been told about how a collar was used to control a slave. I wasn't worried that he would do so as he was with me as my protector, but it was still a worrying thought. Despite knowing what they could really do, I told him to put them on me.

They were surprisingly light. I expected them to be uncomfortable and to weigh down on my neck and wrists, but I could hardly feel they were there. As soon as they were in place, a warmth spread through me. I had been told they had temperature control and it turned out it felt pretty good. I could almost enjoy wearing them, if it wasn't for the fact that I had to take the cloak off.

"Ready?" Tallis asked.

I wasn't, of course I wasn't, but I could find no excuse to delay. I untied the clasp at my neck and removed his cloak. I could feel my face go red as I handed it over to him. I had never been naked in front of a man before, except for Forn.

"I wish I could make this easier for you," he said. I believed him. After all, he couldn't lie, or so he claimed.

Tallis led me out of the inn using the back door, so I could avoid walking through the taproom. We were still in Amanet so not many people walked around naked, though being situated so close to the border, the people living in that particular village were more used to the sight than most.

Daranis was waiting in the courtyard for us, holding our horses. He didn't stare at me, but he didn't turn away either. He acted as though I was fully dressed. Having spent so much time in Sobek, he must have been used to seeing people with no clothes on. The fact that, according to Tallis, he hadn't even looked at another woman since meeting his wife may also have had something to do with his reaction, or should I say lack of reaction. Whatever the reason, I was grateful to him.

"You're riding with me," Tallis said as I moved toward my horse. "Your horse will follow."

"Why?"

"If you ride with me, you can sit across the saddle. Trust me, it will be a lot more comfortable for you. I have been told that having your legs spread across the back of a horse can get quite uncomfortable for a woman if she isn't wearing anything. You're welcome to try, if you like, but I wouldn't recommend it."

I took his word for it.

I felt strangely comfortable with Tallis's arms around me. He even put a blanket over the saddle so my bare flesh wasn't touching the rough leather. He held me securely, but not tightly. As my horse wasn't being ridden, all of our bags were strapped to its saddle, so I didn't have to wear my backpack. I didn't know about riding a horse, but I was sure having my bag on my naked back would have been uncomfortable.

To take my mind off the fact that I was displaying all I had to anyone who cared to look my way, I talked to Tallis.

"How did you always know when I was in the secret passageways? There were times when I was sure you were looking at me, even though I was on the other side of the wall."

"I was. I don't know why, but I can sense where you are. Not once were you able to spy on me without me knowing."

"I didn't spy," I said. He raised a questioning eyebrow at me. "Well not exactly. I was keeping an eye on you, making sure you weren't up to anything you shouldn't have been."

"Why do you hate me so much?"

It was the last question I had been expecting him to ask me. He never gave me the impression of being such a direct person. Or that he even cared about how I felt. Not any longer anyway.

"I don't hate you, as such, I hate what you are. How can I not hate someone who tortures others, who can cause pain with just their mind?"

"I don't cause pain."

"Don't lie to me."

"I can't lie, remember. Sentinels don't cause pain. We can enter people's minds, but we can't affect them physically."

"If you make someone believe they are in pain, that is just as bad. I'm sure it hurts just as much as the real thing."

"Sentinels don't cause pain, Adara. What we do is worse, in some respects."

"But you make people scream."

"But not in pain. We make them see things, horrific things, and the images won't stop until they tell the truth. Closing their eyes doesn't help. Nothing does."

"What sort of things are we talking about? What did you make my sister see?" I wasn't sure I really wanted to know.

"I have no idea. A Sentinel doesn't choose what their victims see, the victims themselves do. Whatever horrifies them the most is what they will see. If you want to know what images filled Rosemerta's mind, you will have to ask her when we find her."

I was glad he said 'when' not 'if'.

"Did you enjoy doing it to her?" I had always believed that he had done, seeing as he obviously detested her, but by then I wasn't so sure.

"No, I hated every single minute of it. I always do, but it had to be done."

"Why did you say that what you do is worse than causing pain, in some respects?"

"Because pain is a momentary thing. Once it's gone you can usually forget about it. Those images, on the other hand, stay with you. Some people have nightmares. Those who resist telling the truth for too long have been known to go mad. Knowing you did that to someone is hard to cope with."

"Yet you still do it."

"It has to be done. It stops a lot of bloodshed."

I didn't want to hear any more. I didn't think I would ever understand Tallis's point of view. We rode in silence until we took our first break. Tallis stopped us by a stream so the horses could have some water.

"Show me," I said as we stretched our legs.

"Show you what?" Tallis asked.

"Show me how you put images in someone's head." I would say I had no idea why I asked him to do that, but I would be lying. I had hated Tallis for a long time for causing Rose to scream in agony, only to find out that that wasn't what he had done. I needed to know the truth so I could go on hating him.

I could see the anger flow through him and he yanked hard on the chain which was connecting the collar around my neck to his wrist. It hurt and I cried out as I stumbled closer to him.

"What I do is not some party trick," he hissed at me. "When will you get it through your head that I hate doing it and I will only ever do it when I have to, when there is no other option. And I will never, ever, do it to you. Do you understand?"

I nodded my head. I could feel tears building up in my eyes, threatening to fall.

"I just thought that I might understand you better if I experienced it," I managed to mumble.

"You won't," he said. Then he put his arms around me and held me tight. "You will never understand what I am," he said gently. I was trembling and he didn't let me go until I had stopped.

Daranis loudly cleared his throat to get our attention. "We should get moving."

Tallis released his hold on me and led me over to his horse. He helped me remount then climbed up behind me and placed his arms around me once more.

"I'm sorry if I hurt you," he said when we had been riding in silence for a while. "It was not my intention."

"I know. And I shouldn't have asked you to use your powers on me. You told me you hated doing it. I guess I'm still not listening."

"You're getting better. Maybe there is hope for you yet."

A few hours later we approached a large village. "Do you want to stop for some food?" Daranis asked. "Or carry on through."

"I think we should keep going," Tallis replied. "We have enough supplies."

"You said that for my benefit, didn't you?" I said. "You don't want me to have to be unclothed in public if it can be avoided." We had met few people as we travelled so not many people had seen my nakedness.

"Actually I don't want you around people when you are supposed to be my slave because I'm worried you won't be able to keep your mouth shut. You're not supposed to speak without my permission, remember."

The way he said it brought a smile to my face. "Wow. It seems you do have a sense of humour after all."

"I'm not joking Adara. I can't lie, remember."

"No," Daranis said. "But he can speak partial truths." He winked at me, leaving me wondering whether Tallis had been serious of not.

The rest of the day passed uneventfully and when we stopped at an inn for the night, Tallis arranged for us to eat in our room rather than in the dining room. The moment the three of us were alone, Tallis removed his cloak and placed it over my shoulders. I pulled it tight, covering up as much of myself as I could.

"Can I put any of my own clothes on?" I asked. While I appreciated no longer being exposed, wearing something more than just a cloak would have been nice.

Tallis shook his head. "If anyone knocks on the door, the cloak can be quickly removed, clothes can't. I can, however, take this off for a while. You won't need it until we leave the room," he said as he removed the chain that connected my collar to his wrist.

"You're handling yourself well," Daranis said. "From what Tal told me about you I didn't think you were going to be able to obey him, but you acted the perfect slave the moment you entered the building."

I had no idea if Daranis was trying to wind me up, but it didn't work. Tallis may have mentioned me to him, he may not have done. Either way, I didn't care. What he said was right. I didn't think I would ever be comfortable acting as anyone's slave, let alone Tallis's, but he was making it as easy for me as he could.

"Are slaves allowed to bathe?" I asked. I had noticed a sign for a wash house out the back as we entered the inn and I longed to relax in warm water.

"Of course," Tallis said. "I will go and organise a bath to be filled for you. I'll have to stand guard over you though, I'm afraid. For you own safety."

I thanked him and he left the room.

It was the first time Daranis and I had been alone and I suddenly felt uncomfortable. I had no idea what to say to him. I knew I was safe with him, after all he hadn't even looked at me while I had been naked, but I just didn't feel at ease.

"Why do you hate Tal so much?" he asked suddenly.

The question took me by surprise. "What makes you think I hate him?"

"We talk. Regularly."

Well I guess that answered that question. I could have argued that he was wrong, that he was only hearing one side of the story, a bias side, but I would have been lying.

"I don't hate him. I hate what he is. I hate all Sentinels. I abhor what they do and, despite many people telling me that they are needed and that their methods are effective, I can't help feeling that there has to be a better way."

"You sound like you think that everyone should be treated well, despite whatever horrific crimes they have committed. In order to get them to confess, you just need to ask them nicely. You believe that everyone is generally good, other than Sentinels that is."

I laughed. I couldn't help it. "Far from it," I said. "I judge too quickly and once I have made up my mind about someone, I am too stubborn to change it." I had never admitted that to anyone before. Maybe it was a sign that I was growing up at last.

"So Tal told me."

"Tallis is a prime example. I decided that I wouldn't like him as soon as I heard what he was and no matter what he did, nothing would change my mind. The fact he is a Sentinel terrified me. It still does."

"Yet you willingly let him have power over you and chain you to him. One word and he could kill you yet you never hesitated to let him put the collar on you. Are you sure you're still terrified of him?"

Thankfully Tallis chose that moment to return. He led me to the baths which were located in a room out the back of the inn. He gave no indication that he knew that Daranis and I had been talking about him. He had arranged exclusive use of the bathhouse, yet he still didn't leave me alone. He refused to leave the room, but didn't watch me. He kept his back to me while I submersed myself in the hot water, despite the fact that he had already seen all I had to offer.

The more I got to know him, the more of an enigma he became.

Once he was sure that I had everything I needed, wash cloths, soap, hair wash, he stripped off his clothes and settle into one of the other baths. I didn't show him the same courtesy he had shown me. I couldn't take my eyes off him as he undressed. I longed to reach out and run my hands down the scarred runes on his back. I had seen him strip off before, but this time he didn't leave his underwear on. He had his back to me and I couldn't help wishing that he would turn around. All too soon he was in the water and out of sight.

Only then did I realise what I was doing. I was ogling a man I despised. I quickly sank down into the water and washed myself. I had only been wearing the shackles for one day, but it felt strange not having them on, or should I say not having the protective shield they provided. Tallis had removed them so I could bathe properly.

The water was warm and relaxing and I felt my eyes close. I was jerked awake by someone washing my hair. Tallis was already dressed in clean clothes and his old ones, having been washed, were hanging in front of the fire to dry.

"As your slave, shouldn't I be doing that for you?" I asked as his fingers massaged my head. "If you had any hair, that is."

"Yes, but we both know that would never happen. You were also supposed to undress me, wash me, then dry me. Why do you think I arranged for some privacy?"

"You're very good at that." I wasn't exaggerating. The only reason I was talking was because it stopped me moaning.

"I've had plenty of practice."

"How?"

"The 'ladies of pleasure' have been teaching me. And the 'gentlemen of pleasure'."

I burst out laughing. "You have been having lessons from whores! What else did they teach you? The best sexual positions?"

I suddenly realised what I had said and how insulting it may have sounded, but it was too late to take the words back.

Tallis, however, wasn't offended. "Not exactly," he said. "But they did teach me how to please a woman."

My mouth was still hanging open when he pushed my head under the water to rinse my hair.

I came up spluttering. "You could have warned me."

"You're right, I could have."

I was too dumbfounded to speak as he helped me out of the tub and dried me off. He was rough, but not unpleasantly so. He wasn't touching me intimately in any way and as soon as I was dry, he told me to stand by the fire to get warm.

He hung the towels up to dry then picked my shackles up off the floor. He didn't say anything as he put them back on me, but his entire demeanour told me he didn't want to do it.

I slept well that night. I was warm and clean, the bed was soft and the pillow hard, just the way I like it.

We left early again the next morning. After a few hours riding, we stopped by a stream for breakfast and Daranis told me more about his family and how he met his wife. I had never seen a man so devoted to a woman, especially one who looked so good he could have almost anyone he wanted. Maybe that was what made him so dedicated to his wife. He could easily have betrayed her every time they were apart, but she had complete trust in him.

One of the reasons he took a job outside of Sobek was because he could not bear to have her as his slave. He vowed never to take her into the kingdom again if he could avoid it.

The sun was just setting when we rode into a village. I had been expecting Tallis to stop at the inn, but he didn't slow down. Instead he led us to a small cottage on the outskirts. He took us around to the back, where we released our horses into a fenced off field. Once the saddles and bridles had been stored in a barn, he strode up to the back door. Without knocking, he walked in.

"Osin," he called out loudly, but there was no reply.

"Maybe he isn't here," Daranis said.

"Maybe," Tallis replied. "He never bothers to lock his door."

He placed his bag on the floor by the kitchen table, then suddenly turned around, grabbed hold of something that I couldn't see and slammed it into the table.

Whatever he was holding shimmered. When the shimmering had stopped, I could see that Tallis was holding someone by the throat, pinning him to the table.

"Adara, meet Osin, my brother."

Sobek

We sat around the kitchen table, drinking coffee, while Osin prepared us a meal. I was once again wearing Tallis's cloak.

Osin had been shocked when Tallis told him who I was. Not just because I was a princess, but because Tallis was treating me as a slave. And I was going along with it.

"There wasn't really much choice, Osin," Tallis said. "The only other option was to leave her at the border and she didn't want that."

"You should have made her stay."

"It's kind of hard to make Adara do anything."

"You're a Shield. Don't try and tell me you couldn't put her in a room and Shield it to keep her in, then drop it after you had left."

"She would have followed us. She's not very good at obeying orders. Though she has been better since I shackled her. Maybe I should keep them on her after we leave Sobek." I must have been imagining things, but I was sure I heard some amusement in his voice.

Osin must have heard something else because he swung around and looked at Tallis, as if he was assessing him. He said nothing though and after a moment he shook his head and returned his attention to the stove.

"Why did you attack Tallis?" I asked. "Didn't you know it was him when we invaded your home?"

It was Tallis who answered. "I've already told you that Osin is a Cloak. Ever since he got his powers, he's been trying to creep up on me."

"And I haven't managed it yet," Osin said. "I have no idea how, but Tallis always knows when I'm nearby, even though he can't see or hear me."

'I know that feeling,' I thought to myself, but said nothing.

I studied Osin as he cooked. Seeing them both together, it was easy to tell that he and Tallis were brothers. He had the same blue eyes as their parents, the colour I kept imagining Tallis to have before his were turned black. He was bulkier than Tallis and a little taller. They had the same facial features, but Osin's were more hardened. Osin's long dark hair, tied back at the nape of the neck, flowed down his back and I found myself wondering if Tallis's used to be the same, before it was removed and runes were cut into his flesh.

It turned out that he was a surprisingly good cook. The meal was great and I had an enjoyable time hearing about the three men growing up together, along with Daranis's brother. I saw a different side to Tallis that night. For a while, he wasn't a Sentinel; he was just an ordinary man enjoying spending time with his friends and family.

The reason for our visit wasn't mentioned until the following morning. Osin understood Tallis's actions, though he didn't agree with them. He thought I should have been left at the palace, under armed guard if necessary.

Despite this, I thought Osin was great. He had charisma and I could understand why he was a hit with women. He didn't flirt in any way, but he was charming and made you want to get to know him better. He wasn't as good looking as Daranis, or Tallis for that matter, but there was something about him that made him the more attractive of the three.

When we had finished breakfast and it was time to leave, Osin surprised us all by saying he would accompany us before Tallis had chance to ask him. It was a good excuse to see his parents and he was between assignments so had nothing better to do. He would visit his commander while he was in the capital.

"What's the real reason?" Tallis asked. It wasn't said in an unfriendly way, but the question was definitely filled with suspicion not just curiosity.

Osin grinned at him. "If you are planning on going into Draygar, you're going to need my help little brother."

Tallis grunted. It felt strange hearing him referred to as a little brother. It made him more human and less a Sentinel, for some reason.

Osin insisted we stop at an inn for lunch instead of picnicking, like we usually did, then proceeded to spend the entire time talking with the barmaid. I was surprised he didn't stay when Tallis told him it was time to go. The look the barmaid was giving him suggested she had been hoping he would.

"Can't you go anywhere without chatting up some young lady?" Daranis asked him once we were on the road once more.

"I wasn't chatting her up." Osin sounded a little too defensive to me. "I was just talking to her. There's a difference."

"Not with you there isn't."

It was mid-afternoon by the time we reached the outskirts of the capital. The number of people on the road had been steadily increasing, as had the number of slaves. I looked closely each time I saw one, but none of them looked unhappy. Most were smiling and those that weren't just seemed caught up in what they were doing. Having so many naked people around made me feel less self-conscious.

Armed men and women guarded the city gates and they welcomed Tallis, Osin and Daranis warmly, greeting them by name. As we rode down the street, many people called out their names in greeting, Tallis more than the others.

"I told you he was a celebrity," Daranis said to me and winked.

"How do they recognise you?" I asked Tallis. People were calling out to him before they had chance to see his face.

"My cloak. It has a unique design on it."

I couldn't help noticing that most of the people trying to attract his attention were female.

"I didn't realise that you were so popular with women," I said.

"He's not," Osin said before Tallis could answer. "Being married to Tal would greatly improve their status, even if they do have to be his slave. He's the most important Sentinel ever to have been born, maybe the most important magic user."

"So they want to be with him just for what he is? That's despicable." For some reason that made me angry.

"Why?" Osin asked. "Don't most women marry for status?"

It wasn't something I had ever given thought to, but I really hoped not. "Well I'm going to marry for love," I declared.

"I hate to shatter your illusions, princess," Osin said, "but you are going to have an arranged marriage whether you want it or not. You will marry for political reasons, not love."

Tallis grunted. "I wouldn't bet on that. Her father is having a few problems in that regard."

"Maybe the king should give her to you in exchange for a lifetime of service to him," Daranis said. "You seem to know how to keep her under control." I could hear the laugher in his voice.

"That will never happen," Tallis snapped at him. "Being married to a Sentinel is not something I would wish on anyone."

He had said something like that before and I was curious about what he meant, but it was something I would have to ask him when we were alone.

When we stopped outside a large wall with a set of metal gates, Daranis said his goodbyes. He planned to go directly to his mother's house and promised to let Tallis know when he could visit with her.

The gates opened automatically as Tallis and Osin rode closer, almost as if they recognised them. "Magic," Osin said, seeing the look of confusion on my face.

The long driveway was lined with rosebushes and ran through ornate lawns. It ended at a large house, where slaves were waiting to take our horses.

"Welcome home Tallis," one of them said and bowed to him. This seemed to irritate Tallis.

"How many times do I have to tell you to stop doing that?" The man grinned at him.

"Just following protocol." He then turned to Osin. "Will you be staying Osin? I can have a room prepared for you."

"Thank you, Faber, that would be great."

"Why didn't he bow to Osin?" I whispered to Tallis.

"He threatened to beat the crap out of him the last time he did it and Faber took him seriously," he said quietly.

"Would he have done?"

"Of course not."

Further discussion was interrupted by Faber addressing Tallis once more. "Would you like me to take your slave for you?"

It took me a moment to realise that he was talking about me.

"That won't be necessary, but please make up a guest room for her. As close to mine as possible."

Faber bowed again, making Tallis sigh in irritation. Both of us could see the smirk on Faber's face, indicating he did it just to annoy Tallis.

"Come on. Let's get you inside and covered up."

The moment the front door closed, Tallis took off his cloak and put it around my shoulders once more.

"Pa is probably in his study," Osin said and walked down the hall, closely followed by Tallis, who took my hand and pulled me after him.

Osin knocked on the door and waited for permission to enter before opening it.

"Osin," Balor said. "This is a nice surprise. And Tallis. To what do we owe this pleasure?"

He stood up and walked around his desk so he could greet his sons, hugging them both tightly. Even in his own house he never wore clothes it seemed.

Then his eyes fell on me. He was about to say something, when they widened in surprise. He rounded on Tallis. "Why is Princess Adara here and why, in the queen's name, is she dressed as a slave?"

"It's a long story, Pa," Tallis said. "Where's Ma?"

"Where do you think she is? In the kitchen. Why we have a cook I have no idea. She never lets the poor woman do her job."

"I'll go and get her," Osin volunteered and left the room.

"It's good to see you, your Highness," Balor said. Instead of holding out his hand, he hugged me. "You have a lot of explaining to do, young man," he said to Tallis over my shoulder.

We retired to the lounge, where Macha greeted me warmly as soon as she arrived.

"Get those shackles off her right now," she said to Tallis. Her tone told me just what she thought of me being treated as a slave.

Without arguing, Tallis obeyed. The moment the shackles were removed, I began to shiver. I had gotten used to the warmth they provided and their sudden removal left me feeling cold.

"Do you have any of your own clothes with you?" Macha asked. I nodded my head.

"Her bag is in one of the spare rooms," Tallis said.

Macha placed her arm around me in a motherly fashion. Tears sprang into my eyes. I had no memory of my own mother ever doing it, though I'm sure she must have. "Come with me," she said.

Tallis's mother led me from the room and up the stairs to the second floor. She tried a few doors before finding the one my bag was in. "He's keeping you close I see," she muttered to herself. I gave her a questioning look. "Tallis's room is right next door."

For some reason that statement was strangely comforting.

I went through my bag and selected some clothes. Macha said she would wait for me outside and left the bedroom, giving me privacy while I got dressed.

I had only been without clothing for a few days, but it still felt strange to have material touching my skin again, especially my most intimate parts. I had gotten used to having the air flowing around me and putting underwear on again felt a little restrictive.

"Has he explained yet?" Macha asked as soon as she walked back into the lounge. She had her arm around me once more. "Does King Andrast even know his daughter is here?"

"Not exactly," Tallis said then told them everything.

"You can't fault his logic," Balor said once Tallis had finished talking.

Macha sighed. "I know, but I want to. There must have been an alternative."

"Can you think of one?"

She couldn't so she turned to Osin. "And what is your excuse for being here?"

Osin grinned at his mother. "You don't think I would let Tal go into a kingdom which isn't part of the alliance alone do you?"

The look she gave him suggested she didn't believe him. "And it's got nothing to do with finding out how easy the women from Draygar are I take it."

The grin didn't leave his face when he said, "Nothing whatsoever."

I was suddenly unsure I wanted Osin to travel with us when we left Sobek. I was beginning to wonder if he would be a help or a hinderance.

Something in my manner or the look on my face must have given away what I was thinking because Tallis leaned close to me and whispered, "Don't worry. His mind will be on the mission. I promise you. He is a professional and won't let anything interfere with what he has to do."

Suddenly Tallis stiffened. He then sat on the floor, crossed his legs, placed his hands on his knees and closed his eyes.

Everyone watched him expectantly. It was the position he took when contacting Daranis so I assumed that this time his friend had contacted him.

He didn't look happy when he opened his eyes and stood up. "Well Nis has managed to get us an appointment with Claudette."

"So what's the problem?" Osin asked.

"It's tonight, at her house. She's having a party and we've been invited to attend."

Party

"You are not going," Tallis said. I could tell he was doing his best not to yell at me.

"Yes I am. I have to be there. What if Daranis's mother wants to see me, to hear what I have to say? After all, I am the reason you are going to see her."

"No, Rosemerta is the reason I am going to see her. The only reason you are even in Sobek is because I couldn't trust you to stay in the palace if I left you behind."

"Yet you trust me to stay here if you leave without me?"

Tallis turned his back on me and walked away. Something told me he needed to get away from me before he did something he would regret.

"Damn it Adara. Why won't you listen to me? Do I have to put the shackles on you again just to get you to obey me?"

"Do you really believe they make any difference?"

"Yes. You act like the perfect slave in public when you are shackled."

"But I won't be in public if you leave me behind."

He swore. A number of times. I still don't know what some of the things he said actually mean.

"Why don't you want me to go?" I asked as soon as he had stopped his rant.

"Are you trying to be funny?" I wasn't. It was a serious question. He didn't wait for me to respond. "It was bad enough making you ride through the streets with everyone able to see your naked body. But then I was holding you tight, covering up as much of you as I could. The party will be different. You will be on full display. I can't put you through that. I won't."

"It's not your decision to make."

Tallis strode over to the door, yanked it open, walked out of the room and slammed it behind him. The discussion was evidently over, but I had no idea what the outcome was.

Almost immediately there was a knock on the door and Osin walked in when I gave my permission. He took a seat on the bed and watched me pace for a while, doing his best not to laugh.

"You need to see this from his point of view," he eventually said.

"And he needs to see it from mine," I snapped. The amusement never left his face, though why he found my anger so funny I don't know.

He tapped the bed beside him. "Come and sit down."

Not knowing what else to do, I obeyed him.

"Tallis has never owned a slave. He abhors everything about slavery. Putting shackles on you was probably the hardest thing he has ever had to do. Yet still did it. Because it was what you wanted. Taking you to a party as his slave will absolutely kill him."

"Then why can't I go as yours?"

Osin shook his head. "It's too late. You have already been seen by too many people. The fact that Tallis now has a slave is already the talk of the town. If you go to that party, everyone there will want to see you, meet you, assess you."

"Surely that's my problem, not his."

"That's not the way he sees it. Everything you have gone through since leaving Amanet and everything you are going to have to face he sees as his fault, his responsibility. His job is to protect you. Taking you naked to a party so everyone can critique you doesn't exactly fit the job description."

"So what's the alternative? I am not going to stay behind. It's my sister we are trying to rescue. If there is any way I can help, I want to do it. I need to do it."

Osin sighed. "He said you were stubborn. I'll talk to him."

"Thank you," I said.

I have no idea what Osin said to Tallis, but when he returned to me, he was no longer angry. He was far from pleased though. Resigned is a good way to describe him.

"Against my better judgement," he said, "I will take you. But Osin goes as well and I will hand you over to him when I have my meeting. Don't leave his side. Ever. Do you hear me?"

I nodded. "And remember," he continued. "Don't speak unless you are directly spoken to. Don't answer any questions about me or yourself. As soon as I pass you over to Osin you will obey his every command and ask his permission before doing anything."

Again I nodded.

"Get undressed and put my cloak on. We are travelling by carriage so you can wear it until we arrive."

Osin and Tallis were both waiting by the front door when I descended the stairs. Tallis had the shackles in his hand.

"You can still change your mind you know."

I shook my head. This was something I had to do. For Rose. If me not being at the party delayed our rescue attempt, I would never be able to live with myself.

The moment the collar and bracelets were in place, a now familiar warmth flowed through me.

It took a while to get to Daranis's mother's house. We had to travel into the centre of the city. There were a lot of carriages dropping people off, some clothed, others obviously slaves. Before anyone could open the door to our carriage, I removed Tallis's cloak and handed it to him. Until that moment the chain that linked me to Tallis, signifying I was his property, wasn't in place. As he attached it to a bracelet on his wrist, his face was unreadable.

"Let's get this over with," he said. The moment the carriage door opened, he stepped out then held his hand out to assist me. I took a deep breath, then left the safety the carriage was providing.

Many people greeted both Osin and Tallis as we entered the house. I could feel eyes on me and could hear the whispers. Most people were surprised by my presence. Obviously the rumours hadn't spread as much as Osin had thought.

The house was filled with the sound of people talking and I could hear music in the distance. Tallis didn't stop to talk to anyone; he led us directly to where he had spotted Daranis.

As soon as Daranis saw us, he broke off his conversation with the man he had been talking to and walked over to us. He looked like he was about to bow to me, but Tallis gave him a warning glance. I may have been a princess, but at that moment I was nothing more than a slave and I had to be treated as one.

"I'm surprised you brought her with you," he said to Tallis.

"So am I," he muttered.

"You are going to have to socialise for a while, I'm afraid," he informed us. "Mother has had an unexpected visitor. The high chamberlain is here."

Both Tallis and Osin looked surprised. I looked at Tallis, asking with my eyes for permission to speak. Tallis nodded his head. "Who's the high chamberlain?" I whispered.

"The queen's chief advisor," Osin said. "I wonder why he is here."

"Maybe Tallis should ask my mother when he goes to see her." Daranis had a huge grin on his face, though I had no idea why.

"Very funny," Tallis said. Then he turned to me. "Claudette is a hive of information," he said. "If she doesn't know something, it's highly likely nobody in the country does. There are rumours that she is running a spy ring, but she denies this. She claims she is just a nosy old woman. She is also good at keeping secrets. She will never disclose to another what someone asked her about. You are banished from ever seeing her again if you ask her to."

"My mother has a lot of integrity," Daranis said.

"Will she be able to help us?" Osin asked.

Daranis shrugged his shoulders. "I don't know. But if she can't answer Tal's questions, she will do all she can to find out the information for him. And not just because I am asking her to. She hates not knowing things."

"So the rumours are true," a voice suddenly said from behind us.

I turned around and found myself face to face with Melantha. She looked me up and down disdainfully. There was no recognition in her eyes. I wasn't surprised. After all, my hair was much shorter, I wasn't wearing any clothes and I was shackled. There was nothing to make her think about a princess from Amanet. All she saw was a slave.

"I expected something much prettier," she continued.

"Go away Mel," Tallis said. "I don't have time for you right now."

Melantha ignored him. "Aren't you going to introduce me to your new play thing?"

"No, I'm not." He took hold of my hand and led me away. He found an empty reception room and dragged me into it, shutting the door behind him.

"I'm sorry about that. I didn't know she would be here. Are you alright?"

"I'm fine," I assured him. "It's how I was expecting to be treated."

"Well you shouldn't have been. Most people have better manners than that."

There was a knock at the door and Daranis walked in. "The high chamberlain just left. Mother will see us now." He glanced at me. "But only us."

Tallis nodded then took the bracelet with my chain on it from his wrist. He handed it to Osin, who had followed Daranis into the room.

"Put this on. I am trusting you to look after her. If anything happens to her, I will hold you responsible."

"She'll be fine," Osin said.

Then Tallis turned to me. "Behave. Obey Osin. Don't do anything without his permission."

"Okay."

The look Tallis gave me suggested he didn't trust me, but he remained silent.

"Come on," Osin said once Tallis and Daranis had left. "Let's get some food."

He said hello to a few people as we made our way to the dining room, where food platters had been laid out. He took two plates and handed one to me. "Help yourself to anything you want," he said.

I looked around and noticed that other slaves were eating, so I took a small amount of the food and put it on my plate. I wasn't hungry, but I forced myself to eat. I felt oddly alone and vulnerable without Tallis, despite the fact that Osin wouldn't let any harm come to me.

I did my best not to shudder when Melantha approached again.

"I'm surprised Tal trusts you enough to leave you in control of his little pet." I have never heard such contempt in one little word.

Osin ignored her hostility. "It's good to see you Mel." He kissed her on the cheek. "Where's your slave?" Only then did I remember that women were not permitted anywhere without an escort, either their father, owner or slave.

"I left him at home. My father escorted me here this evening. He's off socialising with some of his associates. I'm glad you came. I was getting a little bored."

She slipped her arm through his. "Why don't you entertain me by telling me about your latest military conquests." She then looked at me. "Sorry, I'm being rude. Let me get you both some drinks first."

Before Osin could say no, she released his arm and walked away.

"I never understood what Tal saw in her," Osin whispered to me. "I was overjoyed when I heard they had split up. Not that they were ever really a couple, according to my brother."

Like the good slave I was pretending to be, I didn't respond.

Melantha returned, holding out two glasses. I glanced at Osin before taking mine. While it looked like I was asking his permission, in reality I was asking if it was safe to take it. He nodded his head. I hoped he understood what my glance had really been asking.

I waited until Osin had drunk some before taking a sip. It was light and refreshing, so I drank a little more. I didn't think that there was any alcohol in it, but a warm feeling began to spread through me.

Soon, however, it became overwhelming. I felt light headed and was tingling all over. I grabbed his arm to steady myself before I fell over.

"Are you alright?" he asked in concern.

"No. I don't feel good."

He looked sharply at Melantha. When I followed his gaze, I could see she was smiling maliciously.

"What have you done?" he asked.

"I may have slipped a magically enhanced love potion into her drink."

"You've done what? Why?"

The smile remained in place. "I want to see the look on Tal's face when his little sex partner is throwing herself at his brother. This is going to be so entertaining."

"You complete idiot," Osin hissed at her. "Don't you know who this is? I know you've met her; you were with my parents at the time."

She looked me up and down. I could imagine her picturing me with clothes on and longer hair. I saw the moment when realisation dawned. All colour drained from her face.

"Princess Adara?" she whispered.

"Yes. And now your petty little stunt may just have caused a diplomatic incident. I need to get her out of here as soon as I can."

I was only just following the conversation. My entire body was on fire. I was craving for something, but I had no idea what.

Then I noticed Tallis and Daranis approaching and I knew exactly what I wanted. Sex. I wanted to have my hands on him. I wanted to feel him touching me everywhere.

I started to move toward him, but Osin grabbed me. He looked over in the direction I was staring and spotted who I was looking at.

"Oh shit," he said. "This has just gone from bad to worse. If she wants Nis, she won't let anyone else touch her and there is no way he will betray his wife."

"I'm sorry," I heard Melantha stammer. "I would never have given her anything if I knew she was in love. I didn't know she liked Nis, I swear I didn't."

I didn't look at her; I couldn't take my eyes off the approaching men.

"Neither did I," Osin said.

Tallis frowned as he approached. He could see that there was something wrong by the way Osin was holding me.

"What's going on?" he asked.

"This stupid little bitch has slipped her a magically enhanced love potion."

"What in the queen's name possessed you to do that?" Daranis asked her. Tallis couldn't speak because I had thrown myself at him and had my tongue in his mouth.

Intimacy

The journey home was painful for me. Tallis held me tight in the back of the carriage the entire way, but he had placed a Shield around me so I couldn't move. The craving for him was completely consuming me. The throbbing between my legs was agony. Tears flowed down my face as I begged him to kiss me, to touch me.

Whenever Osin looked at me, his eyes were filled with despair. There was nothing he could do to help me. Only Tallis could do that and for some reason nobody would explain to me, he was refusing to do so.

"You're going to be alright," Tallis kept whispering to me over and over again.

'Of course I'm going to be alright' I thought to myself, whenever I was able to think. All he had to do was touch me, caress me, kiss me, make love to me, and everything would be fine.

But he didn't.

"Is she?" Osin asked, as though I wasn't there.

I felt rather than saw Tallis nod. "As soon as we get home, I will extract the potion from her system. She's going to be fine. She'll be tired for a while, but that's all."

When we arrived back at his parents' house, he carried me to the room I was staying in, calling out for his mother as he ascended the stairs. He placed me on the bed, but didn't join me.

"Stay," he said and moved away from me. The Shield was still in place so I couldn't move my limbs, but that didn't stop me rolling over toward the edge of the bed, closer to him.

"Oh no you don't," he said and took hold of my wrists, raising them above my head. I felt his Shield drop, only to be replaced by another one that tied my arms to the headboard. I wasn't going anywhere until he released me.

He then removed his cloak and placed it over me, covering up my nakedness, before removing my shackles. Osin had handed back my chain to him as soon as he could, but Tallis hadn't put it back on his wrist. As soon as he found out what was happening, he simply picked me up and carried me out of the house, doing his best to ignore the fact that I was running my tongue down his neck.

As I could no longer move, Tallis approached the bed once more and sat down. He put his hand on my head, which I moved about in a vain attempt to feel his caress.

"Keep still," he snapped at me, but his voice was filled with worry, not anger.

He then closed his eyes and I felt something enter me. It made its way all through my body, but did nothing to ease my discomfort.

"What's going on?" Macha asked as she ran into the room. Her hair was wet, indicating she had just finished bathing.

Tallis didn't answer her. He was so focused on me I don't think he even noticed that she had entered the room.

Osin quickly summarised, talking about me as though I wasn't there. Not that I cared. All I cared about was the fact that Tallis was touching me, though not in the way I wanted.

Suddenly Tallis removed his hand. "That bitch," he exclaimed. "Somehow she's managed to put a binding spell into the love potion. It's connected itself to her body so I can't remove it." Then he noticed his mother. "Can you help?"

"We both know that you are already a better Healer than I am. If you can't do anything, then I won't be able to."

"Please try," Tallis said.

She sat beside me and placed her hand where Tallis's had been only a moment before. Once again something entered my body. Soon she, too, removed her hand and shook her head.

"I'll try again," Tallis said, but he didn't sound hopeful. "While I do that, can you brew a sleeping potion for her? Anything that will knock her out."

"Nothing I create will be any good. I can't put any magic in it; we have no idea how it will react to the magic Melantha used. Without it, it will have no effect. We have to get the potion out of her."

"What if you both work together?" Osin said.

"It won't help," Macha told him. "Even our combined magic can't undo what Melantha has done."

"What's the point of having two Healers in the house if neither of you can do anything?"

I couldn't understand why everyone was so on edge. All I needed was some physical attention from Tallis and everything would be fine.

Soon I was panting and sweating. I didn't know how much more I could take without getting some relief.

"There's only one thing you can do, Tallis," Macha said.

He glared at her. "You know I can't. It's too dangerous."

"You're stronger than you think. You can do this without letting things go too far."

"You don't know that and nor do I. I will not take that sort of risk."

Osin placed his hand on his shoulder. "I don't see that there is any other option. You can't let her suffer."

"You don't realise what you are asking me to do." Even in my agitated state I could hear the pain in his voice.

"Yes, I do," Osin said.

When Tallis looked at me I could see the distress he was failing to keep inside. Then he looked back at Osin. "No, you don't."

Then he left the room, quickly followed by Osin and Macha. They closed the door. I could hear raised voices, but couldn't make out what they were saying. It sounded like they were both trying to persuade Tallis to do something he really didn't want to do.

Then I no longer cared as the pain I was feeling became too much for me and I began to scream.

The door sprang open and Tallis ran back in. He sat down beside me and gently moved my hair out of my eyes. "Sssshh," he said soothingly.

"Help me. Please," I begged. Tears were streaming down my face.

"Alright," he said then got off the bed, walked over to the door and closed it. The last thing I heard before it shut was his mother telling him to be careful.

When he returned to the bed he leaned over and kissed me. Never had anything felt so good. A tingling sensation started on my lips then slowly spread through me. I wanted more, a lot more.

When his tongue probed tentatively at my lips, I opened my mouth and let him in. It was the best kiss I had ever had. Had I been able to, I would have cried out in ecstasy.

As he kissed me, he pulled his cloak off me and he trailed his hand down my side, making my entire body come alive. The throbbing between my legs became more intense, more urgent, but the pain was slowly reducing.

I longed to run my fingers over his body, to feel his flesh beneath my fingertips, but he didn't release his Shield. My arms were fixed in place and there was nothing I could do to stop him doing whatever he wanted to me. Not that I wanted to stop him.

And then he set about showing me just what he had learned in the brothels about pleasing a woman.

Conviction

When I woke the next morning, I was exhausted. I had never felt so drained in my life. I felt worse than when I was recovering from my fever. I tried to move my arms and found I didn't have the energy.

What Tallis did to my body was unforgettable. He knew just where to touch me, every caress sent me reeling. I didn't know if it was the love potion or Tallis's skill, but he expertly took me over the edge again and again. He used his tongue, his lips, his fingers, even his teeth. Everything he did felt so good I just wanted to scream his name over and over.

Only once I had been completely satisfied and no longer craved his touch did he release the Shield that was holding my arms in place. I was drifting off to sleep when he finally undressed, down to his underwear, and climbed into the bed beside me. He pulled me close to him then covered us over with a blanket.

I fell asleep with his arm around me, our fingers intertwined. I couldn't keep the smile off my face. I never imagined a sexual experience without having full sex could be so enjoyable.

I still had the smile on my face when I awoke. I could remember every touch, every kiss, every caress.

Then I remembered how I threw myself at him, how I shamelessly begged him to satisfy me while we travelled home and I was suddenly glad that I was alone. I didn't know when Tallis had left me, or where he had gone, but I was relieved that he was no longer in the bed with me. I had no idea how I was going to face him.

My musings were interrupted by a knock at the door and Macha's voice calling out, asking if I was awake. When I said I was, she entered carrying a steaming mug.

"You're going to need this," she said. "Are you able to sit up or do you need some help?"

"I can hardly move any part of my body," I admitted.

Macha gave me a knowing smile. "It's the after effects of the love potion. This restorative I made will help."

I was embarrassed when not only did Tallis's mother have to pull me into a sitting position and move pillows behind me for support, but she also had to hold the mug up to my mouth, allowing me to take small sips, as I didn't have the strength to even lift my arm, yet alone take the mug.

"I feel so humiliated," I said between mouthfuls. "You're having to treat me like a baby." Though I could feel my strength returning with each sip I took, I could still hardly move.

Macha put the mug on the bedside table, much to my disappointment, then took me by surprise by hugging me.

"Put it out of your mind," she said gently. "This isn't your fault. What Melantha did was not only petty and cruel, it was also dangerous."

"But the way I acted." I didn't know how to finish the sentence. Luckily I didn't need to.

"You were not in control of yourself. Everyone understands that. Nobody is going to hold you responsible or blame you for anything you did or said while you were drugged."

I didn't realise I was crying until I felt dampness on my cheek.

Macha pulled away from me and picked up the still steaming mug once more.

"Now finish this, then I'll help you get dressed and take you downstairs. Food will do you the world of good."

"Thank you," I said as I wiped my cheeks dry with the back of my hand.

I felt a lot better when I was wearing trousers and a blouse. Until I made the mistake of looking in a mirror. I couldn't hold back the groan. I looked like I hadn't slept in a month.

"Stop worrying," Macha said and put her arm around me once more.

With her support, I managed to walk down the stairs to the kitchen before collapsing into a chair. The cook took one look at me and placed a mug of coffee in front of me, followed by a bowl of porridge with a generous portion of syrup on top.

"Eat it all up," she said before I could say anything. "After what you have been through, you need something nutritious inside you."

I tentatively took a mouthful, then another. It tasted great. "Thank you." The words seemed inadequate. Then I noticed that she was wearing clothes. "You're not a slave," I said in surprise before I could stop myself.

Much to my relief, the cook laughed. "No. I'm one of the lucky ones. I was freed."

"Giada is far too good at her craft to be a slave," Macha said. "She used to be owned by a friend of mine. The moment I tasted her food, I knew I had to have her working for me. I won't mention the price I had to pay, but she was well worth it."

Giada blushed. "Macha didn't only purchase me. I had been seeing a gardener for a while so she bought him as well. He's the reason the gardens here look so good."

Macha continued the story. "When I decided to free Giada, I gave him the option of being signed over to her or I would find someone else to be her slave. He jumped at the chance. They got married and three children later, they are still together. He took to being his wife's slave almost as well as Balor has."

Giada turned her attention back to the food she was preparing for those in the family who hadn't already eaten and I continued my meal quietly.

I had finished eating and was just drinking the last of my coffee when Osin walked into the kitchen. He grinned when he saw me and his eyes shone with amusement.

"So how long have you been in love with my brother?" he asked, making me choke.

"I'm not," I spluttered.

"Your actions say otherwise."

"That was the love potion, not me. Your mother told me I wasn't in control of myself and can't be held responsible for anything I did."

I didn't like the way Osin kept smiling at me.

"Sorry Adara, but that's not the way the potion works. It's designed to make you crave sex so much you will throw yourself at anyone, usually the first person of the opposite sex that you see. Or you own sex, if you're that way inclined. That's why Mel gave you the drink when you were with me. She expected me to be your target."

He took a seat at the table and thanked Giada when she placed a plate full of food in front of him. Then he continued. "The only thing that stops that happening is love. The only explanation for the fact that you wanted Tallis instead of me is that you are in love with him."

I stared at him, trying to work out if he was winding me up or not. Then I replayed every encounter I had ever had with Tallis and every conversation I had about him. From the very beginning I had been against a Sentinel living in the palace. I hated them for what they did. And they terrified me. But did I hate the man? No. I had to admit to myself that I didn't.

The more I got to know Tallis, the more I liked him. It wasn't Tallis I was afraid of, but the fact that I was falling for him. Whenever I was angry with him, it wasn't really him I was angry with, but myself for feeling about him the way I did. I just took it out on him.

When he said he was through with me I was devastated. Finally I understood the reason why. I hadn't just been hiding my feelings from everyone else, but from myself as well. I had treated him so badly just because I couldn't admit to myself how I really felt.

I was stunned. I couldn't understand how I could have deceived myself.

Then I thought back to the time when Tephi took me to meet his son and told me the truth about Tallis. That was the moment that I fell in love with him, that was the answer to Osin's question. I had been in love with his brother ever since that day.

"You didn't know, did you?" Macha said. Something about the look on my face must have given me away. I shook my head.

"How could you not know? Balor knew you liked him the first time he visited. The second time, he knew your feelings had grown. How could he know if you didn't?"

I had no answer to that question. How could I explain to this wonderful woman who had treated me so well that I was so terrified of falling for her son that I managed to convince myself that I hated him?

"So what are you going to do now?" Osin asked. He was still grinning at me.

"Do?" I didn't understand the question.

"About Tallis. I presume you're going to tell him how you feel. Not that he doesn't already know after you threw yourself at him."

I almost said yes, then I remembered what had happened the night before, how he refused to let me touch him or make love to me. "What's the point?" I said with a trace of bitterness. "He doesn't feel the same about me. Last night he did what he needed to do in his role as a Healer, nothing more."

Osin opened his mouth to say something, but Macha held up her hand, silencing him. "You have no idea how hard it was for my son to not let things go further with you. It took incredible amounts of self-control. For a Sentinel, having sex is a risky thing to do, especially if you care about your partner."

"And Tallis cares about you a great deal," Osin said. "I can see it every time he looks at you, talks to you, talks about you. He was scared to be with you last night, terrified that he was going to do you a lot of harm."

I wanted to ask how, but the conversation was interrupted by the man we were talking about walking in. His shoulders were slumped and he collapsed into a chair as though he no longer had the energy to stay standing.

"How did it go?" Osin asked.

"Later," Tallis said. He sounded more than just tired. Something had happened which had upset him. A lot. He looked up at his mother. "How is she?"

"Fine," Macha said. The smile on her face spoke volumes. "Just very tired and food and a restorative is helping with that."

"You could have asked me," I said. I was finding it hard to look at him. I felt embarrassed, not just because of what we did

188

the night before, but also because of my discovery of what I felt for him and the horrible way I had been treating him.

He took hold of my hand and I forced myself to raise my head. It was the first time I had ever really looked into his eyes and I was surprised by what I saw. They weren't just one shade of black. I could see a multitude of differing shades swimming in them. And they were a lot more expressive than I had ever thought possible. I could see pain in them. And concern.

"I didn't ask you for two reasons." His tone was soft and gentle. He was explaining, not telling. "Firstly, I don't trust you to tell me the truth and I'm not going to make you. You are so stubborn that you will tell me you're fine even if you're not."

I wanted to argue with the comment, but he was right.

"Secondly, my mother is a Healer. She knows how you are better than you do."

Giada placed a plate of food in front of Tallis, but he pushed it away. "Sorry, but I can't face food right now."

"What's wrong?" I asked and gripped his hand tightly. Part of me was glad that he didn't want to eat as it would have meant that I would have to remove my hand from his.

"I took Mel to the Council."

I was the only one in the room who showed any sign of being surprised. I had no idea what was going on.

"So what happened?" Macha asked.

"I told them what she did and when they questioned her, thankfully she told the truth."

"I thought Sentinels always had to tell the truth," I said, interrupting.

Tallis didn't seem to mind. "She's still in training. She doesn't have the runes yet so she is still capable of lying. Several Council members are Sentinels and they have a reputation for being ruthless during interrogations. It wouldn't have been pleasant for her if she had lied."

"What's her punishment?" Osin asked.

I don't know what I had been expecting Tallis to say, but the words that came out of his mouth completely shocked me.

"She's been stripped of her magic and they made her a slave."

I couldn't believe what I had just heard. Her life had been ruined and it was all my fault.

"But she didn't mean any real harm. No damage was done."

"But it could have been. Things could have gone very differently."

"How?"

"I'll explain later," Tallis said. I wanted him to explain then and there, but I trusted him to keep his word and he looked like he had more important things on his mind.

"Why did you do it?" I asked. I could see how distraught he was. "It can't have been easy. Why did you put yourself through this? For me?"

"No. Not for you. It had to be done. We never use our magic for our own benefit or petty revenge. Magic should only ever be used for the benefit of others. It is the one rule that should never ever be broken. I had to turn Mel in. She couldn't be trusted. If I hadn't, someone else would have. It was better for her that I did it. I got her the best deal I could. They wanted to execute her."

"Execute her!" Tears sprang into my eyes. "This is all my fault. I should never have insisted on going to that party."

Tallis moved from his chair, knelt before me and took me in his arms.

"No Adara. This isn't your fault. Mel made her own decisions. And it isn't as bad as it seems. Apparently, she was having an affair with one of her tutors. Though frowned upon, it isn't strictly forbidden. He is now her owner and has agreed to marry her."

"That doesn't make it alright," I sobbed.

"No, it doesn't. But it was necessary. This time Mel was lucky and nobody got hurt. That might not have been the case the next time she used magic for fun. She broke the rules once, there was nothing to say she wouldn't do it again. She had to have her magic removed."

"But to be made into a slave? Was that necessary?"

It was Osin who answered. "Yes, it was. Mel knows too much and she can no longer be trusted to keep the academy's secrets.

Making her a slave was the only sensible thing to do. It was either that or, as Tallis has already said, execution."

I didn't want to hear any more. I suddenly felt sick.

"We need to talk," Tallis said to me. I nodded my head. We had a lot to talk about. I didn't think it was the right time, but postponing things wouldn't help and it might take my mind off Melantha.

He took me up to my room and sat me down on the bed. He didn't sit beside me. Instead he paced the room. He kept looking at me, opening his mouth, then closing it again. He had a lot to say but it seemed he didn't know where to start.

"Why didn't you tell me how you felt?" he eventually asked. "I thought you hated me."

"So did I," I admitted. I then told him everything that had gone through my mind from the moment Osin told me what the effect the love potion had on me meant. I poured my heart out to him like I had never done to anyone before. And I couldn't stop apologising for the way I had treated him.

Tallis just let me speak. He didn't approach me or interrupt me.

"I wish I had known," he said when I finished. "I would never have brought you with me. I would have done this on my own."

"I understand," I said. My hands were clenched together in my lap and I stared at them; I couldn't bring myself to look at Tallis. "After the way I treated you, I wouldn't want to be with me either. Especially now you know how I feel. Are you going to send me back to Amanet?"

The next thing I knew, Tallis was sitting on the bed next to me and I was in his arms. He kissed my forehead. "Of course not. Now I know how you really feel, I'm never letting you out of my sight again."

"I don't understand. Why?"

He smiled at me. He really did have a nice smile. "Because I'm in love with you and have been for a long time."

I wanted to believe him, I really did, and I knew he couldn't lie, but something prevented me from doing so.

"But you didn't want to make love to me last night."

"Didn't want to? I've never wanted something more in my entire life. I can't; there's a difference."

He pulled away from me, but left his arm around my waist. "There is something you don't know about Sentinels. When we have sex, we lose control. Our minds have to link with our partner's. We can't stop it. We force our way into the other person's mind. Sometimes the mental attack is too much for them to take and we shatter their mind. Sometimes it leaves them like zombies, able to eat, walk, talk, but not much else. Other times it kills them. If the initial onslaught doesn't damage them, the sensations they feel during sex can be so overwhelming they can't cope and their minds shut down. There was no way I was going to take that risk with you."

"Yet you slept with Melantha."

Did I sound bitter? Maybe a little.

"The first thing magic users are taught is how to shield their minds. We both put up mental barriers to prevent the other one getting through."

"So you're saying you can have sex with any magic user, but nobody else?"

"No. I'm saying it's dangerous for me to sleep with someone else. It has been known for the partner to be able to handle the mental link."

"Maybe I could," I said tentatively.

"Maybe you could, but I'm not going to risk finding out."

I desperately wanted to argue against him, but he was right. Was he really worth risking my sanity? The answer, of course, was yes, but not yet; not until we had rescued Rose.

"Can you at least kiss me?"

He smiled at me again. "That I can do."

It was quite a long time later that we left my room. We rounded up the family and once everyone was in the lounge drinking coffee, Tallis brought up the outcome of his meeting with Claudette. We sat on a sofa together and he held my hand.

"Was it worth everything that has happened?" Osin asked. "Did you find out what you needed to know?"

"Yes, but we can't head off yet."

"Why not?" I asked.

"First we have to go and see the queen."

Queen

"Why exactly am I going with you?" Osin asked as the carriage made its way along the streets to the palace.

"Unofficially, it's because I'm not sure why I have been told to see the queen and I want you by my side in case I need protection," Tallis said. "Officially, it's because you have been dying to meet her ever since I can remember and I will never hear the end of it if I get in to see her without you."

Osin grinned at him. "You're probably right. Did Nis's mother give any indication as to why we need to do this?"

Tallis shook his head. "No. She just said it was something I had to do, if I knew what was good for me, and that I would definitely be given permission to meet her."

"So why am I here?" I asked. Once again I was dressed as a slave. Tallis's cloak was covering me up; he would remove it before we left the carriage.

"Because I couldn't bear to leave you behind," he said. "The fact that Claudette also said I had to take you along is irrelevant."

I cuddled down closer to Tallis. I was amazed at how quickly I had gotten used to being so close to him. I had been in his arms almost constantly since his return from taking Melantha to the Council.

To pass the time, we talked about the queen. She had only been ruling for a few years, but seemed to be doing a good job of it. She had only just turned twenty one when her father died and, as his eldest offspring, the throne was handed over to her.

Neither Tallis nor his brother could describe her to me. It was traditional that none of the royal family ever revealed their faces to the public, choosing instead to wear veils. It meant that, should the palace ever be attacked, the attackers couldn't be certain who was a member of the royal family and who wasn't.

"How do I act?" I asked. I had been taught the proper protocol when meeting a king or queen, but had no idea what a slave was supposed to do.

"Don't do anything different than us. Bow when we do, that sort of thing. It's highly unlikely that she will even notice you, let alone speak to you, so remain quiet."

All too soon we arrived at our destination. Guards stopped us at the gates, but as soon as Tallis told them who he was, we were waved through.

Another guard opened the door as soon as the carriage drew to a halt in front of the main entrance. This one was dressed differently from the others. His uniform was more ornate and a brighter shade. If the stripes on his cuffs dictated rank, then he was very high up indeed.

"Come with me," he said. He didn't introduce himself, but his bearing and the look on his face gave me the impression he was used to being obeyed and refusing to follow his order was not an option.

He led us around the back of the building and through a rear door. Tallis threw a questioning look at his brother, but Osin just shrugged. He had no better idea what was going on than Tallis did.

We followed the guard down corridors and up stairs until he came to a halt outside a set of double doors. Fearsome looking guards were stationed on either side.

"Wait here," the man said. He knocked on the door then entered the room as soon as he received permission, closing the door behind him.

"What's going on?" Tallis whispered to Osin. "I was expecting to meet the queen in the throne room or one of the formal reception rooms. This appears to be her suite."

"I don't know," Osin said. "But something tells me we are in a lot of trouble. Unless I'm very much mistaken, the man who escorted us here is actually the head of the army."

Both of the guards could overhear our conversation, but neither reacted.

We were not left waiting long before the door opened once more and we were told to enter.

The room we found ourselves in was a tastefully decorated lounge. A large curtain separated the room from the rest of the suite, hiding what was behind it from view.

A woman was sitting on a sofa, her head pointing in our direction as if she was regarding us critically. All of her features were obscured by a black lace veil, thick enough to hide her from us but thin enough, I assumed, for her to see us clearly.

The only other person in the room, other than the guard who Osin thought wasn't really a guard, was a woman standing to attention beside the sofa. She was dressed head to foot in black leather, the tight fit enhancing the shape of her athletic body. She was pretty, but not beautiful, with long black hair pulled back into a pony tail. She assessed us, looking us up and down as though she was trying to work out if we were a threat or not. Everything about her screamed Warrior and I found myself looking for a black band on her wrist, but her clothing hid it.

Osin was looking at her just as closely, but something told me he had other reasons for doing so.

"May I present Queen Ariana Druantia," the 'guard' said. "Your Majesty, Sentinel Tallis, his brother Warrior Osin and his slave."

Tallis and Osin both bowed when their names were spoken. Unsure what to do, I did the same thing.

"So you've come to challenge me at last have you Tallis?" the queen said. Her voice was strange. Then I remembered that I had been told that she magically altered it

Tallis was holding my hand and I felt him stiffen. Osin stepped away from us, giving himself room to react if he needed to. He was looking at the Warrior, though this time not with admiration. If an attack came, he had no doubt that she would be the source. He would defend his brother with his life, if he needed to.

"Of course not, your Majesty," Tallis said. "Why would I ever want to challenge you?"

"You have the use of three disciplines of magic, you are the most powerful magic user in our entire history. You have the right to challenge me for the throne."

A pained look crossed Tallis's face. "That may be true, your Majesty, but I have no wish to do so. The country would fall apart if I tried to run it."

The queen laughed lightly. "So why are you here?" she asked.

"I needed some information from Claudette. She suggested that it would be to my benefit to visit you."

"And did she mention why?"

"No, your Majesty, she didn't."

"When she told the high chamberlain that you would come to see me instead of me having to send guards to arrest you, I didn't believe her. I will never doubt her again."

The word 'arrest' made Tallis tense once more.

"Is that why the high chamberlain was there last night? To find out where my brother was?" Osin asked. He, too, was on edge, though he hid it well.

"Yes."

"May I ask why?"

"Because I have a visitor who wishes to see him."

At that moment, the curtain moved back and a man strode toward us. He was dressed well, though not overly formally. He wasn't particularly tall, but had a bearing about him which suggested he was someone important.

Tallis stepped in front of me, shielding me with his body, and Osin relaxed his stance, ready to move if he needed to.

Suddenly I gasped. I knew who was striding purposely over to us. And he did not look happy.

"What exactly did you think you were doing, Tallis, leaving in the middle of the night with my sister?" Then he looked at me and his eyes went wide. "And why in the name of the king is she dressed as a slave? Or should that be undressed? Someone put some clothes on her."

Tallis instantly took his cloak off and placed it around my shoulders.

"Tephi," I said. "What are you doing here?"

"I've come to drag you back home, where you belong."

"She's not going anywhere with you," Osin said, aggressively.

Tallis held out his hand to his brother, palm upward. "It's alright. Tephi's her brother. Let me talk to him."

Osin nodded his head, but didn't relax.

"Your Highness—" Tallis began to say, but Tephi interrupted him.

"Cut the Highness crap Tallis. Now isn't the time. Right now I'm more interested in hearing what possessed you to hand in your resignation and take Adara on some fool's errand instead of locking her up."

"Resignation!" I exclaimed. He had said he had left a note, but hadn't mentioned resigning his position with my father.

"I didn't really have much choice," Tallis said, turning to look at me. "I had no idea how long we would be gone."

"He also wrote that he would return for whatever punishment our father saw fit. If you both lived, that is."

"He wrote what!"

"Isn't she supposed to remain silent unless spoken to directly?" Osin said quietly to Tallis, just loud enough for me to hear.

"Shut up Osin," I practically shouted. I was mad at Tallis and taking it out on Osin seemed like a good idea. "Everyone here knows who I am."

"Please explain what is going on," Tephi said. He was talking to Tallis, not me, which annoyed me even more.

"It's a long story," Tallis said.

"Then I think refreshments are in order," Queen Ariana said. She glanced at the female Warrior, who was still posed as if ready to attack. The woman nodded her head then left the room, returning a moment later.

"This is Tia, my personal bodyguard," Ariana said. Then she pointed to the 'guard.' "General Intep, commander of my army. Now that we all know each other, will you all please sit down."

When we did so, Tallis pulled me close to him. I was surprised that he wasn't keeping his distance, seeing as Tephi was watching us closely.

Tephi raised a questioning eyebrow, but said nothing. He just looked at me pointedly, waiting for me to speak.

"We're in love," I said. I didn't get the reaction I was expecting.

"It's about time you admitted your feelings for each other. Etain and I have a bet about whether you had actually eloped or not. You're not married are you?" I shook my head. "Good. I don't like losing to Etain."

I couldn't believe what I was hearing. It seemed that everyone knew how I felt about Tallis except me and Tallis.

"Will someone please tell me what is going on," Ariana said.

Tallis did the honours. He told her everything that had happened at the palace in regard to Rose's disappearance, the journey to Sobek and the reasons for it, as well as why I was having to be dressed as a slave.

"If it wasn't for the fact she had to remove her clothes," Tephi said, "I would be tempted to leave her here. Being a slave for a while might do her some good."

Tallis had the audacity to smile. "There's no need for that. Now that she knows how she really feels, she understands why she behaved as she did."

Tephi grunted as though he didn't believe what Tallis had said. I huffed indignantly at him.

Refreshments had arrived while Tallis spoke. I had spent most of the oration looking at Osin, who didn't take his eyes off Tia. It was almost as if he didn't trust her. The way she was looking at him suggested the feeling was mutual.

"Why didn't you just lock her in her room?" Tephi asked. "Then told me or my father of her plans."

"What would have been the point? She would have snuck away eventually. She's a lot safer with me than if she had gone on her own. It's not as if I could have put a permanent Shield on her room in order to keep her prisoner until she came to her senses."

"Why not?"

"I'm not going to bother answering that," Tallis said.

"So what did you find out from Claudette?" the queen asked before Tephi could retaliate.

"Nothing good, your Majesty. Count Gillain is the head of a cult. Rumour has it they are demon worshipers who believe that they will be granted powers through sacrifice. Not their own, I hasten to add. They also believe that only the most beautiful women should be allowed to bear their offspring."

"Rose is going to be used for breeding?" I felt sick just asking the question.

Tallis had one arm around my shoulders. With his free hand, he gripped mine. I wasn't going to like what he was about to say.

"Unfortunately not. When I described Rosemerta, Claudette gave me the bad news. The combination of her eye colour and her hair is rare, rare enough that the cultists believe that they make the best sacrifices."

Tephi went pale. "You mean they're going to kill her?"

Tallis nodded his head. "But it may just be a rumour."

"So why are you sitting here instead of going to rescue her?"

"I think that, technically, it's your fault," Osin said. He didn't look at my brother as he spoke; his eyes never left Tia. Tia, I noticed, did her best to hide a smile.

"Do you know where to find him?" General Intep asked.

"Claudette could tell me where in Draygar the cult's headquarters are located. She also let me know that the sacrifice had to be made at a specific time and date. We have until the next full moon."

"Politically, this is a tricky situation." He rubbed his bearded chin as he spoke. "As Draygar isn't in the alliance, we can't officially enter the country and rescue the kidnapped princess." He then looked at Tallis. "We also can't allow magic users to cross the border."

"I'll take care of that," Osin said. He put his arm forward, revealing the coloured bands on his arm. "I'm a Cloak. I can get Tallis into the country. Once across the border, he'll have to wear dark glasses to hide his eyes."

The general nodded his approval. "I'll arrange for you to be absent for a while. You'll need at least one more Warrior with you. Two would be better."

"Daranis will agree to help," Tallis said.

"Is that Claudette's son?" Tallis nodded. "I've heard about him. Not as skilled as Osin here, but still a fair Warrior. I will arrange his extended absence with his employer."

The comment startled Osin. The general grinned at him. "I know exactly who you are. I've been taking great interest in your career. I have plans for you when you get back. If you get back," he added. I was not happy about that last sentence.

"This must be an unsanctioned mission," the queen said. "I have heard of this cult and nothing would give me greater pleasure than removing the leader's head, but there is nothing I can officially do. If you are caught, you are on your own."

"Understood," Osin said.

"Not completely on their own," Tephi said. "I'm coming with you."

"Don't be stupid, Tephi," Tallis said. "You're next in line to the throne. Do you really think you will be able to cross the border without being recognised?"

"Rose is my sister," Tephi snarled. "I have the right to assist in her rescue. If Osin can hide you, he can hide me as well."

"I can," Osin said. "But I won't. You may be prepared to risk your life, your Highness, but I'm not. You will be a liability. There's a chance someone will recognise you and I can't keep you permanently hidden."

"He's right," General Intep said before Tephi could respond.

"I will send Tia with you," the queen said, but she didn't sound like she was happy with the idea. "She is more than capable of looking after herself, and others. On top of that, I'm her mental link so we can stay in contact. If anything happens that Tephi or I need to know about, she can tell me."

"Are you sure that's a good idea?" the general asked, though he glanced at Tia before looking at the queen.

"I am certain." There was steel in her voice when she spoke, leaving little doubt as to who ran the country.

"I will allow her to come along," Osin said, as though he had any say in the matter, "once she has proven her skills."

Tia raised an eyebrow at him. "Is that a challenge?"

"You bet it is."

"Fine," she said. "I'll meet you in the combat arena in a few minutes. You may choose your weapon."

Osin glanced at the general, silently asking his permission. "Is this really necessary?" he asked.

"Yes," Tia and Osin said together. Something told me there was more to the challenge than proving Tia's skills.

"Fine," he said. "But no weapons. Unarmed combat only."

Neither seemed to mind.

"When do you plan on leaving?" Tephi asked.

"First thing in the morning," Tallis said.

"Come here first and collect some weapons," the queen said. "You will be allowed to take anything you want from the armoury."

"Thank you, your Majesty," Osin said, bowing deeply. He had a grin on his face. I had no idea what was in the armoury, but Osin was obviously eager to get his hands on the weapons.

"If there's nothing else, your Majesty," Tallis said, "Adara and I should be on our way. We'll take a detour on our way home to let Nis know he's about to go on a journey."

Ariana gave her permission and wished us all luck.

Tallis stood and held out his hand so he could help me rise.

"I'll come with you," Tephi said as we walked to the door. "Adara can collect her things then I will bring her back here."

Tallis froze, then very slowly turned around. "Adara is coming with me."

"Over my dead body. You can't take her into Draygar. She's coming home with me."

"No, she isn't."

"You work for my father, or had you forgotten? That means you have to do as I say."

"I resigned, remember."

"Adara is not going with you. Her place is at home. Now hand her over or I'll make you." Tephi was issuing Tallis an order. It was an order I hoped he wouldn't obey.

"How exactly are you planning on doing that?"

"Tallis," Osin said in warning. "Don't do anything stupid."

"I won't," Tallis said. Then he turned his attention to Tephi, who had walked up to us and was now only a few paces away. "I want you to look me in the eye and tell me that you can take better care of her than I can. Promise me that nothing will happen to her. Guarantee that she won't slip from your custody and follow me into Draygar, on her own and unprotected."

Both men stared at each other. Tephi was the first to look away.

"I didn't think you could," Tallis said, but there was no malice in his voice.

"She's my sister. If anything happens to her, I will make sure your life won't be worth living."

"You won't need to. Life will be meaningless without her in it."

Departure

To say that Daranis was not happy when given the news is a huge understatement.

"Are you a complete idiot?" he yelled at Tallis. "You want me to go into a potentially deadly situation with the one person I can contact if I need help? You are out of your mind."

"We will have a direct connection to the queen. Should we get into trouble, we can let her know and she can send reinforcements. General Intep will have a couple of garrisons close to the border."

"This is an unsanctioned mission. Do you really think that he will order an invasion of Draygar just to rescue our sorry arses? Excuse the language," he added, quickly glancing in my direction. I grew up with brothers; I was used to hearing a lot worse than that and told him so.

"And how long do you think it would take to reach us?" Daranis continued. "Where we need to go is almost the other side of the country."

"What's the real problem Nis?" Tallis asked. "You volunteered to come with us, if my memory serves me right."

"That was before I found out who the count is. I heard a lot about his cult. They aren't people we should be messing with."

Tallis placed his hand on his friend's shoulder. "I understand your reluctance. You have a wife and child to get home to. But Adara, Osin and I have to do this. We could use your help."

Daranis glared at him. Eventually his face began to soften. His shoulders slumped. "Alright, I'll go with you. Someone needs to watch your back. If we're taking a female Warrior with us, something tells me Osin will have his mind on other things. But something is going to go wrong. Don't say I didn't warn you."

Things didn't go any better for Osin. He was not a happy man when he made it back to his parents' house.

"She's coming with us." It sounded like he was sulking.

Tallis grinned at him. He had been smiling a lot since arriving in Sobek. I liked it and wished he would do it more often. "What happened? Did she beat you?"

"Of course she didn't beat me," he snapped. "But she came damn close. It was going to be an easy win for me, until the general told me that Cloaking was against the rules. What's the point in having a talent if I can't use it?"

"It did give you an unfair advantage," I pointed out to him. He growled at me.

"She's good, though, I have to admit. Very good. While I am far superior in strength, she is more dexterous. She knows how to use her magic to her advantage. And in ways I wouldn't have thought of."

"It's going to be a long journey," Tallis said. "Why don't you spend the time learning off each other?"

"That's what she said. Why do I feel like I'm being ganged up on?"

"Stop sulking, Osin. It doesn't suit you."

Osin growled again and stormed off, making Tallis laugh.

That night, I didn't sleep in my room; I couldn't bear to be parted from Tallis. He seemed to feel the same.

There was a lot of touching and not much sleeping. I loved running my hands over his bare skin. His scars were rough, but not unpleasant. I traced each one with my fingertips as he told me what they did. Most were not very powerful, but combined with those carved next to them on his body, they became very effective. They gave him the ability to do things he refused to talk about. I didn't push him. He would tell me when he was ready. All he would say was that he hoped to never have to use some of his powers, but he would if he had to.

He slept naked and he was close enough to me that I could feel the effect touching me was having on his body. But when I moved my hand closer to his groin, he grabbed it and placed it on his chest.

"Don't," he said. "I'm finding it hard enough to not let things go further as it is."

I wanted him, I wanted him badly, but left my hand where it was. He was terrified of hurting me. I wouldn't push him until Rose was rescued. Then we were going to have a serious talk about being much more intimate.

The next morning, we packed our bags and rode to the palace. Once again I was riding with Tallis. We took my horse along as well so I could ride it as soon as we left Sobek, but until then I had to sit in front of Tallis so he could hide my body with his as much as possible. That was what he claimed anyway. Personally I think he just liked having me in his arms. If so, he wasn't the only one.

We were permitted entry at the gates and were told to head directly to the armoury. Tia, General Intep and Tephi were there waiting for us.

"Oh for Father's sake," Tephi said the moment he saw me. "Put some clothes on."

"You know I have to dress as a slave while I'm in Sobek," I told him as I slipped Tallis's cloak around my shoulders.

"I know, but I don't have to like it."

General Intep gave the order and one of the guards in front of the door opened it. It had been magically sealed with a Shield and I couldn't help noticing the blue band on the woman's arm.

Tia entered the room and immediately began selecting her weapons. Osin whistled before joining her. I must admit, it was an impressive room. Any sort of weapon you could possibly want was there.

A bow was calling to me, but when I reached up to grab it, General Intep stopped me.

"That is a dangerous weapon, your Highness, not a toy."

"She knows how to use it," Tephi said. "My brother and I have been training her."

"She's quite skilled," Tallis said as he handed me a quiver full of arrows. He grinned when I gave him a surprised look. I thought only Etain and Tephi knew I had been learning how to shoot. "I've been watching you more than you realise," he said.

A warm feeling spread through me. I liked knowing that, even though he had told me he wanted nothing more to do with me, he had still been watching me closely.

Osin, Tia and Daranis took a while selecting their weapons. Tallis didn't take any; they would be of no use to him.

"We have packed some food for your journey and Tia has been provided with enough money for inns and warm meals. You will not be sleeping rough." Intep emphasised the 'not'. It was an order not a request.

"What if there is no choice?" Daranis asked.

"There is always a choice. If I find out you have made the queen's personal bodyguard sleep outside, even for one night, I will personally make sure that you explain the reasons why to the queen. And they had better be good."

"And you can also explain to me why decent accommodation couldn't be found for a princess of Amanet," Tephi said.

"Leave your weapons here and I will make sure they are packed correctly on the horses which have been chosen for you. They are the strongest, fastest and smartest in the stables. They have been training to work with Warriors since they were very young."

"Sorry General," Osin said, "but I will be taking my own horse. I have more confidence that he will take care of me than any you can provide."

"Why?" Tia asked. "What's so special about him?"

It was Tallis who answered. "The horse kind of adopted Osin. He was running along the shore of one of the great lakes one morning when he saw a group of young men calling out and laughing. They had chased a young foal into the water and whenever the poor creature tried to swim to shore, they attacked it, making it swim out again. If Osin hadn't arrived, it would probably have drowned."

"What did you do to the young men?" Tia asked. She was playing with a knife on her hip as she spoke.

"Let's just say they weren't able to laugh and joke for a while," Osin said. The general glared at him. "Don't look at me like that," he said. "It was six against one. It was self-defence."

General Intep didn't look convinced.

Tallis continued the story. "Once the men had been dealt with, Osin coaxed the terrified animal out of the water. When he was satisfied that it was unharmed, he walked back home. The foal followed him the entire way. It has been by his side ever since."

"So what happened to the men? Didn't they try to retrieve their property?"

"Oh yes," Osin said, grinning. "One was a baron's son and he persuaded his father that I had attacked them and stole the horse. When his guards came to arrest me, Tallis went with me. He persuaded the baron to hear my side of the story and confirmed that I was telling the truth. He then made his son do the same thing. Hearing his screams was surprisingly enjoyable."

I was disgusted by the comment, but Tia seemed pleased with it. She was smiling almost as much as Osin was.

"Do I want to know how the baron reacted?" Tephi asked.

Tallis shrugged. "He gifted me the foal and said he would deal with his son and his friends. He didn't tell me what he had planned and I didn't ask."

"I'm going to pretend I didn't hear any of that story," the general said. "Just in case you broke any laws."

"We didn't," Tallis assured him.

"If you have everything you need, you should get going," Tephi said.

The general then surprised us all by hugging Tia. "Keep in constant contact with the queen. Claudette has put out her network of spies to try to find out exactly where the sacrifice will take place and how you can get in to stop it. Not that she will ever admit that is how she gets her information. She will keep the high chamberlain informed, who will pass everything on to the queen. Take good care of yourself, and these others."

"I will," Tia said as she extracted herself from the general's arms.

Then Tephi hugged me. "It isn't too late to change your mind," he whispered in my ear.

"From now on I go where Tallis goes. I feel safe with him. What are you going to tell Father?" I asked Tephi once he had released me.

"Nothing," he said. "He isn't even aware that I am here looking for you. What he doesn't know won't hurt him."

Tephi then turned to Tallis. "Promise me you'll look after her."

"I will lay down my life for her," he said.

Tephi's response made me shiver. "Take her into Draygar and you may have to."

Tallis putting his arm around me made me feel better.

The general escorted us out of the palace to where the horses we were to ride were waiting. All of our belongings had been removed from our own steeds and had been securely tied to the saddles. We had to wait a few moments for Osin to move all of his bags back onto his own horse before we could depart.

I returned Tallis's cloak to him and he put it on. Once again I would be riding with him and would continue to do so until we reached the border.

We had only just left the palace when we heard someone calling out to Tallis. A man was leaning out of a coach window and got out when he saw that we had stopped.

He ran over to us and halted next to Tallis's horse. "I just wanted to give you my thanks, for what you did for Melantha," he said.

"It was the least I could do. Please make sure you look after her."

"I will," he said.

"How is she?"

"Coming to terms with what's happened. It's going to take a while. She's taking responsibility, surprisingly. She knows it's her own fault. It's not going to be easy though, without the support of her family. They've all turned their back on her, saying she's brought shame on them."

"Do you want me to speak with them?"

The man shook his head. "Thanks, but that's my responsibility, not yours. You've already done more than anyone could expect, under the circumstances." He then dipped his head in farewell and returned to his carriage.

"Who was that?" I asked.

"Mel's new owner."

"He doesn't seem mad that you turned her in."

"Of course he's not. He understands that it had to be done. He's grateful that I managed to persuade the Council not to execute her. The fact that he now gets to marry her when he didn't think he had a chance may also factor into it."

I laughed lightly.

We headed north through the city. When we were getting close to the outskirts, Osin called out.

"Tal, I think we should make a slight detour. Granny will be mad at us if she finds out we were both in the city and didn't visit."

"You're probably right," he replied.

Instead of continuing northward when we reached the edge of the city, Tallis turned east. A short while later he stopped outside the gate to a small cottage. He dismounted then helped me down.

"You might want to stay here," he said to Daranis and Tia.

"Does the lizard still live here?" Daranis asked.

"Yes, he does."

"I'll look after the horses then."

Osin grinned. "I thought you might."

The exchange had me intrigued. Daranis was a trained Warrior and a good one, from what I had been hearing, so I couldn't help wondering why he would be scared of a lizard.

As soon as we walked into the garden, I found out.

The creature that ran toward us was huge. I was sure it could swallow my leg whole if it wanted to. It ignored Osin and ran directly to Tallis, sticking out its tongue to lick his hand when he held it out. I swear it was as long as my arm.

"Adara, meet Mata. I've had him since he was hatched. He's loveable, but fiercely protective."

Lovable? That wasn't the word I wanted to use. He was a lizard. He was green and scaly and the claws on the end of his feet looked like they could rip me to shreds. I couldn't understand how Tallis could say he was loveable.

The animal seemed so pleased to see Tallis that he was bouncing up and down, trying to lick his face. Tallis must have placed a Shield around himself because the tongue never reached him.

"He lives off magical energy so I had to leave him here when I moved to Amanet. He makes a great guard dog for my granny." He turned to look at me. "Come and say hello."

I wanted to stay where I was and just say 'hello' from a distance, but that wasn't what he meant so I tentatively stepped closer.

"Mata, this is Adara. Friend."

The oversized iguana looked me up and down, making me feel as though he was trying to decide if I was edible. The moment he heard the word 'friend', he rolled out his tongue and licked my hand. It tickled, making me giggle. When I reached out and stroked his head, I was amazed at how smooth it was. Then he started to make the most incredible noise; it was almost like purring. He rubbed his head against my hand, demanding more attention, and I couldn't help smiling.

Suddenly he tensed then backed away, baring his teeth, which were long and pointed, reminding me of fangs. But he wasn't looking at me; he had his eyes fixed on Tia, who had just walked into the garden.

"Tia is also a friend," Tallis said calmly.

The effect on the lizard was amazing. Just one word from Tallis had him going from about to attack to wanting fuss and attention. Tia laughed as she gave him what he wanted.

"What's going on out here?" a voice said from the open doorway.

I looked up to see a short, thin, grey haired old lady. She had to be Balor's mother; the family resemblance was unmissable.

"Osin," she cried out as soon as she saw him. "And Tallis. To what do I owe this pleasure?"

She hugged both of her grandsons affectionately.

"We were passing and thought we should drop in," Osin said. "Let me introduce you to Tia, the queen's bodyguard."

When she took Tia's hand in hers, the sleeve of her dress moved back, revealing a yellow band on her arm. Like her son, she, too, was an empath.

She glanced across at Osin before releasing Tia, a slight smile on her face.

"And this is Adara," Tallis said.

She held my hand for less than a second before she pulled away from me. There was anger in her face as she glared at me. "Take this hussy away," she said through clenched teeth. "I won't have any slave trying to seduce my grandson."

Fight

"Calm down Granny," Tallis said. "This isn't what it looks like. Why don't we go inside and I will explain."

"I won't have the likes of her in my house. You know how I feel about slaves. Ones who have designs on their owner are even worse."

"Grandfather was your slave," Osin pointed out. It might have been my imagination, but I'm sure he was trying not to laugh.

"That was different," the elderly woman snapped at him. "Because of the stupid laws in this country, I had to take him as my slave in order to marry him."

"Things aren't always as they seem," Tallis said. He, too, seemed amused by his granny's reaction to me. He bent down and whispered something in her ear. I have no idea what he said, but it made her go pale.

She looked at me once more, assessing me, then turned her back on me and walked into the cottage.

"Come on," Tallis said as he took my hand. "If I know my granny as well as I think I do, she will have the kettle on by now."

"Are you sure? I don't think she likes me."

He kissed my cheek. "That's because she doesn't know you yet."

Reluctantly I allowed him to drag me into the house; Osin and Tia followed us.

As Tallis had predicted, his granny was in the kitchen, placing mugs on the table. "Will Nis want one?" she asked without turning around. "I take it he is still too scared of Mata to come into the house."

"He'll be fine outside," Tallis said. "If he wants a drink he can damn well come in and get one."

She turned around abruptly and hit Tallis on the arm. "I won't have language like that in my house." Then she hit him again.

"What was that for?" he asked as he rubbed his arm. I noticed that she had managed to hit him in exactly the same place. She looked weak and frail, but I was willing to bet that she was a lot stronger than she seemed.

"That, young man, was for bringing royalty to my house without telling me."

I smiled. It was nice to see Tallis being treated as a naughty schoolboy instead of a Sentinel.

"You didn't exactly give me chance," he argued.

"That's no excuse," she snapped. Then she took a deep breath and turned around to face me. Much to my embarrassment, she bowed low. "Please forgive me, your Highness."

"Don't worry about it," I said. "You were just protecting your grandson. I can understand that. He's worth protecting."

"That he is. Now how do you take your tea?"

It was relaxing spending time with Tallis's granny. Even Tia no longer seemed on edge, ready for a fight. All too soon it was time to go.

"Can we take Mata with us?" I asked. The lizard had spent the entire time curled up under the table, by my feet. "He'll be a great asset."

"Unfortunately not," Tallis said. "He's all the protection my granny has. Not that she really needs protection," he quickly added. "She's one tough old lady. If anyone tried to attack her, I'm sure she would end up getting them to clean her house or mend something for her."

"The other reason," Osin said, "is that Nis is so terrified of him he would refuse to travel with us and while Mata would be great in a fight, Nis would be better."

The lizard came with us when we left the house. As soon as he spotted Nis, who was still patiently waiting outside the gate, he made a beeline for him, his long tail swishing from side to side. Tallis had to throw up a Shield to prevent him leaving the garden.

The poor lizard stood there, pawing at thin air, unsure as to why he couldn't get to his target.

"Mata loves Nis," Tallis said. "He just wants to say hello to him."

Tallis called the creature back. He seemed reluctant to takes his eyes off Daranis, but did so anyway. It looked like he was sulking when he slowly walked back to us. Tallis scratching him behind the ear seemed to cheer him up though.

"Be a good boy and look after Granny," Tallis said to him. We then said goodbye to the old woman, all of us receiving hugs. She made us promise to visit again, even Tia.

"What's your problem with Mata?" I asked Daranis once we were all mounted.

"I don't want to talk about it."

I never did find out why he was terrified of the iguana.

We rode the rest of the day, stopping at a village once the sun began to set.

"My wife's brother lives in the next village," Daranis announced. "Does anyone object to me continuing on and spending the night at his place? I'll meet you back here before sunrise."

Nobody objected so he rode off.

"Will this meet with the queen's approval?" Osin asked when we entered the only inn.

Tia smiled at him. "The queen will approve, but I'm not so sure about the general. Then again, he doesn't need to know."

Unfortunately there were only two rooms available.

"That's not a problem," Tia said. "I am more than capable of sharing a bed with someone of the opposite sex without anything going on."

"Well I'm not," Osin said. "The stable will be fine for me. I'm used to sleeping rough and my horse makes a good pillow."

Tia shrugged. "Suit yourself."

We ate a meal which was surprisingly tasty and filling, then went to the room Tia would be staying in to discuss the plan of action once we reached the border. As Draygar wasn't part of the alliance, Sobek had put a magically enhanced fence in place to prevent anyone entering the country without going through the official crossing places, which were all heavily guarded. Getting Tallis through wouldn't be a problem, as Osin would Cloak him, but we still needed a reasonable story about why we were entering the country.

There was also one other problem; the guards on the Draygar side always checked everyone's arms, looking for the coloured band which identified them as magic users.

"I should have had got Nis to ask his mother how her spies get in," Tallis said. "I'd be surprised if none of them were magic users."

"Why don't we ask her now?" Tia said. "I'll contact the queen and get someone to visit her."

Without waiting for approval from anyone, she sat down on the floor and assumed the same pose that Tallis favoured whenever he mentally talked to Daranis. Nobody spoke as they didn't wish to disturb her.

"Her Majesty will get back to us tomorrow evening," she said when she opened her eyes. "There has been no further word on exactly where the sacrifice will take place, though Claudette is hoping to know before we reach the border."

It had been a long and tiring day, so everyone opted to get an early night and discuss ideas for crossing the border the next day. Tallis and I left Osin and Tia alone. We were staying in the room next door and I couldn't stop myself listening against the wall.

"Well that's disappointing," I said when I heard Osin leave the room.

"I'm sure Tia is thinking the same thing," Tallis said.

Despite our tiredness, neither of us were in the mood for sleep. We may not have been able to make love, but there was plenty of other enjoyable things we could do.

"I wish you would grow your hair back," Tallis said much later as we were cuddled up in bed together.

"Why?"

"I often longed to run my hands through it. It broke my heart when you cut it off."

"But you said it suited me."

"It does. That doesn't mean I didn't prefer it when it was long."

"I hope you understand why I did it."

"I do and I also understand the reason why you haven't grown it back, but I'm hoping that when we return to Amanet, those reasons will no longer be important."

"If you liked my hair so much, why did you refuse to make it grow back?" I was sleepy, but Tallis and I didn't get much alone time to talk and there was a lot I wanted to know.

"It was the right thing to do."

"So you not wanting my father to marry me off had nothing to do with it then."

"That may have been the other reason. The same applies for when you listened in on my conversation with your father about arranging a marriage for you. Everything I said to him was the complete truth. I just neglected to add in the fact that I wanted you to remain at the palace."

"I thought you were interested in Olwen," I said as I ran my fingertips down his chest. "You practically admitted it when Father asked if you would marry her."

"Actually I said that nothing would make me happier than being married to one of his daughters. I didn't say which one. I'd already fallen for you by then."

"So why did you really suggest Forn? Were you jealous of my relationship with him and wanted it to end?"

"Yes and no. Was I jealous that he got to share your bed and I didn't? Of course I was. Did I want to end your relationship with him? No, I didn't. I've only ever wanted you to be happy. That's why I had my father visit. I needed to know how you felt about Forn. I was being honest with you when I told you this."

"I don't get it. You say you love me yet you claim you would have done nothing to prevent me marrying Forn, if that was what I wanted."

"I never let myself even hope that you could be mine. If I believed Forn could make you truly happy, I would have done everything in my power to ensure you two could be together."

"I never thought I would say this, but you are a good man."

Tallis smiled at me. "No I'm not. A good man wouldn't have you naked in his bed." Then he kissed me. It was a long time before we got around to going to sleep.

As he had promised, Daranis met us at the inn for breakfast. He didn't look well rested and hardly ate anything. When I asked if there was anything wrong, he said he was fine then changed the subject.

We rode for a few hours and when we stopped to take a break and water the horses, Osin withdrew some weapons from the back of his horse and handed two to Tia.

"I want to see how good you are with these," he said.

"What are they?" I whispered to Daranis.

"Sai," he said. "They can be used as offensive weapons or for defence. They're quite effective against a sword. Used right, they can protect your arms and your legs. An expert can disarm an opponent."

I watched in fascination as Osin and Tia fought. They certainly weren't taking it easy on each other. If the sounds of clashing metal were anything to go by, if one of them missed a block, they would be seriously injured.

Their strength and speed were amazing. I could clearly see how magic improved their fighting ability. Even Daranis seemed impressed.

Then Tia managed to trap Osin's sword with her sai and twisted sharply, snapping the blade. Daranis started swearing.

"How in the queen's name did you do that?" Osin asked.

Tia grinned at him. "Disarm me and I'll show you."

Osin handed the broken pieces of his sword over to Daranis. "Can you mend this?" he asked.

"Of course," Daranis replied. He placed the two pieces together then asked Tallis to hold them for him. He put his hands over the break and closed his eyes. The metal began to glow and when he removed his hands, it was back in one piece.

"You're handy to have around," Tallis said.

Daranis shrugged. "All Warriors can do that."

While Daranis worked on the sword, Osin had retrieved another one from his horse.

"Really?' Tia said. "You want me to break another sword?"

Osin grinned at her. "I was going easy on you. Now I know what you're capable of I won't make the same mistake again."

"We'll see."

The fight was vicious. If I didn't know better, I would have said they really wanted to kill each other. Both were grinning inanely; they were enjoying themselves.

Then Osin cheated. At least I call it cheating. Both Tia and Osin later confirmed that all's fair in a fight, but I still think it wasn't right. He turned unexpectedly, pointed his sword upward and brought the hilt down on Tia's hand, hard. How he didn't break it I'll never know.

She cried out and dropped one of her sai. Osin didn't step back and give her time to recover; he pressed his advantage and attacked, hard and fast. Somehow Tia managed to defend herself.

Then Osin grabbed the wrist of her empty arm, pulled her close to him and kissed her on the lips. Tia dropped her other weapon, pulled back her arm and punched him in the face.

"What in the queen's name do you think you are doing?" she yelled at him.

He rubbed his chin and looked at her. He had a twinkle in his eye. "Disarming you."

Tia looked down at her discarded weapon. "Oh."

"Didn't anyone teach you about distractions?" Daranis called out.

"So now are you going to tell me how you broke my sword?" Osin asked. I wondered if Tia was going to hit him again, just to wipe the smug smile off his face. Unfortunately she didn't.

She called Daranis over. If she was going to be giving a lesson, he might as well hear it as well.

She demonstrated what she had done, explaining how she had channelled her magic. I didn't understand half of what she said and can remember even less. What I can tell you is that by the time we were ready to start our journey again, both Daranis and Osin had broken each other's swords.

Once both swords had been mended, Tia and Osin returned to the horses to store away all of the weapons they had been using. Osin had just secured his sword in place when Tia turned him around, pushed him up against his horse and kissed him passionately.

"Now that is how you kiss someone," she said when she pulled away. "If you're going to distract someone, make sure you do it properly."

Osin just stared after her, his mouth hanging open, as she mounted her horse. She turned around to look at him. "Are you coming or what?"

Tallis chuckled as he helped me onto his horse and got up behind me.

"Those two are either going to end up in bed together," I heard Daranis mutter, "or they're going to kill each other."

I found myself praying that it wouldn't be the latter.

Mirage

"Your friends and Osin all seem to call you Tal," I said as we rode. "Do you mind? It seems a little impersonal somehow."

"Of course I don't mind. It's just a sign of familiarity, of friendship. It's no different to me calling Daranis Nis."

"Tal," I said. "Tal." Then I shook my head. It didn't feel right; the word didn't sit comfortably on my tongue. "Do you mind if I don't call you Tal?'

Tallis kissed me. "Of course not. You can call me anything you like."

Daranis was riding close enough to hear the conversation.

"Given the situation, 'master' would be a good idea."

"Very funny," I said before returning my attention to Tallis. "So why don't you shorten Osin's name?"

"I did call him Sin for a while, but Ma didn't seem to like that for some reason. It seemed fitting at the time."

I looked over to where Osin was talking with Tia as they rode side by side. "Is he as bad as all that?"

"Not really. He has earned himself a reputation because women throw themselves at him and he dates, a lot, but he doesn't sleep around. Contrary to popular opinion, he doesn't believe in spending the night with a woman then leaving her the next day. We were both brought up better than that."

"Something tells me he's not going to be spending many nights alone on this journey."

Tallis looked over in the direction my head was turned. "I wouldn't bet on that. She's the queen's bodyguard. Even Osin isn't stupid enough to get involved with her. There could be dire consequences."

"Like what?"

"Marriage."

"Oh, so you think marriage is a dire consequence, do you?"

"For Osin it would be, especially if it was ordered by the queen and it wasn't something he wanted to do. I just hope that if things do go further between them, they are both sensible about it."

"They are both Warriors," Daranis said. "They won't let anything distract them from the mission."

The next time we took a break, we stopped by a lake. While Tallis and Daranis fished, Tia and Osin took me aside; they wanted to see how good I really was with a bow.

I demonstrated and they seemed impressed. At least I thought they did, until they spoke.

"Not bad," Osin said. "For a woman." I think he was trying to wind Tia up, not me.

"You mean for someone who isn't a Warrior and hasn't had the same amount of training," she said.

"Something like that."

Tia asked me to shoot again while she watched me, critically eyeing my every move.

"Your technique is good," she said, "as is your accuracy, but you won't be able to shoot like that unless you are standing still. If you are having to duck between trees or hide behind things before and after shooting, you need to learn to do things differently."

"You also won't be able to shoot from horseback easily shooting the way you do," Osin said.

Tia took the bow from me and demonstrated her favourite way of shooting. Instead of drawing the string back with her fingers, she used her thumb. She also didn't stand at right angles to her target, she was at a lesser angle and her feet weren't straight. It looked completely wrong to me.

"You need to learn how to shoot from different positions," she said, then demonstrated leaning to one side. "If you have to shoot around something, for example."

Then she went down on one knee. "Sometimes you can't stand up," Osin said. "It makes you too much of a target."

Every time she released an arrow, Tia hit the same spot, regardless of where and how she placed her body.

"You need to learn how to do that," Osin said.

Tia handed the bow back to me and the torture began. They made me shoot over and over again, all the time issuing instructions.

"Always anchor at the same point."

"Bend your knees more so you lower your centre of gravity."

"Push with your left hand as you pull back with your right."

"Use your shoulders more. Your shoulder blades should be almost touching."

By the time the fish was ready to eat, my arms were killing me and I was exhausted. They both seemed pleased with my progress though.

I was so tired, I fell asleep as we rode. Luckily Tallis was holding me tight or I might have fallen off. We stopped mid-afternoon in a small town, opting to rest for the night in a decent inn instead of carrying on for a few more hours. The inn had a bath, which I took full advantage of, and Tallis gave me a back and shoulder massage as soon as I had finished.

While I bathed, Tia contacted the queen. There was no update on where Rose was to be sacrificed, but a solution had been found in regard to getting the magic users into Draygar. We were given the address of a friend of Claudette's who lived close to the border. He was a magic user who knew a spell to hide the marks on magic user's arms.

I slept well that night. I was so exhausted, as soon as we were in bed, Tallis kissed me goodnight and told me to go to sleep.

We arose with the sun and headed out before the rest of the inn's guests were awake. Osin and Tia worked with me again when we stopped for lunch. This time Daranis joined in as well. By the time we stopped, I was aching just as much as I had been the previous day, but at least I was improving.

When we stopped in the middle of the afternoon to rest the horses, Osin made me try shooting while sitting on one. His horse was so mild mannered I found I could almost aim straight, even when moving.

"If ever we find ourselves in a fight," Osin said later that evening, "immediately grab your bow and swap horses with me.

Mine will know exactly what speed to take and what course to enable you to shoot the enemy."

I went pale. "Will I really need to kill someone?"

"I hope not, but it's best to be prepared. We will all do our best to not involve you, but I can't guarantee we won't need an archer to help us out and, though I hate to admit it, you're a pretty good shot."

We continued to head north for most of the next morning before turning west when we hit a fork in the road. We soon arrived at the address Tia had been given, but none of us thought we were in the right place. It was nothing more than a run-down shack; I couldn't believe anyone actually lived there. We decided to investigate anyway.

"Do you feel that?" Tallis asked as we neared what remained of the building.

Daranis, Osin and Tia all nodded.

"Magic is being used somewhere close by," Osin said.

Tallis was about to knock on the door when it sprang open and an old man stepped out.

"Trespassers," he shouted out. "Clear off. You are not welcome here." He was short and so thin he seemed malnourished. It looked like there was hardly any flesh, let alone muscle, covering his bones. His long white beard was dirty and ragged. I wondered if it had ever seen a brush.

To my horror, when he turned around, I could see that he was naked. His bare behind was not a pleasant sight. I was suddenly glad that his beard was so long.

"Are you Wilbur?" Tallis asked.

"Never heard of him," the man snapped. "Now get off my property."

Unperturbed, Tallis tried again. "Claudette sent us."

The effect the words had on the man was amazing. He straightened his back, rolled back his shoulders then shook his head, making all of his face hair quiver. I just stared at him as his beard became indistinct, as though I was looking at it through water, then disappeared. Flesh which clung to bones suddenly filled out and clothing appeared.

Within seconds, a handsome middle-aged man stood before us instead of a crotchety old curmudgeon.

"In that case," he said politely, "you had better all come inside."

The inside of the shack was nothing like the outside. It was clean and well maintained. And much larger. I looked at him suspiciously. Something was going on.

"You're a Mirage," Tallis said.

"I am," Wilbur confirmed and held out his arm, revealing a red band. "Welcome to my humble abode."

"It doesn't look so humble now we're inside," Tia said dryly.

"Mirages are illusionists," Tallis explained to me. "They can disguise themselves and almost any object. In reality this house looks nothing like a tumbledown shack; he's placed an illusion spell on it."

"And that is why you are here I assume," he said. "You want me to disguise the bands on your arms."

"We need to get into Draygar and my mother told us to visit you," Daranis said.

Wilbur looked at him closely. "So you're Claudette's offspring. I can see the resemblance."

"Will you help us?" Osin asked.

"Claudette is an old friend. I always help those she sends to me. There is just one condition. I don't want to know why you are going into Draygar. Or why you are taking a non-magic user with you."

"That's fair enough," Tia said, "seeing as we weren't going to tell you anyway."

Wilbur then looked at me. "Make yourself useful lass and put the kettle on while I deal with these people."

I have no idea what spell he put on them, or how, but by the time I returned with filled cups, their bands were invisible.

"The spell will only last ten days, two weeks at the most, so you had better be out of Draygar before then or you will be in a lot of trouble."

"It will only take a few days to get to our destination, so that time frame shouldn't be a problem," Osin assured him.

"Can you do anything about my eyes?" Tallis asked. He had his dark glasses with him, but it would be better for us all if he didn't have to wear them.

Wilbur shook his head. "The magic that turned them black is much more powerful than mine. There is nothing I can do."

Tallis shrugged his shoulders as though it was the answer he had been expecting. "There was no harm in asking."

As we drank our tea, Wilbur regaled us with tales of some of the people he had helped get across the border. I wasn't sure I believed anything he said, but he was certainly entertaining.

When it was time to move on once more, Tallis thanked him for his help and promised to drop in to see him again once our business was concluded.

"Good luck," Wilbur said as we left his house. "You're going to need it."

Osin kept inspecting his arm as we rode. "I hope his spell lasts as long as he said it will."

"Stop worrying," Daranis said. "It only needs to get us across the border. We can stay covered up after that."

"No we can't," Tia said. "I've heard rumours that they have armed gangs roaming throughout the country, looking for magic users. They have the right to demand everyone show them their right arms."

"Then I'm back to hoping that his spell lasts," Osin said. "Or that the rumours are wrong."

"Or that we can beat any of these armed gangs in a fight," Tia said with a smile on her face that was almost frightening.

Tallis rolled his eyes. "She's almost as bad as Osin is."

Less than an hour later, Tallis called us to a halt. We were close enough to the border that I could stop pretending to be a slave. Tallis removed the shackles from me and placed them in his saddlebag; we would need them for the return journey. I quickly got dressed while Tallis removed his cloak and stowed that away as well. He would be invisible crossing the border, but he didn't want to wear it once he was inside Draygar. It was unlikely anyone would recognise it, but it wasn't worth taking the risk.

As we rode closer to the border, I grew more and more nervous. I found myself frequently glancing at Tallis's exposed arms, looking for his bands. Wilbur had told us the invisibility spell would last at least ten days, but that didn't stop me worrying. And I missed riding in Tallis's arms. Now that I was no longer having to act as though I was a slave, I had to ride my own horse. I had brought some skirts with me and I was grateful that Tallis wasn't making me wear them. Riding in trousers was much more dignified.

Daranis had been the only one to comment when I got dressed. He was of the opinion that women should only be allowed to wear dresses or skirts and didn't keep his opinion to himself. Tia took him aside and spoke to him. I have no idea what she said but he looked pale when he returned and apologised to me, saying I was entitled to wear whatever I wanted to.

Before we reached the border, Tallis stopped his horse and dismounted. He tied it's reigns to the saddle on Daranis's horse, so it could be led, slipped on his dark glasses and climbed onto Osin's horse behind his brother. I didn't hear Osin say anything, but suddenly they both disappeared, as did their horse.

I knew that they were still there, but not being able to see them made me suddenly feel vulnerable. Even if they had left, I would still be protected by two Warriors, but that didn't stop me feeling empty and alone.

Draygar

When the border came into sight, it was evident that it wasn't as heavily guarded as we had been led to believe. There was a wooden hut on the Sobek side and its mirror image stood just inside Draygar. The fence that stretched each way as far as the eye could see looked strong and impenetrable and was so high it would be impossible to get over, but I couldn't see what was preventing people climbing it. If they walked far enough along it so that they were no longer in sight of the men guarding the gate, anyone could just climb over.

I asked Daranis about it and he explained that it was enchanted, making it impossible to touch, let alone climb. The moment someone came into contact with it, all of their muscles would tense up. That meant that, not only would their hands clench so they wouldn't be able to use them, they would also be unable to make their leg muscles work. It was supposed to be a very painful experience, one I had no intention of trying out.

Which brings me to the gate. While the fence created a protective barrier, preventing anyone entering or leaving Sobek undetected, the gate was nothing more than few pieces of wood nailed together. Not only could it easily be jumped over, even I would be able to break it down. It seemed completely inadequate. It was also standing open.

As we drew closer to it, we must have tripped a silent alarm or something because suddenly four guards came out of the two huts. Either that or they had been watching us from the huts without us being able to see them. The two on the Draygar side were heavily armed with swords, bows and arrows, large knives hung from their belts and a couple of pikes were leaning against the side of the hut.

Those on the Sobek side were unarmed, but that didn't matter. I could see that they were Warriors; their black bands were clearly visible on their arms.

They were standing in front of the gate, blocking the road, so we slowed to a halt.

"Identify yourselves and your reason for entering Draygar," one of them said in a bored tone.

Daranis did all of the talking. He provided a false name and said he was escorting his two sisters to a friend's wedding. The bride had met a merchant from Draygar, fell in love and decided to give up her Sobek citizenship for him. Pretending that we were all related was the only reason we could give for Daranis travelling with women who weren't slaves.

"They don't look much like you," one of the guards said as he looked Tia up and down before turning his gaze to me.

"A fact for which I am truly grateful," Daranis said. "It's hard enough to keep an eye on them both as it is. Imagine how hard it would be if they both looked as good as I do? I would be forever fighting to keep men away from them. As it is, I don't have that problem."

The guard laughed when I gave an indignant snort. Tia was clenching and unclenching her hand. She would have been playing with her knife had Osin not confiscated them all. She couldn't be armed crossing the border. That argument had lasted a while.

"Why do you have an extra horse?" the other guard asked, looking at Tallis's riderless mount.

Daranis gave him a pained look. "To carry all of the luggage for these two. Anyone would think we were going for a month instead of just a couple of weeks."

The first guard laughed again as he moved out of the way of the gate. "I would say enjoy yourself," he said, "but something tells me you're not going to."

Daranis leaned over as he passed him. "If I come back alone," he said so quietly I could only just hear, "you won't tell anyone will you?"

The guard grinned at him.

We passed into Draygar, where we were stopped by the other two guards. They must have heard some of the exchange as they, too, looked like they were trying not to laugh. They gave a perfunctory glance at our arms, but didn't give us a proper inspection before stepping out of our way and welcoming us to their country.

None of us spoke until we were far enough away from the border that nobody could overhear us.

"Was that really necessary?" Tia asked.

"Necessary, no," Daranis said. "Advisory, yes. It never hurts to get guards on your side. You saw how little interest they had in checking our arms. We didn't need Wilbur's magic. Just some concealing make-up would have been adequate."

Tia grinned at him. "I didn't know you carried that sort of thing with you," she said.

"I don't," Daranis said hastily.

A short while later, Osin and Tallis rematerialized. Tallis slipped off the horse while it was still moving and climbed onto his own mount. He leaned forward to release its reigns from Daranis's saddle then steered closer to me.

"It's good to see you again," I said.

"I never left your side."

I smiled at him. "I know, but it still feels good being able to see you. Why did you and Osin have to make yourselves invisible? Why didn't you just teleport yourselves across the border?"

"A number of reasons. Firstly, we wouldn't be able to teleport the horses and the guards would never have believed that you needed two spare mounts. Secondly, we have to have been somewhere in order to teleport there or be able to lock onto a marker. A magic user has to picture their intended destination in their mind. Neither I nor Osin know anywhere in Draygar we could both have pictured accurately enough."

"And?" I asked. I could tell he had more to say.

"And nothing would have persuaded me to leave your side. I trust Daranis and Tia to protect you, but that doesn't mean I would ever willingly leave you alone."

I cannot put into words how good that made me feel.

When we stopped for a break, we discussed what our next steps were. We knew where we needed to go, but still hadn't received any word on exactly where the ceremony was to take place. Without knowing the layout, we wouldn't be able to formulate a plan.

While Tallis didn't need to be that close to Shield someone, as he had demonstrated when saving Tephi's life in the training arena, he wouldn't be able to do so while he was invisible as Osin's Cloaking magic blocked everything; sight and sound, but also other magic. That meant that he would have to be close enough to get to Rose as soon as he revealed himself, not just close enough to Shield her.

Getting away was another problem. One option was for Tallis to force his mind into Rose's so he could teleport her out, but it was a risky thing to do and he would only do that as a last resort.

Before we continued our journey, Tia contacted the queen once more. She had no update for us, but did let us know that Claudette had requested that the high chamberlain visit her that evening so she was hopeful of being able to deliver details later that night.

The Draygar countryside was lovely. We rode past meadows and streams and fields full of cattle. We planned to avoid the cities and larger towns, choosing instead to go cross-country as much as possible. As we didn't have a wagon there was no need for us to stick to the roads. It meant finding decent accommodation would be more difficult, but it would save a lot of time and time was the most important factor. Not only did we have to reach our destination by a specified date, we had to know exactly where to go, at what time and how to get in, grab Rose and get out without being caught. I tried not to think about any of that as I rode.

I had been hoping that, as we were no longer in Sobek, my archery lessons would end. They didn't. As we rode, Osin, Tia or Daranis would pick a target in the distance and I would have to try to hit it with an arrow while still riding. I didn't hit many, but my shots were close enough that I didn't lose any arrows.

As the sun descended, we rode into a village which, thankfully, had a semi-decent inn. The beds were clean, the beer wasn't watered down and the food was hot and filling. The mattresses were thin and the food was lacking in flavour, but you couldn't have everything.

That evening, once we were alone in the room Osin was sharing with Daranis, Tia contacted the queen once more. She had good news; the exact location of the ceremony had been discovered. Details were discussed and plans were made on how to rescue Rose. Nobody asked how Claudette had obtained the information.

The sacrifice would happen in a clearing surrounded by low hills, locally known as the Bowl. There would be nothing to stop us attending and watching from above, but we would have to get down into the Bowl, surrounded by cult members, if we were to get to Rose. Getting out would be a problem as we would be heading uphill.

Tallis insisted that I didn't descend into the Bowl, instead remaining an observer only. I wanted to object, but he was right; I would only be a liability. How could Tallis rescue Rose if he was concentrating on safeguarding me?

He asked Daranis to stay with me, but he refused. "You need me down there," he insisted. "While Tia is a formidable Warrior, she doesn't have the battle experience I have. It would be better if she guards Adara."

"We need someone to watch our backs, to let us know if our exit is blocked, that sort of thing," Tallis said. "Only you can do that. Our link will allow you to warn me."

"Not while you're Cloaked, it won't. Not only will it block our communications, it will also stop me knowing where you are."

"He has a point," Osin said.

"Alright. Daranis comes, Tia stays, unless anyone objects." Nobody did. "Now, we need to get hold of some of those cloaks Claudette said the cult members wear. It's more or less guaranteed that they will be wearing them for the ceremony."

"Leave that to me," Daranis said. Tallis nodded.

"Did Claudette have any idea how many members will be in attendance?" Osin asked Tia.

"Her best guess is a few thousand."

Osin whistled. "Let's hope it doesn't come to a fight then. I'm not sure even Daranis and I can fight off that many."

"If things go wrong," Tallis said, "we will need help getting out. Tia and Adara both know how to use bows. It will be a long distance, but accuracy won't be that important. Just get the arrows close to us and hopefully people will run for cover."

"I can do that," Tia said. "I can also enchant Adara's bow to make the arrows go further. She won't have the strength to shoot the distance we are talking about, but with the spell I have in mind, she won't need to have."

"How will we know where you are if you manage to Cloak yourselves again?" I asked.

"Good question," Tallis said. He looked at Tia and smiled. "I can sense where my brother is, even when he's Cloaked. You need to learn how to do that."

"I'll try," she said, but she didn't sound hopeful.

The next day, every time we stopped for a break, Tia and Osin fought. The closeness of the combat would make Tia more aware of Osin, more in tune with him. Not once did he manage to beat her, until he Cloaked himself, then she had no idea where he was so he easily overcame her.

Once, while Cloaked, he went after Tallis instead of Tia, but Tallis sensed him and moved out of his way.

"How did you do that?" Tia asked in amazement.

"As I said, I can sense him. You need to get close to him. Spend all of your time as close to him as you can get. Ride next to him. Talk with him. Get to know him better. Continue your training with him. We have a few more days."

Tallis did not look confident. Nor did Tia. Osin couldn't keep the smile off his face.

Two days later, we arrived at our destination. Tia was still unable to sense Osin when he was Cloaked and she was beginning to get frustrated.

It was early afternoon, so we took rooms at the only inn then went to the Bowl to check the layout. It was as we had been expecting; a large grass-covered meadow surrounded by small hills. Standing at the top of one, I looked down. It was a long way to the bottom. I was never going to be able to shoot that far.

When I commented, Tia took my bow from me and placed her spell on it. "Try it," she said when she handed it back. I did as she asked, expecting to only get half way and swore loudly when my shot reached the edge of the base of the Bowl.

I then looked at the four magic users and grinned. "Now which one of you is going to retrieve my arrow for me?"

Osin rolled his eyes then vanished. I saw him appear far down below then vanish again. When he rematerialized next to me, he had my arrow in his hand.

"What do we do now?" I asked. The ceremony was due to take place when the sun was at its highest the day after next.

"Now," Tallis said. "We wait."

Ceremony

The next day, people started arriving. The inn filled to overflowing and the surrounding meadows became fields of canvas as tents were pitched.

Later that evening, we were eating a meal in the taproom when a man and his wife asked to join us. There were no spare tables and we didn't want to draw attention to ourselves, so we agreed. They didn't introduce themselves.

The man was short, for a male, with long dark hair which looked like it hadn't been washed in far too long. His wife was thin and pale and never spoke the entire time they were at our table.

"Are you here for the ceremony?" the man asked.

"We are," Tallis said. He wasn't lying; we were just there for different reasons than everyone else.

The man grunted. "This had better work. It's my wife's last hope."

"What's wrong with her?" I found myself asking. I wish I hadn't. She had an incurable illness. They had travelled to Sobek, but the best Healers had not been able to help. She was slowly deteriorating. If no cure could be found, she was facing a long and excruciating death.

I began to wonder how many others had similar reasons for joining the cult. Maybe it wasn't about power and dominance and devil worship, as I had been led to believe. Maybe it was just about people struggling to help their loved ones. If it wasn't for the fact that it was my sister who was to be sacrificed, and also that I didn't believe for a moment that it would work, would I have let it go ahead? I like to think I would still do all I could to save the victim, regardless of who she was, but if, by some miracle, it did work, how many would I be condemning by saving the one? I forced myself to stop thinking about it.

"What's with the glasses?" the man asked before taking another mouthful of his meat. He pointed his fork at Tallis as he spoke. I wondered how Tallis was going to able to answer without lying.

"Something happened to me a while ago. As a result, I have to keep my eyes covered."

The man didn't look convinced, so Osin took over. "He's oversensitive to light. Even the dim light given off by candles hurts his eyes and gives him terrible headaches. Like your wife, the Healers can't fix it."

The man must have been satisfied with Osin's explanation as he asked no more questions. As soon as we had finished eating, we bid the couple a good night and retired to our rooms.

Once again, Osin Cloaked himself, making himself invisible, but Tia was still unable to sense him. Tallis told her not to worry about it. He had had years to perfect it while she had only had a few days. It wasn't really a big deal; it just meant that we would have no idea where they were while under Osin's Cloak. We would just have to keep scanning the edges of the crowd until they appeared.

Tia seemed dejected when Tallis and I headed to our room.

For obvious reasons, I was unable to sleep. "I feel sorry for that woman," I said as I lay in Tallis's arms. "Whether we succeed in rescuing Rose or not, she faces a horrible death."

"I would never allow you to go through something like that," he said. "I would put you out of your misery before the pain became too severe."

"You mean kill me." I wasn't sure if I was shocked by his words or pleased.

"If it was the choice between that or you suffering agony with no hope of recovery, yes. I hope that you would do the same for me."

I thought about it for a moment. "Now I know that is your wish, I would make sure it was taken care of, but I wouldn't be able to do it myself. I would have to get someone else to do it." I then turned so he could see me grinning at him. "I'm sure there would be lots of volunteers."

"Very funny," he said and kissed my forehead.

"I don't think I could ever take someone's life."

He wasn't smiling when he said, "Tomorrow you may have to."

The next morning was cloudy with signs that it might rain. Part of me hoped that it would stop the ceremony going ahead, but Daranis said that it was due to clear up before midday and it was highly unlikely the ceremony would be put off just because of a little rain.

Unfortunately he was right and by mid-morning the sun was shining brightly.

When we went downstairs to request food, there were no spare tables, so the owner said we could eat in our rooms and he would send trays up as soon as he could. We readily agreed as I'm sure I wasn't the only one feeling uncomfortable in the taproom. Everywhere I looked I saw cloaks, all the same shade of brown.

"Blood cultists," I heard the owner mutter. I hoped that he wouldn't be around the next time we descended the stairs as we, too, would be wearing the same cloaks. Daranis never said where he got them from and none of us asked, but the previous day he had gone out for a while and returned with five of them.

We stayed in our rooms until we were sure that most of the cultists would have left. It would take a good few hours to walk to the Bowl and most didn't have horses. We would be taking ours, not only to carry the weapons, but we might need to make a fast getaway.

The taproom was deserted by the time we left. I was glad that the innkeeper wasn't around to see us. I felt ashamed to be wearing the cloak of a cultist even though I knew it was only a disguise. The man had been polite and friendly to us and I didn't want him to think we were something we weren't.

We rode slowly, not wishing to draw attention to ourselves. As we got closer to the Bowl, we began to see people, the last few stragglers making their way to the ceremony.

It was a hot day and the thick cloaks we were all wearing were heavy and uncomfortable. I was glad I wasn't walking. Some people gave us odd looks when we moved around the top of the bowl instead of going down into it, but they said nothing. Maybe they just assumed that we were trying to find somewhere to tie our horses before we walked down the hill. Or maybe they just didn't care enough to comment.

There weren't many trees about, so we dismounted under the first one we came across. It was tall and majestic and it had a large canopy which would provide adequate shade for me and Tia.

I glanced down into the Bowl, which looked like a sea of brown. There were a lot of people down there. At the far end, Count Gillain had set up some sort of stone altar; at least that's what it looked like from a distance. As I watched, a man carried the slumbering form of a woman, dressed all in white, and laid it on the flat surface. From the colour of her hair, I assumed it was Rose, but I couldn't be sure.

I couldn't supress a shiver that ran through me, making me cold inside and causing goosebumps on my arms. Tallis walked up behind me and placed his arms around me. It didn't help me warm up. Nothing would until Rose had been rescued.

"Everything is going to be alright," Tallis said, taking my hand and squeezing it tight. I was too scared to speak so I just nodded my head.

I forced myself to look away and saw that Osin and Daranis were arming themselves, as was Tia. She handed me my bow and a quiver of arrows. I removed my cloak so I could put the quiver on my back. I might need easy access and the cloak would get in the way. We were far enough away to not be noticed by those in the Bowl and they were all looking the other way anyway. I held my bow tightly in my hand.

"Look after her," Tallis said to Tia.

"I'll protect her with my life."

"You'd better."

"Are you ready?" Osin asked. Tallis and Daranis both confirmed that they were. Osin held out his hands. "Grab hold of me and don't let go. I can only keep you hidden while we are in physical contact."

The two men did as instructed then all three disappeared. All I could do was watch the proceedings and pray that they made it to the altar in time. And that they somehow managed to free Rose and escape. I had my bow on my shoulder and my quiver of arrows on my back. The moment Tallis came into view once more I would be ready to shoot whoever I needed to to ensure they all managed to get away.

Tia put her arm around me. We both watched the ceremony, hoping it would last a long time. Rose still hadn't moved; she must have been unconscious. I was glad that she didn't know what was happening; she would have been terrified.

I kept looking into the crowd, but I had no idea where Tallis and the others were. I assumed that they were working their way around the outside, to avoid walking into anyone, but there was no way for me to tell.

"Where are they?" I said to myself.

"I can feel Osin," Tia said. She sounded proud of herself and I could understand why. She had been trying so hard to sense him when he was Cloaked and I was pleased for her that she finally could.

"Where?" I asked.

"Just keep watching along the edge. Tallis will reveal himself soon. Do not watch what is happening on the altar."

It was good advice and I tried to follow it, but my eyes kept moving back to Count Gillain. From where I was standing, I couldn't hear what he said, but he seemed to have the crowd mesmerised. When he drew a dagger from his robes, I gasped. I couldn't help thinking that they were going to be too late.

Then I saw movement at the side of the crowd, close to the altar. My eyes focused on it and I breathed a sigh of relief when I saw Tallis. He was close enough to Shield Rose. Osin and Daranis remained hidden and would do so until they were needed. I assumed they were making their way closer to Rose, but I couldn't be sure.

I watched as Count Gillain raised the dagger high over his head and brought it down swiftly. It bounced harmlessly off Tallis's Shield, causing the count to look around in confusion.

Only that's not what happened.

Instead, as the dagger made its descent, Daranis suddenly appeared; he must have let go of Osin for some reason. I couldn't understand what was happening as I saw him run at Tallis and tackle him to the ground.

I later found out that the surprise assault broke Tallis's concentration enough to shatter the Shield. There was nothing to stop the dagger entering Rose's body.

She didn't react as the sharp metal slid between her ribs, into her heart. Blood spurted everywhere, covering Gillain as he withdrew the dagger. I could only watch in horror as Rose's life flowed out of her.

Traitor

I couldn't help myself; I screamed. My eyes darted back to Tallis, who placed his hands around Daranis's head and forced him to look at him. Then they both vanished. Initially I thought that Osin had reached them, but I was wrong.

"We have to get out of here," Tia said.

"We can't leave them alone down there," I cried out.

"They're not down there anymore. They've teleported." She took my hand and pulled on my arm. "Come on. We have to leave. Now."

I was in a daze as Tia forced me onto my horse. I have no memory of riding back to the inn we were staying at, leading the three riderless horses behind us. We didn't hurry as Tia didn't want us to draw attention to ourselves.

Three words kept running through my mind. Rose is dead. My mind couldn't come to terms with it. I had failed. We all had failed. We had travelled through three kingdoms, deserted my family, put ourselves in danger, all to rescue Rose. And we had failed.

I walked like a zombie as Tia led me to the room I was sharing with Tallis. It was empty, so we tried Tia's room. That, too, was unoccupied. I should have been worried, but I was too numb to feel anything.

We found the men in the room Daranis was sharing with Osin. From the way he was sitting in the chair, it looked like he was tied in place by Shields. His hands were behind his back and his legs were against the legs of the chair. His head was bowed low. He wasn't asleep or unconscious; he was just avoiding looking at anyone. Tallis was pacing up and down while Osin sat on the bed, glaring at Daranis.

"Thank the queen," Tallis said when he turned around and saw me. He took me in his arms and held me tight. "I am so so sorry."

Only then did the tears begin to flow. I had been holding everything in, but being with Tallis made me feel safe enough to surrender to my emotions. As I sobbed into his chest, I heard him thank Tia for getting me back to the inn safely.

"What happened?" she asked.

"We don't know yet," Osin said. "Nis attacked Tal, stopping him protecting Rose. We have no idea why. As soon as we knew we had been compromised and there was nothing we could do to save Rose, we teleported here. Due to their connection, Tal was able to link his mind with Nis's and bring him with us. He hasn't said anything and we wanted to wait until you were back before questioning him."

"Please let me do it." Even through my crying I could hear the venom in Tia's voice.

It took me a while to get myself under control enough for Tallis to let go of me. When he did, he asked me if I wanted to stay for the interrogation. I didn't, but I said that I did. I didn't want to be parted from Tallis. I also wanted to hear what Daranis had to say first hand.

"It's time to start talking," Osin said and kicked Daranis's leg to get his attention.

When his head raised, I didn't see the smug look I had been expecting to see. He looked devastated.

"Please don't torture him," I suddenly said. The man was responsible for my sister's death, but I couldn't bear to witness the truth being forced out of him.

"I can't," Tallis said. "Unless he lies. And something tells me he isn't going to be that stupid."

"Well I can," Tia said and slipped a knife out of her boot.

Osin got off the bed, walked over to Tia and placed his hand on her arm. "Not yet sweetheart."

That comment dragged me from my misery. Why was he calling her sweetheart? Before I had chance to ask, Daranis started speaking.

"I told you that something was going to go wrong." There was no emotion in his voice. I have never heard anyone sound so dead when speaking. He had won, had prevented us from rescuing Rose, yet he seemed defeated. He looked at the wall as he spoke, instead of at anyone in the room.

"I have been a member of the cult for a while. It's not what you think. We are not devil worshipers and have never sacrificed anyone, until now. It's just a group of desperate people, all wishing to change something in their lives. Count Gillain promised me everything I could ever want; the power to take away slavery in Sobek. I would be able to take my wife home as an equal, not as my property."

"How?" Osin asked.

"He swore that the right sacrifice would give us power. Those of us with magic would become unstoppable. I would be able to destroy the Council and abolish slavery. The running of the country would be handed entirely over to the queen and I would have the power to make sure she brought in the new rules."

"And what then?' Tia asked. I didn't like the way she was playing with her knife. "You would run the country with her as your puppet?"

Daranis moved his head to look at her. "No. I have no interest in running the country. I just want an end to the slavery."

"He's telling the truth," Tallis said.

"We all want that," Tia said. "But it isn't as easy as it sounds. It's how the Council keeps control. There would be anarchy without that control."

"There has to be a better way." I found myself agreeing with Daranis, though I hated myself for doing so.

"And it is being looked into," Tia said.

"Why Rose?" I asked. My voice sounded small and pathetic, but I didn't care. "Why did Rose have to die?"

"I am sorry for your loss," Daranis said. "I truly am. But Count Gillain found an ancient text. It told him what he had to do, how he had to do it, when he had to do it and who the sacrifice had to be. I myself saw the scroll. It described your sister perfectly, even down to the fact that she was of royal blood."

"Are you feeling proud of yourself?" I spat at him.

He shook his head. "No. It's all been for nothing. The document was a lie. The sacrifice didn't work. I should have felt the power enter me the moment the knife pierced the sacrifice's chest.

"The sacrifice!" I screamed. I tried to get to Daranis. I wanted to hit him, I wanted to pound his face with my fists, but Tallis held me back. "She has a name."

Daranis looked even more devastated than he already did. "I know. I'm sorry."

"So Count Gillain lied to you," Osin said.

Once again Daranis shook his head. "No. He has been deceived as well. He was as much a believer as the rest of us. To prove it he had a Sentinel confirm that he was telling the truth. He asked me if Tallis would do it, but I knew that the moment Tal found out what was going on, he would do something to stop it."

"Why did you do it?" I asked. "Is stopping slavery really worth killing my sister, because that's what you have done. You may not have made the killing blow, but you are just as responsible."

"You think it was an easy decision to make?" The despair in his voice almost made me feel sorry for him. Almost. "I didn't want to come with you; I didn't want to have to make this decision, but I couldn't let Tal down, not when his life might be at risk. When I went to see my wife's brother, I hoped that he would make the decision for me. He's also a member of the cult. But he didn't. He said I had to do what I believed was right. I had to choose between your sister and my wife. I couldn't have made any other choice." By this time, tears were flowing down his face.

"You could have spoken to me," Tallis said.

"And what could you have done?"

"I could have met with Count Gillain. I could have seen this document you are talking about. I could have convinced you both that it was nonsense."

"And that is why I didn't tell you. You would have taken away the only hope I had of living a normal life with my wife."

"So instead you let a woman be executed," Tia said. "And look where that got you. You are probably never going to see your wife again."

Tallis looked at her sharply. "What does that mean?"

"When I tell the queen what has happened, he's going to be arrested the moment we re-enter Sobek. Murder is still a crime there, or had you forgotten?"

There was real anger in her voice. She hated Daranis as much as I did. As I should have.

It was then that I realised that I didn't hate him. I hated what he had done, but not him. He did what he did to help his family. Would I have done any different?

Daranis said nothing to defend himself. Tallis did, however. "You wouldn't be saying that if you had ever experienced having to own someone you care about. You have no idea what it's like having to treat the person you love like a slave, to have to put a collar on their naked body and chain them to you. You are ignorant of the reality and have no right to speak about it. Experience it, just once, and then tell me if you are still so quick to condemn Nis."

Tia said nothing.

"I don't want to hear any more," I said. I was tired. I was completely worn out. I just wanted to go so sleep. I hoped that things would be better in the morning, but I wasn't holding out much hope.

I turned around to leave the room, but Tallis grabbed my shoulder. "Just give me a minute, then I'll join you." I didn't turn around to look at him; I just nodded my head.

I have no idea what went on after I left the room, but Tallis wasn't happy.

"Tia has agreed not to tell the queen about Daranis yet, though I don't know how long I can stop her for. I've released him, but Shielded the room so he can't get out. He can't even teleport. I've confiscated all of his weapons so he can't do something stupid to himself. He wasn't lying when he said he wouldn't, but that doesn't stop him changing his mind during the night."

"Osin will keep an eye on him."

A smile almost made it onto his face. "Osin isn't staying in the room. He's sleeping in Tia's tonight. Apparently, he slept there last night as well."

Under other circumstances I would have found that amusing, but right then nothing would have made me smile. "The queen won't be happy when she finds out," was all I could think of to say.

"Are you hungry?" Tallis asked. I hadn't eaten since breakfast, but I couldn't face food. I told Tallis to go and get something, but he wouldn't leave me alone.

He sat on the edge of the bed and pulled me down beside him. How long we were like that before there was a knock on the door, I have no idea.

Reluctantly Tallis got up to open it. Osin was on the other side with a tray. "You need to eat," he said. Tallis didn't argue. He thanked him then closed the door.

I watched while Tallis ate, not that he ate much. He didn't try to force me to eat anything. He did suggest I should have some of the wine, to help me get to sleep if nothing else. I declined. Drinking on an empty stomach was not a good idea. I did, however, have some water when he insisted.

Tallis moved the tray of mostly untouched food onto the floor in the far corner of the room, then undressed. Despite the way I was feeling, I couldn't help admiring his body. Even now I still feel ashamed at the thoughts that went through my mind as each article of clothing was removed. I should have been mourning my sister not lusting after the man I was in love with.

I didn't have the energy to undress myself, so Tallis did it. I should have done it myself. I was getting more and more turned on with each garment he took off me. I don't think I was the only one. He couldn't help kissing or caressing each piece of flesh as it was revealed.

"Let me take your mind off things for a while," he said. He didn't mean what I wanted him to mean, but right then I didn't care. All I could think about was how good he was making me feel.

He kissed me, licked me, caressed me, but it wasn't enough. I wanted more, much more. He didn't resist as I rolled us both over so I was on top. The way I kissed him told him exactly what I wanted.

"Don't Adara, please don't," he said when he turned his head away from mine. "It's too dangerous."

"I trust you."

"I don't trust myself."

"You won't hurt me." He must have been able to hear the conviction in my voice because he did nothing to stop me as I made my way down his body, leaving a trail of kisses down his chest and abdomen until I reached his groin.

I was about to take him into my mouth when he moved away. "No, not that. If I'm going to lose control, I want it to be while I am inside other parts of your anatomy."

He gently pushed me down onto my back and climbed on top of me. I swear the kiss he gave me had me moaning into his mouth. He didn't stop kissing me as he slowly slipped inside me. He did it tentatively, almost delicately, nothing like I was used to.

Then his mind crashed into mine. When he took my memory of Rose's cat being killed, it was a gentle probing, a 'may I enter'. This was something completely different. Even if I had been taught how to shield my mind, I don't believe I would have been able to keep him out. Suddenly I understood why he was so scared to make love to me. If I hadn't been prepared for it or if I had tried to fight against it, he would have shattered my mind.

It was overwhelming. I couldn't read his mind, but I could feel everything he was feeling, emotionally and physically. I could feel his terror, and his joy. I could feel him moving inside me but I could also feel what he was feeling as he did so. The combination of sensations was almost more than I could take.

He must have been able to feel me the same way I could feel him because he started to pull away. I hooked my leg around him, put my arm around his back and pulled him closer. "You're not going anywhere."

I was being stimulated both physically and mentally. I can't even begin to describe how good it felt. I climaxed much sooner than I ever had before and I could feel the effect the tightening of my inner muscles was having on him. He didn't last much longer before he, too, reached orgasm.

"That was amazing," I gasped.

He grinned. "You haven't seen anything yet." He was still inside me, both mentally and physically, and I could feel that he was already ready to go again.

I had never cried out in ecstasy so much in my life and I began praying that he had found a way to soundproof the room.

The amused look on Osin's face the next morning told me he hadn't. "Sleep well?" he asked.

"Very well thank you." I wasn't lying. When Tallis and I finally had enough of each other for one night, I was so exhausted I fell straight to sleep. "And you?"

The blush on Tia's face answered my question.

After breakfast we took food up to Daranis's room. Tallis was pleased to see that he was still alive, though he looked like he hadn't slept. I could hardly blame him. Not only was he responsible for my sister's death, he also had no idea what was going to happen to him.

He refused to even try any of the food Tallis had brought up on a tray for him until Osin said he could either eat it willingly or he would force him to.

I didn't believe that Osin would really follow through on his threat, but Daranis did.

"What do we do now?" I asked. Our mission was over, yet just leaving felt wrong.

"I have spoken to the queen," Tia said. "She knows what happened and sends her deepest sympathy. She has also told your brother."

I thanked her. I hadn't been looking forward to letting Tephi know that I had failed to save our sister. Suddenly everything came crashing back into me. Tallis had successfully taken my mind off what had happened, but only for a while and now that while was over. My bottom lip began to quiver and tears filled my eyes. Before any could fall, Tallis had his arms around me.

"Did the queen say anything about what she wants us to do now?" Osin asked.

"Yes." The tone of Tia's voice made me look up at her. She was grinning. It wasn't a nice grin. "She wants us to find Count Gillain and kill him."

Plan

"Is she insane?" Osin exclaimed. "We can't just assassinate someone. Yes, he's a murderer, but he should stand trial. We can't be judge, jury and executioner."

"We can't kidnap him and take him back to Sobek," Tia said. "Even if we did somehow manage to get him across the border, it would cause a political nightmare, maybe even war."

"And we can't let him get away with Rosemerta's death," Tallis said. "If we do nothing, there is a risk that he will sacrifice someone else."

"The other reason we need to kill him," Tia said, "is that Claudette's sources believe that removing the leader will disband the cult and the cult is becoming too big and dangerous to be ignored."

"She's right," Daranis said. "The cult is devoted to their leader, without him they will have no purpose, no reason to continue. He doesn't have a second-in-command. Nobody will take over control if he's removed."

"There has to be a better way," I said. I wanted Gillain punished, but I had to agree with Osin; assassination was not the answer.

Tallis sat on the edge of Daranis's bed and pulled me down beside him. He had a thoughtful look on his face.

"Maybe there is. We need to get a message to Claudette."

"What are you thinking?" Osin asked.

When Tallis told us, we all nodded our agreement, even Daranis.

"I'll make the arrangements," Tia said then sat down, crossed her legs, placed her hands on her knees and closed her eyes. It felt like she stayed in that position for hours, but in reality, it was only a few minutes. Osin's pacing up and down was irritating and finally Tallis snapped at him to either keep still or leave the room. Osin glared at him, but did as instructed.

"Claudette will be contacted as soon as possible," Tia said when she finally opened her eyes. "Now all we can do is wait."

"No," Osin said. "We can't afford to wait. Now that Count Gillain knows that the sacrifice didn't work, we don't know what he will do. He may leave and if he does, we won't know where to find him. I say we go and get him now."

"And do what?" Tia asked. "Bring him here?"

Osin shrugged. "Why not? Tal can Shield the room so nobody will hear him if he tries to call for help."

"It will give us the opportunity to question him," Tallis said. "I, for one, want to know where he got that scroll. I find it a little too convenient that it made Rosemerta the target. There is more here than meets the eye."

"I don't know if the queen will agree to that," Tia said. "She was adamant about not acting until she has heard back from Claudette."

"The queen doesn't need to know." Tia stared at Osin as though trying to gauge whether he was serious or not.

Eventually she shrugged her shoulders. "Alright." She didn't sound happy about agreeing.

"So how are we going to do this?" Tallis asked. "Did Claudette tell you where Gillain lives or where the location of the cult's headquarters is?"

Tia shook her head. "No, only that he runs the cult from his estate and it's located somewhere near here."

"Maybe we could ask around," I suggested. "Someone is bound to know where it is."

"I'd rather not draw attention to ourselves if we can avoid it," Tallis said.

"I can tell you," Daranis said. "I have never been there, but I know where it is."

We all looked at him. Why it never occurred to any of us that he would know, seeing as he was a cult member, I have no idea, but his comment seemed to take us all by surprise.

"Where?" Tallis asked.

Daranis gave the location. "I have been told that it's hard to get in. Nobody is allowed to see Count Gillain without an appointment and there are a lot of cult members located there to protect their leader. They want to keep him safe."

"Don't you mean 'we'?" Tia said viciously. Daranis winced.

"That wasn't called for," Tallis said by way of reprimand.

"Maybe, but it's still true."

"Can we deal with this later?" I asked. "Right now we should be discussing how to get hold of Gillain."

Tia mumbled an apology then the discussion returned to where it should have been. Options were suggested then discarded. With only two warriors, three if you included Daranis, which Tia refused to do, a Sentinel and a non-magic user, brute force wasn't going to get us onto the estate. Soon it became obvious that we would need Daranis's help. As a member of the cult, he would be able to get us in.

Tia, however, wouldn't even consider the possibility.

"That man is a traitor. He could easily lead us into a trap."

"I trust him," Tallis said.

"And look where that got you."

"This is different. Nis and I are blood bonded. He won't put my life in danger."

"Hasn't he already done that?" Tia argued.

"No. He stopped me rescuing Rosemerta, but that was all. He could easily have shouted out a warning. There were enough cult members around us that we wouldn't have been able to defend ourselves if he called for help, but he didn't. He wanted the sacrifice to go ahead, not for me to get harmed."

"I still don't trust him."

"You don't have to." Tallis turned to his bother. "Osin, what's your opinion."

"I hate to say it, but Tal is right. You could argue that Nis betrayed Rose, or even Adara, but not Tal. And he only did that for the sake of his family. Nis would never lead Tal into a trap."

Tia growled in frustration. "I still don't like it and nor would the queen."

"Who said you have to like it? You just have to agree. And if you don't, you can stay here. You don't have to be part of this."

"If you are going to do this," Tia said, "you're not going to do it alone."

I waited for Tallis to say I had to stay behind, but he didn't. Daranis grabbed his cult cloak and put it on; he would need it if he was going to gain access to Gillain.

"Make sure you stay close," Tia said to him. "And don't do anything stupid. If I even think that you are betraying us, again, I will put a knife in your back."

"Understood." For someone who was having his life threatened, Daranis didn't seem nervous. I took that to be a good sign. He obviously didn't think he had anything to be nervous about.

He placed his hand on Tallis's shoulder as he went past. "Thank you for trusting me."

"If you make me regret it, Tia won't be the only one after your blood." Tallis spoke so calmly I wasn't sure if it really was a threat or not.

We collected our horses from the stable then took the road north, with Daranis in the lead. We would ride to the estate and hope that nobody would think to place our horses in the stable or someplace else where we wouldn't be able to easily get to them; we would need them if we were to make a swift exit.

Weapons were securely tied to the saddles then hidden with blankets. We didn't want to arouse anyone's suspicions by being obviously heavily armed. What we would do if we were searched, I had no idea, but I didn't doubt that the magic users had a plan.

Nobody spoke as we made our way along the road. We passed the occasional traveller, most of whom were wearing brown cloaks. Those that were, nodded their greetings to Daranis. Nobody looked happy. They all looked downcast. It wasn't a surprise; they had been expecting great things from the sacrifice. They had pinned their hopes on it working and had been let down. I began to wonder if getting to Gillain would be easier than we had thought. Maybe all of his followers had deserted him.

We weren't that lucky. We could see cloaked people guarding the entrance to the estate as we got near. One stepped out when we were close enough to be addressed without the need to shout.

"What is your business here?" a man asked. His bushy beard hid most of his face.

"I've come to see the leader," Daranis said. "These are potential new recruits."

The man grunted. "I didn't think anyone new would want to join after last night's failure."

"Who says it was a failure?" Daranis asked him. "It may just take longer to work that we expected. You need to have a little faith."

"I have faith," came the reply. "I wouldn't be here if I didn't."

A woman wandered over. She was carrying a sword and looked like she knew how to use it. She was also carrying a lamp, even though it was a bright and sunny day.

"How do we know you are a believer?" she asked Daranis. I had been worrying about that. Anyone could get hold of a cloak and pretend to be a member of the cult. After all, we ourselves had done so the previous day.

Daranis held out his left hand, palm facing upward, revealing his wrist. The woman lifted her lamp high and inspected Daranis's skin under its light. I almost gasped when I saw it reveal a scar running across the entire width of his wrist. I had never seen it before.

The woman nodded in satisfaction. "You may enter, but it's unlikely Count Gillain will see you. He has been refusing all visitors. You may, however, be allowed to make an appointment for a later day."

The news wasn't quite as bad as it sounded. At least we now knew he was in residence. There had been a possibility that he wasn't there and none of us relished the thought of having to track him down.

As we rode down the long driveway, I manoeuvred my horse closer to Daranis's.

"Why have I never seen that scar before?" I asked quietly.

"Because it's not visible in normal light. It was caused by an enchanted dagger and can only be seen using flames created by burning a specific combination of elements. If that woman had been holding a normal lamp, it wouldn't have revealed it. It's the way cult members identify each other."

I wanted to ask more, but the driveway wasn't long enough for an extended conversation. More cloaked people guarded the door to the house. One of them came forward and offered to take our horses.

"I don't think we will be staying long," Daranis said. "From what I have been told, it looks like I will just be able to make an appointment for another time. Would you mind looking after them for a few minutes while we go inside?"

A couple more cult members came forward and held our horse's bridles while we dismounted. From the look Tia was giving the blanket hiding her weapons, she wasn't happy about going into the house almost unarmed. I say almost because she had knives secreted down both of her boots as well as inside her tunic, as did both Daranis and Osin. Only Tallis was completely unarmed as I also had my knife on me.

We were given instructions to find the man who took care of scheduling Gillain's appointments and were permitted to enter the house unescorted.

"Any idea where to go?" Tallis asked as soon as we closed the door behind us.

"Quiet," Tia said. "I can hear voices. I think they are coming from down the corridor on the left."

She moved her head to one side as she listened, then straightened it before nodding.

"I guess we head toward them then," Osin said.

Two figures came into sight, both cloaked. One was tall and thin and towered over her shorter companion. They were walking away from us so Osin called out to get their attention.

"Excuse me. Could you point us in the right direction please?"

They both spun around, revealing a stern faced woman and a cheery looking man with a round face and rosy cheeks. The woman looked down her nose at us as though she was superior to us. I would love to know how she would have reacted had she known that she was in the presence of royalty.

Her smaller companion, however, seemed more friendly. "Where do you need to go?" he asked.

"We are looking for Count Gillain," Tallis said.

"You will need to speak with Kelvin. Nobody sees the count without his permission."

"Of course," Tallis said pleasantly. "And where can we find him?"

"Come with me," the man said and smiled at us. The woman looked at him in disgust as he turned away from her and led us back the way we had come.

"You came at just the right moment," he said once we were far enough away from the woman for her not to overhear. "I can't abide that woman. You gave me a good reason to leave."

Osin chuckled and I couldn't help breaking out in a smile.

The man led us down a different corridor and stopped outside a large wooden door. "This is Kelvin's office. He's usually there. If he isn't, you are welcome to wait inside for him."

Osin thanked the man, who walked off in a completely different direction to the one that he had been taking with the shrew-faced woman.

Daranis knocked on the door and waited for a reply. A deep voice called out, "Enter."

As the only one of us who was obviously a member of the cult, Daranis was the first one into the room.

Like everyone else on the estate we had seen so far, Kelvin was wearing a brown cloak. He was seated behind a large desk which was strewn with papers. He had more in his hands and was frowning at them.

He had a neatly trimmed beard and when he looked up at us, I noticed how well his eyes matched its colour. He appeared to be middle aged and looked underfed.

"How can I help you?" The deepness of his voice was in complete contrast to his physique. Had I not already heard him speak, even if it was through the door, I would have expected something much higher pitched.

Daranis held out his hand. Kelvin ignored it. "I have some potential new members who would like to speak to Count Gillain."

"You will have to come back next week." His attention was once more on his paperwork.

"That's not possible I'm afraid," Osin said. "We need to see the count today."

When Kelvin looked up again, he seemed annoyed that we were still in the room. "Then you are going to be disappointed. The count isn't seeing anybody today, nor for the rest of the week."

"But he is here?" Tallis asked.

"Yes, he is. Not that it is any of your business."

That was all that we needed to hear. As soon as Kelvin's head lowered once more, Osin Cloaked himself. I watched Tia, who seemed to be watching Osin, even though she couldn't see him. She could sense him and her eyes tracked him as he made his way around the desk.

Kelvin's head was suddenly pulled back. When Osin reappeared, he had a knife to Kelvin's throat.

"Now let's try again shall we," Osin whispered menacingly in his ear, just loud enough for us all to hear. "Where can we find Count Gillain?" He moved the knife away just far enough that the man could speak without it cutting his skin.

"He..he..he's in his study," Kelvin stammered.

"Very good. Now you are going to take us there. I will be standing behind you. If you so much as look at anyone in warning, this knife will go straight into your kidneys. My next one will go through your heart."

"And don't even think about trying to run," Tia said. She had also drawn one of her knives and was holding it up for Kelvin to see. "I'm a very good aim."

When Kelvin nodded his head, Osin stood back. He took hold of Kelvin's arm and made him stand. The man looked terrified.

It didn't take us long to reach Gillain's study and we met nobody on the way. Which was lucky for us as if anyone saw Kelvin, they would instantly know that there was something wrong. The man was physically shaking.

When he indicated which was the correct door, Tia opened it and walked in.

"Haven't you heard of knocking?" Count Gillain said before he had chance to take in who had just entered the room.

We closed the door behind us and Osin pushed Kelvin away from him.

Gillain looked much as I remembered him, except he no longer had the air of arrogance about him that I recalled, though whether that had been real or just something my memory had conjured up, I couldn't be sure.

Osin looked at Tallis, who nodded. He had Shielded the door. We were free to say anything we wanted without fear of being overheard or disturbed.

"What is going on here?" Gillain asked.

"I'm sorry count," Kelvin said. "They threatened my life."

"It's alright Kelvin. This isn't your fault." He returned his attention to his visitors. "What do you want?"

Then his eyes fell on me and he went pale. "Princess Adara," he said and bowed.

"P..P..Princess?" Kelvin stammered.

"Yes," I said. "I am the daughter of King Andrast of Amanet, sister of Princess Rosemerta, the woman your leader killed yesterday."

Kelvin fainted.

Tallis removed his glasses and looked at Gillain. Recognition showed on his face and he collapsed back into his chair.

"All I have to do is scream and dozens of armed guards will be in here within seconds. You can't possibly fight that many."

Tallis smiled at him. "Go ahead and try. I have the room Shielded."

"I suppose you've come here to kill me," he said. He sounded defeated rather than scared.

"Unfortunately not," Tia said. "While nothing would give me greater pleasure, I have been persuaded not to. At least not yet."

"Who are you?" he asked.

"The Queen of Sobek's personal bodyguard. It seems you have pissed off two royal families. I wouldn't like to be in your shoes."

"We are going to take you away to answer some questions," Tallis said.

"You will never get me out of here. There are too many people here to stop you."

"Maybe, maybe not," Osin said. "But we are certainly going to try. Now are you going to come willingly or unwillingly?"

"Of course I'm not going to go willingly."

Osin smiled at him. "I was hoping you were going to say that." He walked up to him, placed one hand partially around his neck, where it met his left shoulder, and squeezed. Count Gillain slumped onto his desk, unconscious.

Kidnap

"Was that really necessary?" Tallis asked.

Osin shrugged. "It seemed like a good idea to me. Now all we have to do is walk out of here. Will you be able to Shield the room after we leave?"

"I can," Tallis said, "but it will wear off before we get too far away. There's a limit to the range I can maintain it from."

"Then let's hope nobody tries to get in for a while," Daranis said.

"And that he doesn't wake up too soon." Tia nudged Kelvin's inert body with her foot. He showed no sign of regaining consciousness.

"Do you want me to tie him up with a Shield?" Tallis asked his brother, but Osin shook his head.

"There's no point. Even if he does wake up, he won't be able to get out of the room or call for help and any magical bindings you put on him will fail at the same time as the Shield you put on the room."

Nothing more needed to be said, so Osin picked Gillain up and hoisted him over his shoulder like he was a sack of grain. Then they both disappeared.

Daranis opened the door and peered out. There must have been nobody in sight because he opened it wider and strode out. We all followed him. At least I assumed that we all did. The way Tia kept looking to her left indicated that Osin was with us.

"The door's Shielded again," Tallis said quietly as we made our way down the corridor.

It all felt too easy to me. Something was bound to go wrong and I couldn't shake the feeling that we were overlooking something. As soon as we exited the house, we found out what. The three cult members were still holding our horses for us and seemed a little surprised when we took the reins from them.

"Where's the other one?" one of the men asked.

Daranis was a fast thinker. "He's still with Kelvin and will be for a while. His wife is feeling ill so he asked us to take her home. If you place the reigns of his horse over his neck, he will follow along behind us. He's a well trained stallion. I'll bring him back later to collect my friend."

"Why not just leave it here?" the man asked suspiciously.

"I would love to but he's the mate of my mare and can't bear to be parted from her. He might become aggressive if he has to stay here without her."

Almost as if the horse had understood what Daranis had said, he pulled back his top lip and showed his teeth. The man holding him quickly did as Daranis had requested then stepped away.

I could only assume that Osin placed Count Gillain's body over the back of his horse then mounted up behind it as the animal showed no reaction until Tia said, "Let's go."

We rode slowly down the driveway, though I'm sure I wasn't the only one who wanted to gallop. Once we were out of sight of those guarding the entrance to the estate, Osin reappeared.

"That was way too easy," Daranis said.

"We're not safe yet," Tallis said. "It won't be long before my Shield fails and if Kelvin has regained consciousness, the cult may give chase."

"We should hurry then," Tia said.

"Hold up Adara," Osin called out and I pulled my horse to a halt. He instructed me to dismount then put the count on my horse. He retrieved my bow and arrows and handed them to me.

"Take my horse," he said. "If we are followed, you can concentrate on shooting at our pursuers. He won't let you fall off."

I wasn't happy about the thought, but said nothing as I placed my weapons on my back and mounted the stallion. He was taller than mine and Osin had to help me.

"Get back to the inn as fast as you can," Tallis said to him. "If we're chased, we will lead them on a different route."

"I'll see you soon," Osin said then made himself, Gillain and the horse disappear.

The rest of us continued our ride at a sedate pace. While there weren't many fellow travellers about, there were enough for us to draw attention to ourselves if we hurried.

It wasn't long before we heard shouting behind us. I looked around and saw mounted cult members galloping toward us.

"Get off the road," Daranis yelled and turned his horse into the nearest meadow then galloped away. Tallis, Tia and I followed his lead.

There were a lot of cultists following us and they were closing the gap. "Try distracting them," Tallis called over to me.

Tia was riding next to me and already had a bow in her hand. "Don't try to hit anyone," she said. "Just try to discourage them from following us. We don't want to kill anyone unless we have to."

As soon as she had finished speaking, she twisted around and shot behind her.

"Aim to miss," I said to myself. Even I could manage that.

I was wrong. My first shot got someone in the arm, by the look of things. The next hit a rider in the chest and he fell off his horse onto the ground. He didn't get up again.

I was so shocked I almost dropped my bow. I felt sick. I felt faint.

"Don't worry about it," Tia called out to me.

"But I think I just killed someone," I cried out. Tallis looked across at me in concern.

"I'm sure he's just hurt and will fully recover," Tia said. We both knew she was lying.

"Pull yourself together," Daranis shouted at me, earning himself a glare from both Tia and Tallis. He was right, however. I couldn't worry about what had happened. There was plenty of time for that after we had escaped.

Our shots had made our pursuers pull back a little, but not enough for my liking. And there were still a lot of them.

"We should split up," Tia said and Daranis agreed.

"There's a hill in the distance," she continued. "I'll teleport myself there and shoot anyone who gets close to Daranis or Adara. Tallis, teleport to the inn, now."

"Don't even think about arguing," Daranis yelled out. "We need you to Shield the room ready for when the count wakes up. We'll look after Adara, I promise."

Tallis gave me a pained looked, then vanished. His horse, now riderless, kept running along. Then Tia disappeared. I heard screams from behind us and some of the cult members pulled to a halt. They had seen what had happened and I guess they didn't want to fight magic users.

About half of them were still chasing after me, Daranis and the two riderless horses. I shot back at them one more time and managed to miss everyone, though I did make one of the riders swerve.

Soon arrows were flying over our heads. If Tia was aiming to miss, she was doing a bad job of it. I glanced behind me to see riders falling from their horses.

By the time we reached the hill Tia was on, there were only half a dozen left following us. As we rode by she teleported to the next hill in the distance.

This continued on for a while. At one point I had to pass her my quiver as she had run out of arrows. By the time we reached the fourth small hill, we only had one person on our tail. Tia got him in the thigh and he gave up the chase.

Once we were out of sight, we pulled to a halt. The amount of shooting and teleporting Tia had been doing had exhausted her and she needed to catch her breath.

I felt numb inside. I had killed someone. Daranis dismounted and pulled me from Osin's horse. He hugged me tight. I was shaking all over and my legs could barely support me as I began to sob.

"It's alright," he whispered in my ear. "Everything is alright. It wasn't your fault. You were just protecting us and yourself. If they had got us, they would have killed us."

I found that highly improbable. From what I had seen, the cult was made up of normal people who were so desperate they joined the cult in the hope that it would help them. Daranis was just trying to make me feel better. Through my tears, I managed to voice my opinion.

Daranis let go of me and held me at arms length, his hands holding my shoulders. "Look at me." I obeyed. I had never seen him look so serious about anything. "I was a member of that cult. I know what I am talking about. You are right, most of them are just desperate people, but desperate people do unexpected, extreme and sometimes violent things. They also make great fanatics and, believe me, some of the cult members are very fanatical. They would do anything to get Gillain back. Anything. Yes, you killed someone, but you saved four lives by doing so."

At best Daranis was exaggerating. At worst he was lying. But his words made sense and they did bring me a little comfort. I didn't fully believe them, but if I clung to them, I knew I would be able to get back to the inn before completely breaking down.

I pulled away from him and dried my dyes with my sleeve. Tia handed me a water bottle. Drinking from it helped a little.

She smiled at me, her face full of sympathy. "You may want to think about washing your face as soon as we get back," she said. "I don't think you want Tallis seeing you like that."

I couldn't help smiling at the comment. I didn't care what my face looked like. Nor would Tallis. As long as we were together, nothing else would matter.

It took a long time to get back to the inn. We had led our pursuers in the wrong direction so we had to back-track. Nobody spoke as we travelled, we just concentrated on getting back to Osin and Tallis. Tallis's horse didn't need to be led; it just followed behind us.

Tallis was in our room, pacing up and down, when I entered. He took me in his arms the moment he saw me. "I have been so worried," he said. I then felt him raise his head. "Thank you for looking after her."

I wasn't sure if he was talking to Tia or Daranis. Probably both.

As soon as we were alone, I broke down again. Tallis just held me as I cried. He didn't say anything. He instinctively knew that all I needed was to be in his arms.

I was shivering, so he placed his cloak around me, using its magic to heat me up. I didn't realise how much I had missed wearing it, but having it on me again gave me great comfort.

When I had cried all of the tears I had in me, I washed my face and got changed. I would cry again over what I had done, many times, but right then I just wanted to try to put it behind me.

Tallis took hold of my hand. "Come on. It's time to interrogate the count."

Scroll

Tia, Osin and Daranis were in Daranis's room. I was pretty sure that Osin would be sharing a room with Tia from then on. Count Gillain was sitting in a chair, his hands behind his back, held in place by Shields. I expected him to look smug and arrogant, or even scared maybe, but he didn't. He looked how Daranis had when Tallis interrogated him; completely and utterly defeated.

"Do whatever you want to me," he said in a resigned tone. "My life is no longer worth living anyway."

"All we want is some answers," Tallis said. "Tell the truth and I won't use my powers on you."

Gillain shrugged. "What would be the point in lying?"

"Why did you do it? Why did you sacrifice my sister?" I asked. I didn't like the way he was acting. I wanted an excuse to hit him, but he wasn't giving me one.

"I had to. The scroll told me it would work, that sacrificing someone would give me the power I need. Your sister matched the criteria perfectly."

"The power to do what?" Tia asked. She was playing with her knife again. Gillain didn't even seem to notice.

"To bring my wife and children back."

"Back from where?"

"The other side. Plague swept through our town, taking most of its residents with it. Some people say I was lucky. I couldn't disagree more."

"I want to see this scroll," Tallis said. "It seems a little too convenient that it describes the necessary sacrifice so perfectly that only Rosemerta matched the criteria."

"Be my guest. I keep it in the top draw of my desk in my study."

Count Gillain was being too nice, too helpful for my liking. I thought he had to be up to something. Whatever it was, he wasn't telling lies; Tallis would have known.

Osin looked at Tallis and raised a questioning eyebrow. He nodded his head then glanced between Osin and Tia. "You both go. I don't want to risk his study not being empty. Be careful. Take no unnecessary risks."

"We won't," Osin said then both he and Tia disappeared. I assumed that they teleported themselves to Gillain's residence.

While they were gone, Tallis continued his questioning.

"Where did you get the scroll?"

"After I lost my family, I travelled around aimlessly. I couldn't stay in the place where I had lost everything, including my reason for living. I abandoned my family home and what was left of the people of the township I was supposed to administer. My brother understood my reasons and took over for me. He knew I would be back."

"That doesn't answer the question," Tallis said.

Count Gillain continued as though he had not been interrupted.

"I ended up travelling through different kingdoms. Each place I visited, I found people like me, people who needed the power to change things in their lives. That's how the cult got started. Initially it was just a group of men and women banding together, looking for something they couldn't find on their own. I ended up seeking them out, recruiting wherever I could. I thought that there must be something out there to give us all what we needed and if we worked together, we would find it."

"You preyed on the weak and the vulnerable," I said, but Gillain shook his head.

"I didn't prey on anyone. I just spoke to people. I didn't get anything out of people joining the cult, but they did. They became part of something, they were no longer alone. I never made any promises, at least not until I got hold of the scroll."

"Are you ever going to tell us where you found it?" Tallis asked.

"I was in northern Amanet when I came across a young man who desperately wanted to change his life. He had been falsely accused of a crime and his father had disowned him. He claimed to have found the scroll in his father's study, which he searched before he was kicked out of his home, and believed it had the power to give him what he needed, he just didn't know how to go about using it."

"And you believed him?"

"When you're desperate, you are prepared to believe anything."

"So he joined your cult," Tallis said.

"No, he just handed it over. All he wanted was the promise that I would help him once I had found a way of releasing the power."

"What was this man's name?"

"Akar. Akar Penbroke. He claimed that he was the son of the local lord."

Tallis turned around and looked at me. The shock I was feeling was mirrored in his face. The man who had attacked Olwen was behind the scroll. It couldn't be a coincidence that it practically named Rose as the victim. But I had no idea what he had against Rose. I could understand if it had been Olwen it had described, but not Rose.

"Do you know this person?" Daranis asked.

"Know him?" I said. "He raped my other sister."

"Was falsely accused you mean," Count Gillain said.

Tallis had to grab me quickly before I hit him. "He was guilty," I spat at him. "I was there. He admitted it."

"He said he was forced to confess by a Sentinel. Lying and saying he did it was the only way to stop the pain."

"You idiot," Daranis said. "That's not how a Sentinel's power works. They can only make people tell the truth. They have no power over someone unless they are lying."

"How was I to know? It's not as if we are taught about magic where I come from."

Osin and Tia suddenly reappeared in the room. Tia handed a parchment over to Tallis, who exclaimed the moment he took it.

"This is enchanted," he said. He then looked at Daranis. "How did you not detect it?"

"I said I saw the document. I never touched it."

Tallis unrolled it and scanned its contents. "This is a very accurate description of Rosemerta," he said. "The hair and eyes alone would narrow it down, as would the height. Even the shape of her nose is described. All of this combined would make the intended sacrifice one of very few people. The fact it states she has to be of royal blood guaranteed that Rosemerta would be chosen."

He handed the scroll to me and I felt nothing odd about it. Then again, why would I? I had no way of detecting magic.

I read it through. Tallis was right, it really did describe Rose perfectly. Akar had guaranteed she would be the victim when he had the document created.

"How did you even know about Rose?" I asked Gillain.

"Akar told me about her. He said he had heard about her, but hadn't seen her himself so he couldn't be sure. I went straight to the palace to see her for myself."

"He was lying. Not only did he meet her, he stayed at the palace. That's where he attacked my other sister."

Count Gillain shrugged his shoulders, as if it was of no importance. "What does it matter now? If I had known, would I have made a different choice? No, I wouldn't. I would be more wary in regard to the document's authenticity, but it wouldn't stop me doing what I did. I would have to take the chance that it was genuine."

I couldn't understand his attitude. He had murdered a woman in cold blood and was now being held hostage and interrogated by people who could easily kill him, but he didn't seem to care about any of it.

"Does my sister's death mean nothing to you?" I couldn't stop myself asking.

"Compared to my family's? No. To me, she was a tool to use, nothing more. I regret that her death has been for nothing, but that is all I regret."

"What happened to her body?" I had to know if we would be able to retrieve it and give her a funeral.

"We burned it on a pyre and scattered her ashes in my rose garden. It was dignified."

Tears formed in my eyes and Tallis hugged me tight. I hated what Gillain had done, but I couldn't hate the man. He had been used just as badly as Rose had and he was suffering for it, emotionally at least. If I had lost my entire family, would I have behaved any differently? It was a question I was unable to answer.

"I have told you everything I know," Count Gillain said. "Will you now please just kill me."

"Not yet," Tallis said. "There is one more thing I want to know. How did you manage to kidnap the princess?"

For the first time since he had been taken, Gillain looked surprised.

"Kidnap her? I didn't kidnap her. The king gave his permission for me to take her. He even administered to her a sleeping drug I gave him so she wouldn't wake until I was far away from the city."

"You're lying," I growled.

Tallis appeared uncomfortable when he said, "Actually he's not."

I couldn't believe what Tallis had just said. "But he has to be. My father would never do that. He must have lied to him about the reasons for wanting Rose."

I expected Gillain to smile smugly, but he didn't. "He knew why I wanted your sister. I told him everything. By now the cult is large enough to amass a small army and many rulers are getting worried."

I saw Tallis and Osin both glance at Tia, who nodded her confirmation that her queen also had concerns.

"What did you promise the king?" Tallis asked when he returned his attention to Gillain.

"To stay out of his kingdom. In exchange for his daughter, I would do no more recruiting in Amanet and would immediately leave the kingdom and never return."

I felt like someone had stabbed me in the stomach. The coldness of the imaginary steel spread through all of my body. My father had willingly let my sister be murdered. If Tallis hadn't been supporting me, I'm sure I would have collapsed.

"He was just protecting his people," Gillain said.

Tia strode up to him and was so close to him when she spoke that he must have been able to feel her breath on his face.

"Don't you dare defend him. No ruler should allow one of his people to be sacrificed, even for the good of others. Where does it end? If one is okay, what about two? Ten? A hundred? Where do you draw the line? The queen would never do something like that."

"Have I come at a bad time?" a voice sounded behind us, making us all spin around. Tia, Daranis and Osin all had knives out. "What sort of welcome is that?" the man continued.

"Sorry," Osin said as he put his knife away. "You took us by surprise. We weren't expecting you so soon."

"I came as soon as I got Claudette's message," Wilbur said. He then looked at Gillain. "So is this the piece of shit that I am supposed to impersonate?"

"It's good to see you again," I said. "But how did you get here?"

"Magic," he said and winked at me.

"I mean, how did you know where to find us?" I knew that all magic users could teleport themselves and that Sentinels could also teleport others if they linked their minds, but I was under the impression that they had to know their destination. I couldn't understand how Wilbur not only knew what inn we were staying in, but which room we were in.

He moved closer to Tia and held up her arm, pointing to where her black band was still invisible. "I can locate my magic," he said. "And while I'm here, I might as well renew it if you are planning on staying in this cesspit of a country."

"I think we have everything we need from our prisoner for now," Tallis said. "Have you eaten?"

"Yes," Wilbur said. "But I could do with a tankard of ale."

"Then let's retreat to the taproom."

"What?" Gillain said. "You're just going to leave me here, tied to this chair?"

Before leaving the room, Tallis put Shields on the window and the door, then released the Shields which held Count

Gillain's hands tied behind his back. "He won't be able to leave the room," he said before slipping his dark glasses on.

He took my hand and we all went for a drink. After what I had heard, I needed alcohol. The taproom was nearly empty and we found a quiet corner in which we could talk undisturbed.

While we drank, Wilbur was brought up to date on all that had happened. "And why exactly are we sharing a table with a traitor?" he asked, glaring at Daranis, who dropped his head in shame.

"Because, for now, we need him," Osin said. "And we also understand why he did what he did. If he enters Sobek, he will be arrested. Daranis knows what his fate is to be and has accepted it. He will do all he can to help us until then."

"Fair enough," Wilbur said.

I had one drink, but couldn't face any more. Tallis took me back to our room as soon as I had finished, but went to check on Count Gillain first. He walked into the room without knocking, then immediately started swearing.

"Get the others," he shouted at me. I ran down the stairs. I had no idea what was wrong and didn't stop to find out. The rest abandoned their unfinished drinks as soon as I told them that Tallis needed them.

I was the last one to arrive back in the room. I got there just in time to hear Osin exclaim, "Shit. What do we do now?"

Imitation

Count Gillain lay on the floor. His body was rigid and contorted and there was foam around his mouth. His eyes were wide open, staring at nothing. There was no doubt in my mind that he was dead.

"Don't touch him," Tallis cried out as Osin moved closer to the body. "We don't know what he took. The foam coming out of his mouth might be deadly."

Tia rounded on Daranis. "Did you know about this?" she demanded. "Do all cult members carry poison pills on them to take if ever they are interrogated. Is death preferable to answering questions about the cult?"

"Of course not," he replied, his voice full of disgust at the accusation. "Why would anyone want to kill themselves instead of answering a few questions? Besides, he had already told us everything we needed to know."

"Did you have any idea he planned on killing himself?"

Daranis shook his head. "No. I don't even know where he got the poison from. I can understand it though. He's lost everything, even hope. And on top of that he was manipulated into murdering an innocent young woman. What did he have to live for?"

"Revenge?" Osin suggested.

Again Daranis shook his head. "He wasn't that sort of man."

"What happens now?" I asked. I looked at Wilbur. "Do you need him alive to impersonate him?"

"No. I know what he looks like and I've heard him speak. I can make myself look and sound like him. His personality will be a problem though."

"Don't worry about that. We'll make sure you are never alone with anyone and he won't act like his normal self after having been kidnapped."

"So when do you want to do this?" Wilbur asked. "Sooner rather than later would be better, before anyone finds him here."

"Let me dispose of the body first," Osin said.

He took a blanket off the bed and wrapped the corpse in it, making sure he didn't touch it. He then picked it up. "Someone will need to open doors for me."

"No problem," Tia said.

Osin made himself and the bundle he was carrying invisible, then Tia left the room.

"How will she know where he is if she can't see him?" Wilbur asked.

"She can sense him," Tallis said.

Wilbur raised an eyebrow. "How?"

"They've become close," I said.

"She means they're sleeping together," Daranis said.

"Oh," was Wilbur's only reply.

As soon as Osin and Tia returned, stating that the body had been buried deep enough that it wouldn't be found, Wilbur said, "Let's get this over and done with shall we?"

I couldn't help staring at him as he shimmered. Soon Count Gillain stood in his place. Had I not known that the man was dead, I would never have known the difference.

"How do I look?" Wilbur asked. He sounded so much like Gillain it was creepy.

"That is unnerving," Osin said. "How do you change your voice and appearance like that?"

"I don't. It's an illusion. You just think you are seeing and hearing the count. In reality, I haven't changed at all."

"Well I'm convinced," Daranis said. "You'll definitely fool almost any cult member, as long as you don't spend too much time with them."

"Almost?" Wilbur asked.

"My only concern is Kelvin, the man who looks after all of his affairs. Hopefully we can find a reason to keep him out of the way."

"Remember to respond when someone calls Gillain's name," Tia advised.

Wilbur rolled Gillain's eyes. "I have done this before you know."

"Does anyone know what Gillain's personal name is?" Tallis asked.

It was a good question. I had only ever heard him referred to by his family name, Gillain, or his title, count.

Everyone looked at each other, then at Daranis, who shook his head. "He never told me and nobody called him anything else in my presence."

"Let's hope that applies to people in his own household as well then," Tallis said. Then he gave Daranis a serious look. "Time to go."

It had been decided that Daranis would escort Wilbur to Gillain's estate, claiming he had been forced to help in the kidnapping and that he had freed the count. With everyone believing Wilbur was Gillain, him verifying the account should prevent any awkward questions.

As soon as they were both safely alone in Gillain's study, Daranis would contact Tallis and we would all teleport there. I wasn't looking forward to it. Tallis assured me that there was no danger and I believed him, but I was still nervous.

The waiting was unbearable. We had no way of knowing what was happening. There was a chance that things could go wrong, that the cult members would recognise Daranis and attack him before he was given the chance to tell his story, but he was aware of that and was prepared to take the risk.

Time crept by. Tallis desperately wanted to contact Daranis to find out how things were going, but it would have been dangerous. He might distract him at just the wrong moment.

Eventually Daranis got in contact. Everything had gone well and they were alone in the count's study.

As soon as Tallis informed us that it was time for us to leave, Tia and Osin disappeared.

"Ready?" Tallis asked me. I wasn't, but I said yes anyway. "All you have to do is let me into your mind, the same as you do when we have sex."

"This isn't going to be as much fun though, is it," I said, which made him chuckle.

He took me in his arms then I felt his mind entering mine. The next thing I knew I was in Count Gillain's study. I hadn't felt a thing.

"Can we travel like that more often?" I asked. "It's a lot quicker than riding."

Tallis kissed me then released his hold on me. "Only if you don't want to take anything with you that you can't carry." He then turned to Daranis. "How did it go?"

Between them, Daranis and Wilbur explained that the guards had bought their story and had not asked any questions. Kelvin wanted to know more, but when Wilbur had said he was badly shaken and wanted to be alone with his rescuer for a while, he hadn't objected. Wilbur asking how he was after he had fainted and saying he looked like he needed some rest successfully got him out of the room.

"What happens next?" I asked.

"We give it about an hour then send someone to find Kelvin," Daranis said. "The count here will ask him to arrange another gathering for first thing in the morning. Then he will address everyone and disband the cult."

"Will it work?" Tia asked.

"Hopefully," was not a very reassuring reply.

Wilbur sent Daranis out of the room to order refreshments and we discussed exactly what he should say to the crowd in the morning. Between us, we got a speech written, then Daranis was sent away again, this time to seek out Kelvin. Unsurprisingly, he was in his office.

Tia, Tallis and I took hold of Osin when there was a knock on the door and he Cloaked us, making us invisible.

When Wilbur told him what he wanted him to do, he didn't ask why; he just said he would organise it. Messengers were sent out in every direction. A lot of the cult members hadn't returned to their homes after making their journey to witness the sacrifice so they wouldn't be difficult to track down. Once Wilbur had delivered his speech, word would spread and eventually every cult member would hear about it.

"What do I do now?" Wilbur asked once we were alone once more and Osin had made us visible again.

"I suggest you retire to your room. After what you have supposedly been through, nobody is going to question you wanting to get some sleep. The rest of us will head back to the inn."

"I'll stay with you," Daranis said. "That way we can get a message to Tallis if we need to."

"Alright," Wilbur said, then he had a sudden thought. "How do I know which room to go to?"

"Can you play dead?" Daranis asked. Wilbur nodded. "Then pretend to faint. I'll carry you to your room, asking directions from the first person I see. I'll make sure everyone sees me leave, then I'll teleport back in."

"I'll come too," Osin said. "That way I can get to the room in a hurry if Nis calls for help."

Osin Cloaked himself and Daranis picked Wilbur up, who made himself go limp. If I hadn't known better, I would have been convinced that he had fainted.

I assumed that Osin must have opened the door, as I'm pretty sure it couldn't open by itself, then Daranis left the room, carrying Wilbur's limp body.

"Can I have some help here please," he called out loudly.

Tia vanished then Tallis told me to open my mind again. He took me in his arms and transported us back to the inn.

"I don't like this," Tia said as soon as we materialised. "Daranis could still betray us."

"If he was going to, he would have done so by now," Tallis said. "Now stop worrying."

Tia growled at him and paced the room until Osin arrived. I'm sure I saw her eyes light up.

"So far so good," he said. "Nobody questioned Count Gillain's collapse, after what he has allegedly gone through, and Daranis managed to persuade them not to call a healer and that all he needed was some sleep. He left the room then teleported back there. He will be in touch if he needs anything."

"So what do we do now?" I asked.

"Enjoy the rest of the day and hope that tomorrow goes as planned," Tallis said.

"What did you have in mind?" I asked.

"I thought I might take you for a ride in the countryside. We haven't had chance to spend some time alone doing that sort of thing since we became a couple."

"Well I'm exhausted," Tia said. "I'm going to go to bed for a while."

The smirk on Osin face told me she wasn't going to be alone and sleep was not on the agenda.

Disbanded

We didn't hear from Daranis until the next morning, when he informed us that everything was still going according to plan. The 'count' had 'regained consciousness' after a few hours, but decided to rest in his room. Food was delivered and there was enough for two, so Daranis stayed with Wilbur, hiding in the bathroom whenever anyone knocked on the door.

Wilbur asked after Kelvin and was told that he was resting, but could be disturbed if he wanted to see him. Wilbur insisted that the man deserved some peace for a while. He did, however, ask about the arrangements for his speech and was told that everything had been organised.

Once again we donned the cult cloaks that Daranis had obtained for us and snuck out of the inn without the innkeeper seeing us. I didn't like sneaking around, but I didn't want the man to think we were something we weren't.

We returned to the 'Bowl', but this time we weren't going to watch the proceedings from a distance. We left our horses on the same hill we had used last time then walked down to join the rest of the cult members.

There were a lot of them, nearly as many as there had been for the sacrifice. The altar was still in place and I couldn't help shivering when I laid eyes on it. Tallis hugged me tighter to him, but said nothing.

He suddenly stiffened, then relaxed. "Nis and Wilbur are in place," he said quietly.

A few moments later, a hush fell over the crowd and Kelvin appeared behind the altar. He thanked everyone for coming at such short notice, then stepped aside so the man everyone thought was Count Gillain could take centre stage. Daranis stayed off to one side, his hand on his sword, ready to react if he needed to.

Instead of standing behind the altar, Wilbur climbed on top of it, giving everyone a good view of him.

Then he began to speak. His words were loud and clear and I couldn't help wondering if he was using a little bit of magic to project his voice.

He spoke of the strength and joy being the founder of the cult had given him, how he shared the despair and hope he knew filled every member. He went on to talk about how much faith he had put in the scroll he had used for the sacrifice and how devastating it was when it failed.

He then announced that he was disbanding the cult. There were gasps from a number of different directions. He waited for the noise to die down before continuing.

He explained the reasons why he had made the decision. He spoke of how he felt he had let everyone down. They had believed in him, just like he had believed in the scroll, and it had gotten them nowhere.

People cried out, telling him it wasn't his fault and that nobody blamed him. One woman begged him not to step down, saying she needed him.

He smiled down at her and told her that she didn't need him. Through the cult, she had made many friends and companions and that, even though the cult would be no more, they would all still be there for her, as she would for them.

"You don't need a cult anymore," he cried out. "You just need each other. This cult was formed by desperate people who needed help. I have failed to give you the help you wanted, but you do now have the help you need. Talk to each other, rely on each other. It won't fix your problems, but it will make them easier to deal with."

"What are you going to do now?" someone called out. It wasn't a question that had been discussed.

Wilbur, however, handled it well. "Me? I'm going to begin my travels once more. I still believe there is an answer out there and if, no when, I find it, I will be back in contact and the cult will be reformed."

It was a nice touch. It still gave the people hope and effectively shut down anyone else trying to take over. We had been prepared for uproar, for infighting, for aggression, but there was none. Everyone just accepted what Wilbur told them. Nobody seemed to doubt he was Count Gillain. All I can assume is that it was the sort of speech he was likely to have delivered.

Wilbur asked if there were any more questions. There weren't, so he requested that everyone spread the word. He then thanked them all once more and climbed off the altar.

The crowd began to disperse and we made our way up the hill to our horses. By the time we got back to the inn, Daranis and Wilbur were both there. Wilbur still looked like Count Gillain.

"I have some bags packed," Wilbur said, "so it will look like Gillain is leaving again, as he said. Daranis and I will head in different directions before making our way here. At some point, I will remove my disguise so people won't see Gillain here if anyone goes looking for him."

"I'll meet you outside the gates," Osin said. "I don't want you travelling alone. You won't be able to see me, but I will find a way to let you know I'm there."

"We," Tia said. "I'm coming with you."

Osin didn't argue. "Bring your bow then," he said. "Just in case."

They left immediately as it would take them a while to get to Count Gillain's estate.

Wilbur and Daranis stayed with us for a while, then teleported themselves back to Gillain's study.

As there was nothing for Tallis and I to do, and wouldn't be for a while, we went to bed. As we lay there in each other's arms, we talked about the future. Tallis had no idea if he was still employed by my father or how he would react when we eventually returned, but he swore to me that, no matter what, he was going to make me his wife and spend the rest of his life with me. He would have done so a long time before had he not been so worried about the physical side of things.

"Do you think Tephi will object?" he asked.

I shook my head. "You saw how he reacted to seeing us together. He was pleased for us. Other than the fact I was naked and was chained to you."

"Marrying you is different."

"He'll be fine," I assured him. "He was accepting of Etain and Simion. And he likes you. If he causes any trouble you can always threaten to tell Father about Cara."

The look of shock on Tallis's face was hilarious. "I would never do that." He didn't realise I was just teasing him until I burst out laughing.

"Stop worrying about Tephi," I said when I had regained my composure.

"You do realise that you will have to act as my slave whenever we go to Sobek."

I shrugged my shoulders. "It isn't so bad. You kind of get used to being naked after a while. I also like showing everyone that I am yours."

"Well I don't," Tallis said. "Not that way, anyway. I want people to know you are mine because we love each other, not because I own you."

"You'd better get used to it, unless the laws change," I said then kissed him. Soon we were too busy to talk.

By the time Daranis arrived, we were dressed once more. We had to wait a while longer for the rest to join us, then we discussed where to go next.

"I want to have a few words with Akar," Tallis said. Something told me Akar wasn't going to enjoy those words.

"I need to see the queen first, to give her my update in person," Tia told us. Then she looked at me. "I have a feeling your brother may want to join us."

"Us?" Osin asked.

"What? You think I'm not going with you to hunt down the person who caused Rosemerta to be taken? I think the queen will want a representative there."

"Tallis and I count as Sobek representatives."

"Are you trying to find reasons for me to stay behind?" There was a twinkle in her eye that suggested she was teasing him.

Osin grabbed her by the waist and pulled her closer to him. He kissed her on the lips then said, "Of course I want you there.

I never want you to leave my side, but aren't you supposed to be protecting the queen? I don't want to get you into trouble."

"She has plenty of other protectors."

"What happens to me?" Daranis asked. Tia hadn't mentioned having him arrested in a while, but that didn't mean she wasn't still thinking about it.

She released herself from Osin and looked at him. "You will be arrested the moment you set foot in Sobek. If you plan on joining us in Amanet, I suggest you teleport to somewhere in the kingdom where we can meet you."

"I may be needed at the border into Sobek, in case the same guards are on duty and recognise you or Adara."

"Good point. Cross the border with us, then leave. I won't tell the queen you entered her kingdom."

"Fair enough," he said. "When do we leave?"

"It's a long journey. We should probably head off as soon as we can," Tallis said. Then he held his hand out to Wilbur. "Thank you for everything."

Wilbur shook his head. "You're not getting rid of me that easily. You might need me to pretend to be Count Gillain if you want Akar to confess."

"We will have to get you a horse from somewhere then."

Wilbur looked at him as though he was insane. "If you think I am riding all the way back to Sobek, you're mad. You can pick me up from my house as you go past it."

"We don't go past it," Tallis pointed out. "The only reason we went there was because Claudette told us to."

"Then make a detour," Wilbur said then vanished.

"I guess we're going to his place once we cross the border," Osin said sarcastically.

We packed our bags, making sure we had our cult cloaks with us; you never knew when they might come in handy. Then we paid the innkeeper for our stay, thanked him for his hospitality and headed out. It was going to take us just as long to travel to the border as it had taken us to get to the location of the ceremony, but at least this time I could enjoy the ride. This time I wasn't worried about whether we would arrive in time or how we would rescue my sister. And I didn't have to suffer archery lessons whenever we took a break.

Thinking about them made me think of the man I had killed. It's something that still haunts me. Would I have killed him if I had been a better shot? Or a worse one? They were questions I would never be able to answer, but I couldn't stop myself asking them.

"Have you ever killed anyone," I asked the group when we stopped for lunch.

"Once," Tia said. "An assassin managed to get into the palace. I didn't enjoy doing it, but it had to be done. I don't let it bother me and I won't let it stop me doing it again, if the need arises."

"I've killed a few men in battle," Daranis said. "It's what I'm trained to do."

Osin nodded his head. "I killed someone in training once. It was an accident. He hadn't put his helmet on properly. That I still struggle to cope with, but that's the only one. When you're a Warrior, you are trained to kill."

That just left Tallis. I expected him to say he hadn't, but he didn't. "I haven't actually killed someone with my bare hands, but I am responsible for someone dying."

The confession seemed to take Osin and Daranis by surprise as well. This was obviously something he hadn't talked about before.

"I was nearing the end of my training when a man was brought to the academy, accused of raping a young boy. He denied everything so my assistance was sought. I used my talents on him, but instead of telling the truth, he managed to get a knife off one of his guards and slit his own throat."

Silence filled the clearing. None of us knew what to say.

"I did my job," Tallis continued. "The man chose to end his own life. You could argue that, technically, I made him, but he could have just told the truth. He was lying about hurting the boy. I knew that the moment I saw him. It happened once and, had he lived, it could have happened again. I don't think about it. My actions stopped other innocent young children being hurt."

Then he turned to me. "Just like yours may well have stopped another woman being sacrificed."

I didn't say anything. What he said made sense. Would we have been captured if I hadn't fired my arrow? I had no way of knowing. I vowed to stop thinking about it. It was a vow I would break many times, but it did get easier over the years.

Before we got to the border, Tallis once more joined his brother on his horse and Osin Cloaked them both. One of the guards on the Sobek side had been there when we had crossed into Draygar and remembered Daranis.

"You didn't manage to leave them behind I see," he said, grinning at Daranis.

He sighed theatrically. "Unfortunately not. I'm sure I must have done something wrong in a past life and this is my punishment."

The guard chuckled as he waved us through, without bothering to search us.

As soon as we were out of sight, Osin and Tallis rematerialized and Tallis removed his glasses. "Thank the queen I don't have to wear those anymore."

"There's something I have to wear though," I reminded him. He did not look happy as he retrieved the shackles from his bag while I undressed.

"I really hate doing this," he said as he put the collar on me and attached the chain to his wrist.

"I know," I said. "But it's a good excuse to ride together."

"Who needs an excuse?" he said as he helped me mount up. He climbed up behind me and I settled down in his arms. I felt warm and protected as he held me tight.

Daranis then left us, having arranged where in Amanet we would meet him. We promised to take his horse and all his things to him. He teleported back to his home so he could spend time with his wife and son while waiting for Tallis to contact him, to let him know that we had left the palace and were on our way to Amanet.

We took the necessary detour to collect Wilbur and it was good to see him looking like himself again. Tallis asked if he could somehow make me look like I was naked and shackled so I didn't actually have to be, but Wilbur shook his head. He could change his own appearance and had found a way to hide magic users bands, but that was all. There was nothing he could do in regard to what Tallis wanted. While we were in Sobek, I would have to remain his slave.

Return

"What in the king's name is she doing naked again?" Tephi yelled as soon as he saw me. Tallis had forgotten to put his cloak around me before entering the throne room. As soon as we got to the capital, we had headed straight to the palace and had been warned that my brother was still visiting with the queen, but it had slipped our minds to cover me up.

"Sorry," Tallis said and hastily removed his cloak and handed it to me. "I hate this just as much as you do, you know."

"If you want to do something about it," I said sweetly to my brother, "you will have to speak to the queen about changing the law."

Tephi grunted. "Or I could just take you home."

Tallis stepped in front of me. "We've already been through this. Don't make me do something we will both regret."

Tephi waved away his concern that he was going to cause trouble. "I have no intention of coming between you two. I happen to think you're good for her, though I'm sure you could do better for yourself." He winked at me when he said that last bit. I glared at him.

"We won't be here for much longer anyway," Osin said. "We are only here to give her Majesty an update."

"I will speak to Tia alone," Queen Ariana said. "The rest of you may retire to one of the reception rooms." I noticed that Osin and Tia were keeping far away from each other.

Without saying anything more, she stood up and we all bowed to her, even Tephi. As she left the room, with Tia by her side, I noticed that Osin's eyes never left them.

"Come with me," Tephi said and strode out of the room without bothering to check that we were following him.

"You've made yourself at home I see," I commented dryly as soon as I caught up with him.

"Well I have been here a few weeks and the queen has been very accommodating. I have been in constant contact with Etain so I know that I'm not needed back home yet."

"Why Etain not Father?" I asked.

Tephi grinned at me. "Father still thinks I'm looking for you."

"So you didn't tell him the truth then."

"I decided it wouldn't be a good idea. I'm not sure his heart would cope with being told Rose was to be sacrificed. I have no idea how to tell him that it couldn't be stopped."

There was something I had to tell Tephi and I knew he wasn't going to like it.

"He already knows," I said quietly.

Tephi stopped outside a set of doors, opened them and walked in. Inside was a number of sofas and chairs. Platters of fruit and cakes were on the table along with glasses and jugs of wine, water and ale.

"Help yourself to refreshments," he said. "Then you can tell me what went wrong." I had no idea how we were going to explain why we couldn't save Rose, but I did know that none of us were going to mention Daranis's part in it.

While the others went over to the table, Tephi took hold of my arm and pulled me into a corner.

"What do you mean Father already knows?" he asked me.

I really didn't want to speak, but I knew I had to. My words were going to hurt Tephi deeply.

"We interrogated Count Gillain. Rose wasn't kidnapped. Father gave the count permission to take her. He even gave her the drug Gillain provided to keep her unconscious until he was well away from the palace."

"Father would never have allowed that if he knew what Gillain had planned."

"He knew, Tephi."

Tephi looked at me in disbelief. "Count Gillain had to be lying."

"Tallis said he wasn't."

Tephi strode over to Tallis. "Is a Sentinel ever wrong?" I could hear the desperation in Tephi's voice. He longed for Tallis to say yes, but deep down he knew he wouldn't.

"I'm sorry, but no. Count Gillain was telling the truth." He hadn't been able to overhear our conversation so must have guessed why Tephi was asking.

Tephi collapsed into the nearest chair. "How could he?"

"He was protecting his country," Tallis said. "The count promised to keep the cult out of Amanet if he could have Rosemerta."

"That's no excuse. Father sacrificed his own daughter. He might as well have used the knife on her himself."

"Calm down," I said as I moved behind him so I could rub his shoulders. "Now isn't the time for this."

"I know. But as soon as I get home, Father and I are going to be having a few words."

"There's somewhere else we have to go first," Tallis said.

Between us, Tallis, Osin and I told Tephi about Akar and how he was involved in Rose's death.

"Why Rose?" Tephi asked when we had finished.

"We have no idea," Osin said. "It's one of the questions we are planning on asking him."

"I'm coming with you."

Tallis grinned at him. "I thought you would say that. It's one of the reasons we came here first."

"When do we leave?"

"As soon as Tia is finished with the queen."

"I'll go and pack," Tephi said and left the room. He had obviously forgotten about wanting to know why we failed to rescue Rose.

Almost as soon as Tephi left, the door opened once more and Tia entered. "Did the queen give you permission to hunt down Akar with us?" Osin asked.

"She did. I'm going to bathe, change clothes and repack my bags." She looked Osin up and down. "I suggest you do the same."

I expected a witty retort, but instead he just nodded his head.

Wilbur remained at the palace while the rest of us headed to Tallis's parents' house. We gave them a quick update on all that had happened and they couldn't help noticing that Tallis and I were holding hands.

"Things are going well between you two I take it," Balor said.

"Better than expected," Tallis said. The look he gave me made me blush.

"I see," Macha said. She had a knowing smile on her face.

We washed ourselves and as quickly as they could, the men put on clean clothes before we repacked our bags. I didn't have many spare clothes with me so Macha took my already worn ones to a friend of hers who was a magic user who could clean clothes quickly. By the time I was bathed, she returned with all of my clothes clean and wearable.

Tallis and Osin both always left a few changes of clothes at their parents' house so packing new clothes posed no problem for them.

We returned to the palace and found Tia and Tephi both impatiently awaiting our arrival. Wilbur was lounging on a sofa as if he hadn't a care in the world.

"Can we take a detour on the way?" Tia asked.

"Where to?" Osin asked suspiciously. He had heard the tone in her voice as well as I had.

"I was wondering if we could visit your granny again."

"Why?" He was now on edge as well as suspicious.

"So we can pick up Mata."

"Why?" Osin asked again.

"I want to feed Akar to him once he has finished confessing his crimes."

Osin grinned at her comment while Tallis indignantly said, "Mata does not eat humans."

"I think she's joking," I told him. I hoped she was joking.

"Who's Mata?" Tephi asked.

"Tallis's pet lizard," I told him. "He's big enough to swallow your arm whole."

"I don't want to hear any more."

"He is not coming with us," Tallis said to Tia, who just shrugged her shoulders.

"It was just a suggestion."

"She wouldn't really have done it, would she?" I whispered to Osin.

"I have no idea," he said. He never took his eyes off Tia as he spoke.

"Are we ready?" Tephi asked. We all nodded. "Then let's go."

"I think your brother is in love," I said to Tallis when he took my hand and led me from the room.

"I doubt it," Tallis said. "But stranger things have happened."

Fresh horses were waiting for all of us except for Osin when we got to the stables; Osin insisted on taking his own horse again. They had been packed with provisions to last us a couple of days. We also took Daranis's horse with us.

It was going to be a long and boring journey and I was getting fed up with travelling. I made Tallis promise me that we would settle down somewhere together as soon as Akar had been dealt with.

Tephi overheard the comment. "It had better be in Amanet," he said. "I will not let Adara live in Sobek if she has to be a slave."

"We will live wherever she wants to," Tallis said.

The days passed surprisingly quickly and we crossed the border into Amanet without any problems. Tallis immediately removed my shackles and I got dressed. Tephi rolled his eyes when I put on trousers instead of a skirt.

We met Daranis not long after and he was grateful to have his horse back.

During the long trek north, Tephi got around to asking about what had happened in Draygar. Tia remained quiet, allowing the rest of us to say whatever lies and half-truths we wanted. We mainly stuck to the truth and he seemed to believe what he was told. Telling him about Daranis wouldn't have done anything other than cause problems for Daranis.

Tephi was intrigued with Wilbur and his ability to make himself look like anyone or anything, almost, that he wanted to.

He turned into Count Gillain once more and Tephi was stunned by how believable he was.

He wasn't disappointed with what happened to the real count. He would have liked him to have stood trial for his crime, but didn't complain that he was dead.

Via messenger birds, Tephi kept in contact with Etain. He told our brother everything, including where he was going and why, but Etain passed nothing on to our father. As far as the king was aware, Tephi was still looking for me. He didn't even know that Rose was dead. That news was something Tephi wanted to give to him in person.

Our journey was delayed for a few days due to the weather. It rained so hard we were more or less trapped in an inn until it had cleared up. Other than that, the weather was fine and the temperature pleasant.

We eventually reached our destination and took rooms at an inn. If anyone recognised Tephi, they kept quiet about it. He didn't visit the northern provinces often so, while it was likely that nobles would know who he was, the general populace wouldn't. Besides, they would never believe that a prince would be staying at an inn.

I wasn't worried about being recognised as I had never gone north. I had hardly ever left the capital until I ran away with Tallis.

Tallis didn't bother to hide what he was. There was no need for him to wear his dark glasses in Amanet and anyone who knew anything about magic users knew what his eye colour meant. Nobody who saw him mentioned it and they didn't seem to be avoiding him. Maybe they didn't know about Sentinels. Or maybe they were just happy minding their own business.

A few discrete questions to the right people informed us that Akar was still living on his father's estate, though not in the main house, so we arranged for a letter to be sent there, requesting he visit Count Gillain at the inn the following afternoon.

"Will he really come, do you think?" I asked once the messenger had been dispatched.

"I hope so," Tephi said. "I don't really want to have to confront him on his father's estate. The poor man has suffered enough because of his son's actions already. I will if I have to though."

We stayed up late, drinking ale, but not enough to make anyone suffer the next morning. In front of everyone, Tephi asked Tallis about his plans for the future, in regard to me. I kicked him under the table. Tallis, like the true gentleman it took me so long to realise he was, answered the question completely and honestly. Marriage was on the cards, with or without my father's agreement, and he hoped we would have children one day.

"Children? So you two have…" He pointed his finger at me, then moved it toward Tallis, before moving it back and forth a few times. It was obvious what he meant and I wondered if Tallis was going to make him say the words.

He didn't.

"Yes, we have had sex."

"Wasn't that taking a huge risk?" He sounded worried rather than angry.

"Speak to your sister about that, not me," Tallis said.

I didn't feel comfortable talking to my brother about my sex life, but I did so anyway.

"Yes, it was a risk, but it was a risk that was worth taking, at my insistence not Tallis's. He was reluctant, for obvious reasons. I had just watched my sister's murder. I needed him. I needed more than just to be in his arms."

Tephi said he understood, gave his blessing, then changed the subject.

Nobody seemed to be looking forward to the next day. Count Gillain may have killed Rose, but Akar was the man who was responsible for her death. I began to wonder whether Akar would turn up and, if he did, whether he would leave the inn alive.

Akar

There was a knock on the door and everyone tensed. We were in a meeting room at the inn that the innkeeper let us borrow for a while. Wilbur had given his name as Count Gillain to the innkeeper and had let him know that he was expecting a visitor.

Wilbur was disguised as the count once more and Tia and Daranis were with him, both wearing cult cloaks. Tallis, Tephi and I were standing in a corner of the room, holding onto Osin, who had us all Cloaked. We wanted Akar to admit to his crime before he found out who he was really confessing to.

"Count Gillain," Akar said as he entered the room. "This is an unexpected and pleasant surprise. I was not expecting to see you again so soon."

The sound of his voice made my skin crawl. My mind went back to when he denied attacking Olwen before Tallis made him confess. My eyes wandered down to his crotch and I couldn't help wondering how he was coping without his penis.

"Akar Penbroke," Wilbur said in acknowledgement. "My request to see you may have been unexpected, but I can assure you it will be far from pleasant."

"And who are your companions?" he asked, taking a seat at the table without it being offered. He gave the impression that he believed he was in control of the conversation. That would soon change.

"Loyal followers," Wilbur said. "They are here to find out why you gave us this worthless piece of parchment." He threw the scroll Count Gillain had used when he sacrificed Rose onto the table. "I followed it word for word and nothing happened."

Tallis had to grab hold of me when I saw Akar's eyes light up. "Rosemerta is dead then." His face was full of glee.

"Yes, unfortunately she is. And it got us absolutely nothing. I want an explanation."

Akar rubbed his hands together in delight. "Does her sister know yet? Olwen?"

"I have no idea and I don't care. Now are you going to answer my questions or are my companions going to have to persuade you?" I could see Tia playing with her knife in a threatening manner.

Akar leaned back in his chair and put his booted feet up on the table. "Ask away," he said casually. "I will answer all of your questions. I have nothing to hide."

"Where did you really get this scroll?" Wilbur picked it up and held it out to Akar, who refused to take it.

"I paid a magic user to create it for me. She made it look old and authentic. She did a good job by the look of things. It fooled you and I'm sure you showed it to others."

Wilbur faked looking confused. "But why? And why give it to me?"

Akar took his feet off the table and leaned in closer to Wilbur. "Because I knew you would do whatever it said you had to."

"So I've killed someone just because you wanted her dead? Why did you want her dead? Why her? Why didn't you do it yourself? Why did you use me?"

Akar leaned back again. "Tut tut count. One question at a time. Let's start with the last one shall we and work our way backward."

He sounded so smug it made me sick. He had gotten what he wanted and was arrogant enough to think he would get away with it. Tallis had to hold me tight to stop me from going for his throat. Osin had a tight hold on Tephi.

"Not yet," I heard him whisper in his ear.

Akar's voice droned on. "I used you because I could. You were so easy to manipulate it was laughable. And why should I do it myself? This way you get punished, not me. Nobody will be able to tie any of this back to me. Even if you told someone, they wouldn't believe you."

He then looked at Daranis and Tia. "Nor your witnesses. I have witnesses that will swear on their mother's graves that I am with them right now instead of meeting with you." He laughed.

It sounded a little maniacal. I glanced at Tia, who looked like she wanted to put her knife in his throat.

"Now I think you had three more questions. Did you kill someone just because I wanted her dead? Yes."

He sounded so cold and callus. I'll never understand how anyone could talk about murder with so little feeling. I had killed someone, but I hadn't meant to. I felt terrible about it, but right then I believe I could easily have killed again without a second thought. Akar didn't deserve to live. How Wilbur didn't react, I have no idea.

"Now to question number two," Akar continued. "Why did I want her dead? Because I wanted Olwen to suffer and killing her sister would achieve that." Emotion crept into his voice at last. He was almost shouting and spittle was flying from his mouth as he spoke.

"It didn't matter which one. I chose Rosemerta because she was the most distinct, the most recognisable by her description. I could easily have chosen Adara instead, but too many other women have her hair and eye colouring. By my description, I made sure that Rosemerta was the only one that would meet your needs."

By this point he was ranting. He stood up and leaned on the table. "That little bitch Olwen should have willingly given me what I wanted, what I deserved, but instead she ran to her family saying I attacked her and they had the audacity to use a Sentinel against me. Me! How dare they? That bastard not only forced me to confess, he mutilated me."

"Well I won't have to force you to confess this time," Tallis said as he stepped away from his brother, revealing his presence.

Akar jumped in surprise. As soon as his eyes fell on Tallis, all of the blood drained from his face and his legs gave way.

"No, no, no, no, no," he stammered. "You can't be here."

"Well it appears that I am. And I'm not alone. Osin."

As soon as Tallis said his name, Osin dropped his Cloak, revealing himself as well as me and Tephi.

"I haven't done anything wrong," Akar blurted out. "Whatever these people say, they're lying."

Tephi shook his head at him. "I've been here the whole time Akar. I heard everything. I heard you confessing to arranging my sister's murder. In this kingdom, that carries the same punishment as if you had performed the act yourself."

"He's the guilty party," Akar said, pointing at Wilbur. I could hear the panic in his voice. "He's the one you should be interrogating."

"Actually, I'm not who you think I am," Wilbur said. "Watch."

Akar went from white to green as he watched Count Gillain shimmer and be replaced by Wilbur. Akar began to whimper.

"Let me introduce you to everyone," Tephi said. He sounded like he was almost having fun. "Wilbur here is a Mirage. Count Gillain killed himself so Wilbur volunteered to help us out. Osin and Daranis are both Warriors, as is Tia, who is also the Queen of Sobek's personal envoy on this mission."

Tephi stepped closer to the trembling man. "You'll never prove anything," Akar said. He was surprisingly defiant, given his obvious terror.

"I don't need to prove anything. You have confessed to your crimes in front of two members of the royal family of Amanet as well as someone whose word Queen Ariana trusts more than yours. Not to mention there were also four magic users in the room who heard everything."

"There still has to be a trial," Akar insisted. Tears were flowing down his face.

"Oh I intend to make you stand trial. Which is why we are going to escort you to your father. He will be the one to convict you, not us."

Akar's mouth opened and closed, but no sounds came out.

Tephi nodded at Daranis and Osin. They took hold of one arm each and dragged Akar to his feet. His legs seemed unable to support him so they had to more or less carry him from the room. They took him out of the inn and slung him over the back of his horse, tying him in place with rope. This was more to stop him falling off than making sure he didn't get away.

We rode to Lord Penbroke's estate. The guards almost didn't believe Tephi when he announced who he was. Luckily for them, they didn't stop him entering.

Word passed quickly and Lord Penbroke was at his front door, ready to welcome his visitors, by the time we had ridden down his driveway.

"To what do I owe this pleasure, your Highness?" he said. "I wasn't expecting a visit." Then he saw his son tied across the back of a horse. "What is going on here?" he demanded.

"A trial, Penbroke," Tephi said. "Your son arranged for my sister to be murdered and, as the highest ranking member of the aristocracy in this province, it is down to you to arrange it."

Penbroke looked perplexed. "Your sister has been murdered?" he asked in disbelief. "And you believe my son did it?"

"We all heard him confess," Tephi said, looking around him at us all. "Without Tallis's help, I hasten to add."

"Release him at once," the lord ordered. "I will get to the bottom of this."

Tephi nodded at Osin, who untied the ropes which were holding Akar in place. I was quite disappointed when he didn't fall to the ground.

Lord Penbroke walked up to his son and embraced him. "Tell me you didn't do it son, tell me this is all a misunderstanding."

Akar tried to smile at his father when he released him, but couldn't manage it. "I didn't kill anyone," he said. "I may have given someone the incentive to do it, but that's all. I'm no murderer."

"What do you mean by incentive?" Akar refused to answer so Lord Penbroke turned to Tephi. "What exactly are you accusing him of, your Highness?"

Tephi told him everything that Akar had said, stating it was more like gloating than confessing. Penbroke's face became grimmer and grimmer.

"And you expect me to put my own son on trial?" he asked in disbelief when Tephi had finished. Tephi nodded. "What about this Count Gillain person?"

"Dead I'm afraid."

"So you want to punish my son because you can't get your revenge on the real killer."

"No," Tallis said. "Your son is a criminal. Arranging a murder is still a crime."

Lord Penbroke rubbed his hand down his face then nodded his head. He then walked back over to his son, drew a dagger from his belt and thrust it into Akar's heart.

Declaration

We left Lord Penbroke alone with his grief. Justice had been done and nobody wished the man to suffer more than he already was. It was a quiet procession who made their way back to the inn. Nobody was in the mood for eating, but we forced ourselves to anyway.

After we had finished our meal, Tia contacted Queen Ariana to give her an update.

"I've been ordered to go back to Sobek immediately," Tia said when she rejoined us, her packed bag slung over one shoulder.

"We'll leave in the morning," Osin said.

Tia shook her head. "No, I mean immediately. I have to teleport back at once."

"No," he cried out. "You can't. Not yet."

Tia walked up to him and placed her palm on his cheek. "I have to."

He covered her hand with his own. "Then I'm coming with you."

"You can't."

He took hold of her hand and kissed the back of it. "Just one more night. Please."

She closed her eyes. When she opened them, they were filled with tears. "I can't. I'm sorry."

"You were told to leave immediately," a voice sounded from behind us. We whirled around to see a stern looking man standing there, his arms crossed and a scowl on his face. His black eyes identified him as a Sentinel. General Intep was with him, looking just as unhappy.

The Sentinel grabbed hold of Tia's arm. "Either you come with me now or I will make you."

"Take your hands off her," Osin said and stepped menacingly forward.

Tallis grabbed him. "Don't," he warned.

"You should listen to your brother," the general said. "Tia has to return to her duties guarding the queen and as for you, as soon as you are back in Sobek, come and see me. I have an assignment for you."

Osin scowled at him. I wondered for a moment if he was going to hit him. I think a number of us breathed a sigh of relief when he backed down.

"A wise decision," the general said. He then turned to the Sentinel and Tia and nodded his head. Both vanished. "Make sure you bring Tia's horse back," Intep said before he, too, disappeared.

"No," Osin roared and slammed his fist down on the table.

"What just happened?" Tephi asked.

"Tia has been recalled to the palace," Tallis said. "The Sentinel was here to make sure she complied. If she didn't, he would force his way into her mind and teleport her there with him."

"How did he know where we were?" I asked.

It was Wilbur who answered. "The amulet she wears is a tracking device. They teleported here the same way I managed to teleport to you when you were in Draygar."

"So what do we do now?" I asked.

"Head back to Sobek and go and see the queen I guess." Tallis looked at Tephi. "Are you coming with us or will you head home?"

"I'll go home."

"As will I," Wilbur said, "now that my services are no longer needed."

"We should all leave first thing in the morning."

"Well I'm not waiting that long," Osin said and vanished.

"Shit," Tallis exclaimed. "I'd better go after him before he does something he'll regret."

Daranis grabbed his arm to get his attention. "I'm coming with you."

"You can't. You know you'll get arrested the moment you set foot in Sobek."

"I know, but I can worry about that later. Right now, Osin is more important. Where will he have gone?"

"Thank you. My guess is he's gone straight to the palace, probably the throne room. The room itself is Shielded, but you can teleport to just outside it. It's the only place inside the palace that you can. They have never Shielded that area so people can get there quickly if they need to. The royal family are never in danger of attack as it's the most heavily guarded part of the building."

Daranis nodded his head then vanished.

Tallis turned to me. "Open your mind," he said.

I did as he requested and I felt him entering my head as he put his arms around me. The next thing I knew I was standing outside Queen Ariana's throne room.

Osin was there, shouting to be let in. Daranis was doing his best to hold him back while the guards in front of the doors were struggling not to laugh.

Tallis let go of me and helped Daranis pull Osin away from the door.

"Calm down," he said. "This is not going to help."

"I want to see Tia," he yelled out. "I demand to see her right now."

"You are in no position to demand anything," a voice said. It was coming down a corridor on the right. We turned toward it and saw General Intep striding over to us.

"I just want to see her," Osin said.

"You will see her when and if the queen allows it." He then turned his attention to me and bowed. "Your Highness, your presence has been requested in the throne room."

"What?" I stupidly asked.

"Please come with me."

I looked at Tallis, who nodded his head. I then followed the general down the corridor, which led to a side entrance to the throne room. This was just as heavily guarded. The men stepped aside as soon as General Intep approached.

I have no idea why but I was nervous when I went into the room. The queen was inside, as was Tia. I could clearly hear Osin shouting to be allowed to see her. There was no concern on her face. Like the guards, she appeared to be trying not to laugh.

"He can be quiet entertaining, can't he," she said.

I quickly bowed to the queen. "Your Majesty. Please will you allow Osin to see Tia. I think he's in love with her."

"Very well," Queen Ariana said. "I will allow it." She turned to the general. "Please escort my visitors into the throne room, but make sure Osin is kept under guard."

"At once, your Majesty." The general was grinning. I felt like something was going on that I wasn't part of, like someone had told a joke but hadn't explained it to me. He left the room using the same door we had entered by.

A short while later, the main doors opened and Tallis, Daranis and Osin walked in, followed by Intep. Both Daranis and Tallis bowed; Osin didn't.

"Forgive my brother for not bowing to you, your Majesty," Tallis said, "but he is unable to do so. I have him Shielded."

Tia burst out laughing. It was hard to tell under the veil, but I'm sure the queen smiled too.

"What do you want with my bodyguard?' the queen asked Osin.

"I just want to be with her, to tell her how I feel."

"I cannot allow you to be together. She is my bodyguard and as such she can't be anyone's slave. And you know the law. One has to be the owner and the other the slave."

"Then I will be the slave," Osin said.

"What!" Tia exclaimed.

"Are you saying," the queen said, "that you are willing to give up your freedom for this woman, to forego wearing clothes, to wear shackles and let everyone know that she owns you?"

Osin didn't hesitate in replying. "Yes."

"But she's just a bodyguard, nobody important. She doesn't outrank you."

"She's not 'just' anything," he said. "That is one word you can never use when talking about her. And don't ever tell me she isn't important."

The queen and Tia looked at each other. Tia smiled shyly.

"You are a member of my army," General Intep said. "As such, you cannot be anyone's slave."

"Then I resign."

Tallis placed his hand on his brother's shoulder. "Have you really thought about this?" he asked. "Do you really understand what you are saying?"

"Yes. I have thought about nothing else since we crossed the border back into Sobek."

"I'll support you whatever you decide to do, you know that. Is this what you really want?"

"Yes." I have never heard a single word contain so much emotion.

"What make you so sure she wants you as her slave?" the queen asked.

Osin smiled. "I just know." Tia blushed once more.

Ariana then surveyed the room. "Leave us," she commanded. The guards who had accompanied the three men instantly obeyed her. She then turned her attention to Daranis, who swallowed, but didn't look away.

"I am pretty sure that you were told if ever you set foot in Sobek again you would be arrested."

Daranis said nothing.

"However," the queen continued, "given your more recent actions, I am prepared to delay the order. Leave now and I will pretend you were never here."

"Thank you, your Majesty," he said, bowed low, then left the room.

"I think you have some things to talk about," the queen said. "I will leave you alone."

We just watched as she left the room via the side door. None of us were sure what was going on.

"Tallis," Osin said, to get his attention. When Tallis looked at him, Osin just raised his eyebrows.

"Sorry," Tallis said and removed his Shield.

Osin ran over to Tia, took her in his arms and kissed her deeply.

"Will you have me as your slave?" he asked when he let her go. "I promise I will obey your every command."

She pulled away from him, suddenly looking uncertain. Osin looked at her in concern. "You do want me, don't you?"

"Yes, but—" she started to say, but Osin interrupted her.

"But nothing. That's all I needed to hear."

Tia put her fingers over his lips. "But," she said in a serious tone, "there is something you need to know, something I need to tell you."

"If you are going to say you need permission from Queen Ariana, I already thought of that. The fact she left us alone to talk indicates that she will agree," Osin said.

Tia shook her head. "No, I don't need permission from the Queen of Sobek. I am the Queen of Sobek."

Tia

"What?" I exclaimed. I couldn't believe what I had just heard. Tallis and Osin both stared at Tia as though they were frozen in place. I'm not sure they even breathed.

"She's telling the truth," General Intep said.

Osin opened and closed his mouth like a fish. He appeared to be in shock. Then his face changed. Fury filled it.

"You complete and utter bitch," he hissed at Tia. "You think it's funny playing with someone's emotions? Is it entertaining to you to lead someone on? You had plenty of chances to turn me down, to tell me we couldn't be together, yet you didn't. You knew I was falling for you and you did nothing to stop me. I was prepared to be your slave, but I won't be your toy, something you can play with whenever you see fit and discard the rest of the time. You make me sick."

He turned his back on her and strode toward the door.

"Osin wait," Tia cried out.

Osin ignored her. As soon as he got to the door, he pushed on it, but it refused to budge. He swung around and glared at Tallis. "Tallis," he snarled. "Unshield this door, now."

Tallis remained calm. "No. I am not going to let you walk away from the best thing that has ever happened to you just because your pride has been dented."

"My pride! You think this is about my pride?"

Tallis shrugged his shoulders. "What else could it be about? She didn't tell you the truth about her and you don't like being lied to."

"This has got nothing to do with what she has or hasn't done. This is about what she can and can't do. I'm just a commoner. We both know she could never be with someone like me, even if she wanted to. All I can be to her is someone to have a little fun with occasionally."

"If?" Tia said. There was steel in her voice. "Did you just say 'if?'"

Osin was wise enough not to reply.

"I rule this country and I can damn well be involved with whoever I want to. I don't have a father who wants to marry me off for political gain. I am in charge. Now are you going to come here and kiss me or do I have to have you thrown in the dungeon until you come to your senses?"

I almost suggested throwing him in the dungeon anyway, just for fun, but stopped myself just in time.

Osin looked like he had no idea what was happening. "You…you…you…" He took a deep breath and tried again. "You really want to be in a relationship with me? But I'm a nobody."

"Of course I do you idiot." She walked up to him and placed her arms around his neck.

"I don't understand," I said, turning my attention to General Intep so I didn't have to see them kissing. "How can Tia be the queen?"

Tia heard the question and pulled away from Osin. "Let's find somewhere more comfortable to talk," she said and took hold of Osin's hand. He grinned like a schoolboy who had just had his first kiss.

She led us to a curtain behind the throne and pulled it back, revealing a door. Behind the door was the queen's private sitting room.

"I come here whenever I want some time alone," she said and pushed Osin down onto one of the sofas. He dragged her down after him and placed his arm around her as soon as she was seated.

Tallis and I took the sofa opposite. Despite there being available chairs, General Intep opted to remain standing.

"What you are about to hear," he said, "is only known to a handful of people. You can tell nobody. Not even Daranis. Or Tephi."

"You have our word," Tallis said.

"The woman you all thought was the queen is actually Jade, her decoy. They are blood bonded so can talk telepathically. However, their bond goes deeper than normal, so they can silently communicate whenever they want, without revealing that they are doing so. Whenever Jade is acting as the queen, she always has her bodyguard close by. Tia tells her everything she wants her to say."

"Why?" I asked.

"It's a good way to keep her safe," Intep said. "Nobody suspects that Tia is anything more than just another well trained Warrior. She doesn't use Jade often, usually just when she wants to be able to socialise with her visitors without them suspecting who she really is. Or when she wants to go off on an adventure," he added, frowning at her. She looked away, blushing once more. The additional colour in her cheeks suited her and I had a feeling Osin would make sure it happened often.

"You allowed the Queen of Sobek to travel with us into Draygar!" Tallis said incredulously. "How could you do that? You knew it was going to be a dangerous mission. She could have been killed."

"It was the queen's decision. I couldn't have stopped her. We did argue about it but, as usual, she won." He then turned to Osin. "In some respects I feel sorry for you."

"General!" Tia exclaimed. He winked at her. He was obviously more to her than just the commander of her army; they were good friends as well.

"Why do you call yourself Tia? Tallis asked.

"It's a nickname my father used to call me when we were alone. My name is Ariana Druantia, Tia for short."

I was still confused. "How does this work. Surely all of the servants know who sleeps in the queen's suite."

"Tia and Jade each have their own bedroom in the suite. They are very good friends and get on well so sharing the suite isn't a problem. The few servants that are allowed in there know what Jade looks like, but all think she is the queen. She is always veiled whenever she leaves the room. The two women are roughly the same size so nobody suspects it is usually Tia under the veil."

"Does that mean that Jade has to remain in the suite whenever Tia is being the queen?" I asked.

"No, she's a magic user. She can teleport so nobody sees her leaving."

"Oh." It was an obvious answer and I was a little embarrassed that I had asked the question. "So what happens now?"

"Good question," General Intep said. He turned to Osin. "As I said earlier, I have a mission for you."

"I resigned from the army."

"And I don't accept your resignation. But I think you are going to like your assignment. From now on, you are personally responsible for the queen's safety, though I may, occasionally, need to borrow you from her side and I want you to help with the training of new Warriors. With her Majesty's permission, of course."

"Of course," she responded, but her tone suggested the general would use Osin with or without her permission. After all, he was, technically, still employed by the army.

"What if she wants to do something I deem too dangerous, like going into Draygar again?" Osin asked. "Can I order her not to?"

"No, you will have to persuade her. Use your charm. I've heard you're good at that."

"Where will I sleep?"

"In my suite, in my bed," Tia said. "Unless you annoy me, in which case I will kick you out until you apologise." Sorry for keep referring to her as Tia instead of Queen Ariana, but that's the way I still see her. Besides, General Intep kept calling her Tia so I just took it for granted that the rest of us could as well.

"How will that work?" Osin asked.

"You will be given your own bedroom," Intep told him. "Not that I expect it will be used very often. Tia's personal maids will know the true sleeping arrangements, but nobody else. You will also be given your own private sitting room to do with whatever you wish."

"You're going to have to be very careful what you call me," Tia said. "Whenever I am wearing my veil, you have to call me Majesty or Ariana. Never Tia."

"I can manage that."

She then addressed me and Tallis. "That goes for you as well."

"No problem," I said and Tallis nodded his head.

"I'll arrange for someone to collect my things from my house," Osin said. "Then I'll sell it. It's not as if I'll need it anymore."

"What happens if she kicks you out?" Tallis asked. He was only teasing and Osin took it well.

"I guess I will have to come and stay with you."

"One more thing you need to know," General Intep said. "As you will be her bodyguard, you won't need to be her slave."

"That's a relief," Tallis said. "His naked body is not a pretty sight."

"You're wrong there," Tia said, then realised that she had spoken out loud and blushed once more.

A thought suddenly occurred to Osin. "Are you and Adara going to be teleporting back to Tephi?" he asked his brother.

"We'll have to soon. He'll want to know what is going on. Why?"

"Can you bring my horse back here for me? And my things. I don't want to have to do all of that travelling if I can avoid it."

"That means a large detour for us. I was planning on heading straight to see Adara's father."

"I could always ask Tia to make it a royal command." He looked at Tia who nodded her head. She was happy to comply with his request.

"Are you going to do that whenever you don't get what you want from me?" Tallis asked.

"I think that is more or less guaranteed." He grinned at his brother.

"Good job I know that Tia is more sensible than to agree with everything you ask for." He turned to me. "We really should get back to your brother. He's probably calling us some very unpleasant names right now."

With Tia's permission, we retreated to the area outside the throne room so we could teleport. Tallis put his arms around me and I felt his mind pressing against mine. I let him in and the next thing I knew I was back in the inn we left Tephi at. There was no sign of him, so Tallis and I headed down to the taproom, where we found him having a drink with Wilbur and Daranis.

"What took you so long?" he asked when he saw us. "Daranis got back ages ago."

"It's a long story," I said as I took a seat. Tephi signalled to the innkeeper and he sent a serving girl over with two more tankards of ale.

"What happened to Osin?" Daranis asked once our drinks had been served. I ignored the way the barmaid was looking at him.

"He's now the queen's new bodyguard," I said. "He'll be working closely with Tia." I had to do the talking as Tallis couldn't lie. He was clever enough to be able to avoid doing so, but I didn't want to put that sort of pressure on him.

"That sounds like an interesting story."

"Not really," Tallis said. "It was the only way he and Tia could be together." It was the truth, but lacked a lot of detail. Thankfully nobody asked anything more.

"When's he joining us?" Wilbur enquired. "If we wait around for him for much longer, some of us will be in no condition to ride."

"You could start drinking coffee instead of ale," I said. My suggestion was rewarded with a growl.

"He's not," Tallis said. "I have to take his horse and the rest of his things back to him."

"Before or after we confront my father?" Tephi asked.

Tallis thought about it for a moment. "After I think. He can do without them for a while."

We finished our drinks, packed our bags, then headed off. We didn't need to lead Osin's horse; Tallis told it to follow us and it did.

We all travelled together for a few days. First Daranis left us to take a faster route home, then Wilbur did the same. Both promised to stay in touch. We didn't ride fast; we were in no hurry to reach the palace. I don't think any of us were looking forward to confronting my father.

As we rode, we made plans. It would have been nice to have Osin with us as Tephi wished to speak to Father without him knowing that Tallis was there, but without Osin to Cloak him, that wasn't possible.

Neither Tallis nor Tephi wanted me there, but I insisted and eventually they backed down when I argued that Father would take the news about Rose's death better if it came from me. I wasn't sure I was telling the truth, but it was a plausible story.

Eventually we reached the palace. It had been a long and tiring journey so we decided to bathe and eat a meal before meeting with Father.

We met outside his study. "Ready?" Tephi asked and knocked on the door before I had chance to answer.

Confrontation

Father seemed both surprised and pleased to see us when we entered his study. He stood up and hugged me tight. "I didn't think I was ever going to see you again." Then he looked at Tallis. "Thank you for bringing her home."

"I think you should sit down, your Majesty," Tallis said. "We have something we need to tell you."

Father indicated with his hand that we should all sit. "I should let you know that I have Shielded this room," Tallis said. "Nobody will be able to overhear this conversation."

"That sounds serious," my father said. "What's happened? Did you find Rosemerta?"

"That's what we need to speak to you about," I said. Tallis took my hand and squeezed it. Talking about Rose's death wasn't going to be easy. Father raised his eyebrows in surprise at Tallis's tender gesture, but said nothing.

"Rose is dead." Blurting it out was the only way I was able to get the words to form in my mouth. If I had given any thought to what I was going to say, I wouldn't have been able to speak.

All colour drained from the king's face. "What happened?" he asked.

Between us we gave him the full story. We explained how we found out that Count Gillain ran the cult and that he planned on sacrificing Rose. We told him everything, leaving nothing out except for Daranis's involvement and Tia's true identity. Tephi didn't know about those two things and there was no need to tell my father. The only other thing we failed to mention was the fact that Count Gillain had told us that my father knew what he had planned for Rose and that he gave his permission for her to be taken.

"So Rose died for nothing?" Father asked. He seemed a lot more upset than I had been expecting, bearing in mind that he knew that Rose was destined to die. I nodded my head. My mouth had gone dry and I couldn't force myself to verbally confirm what my father had just said.

We went on to speak about our meeting with Akar and the fact that his father killed him once he had heard what he had confessed to.

"Good riddance," Father said. "If he hadn't executed him, I would have done. I should have done it when he confessed to attacking Olwen."

"You did what you thought was right at the time, your Majesty," Tallis said. "You couldn't have foreseen what would happen."

"You could, however, have prevented it," Tephi said.

I'm sure I saw my father tense. "What do you mean? How could I have prevented it?"

"By not giving Rose over to Count Gillain."

I watched my father as Tephi spoke, but he showed no reaction.

"I don't know what you are talking about."

Tephi and I both glanced at Tallis, who shook his head. My father wasn't telling the truth.

"Let me tell you a little story," Tephi said and narrated everything that the count had told us about the king's involvement in Rose's kidnapping.

"That is preposterous," he shouted, jumping to his feet. "Of course I didn't give him permission to take Rose. I didn't even know he wanted her."

"Would you like to reconsider what you have just said?" Tallis asked calmly.

My father looked at him and shivered. "Don't you dare use your powers on me. I am the ruler in this country and your employer. You have no right."

Tallis remained calm. "Actually I resigned so you are no longer my employer."

"I never accepted your resignation, therefore you still have to do as I say."

Tallis smiled. "I was hoping you would say that." He then took a piece of parchment out of the inside pocket of his cloak and scanned through it.

"This is my employment contract," he said as he perused the contents. "Which you have just stated is still in effect."

He continued reading until he found the paragraph he was looking for. "It clearly states that I can take any action I deem necessary for the good of the kingdom. Finding out just what the king is lying about in regard to the kidnapping of one of his subjects is covered by that. Would you like to take a look?"

"I would," Tephi said and took it from Tallis's hand. "It seems to be in order to me." He held it out to Father, but he refused to take it.

"You wouldn't dare," he said to Tallis.

"Try me."

"If you even think about using your powers on me, I will have you executed."

Tallis shrugged his shoulders. "That's a risk I'm willing to take. Now I will ask again, would you like to reconsider telling us the truth instead of lying to us?"

My father glared at him. His face was red with anger. I don't think he had ever been spoken to like that before. "You will regret this," he snarled. "I will make sure nobody in any kingdom will ever employ your services again."

If his words bothered Tallis, he didn't let it show.

"Alright," my father eventually said as he sank back into his chair. "I knew that Count Gillain wanted Rosemerta, and why. Though I never believed for one second that he would actually go ahead with it. I did nothing to stop him taking her."

"Nothing to stop him!" I said incredulously. "You practically arranged it. Admit it."

Father nodded his head. "Yes, I helped him take her, but it was for her own good. She would have been terrified if she had known what was happening."

Tears formed in my eyes and rolled down my face. I knew that he had been involved, but actually hearing him say the words was hard to take.

"You sacrificed your own daughter," Tephi said. "Why? Did you really want to get rid of her that badly?"

"Of course not. I loved my daughter. I never wanted anything bad to happen to her, but I had to put my kingdom first. The cult was becoming too big, too powerful. If handing over one woman was all it took to keep them out, then I would do it again without hesitation."

"And what if it was two women, or a child?" Tephi asked. "What if it was my child?"

"But it wasn't," Father said. If he was trying to justify his actions, he wasn't doing a very good job of it.

"Where do you draw the line Father? Sacrificing one person is alright, what about ten, twenty, fifty? What will it take next time?"

"There won't be a next time."

"You are not fit to be king," Tephi said.

"I did what any king would do," Father shouted at him. "I protected my people."

"Sacrificing the few for the sake of the many isn't protecting them. You are supposed to look after everyone in your kingdom not send them away to be killed. The fact that Rose was your daughter is irrelevant. She was one of your subjects and you treated her like nothing more than a disposable pawn in a game of chess. You have no right to play with people's lives like that."

"I have every right," Father yelled. He stood up once more and slammed his fist down on his desk. "I am the ruler here and I can do whatever I deem appropriate for the good of this kingdom."

Tephi shook his head at him. "That makes you a dictator not a ruler."

Father stepped from behind his desk and approached Tephi. For a moment I thought he was going to hit him, but he didn't. "Get out," he shouted, pointing at the door. "I don't care if you are my son, nobody speaks to me like that, especially in my own palace. Get out and I will decide what to do with you later."

What Tephi did next happened so fast I almost didn't see it. Or maybe my mind just didn't want me to see it. One minute my father was standing in front of my brother, the next he was in his arms with a knife in his heart.

"What have you done?" I cried out as my father's body fell from Tephi's arms. He was dead before he hit the floor.

"What I had to do." Tephi sounded as stunned by his actions as I was. "Call the guards," he said in an emotionless voice. "I need to be arrested."

"Are you insane?" Tallis hissed at him. "You will be executed for this."

"I know. But it was the only way. Father couldn't be allowed to continue ruling this country. Not after what he did to Rose. Not after he admitted he would willingly sacrifice others. Not after he said he could do whatever he wanted to. There are laws in place for a reason and no man is above them."

"But if you are executed, who will run the country?"

Tephi smiled. "Etain will make a great ruler. Once he has been crowned king, he can change the law to allow him to marry a man."

"You can do that when you are king," Tallis said. "I am not going to let you just hand yourself over."

He knelt beside my father's body, removed the knife and handed it to Tephi. He then placed his hands on either side of my father's head and closed his eyes. Tephi and I remained silent. We had no idea what he was doing.

A few moments later, he stood up. "Clean that knife on your father's clothes," he told Tephi, "then put it away. Then I need you to remove his tunic. And make sure you don't get any blood on you."

He crossed the room and locked the door. "I have to remove this Shield so I can teleport out of here. Don't let anyone in while I am gone and don't say anything loud enough to be overheard."

Then he disappeared. Tephi and I just looked at each other. Neither of us knew what to say. We couldn't even begin to guess why Tallis wanted my father's dead body undressed.

"We'd better do as he says," Tephi finally said. "Tallis obviously has a plan."

He found a piece of Father's tunic which wasn't covered in blood and wiped the knife clean before placing it back in its holder on his belt. Then he set about removing the tunic. I know I should have helped, but I couldn't bring myself to do so.

When the clothing had been removed, revealing my father's naked torso, I gasped; there was no sign of the stab wound. Tallis reappeared carrying a clean tunic from my father's wardrobe, a bowl of water and a cloth. He handed the tunic to me then set about cleaning the blood off the corpse.

As he worked, he explained what he had done. "There was enough life left in the body for me to use my powers to heal the wound. The heart still has a hole in it, but nobody is going to cut the body open to examine it. As soon as I am done here, I will need you two to redress him."

Once his task was finished, he picked up the discarded bloody clothing, the bowl and the cleaning cloth. "I'll dispose of these," he said then disappeared once more.

By the time he returned, my father was fully dressed. There was no sign of blood anywhere, or that he had been attacked. Tallis nodded his approval.

"Now pick him up. We are going to pretend he collapsed and that we have to get him to my workroom as soon as we can. Call out for someone to find Etain as we go."

Tephi did as instructed and I unlocked and opened the door as soon as he indicated that he was ready. He rushed from the room, calling out for help.

"My father just collapsed," he said to the first servant he saw. "Find Etain and send him to Tallis's workroom."

Tallis ran ahead and had the door open by the time Tephi and I arrived. Tephi placed Father's body on the table and Tallis made it look like he was trying to save him.

"What happened?" Etain asked as he ran into the room.

"Father collapsed when we told him about Rose," Tephi said, loud enough for anyone standing outside the room to hear. "Tallis is trying to save him."

I closed the door and Tallis stopped what he was doing. Then Tephi told Etain the truth. He took it surprisingly well.

He placed his hand on Tephi's shoulder and squeezed it. "You did the right thing." Then he turned to Tallis. "Thank you. For everything. Your actions have saved my brother's life."

'So what happens now?" I asked. I felt numb. I had just lost a sister and now I had lost my father. At least I wasn't going to lose my brother as well.

"Give me a few minutes, then Tephi will have to leave the room and announce that the king is dead." Tallis then looked at me closely. "I'll get you out of here as soon as I can. Right now you are in shock. Everything is happening too fast for you to process. As soon as it hits you, you are going to fall to pieces and I would rather you didn't have to do that with others watching you."

He was right. He didn't move away from Father's body to take me in his arms. It was almost as if he knew that the moment he did so, I would lose my self-control.

It felt like hours passed by, but it couldn't have been more than a few minutes before Tallis announced that it was time. Tephi took a deep breath then opened the door. He and Etain went searching for the chief steward and told him the news. Arrangements would have to be made for the removal of the body.

The moment they left the room, I burst into tears.

Ceremonies

Tallis teleported me to my room, then reluctantly left me alone. He had to officially confirm the cause of death. He said it was problems with the king's heart, which wasn't a lie; he just neglected to mention that the problem was that it had a hole in it. He returned to me as soon as he could.

The following few days were hard as arrangements were made for a funeral then a coronation. Tallis teleported us to where Olwen lived with Forn so I could tell her the news in person. We didn't tell her the truth. She took it better than I had expected. She was sad, but not devastated. She was so overjoyed with the baby growing inside her that almost nothing could stop her being happy with her life. I was glad. She deserved some happiness.

Olwen didn't make it to the funeral, nor did Forn. Her pregnancy was causing her to tire easily and she was still suffering from morning sickness, though she called it morning, noon and night sickness as she couldn't eat anything without being ill. She and Forn both decided that the trip would not be good for her. Forn's father attended, to pay his respect to the family and offer his condolences.

The funeral was a sombre affair. Queen Ariana attended, along with her bodyguard. Tallis and I made sure we never called her Tia, even when we were alone. With Tephi's permission, we told them both the truth about my father's death. They understood Tephi's actions and agreed that Tallis had done the right thing by covering it up.

Rulers from all of the kingdoms in the alliance attended, as did nobles from the entire kingdom of Amanet. Akar's father was there, though he avoided me and Tallis. He even managed to not speak with Tephi. He was probably the only person who attended that did, at least that's what it felt like to Tephi.

"If one more person offers me their condolences, I am going to scream," he complained before the funeral had even started.

Daranis also came, though he made sure he stayed as far away from Queen Ariana as he could. She had no authority over him while he was in Amanet, but he wasn't prepared to take any risks.

Tallis's parents teleported in. The palace was so crowded with guests that there were no spare rooms, so Tallis offered them his. He slept most nights in my room anyway.

Simion arrived as soon as he heard the news of the king's death and never left Etain's side. With Tephi's permission, he stayed in Etain's room and was seated next to him for all of the official ceremonies. They got a few strange glances, but nobody questioned his presence.

A few days after our father was laid to rest, Tephi was crowned king. Everyone who came for the funeral, stayed for the coronation.

Tephi's first act as king was to change the law so that same sex couples could live together and marry. No longer would they need to hide their feelings from the public. Etain's wedding date was announced a few days later.

His second act as king was to change the bastard law. Any child born out of wedlock would be officially recognised if the parents later married. The word bastard would no longer apply to his son, and many other children. A lot of marriages were the result of unexpected pregnancies and many members of the public approved of the legal change of status of their offspring.

Less than a week later, Cara and Tephi were married and Kiran was introduced to the kingdom as the next in line to the throne. There was much rejoicing and the masses embraced Tephi's decision to marry for love instead of duty.

After all of the ceremonies, I needed to get away for a while, so Tallis and I went to Sobek with Osin and Tia when they departed. As we didn't have to take much with us, we teleported. I was really getting used to travelling that way.

We had only been visiting with Tallis's parents for a few days when visitors came calling. It was Melantha and her new husband; they had married while we were away. I was a little apprehensive about seeing them, but it went well. Melantha was happy with her new life and was pleased that Tallis and I were in a relationship. She wished us all the best and she gave me no reason to doubt her sincerity.

We also visited Tallis's granny. She was thrilled that Tia and Osin were together. She was never told Tia's real identity, but something told me she suspected there was more to Osin being named as the queen's bodyguard than she was being told. She was a shrewd woman. She knew that Tallis and I were sleeping together the moment we entered her cottage. She spent ages lecturing him on how he should treat me.

Mata, the lizard, was also pleased to see us. He seemed to take a liking to Tia and never left her side. She tried to persuade Tallis to let her take him to the palace, but Tallis refused, saying his granny needed his protection. I had a feeling the argument wasn't over. He did, however, relent and allow her to take him for a couple of weeks, stating that the lizard deserved a holiday. And so did his granny.

The day before we were due to return to Amanet, we were summoned to the palace. We were shown to Queen Ariana's suite, which Osin now shared. Both seemed happy and relaxed when we entered the room, as did General Intep, who was also present. Mata was laying at Tia's feet. We both bowed low.

"Cut that out," Tia said, removing her veil as soon as our escort had departed, closing the door behind him. "Come here and give me a hug. After all, we are family."

I couldn't help grinning as I obeyed her. She and Osin would never be able to publicly marry, but they had held a secret ceremony a few days previous, which we attended, so Tallis was now related to her by marriage legally, but not officially.

"What can we do for you, your Majesty?" Tallis asked her.

"You can stop calling me that for a start. I'm just Tia when we are alone."

"Is that a royal command?" he asked, with a twinkle in his eye.

"Yes," Tia said. "And if you disobey, I will have you arrested. I'm sure Intep will be more than happy to carry out my wishes." She was just teasing him. At least I hoped she was.

"So how can I be of service, Tia?" Tallis asked.

"I need you to contact Daranis. I am ordering him to come for a visit."

Tallis immediately tensed. "You said he would be arrested the moment he set foot in Sobek."

"I know, but there is something I need to talk to him about."

A pained expression crossed Tallis's face. "I'll speak to him, but he may refuse to come. Even if you make it an order."

He sat down on the floor, crossed his legs, placed his hands on his knees then closed his eyes. He stayed in that pose for a long time. When he eventually stood up, his legs had stiffened up and he had to stretch them out.

"He's on his way," he said. "But I did have to promise that he wouldn't be arrested. Please don't let it be a lie."

"He will be allowed to teleport home," Tia said.

A short while later there was a knock on the door. Tia quickly put her veil back in place before Daranis was escorted into the room. He bowed to the queen, then to me.

He seemed anxious, which was understandable. Then his eyes fell on the lizard and panic took over. He turned and ran to the door, but was unable to open it.

"Mata won't hurt you," Tallis said. "Now if I remove my Shield, will you promise to remain in the room?"

"Not while that thing is here."

Osin rolled his eyes. He then bent over and spoke to Mata, who reluctantly got up. He looked mournfully at Daranis before following Osin to another door and leaving the room when it was opened for him.

"So why am I here?" Daranis asked once the room was devoid of reptiles.

"I have a proposition for you," General Intep said. "I had lined up Osin to take over my role as head of the army, but due to his role as personal bodyguard to the queen, I don't think it will be a good idea. He has recommended you."

"I don't see how I will be able to command the army from a prison cell," Daranis said.

"You won't. Queen Ariana has agreed to rescind her orders for your arrest if you agree to the promotion. I don't plan on retiring for a few years, but it would be a good idea to start your training now."

"While I appreciate the offer, I must decline."

None of us needed to ask why. He would have to be based in Sobek and he didn't want his wife to be his slave.

"I think you may reconsider once I have told you of the new law that will be coming into effect shortly," Tia said. "I cannot abolish slavery, at least not yet, but I can change the terms of it. While married couples will still have to have the master-slave relationship, the slave will not have to wear shackles or be naked. They will, however, still have to obey their spouse's commands, in public anyway."

Daranis looked stunned. "Are you saying I will be able to bring my wife here and treat her as a wife not a slave?"

"Not exactly. She won't have the same freedom as a wife in another kingdom, but she will no longer have to visibly show that she is a slave."

Daranis smiled. "That's good enough for me." He turned to General Intep. "I gratefully accept your offer. When do you want me to move back to Sobek?"

"It will take me a few weeks to cancel your contract with your current employer. That should give you enough time to find somewhere to live."

"That won't be an issue," Tallis said. "I have a house that I'm not using. He can live there for as long as he likes."

Tallis had said that Etain could have the house, but now that the law in Amanet had been changed, he had no need of it.

"You're not planning on moving back to Sobek then?" General Intep asked.

"No. I have a contract with Tephi. Sorry, I mean King Tephi. It's going to take me a while to get used to calling him that."

"And that's the only reason for you remaining in Amanet is it?" Osin asked.

Tallis refused to answer.

When we returned home, Tephi organised some remodelling of the palace. He moved into the king's suite with his wife and son, which left his old suite free for Etain and Simion. After their wedding, they had need of the extra bedrooms as they decided to adopt a couple of orphans, a young brother and sister whose parents had died of a sickness which ravaged the city a few years previous.

That left me and Tallis. I could easily have moved into his suite, but Tephi insisted that no princess would live in the guest wing. A few changes were made to my room and those next to it to make another suite.

Tallis began to teach me about healing, continuing what he had started on our journey to Sobek. I was a fast learner and enjoyed it. I would never be as good as he was, as I lacked magic, but I became a competent helper. I began to attend all of his visits with him, even when he went to the whore houses. He even managed to teach me how to thread a needle, so I could sew up wounds, something my needlework teacher had failed to accomplish.

I also started working in his orphanage, teaching the children how to read and do their sums.

We got married in a private ceremony with only immediate family attending. Tephi wanted to give us a full state wedding, but it wasn't what either of us wanted.

Would I have married him if I had known that within a year I would be dead by Tallis's hands? That's a question I will leave until later.

Olwen was still unable to travel, so we went to visit her straight after the wedding.

The journey took longer than anticipated. We were supposed to teleport, but as soon as Tallis took me in his arms and entered my mind, he immediately let go of me and backed away.

"I can't teleport you," he said.

"Why not?" I was concerned that there was a problem.

Then he grinned at me. "You're pregnant."

Death

"How do you know?" I asked. I had no clue that I was with child so how did he know?

He took me in his arms once more. "As soon as I entered your mind, I could feel another presence. You are either pregnant or you have an intestinal worm."

I tried to hit him, but he was holding me too tightly. Then he kissed me. That kiss told me how pleased he was.

"We will have to ride to see Olwen," he said when he ended the kiss. "I can teleport you, but not our baby. No more teleportation for you for the next few months."

He knew that I loved being teleported and would miss it, but right then I didn't care. I was pregnant! I was expecting Tallis's child. I was so excited I wanted to climb to the top of the palace and shout it out for all of the world to hear.

Thankfully Tallis was more sensible and persuaded me that we should wait a few more weeks.

Tephi, however, guessed when he found out that we had arranged for a carriage to take us to visit Olwen. We could have ridden, but Tallis didn't want me doing anything too tiring, including riding long distance.

Tephi congratulated us and promised not to mention it to anyone. It was a promise he didn't keep. Etain knew before we even left the palace.

While the carriage was being made ready, Tallis teleported himself to Forn's estate so he could let them know that our arrival would be delayed. He refused to tell them why, stating only that I would explain when I arrived.

"You had better let your family know," I said as we travelled west, heading to Forn and Olwen's estate. "If I don't tell Olwen and she hears from Tephi or Etain, she will never forgive me."

Tallis agreed and promised to pay them a quick visit while we were with Forn and Olwen.

Olwen was thrilled for us. She was due to give birth sometime in the next few weeks and waddled up to me as soon as I arrived. Once he was sure I was settled in, Tallis departed for a few hours. He went to the palace while he was in Sobek, as well as his parents' house and his granny's cottage. Everyone wanted to see me to make sure he was looking after me properly so he had to promise to get a message to them as soon as we were back home so they could visit.

Our return to Tephi's palace was delayed when Olwen went into labour early. Personally I think she did it on purpose, though I have no idea how, just so Tallis could be there. He was the best Healer she knew and she trusted him completely.

For a first time mother, it didn't last too long and there were no complications. I had to hold her hand and talk her through her breathing because Forn fainted as soon as she started having contractions.

Everyone was exhausted by the time the baby arrived a few hours later. Tallis examined her, announcing that she had the right number of fingers and toes and appeared to be in good health.

"And she has a good set of lungs on her," he added when she began to scream.

Tallis wrapped his niece in a blanket then handed her to Olwen and left the room. The baby quietened as soon as she was in her mother's arms.

"What are you going to call her?" I asked.

"Tulia Rose," Olwen said. "Tulia was the name of Forn's sister who died when she was very young."

"It's a beautiful name," I said as I wiped away a tear which had fallen down my cheek.

When Tallis returned, he had a sheepish looking Forn with him.

"You're not going to tell Tephi about me fainting, are you?" he asked me. "He'll never let me hear the end of it."

"Your secret is safe with me," I assured him. I then noticed the way Tallis was grinning.

"I however," he said, "plan on speaking with the king as soon as I get back to the palace. After all, I do work for him and I feel this is important information that he needs to know."

"You're a bastard," Forn said, but the smile on his face suggested he didn't mean it.

Then he turned his attention to his wife and child. The amused smile turned to one of absolute adoration. He sat on the bed next to Olwen and kissed her on the forehead.

"You are amazing," he said, then gazed down at his daughter. "She's beautiful."

"I think we should leave the new parents alone for a while," I said and took Tallis's hand and led him from the room. I don't think either Olwen or Forn realised we had gone.

We stayed for a few days to make sure that mother and baby were doing well before returning to the capital. The first thing Tallis did when we entered the palace was hunt out Tephi so he could tell him everything. A few days later a letter arrived for him from Forn. Tallis opened it then burst out laughing. All it said was 'I thought you were joking'.

I never did find out exactly how Tephi made fun of his friend, but the fact that he fainted was brought up whenever he visited from then on.

As for my pregnancy, it progressed at a normal pace. I was lucky enough to not suffer from morning sickness at all, nor the tiredness that Olwen had been afflicted with.

I continued to work with Tallis and spent as much time at the orphanage as he would let me. He kept insisting I was doing too much and needed to rest, but I felt fine. His mother visited regularly to check on my progress and to make sure he was looking after me. She brought her husband with her most times. Despite the law change, Balor still wore no clothes. He said that he was so used to being naked that he couldn't feel comfortable without fresh air on his body.

Everything went well until a little under a month before my due date. I felt exhausted and had to leave the orphanage early. Tallis had been administering to one of the sick servants so wasn't aware that I was back until he found me in our bed.

"I don't feel so good," I said.

He leaned over and kissed my forehead, then jumped back as though he had been stung.

"You're burning up," he said. He placed his hand on my forehead, then down my face, then arms. He took hold of my chin and moved my head from side to side, looking in my eyes as he did so. I didn't like the look on his face.

He quickly left the room and I heard him open the door to our suite and shout at whoever he found on the other side that he needed to get a message to his mother immediately. She had to drop everything and come at once.

"What's wrong?" I asked once he was back by my side. I had never seen him so worried.

"You have a fever," he said. "The same fever you had before."

I wasn't sure what the problem was. He had cured me the last time, so why did he need his mother's help this time? It took me a moment to realise why he was so concerned.

"Is the baby in danger?" I asked. My arms instinctively went to cradle my bump.

"From the fever, no. However, what I used to cure you last time will kill him or her."

"No," I said. "No, no, no, no, no. You can't let that happen."

He took me in his arms. "I may not have a choice. That may be the only cure and without it you will die. I barely managed to save you last time."

I began to cry and he gently rocked me.

By the time his mother arrived a few hours later, I was drifting in and out of consciousness. I heard him talking to her, but couldn't make out what they were saying.

I have no idea how much time had passed before I opened my eyes and found both Tallis and Macha in the room. Tallis was on the bed, holding my hand. He looked like he had been crying.

"How are you feeling?" he asked as he brushed my hair away from my face with his hand.

"Not good." My mouth was dry and speaking was difficult. He helped me to sit up and put a cup of water to my lips. He only let a little trickle down my throat and I wanted so much more.

"Are you up to talking?"

I nodded. I didn't have the strength to speak again.

"I have prepared some medicine for you. I need you to take it. But it has to be your decision. I won't force you to."

I shook my head. If it had been harmless to my baby, our baby, he wouldn't have given me a choice.

"You have to do this," Macha said. "There is no other way to cure you. If you don't take it, both you and the baby will die."

I could hear the tears in her voice. "You can have other children," she continued. "But only if you live."

"There must be something else you can do," I managed to croak. Tallis allowed me to have some more water before he told me that there was. He could cut the baby out of me. I was far enough along that there was a chance that it would survive. I probably wouldn't.

"That is not an option," his mother snapped at him.

His voice was filled with pain when he said, "Unfortunately it is."

"You will kill your wife in order to save your unborn child, which probably won't survive anyway?" She sounded horrified.

"I don't know," he said. "I really don't know."

Macha stood up. "Then you have a decision to make and it can't wait much longer. You either have to do the right thing and save your wife or you have to try to save your child."

Tallis didn't look at her as he shook his head; his eyes never left mine. "It's not my decision to make. It's ours."

"Save our baby," I begged. My voice was barely above a whisper. It was taking all of my effort to keep my eyes open.

"I love you," I heard him say and I felt him kiss my forehead. Then I drifted off once more.

I woke up to find myself in his workroom. He was talking to his mother, giving her instructions.

"Are really sure about this?" I heard her say.

"No," he said. "Of course I'm not."

I had no idea what decision he had made and was in no position to argue against him if it wasn't what I wanted. Then Macha was by my side, placing a cup to my lips.

"You need to drink this," she said. "It will help with the pain."

I looked at Tallis, silently asking him if it was safe. He must have understood me because he nodded his head.

"It won't harm our baby, I promise you. You know I can't lie."

I drank a little, then a little bit more. I didn't like the taste and it made me feel even more woozy than I already was.

"It's time," Tallis said. "Ma, you know what you need to do. As soon as the baby is delivered, it's your job to make sure she or he survives. Do whatever it takes."

She didn't sound happy when she agreed.

Tallis took my hand and kissed the back of it. "I'm going to put a Shield inside you. It will hopefully stop you bleeding too much. It will also block some of the pain. I'm going to have to cut you open to get our baby out of you. Then you are going to drink everything I tell you to. Do you understand?"

I nodded. I could feel tears flowing down my face. I knew that it was unlikely that I would survive and I wasn't ready to die. But I had to take the risk if there was any chance of my child living.

"I love you," I said, though whether the words were loud enough for him to hear, I don't know. They were the last words I would ever speak.

Tallis kissed me gently on the lips, then he let go of me. He placed his hands on my swollen abdomen and I felt warmth flow through me. Then I could feel nothing at all below my waist. I tried to move my toes, but I couldn't.

I saw him pick up a knife, but didn't feel him using it on me. I'm not sure if I stayed awake through the whole procedure or not. At one point I'm sure I heard Macha cry out, "She's losing too much blood," but I can't be sure it was real.

Then I heard a baby crying. I have never heard anything so wonderful in my life.

"It's a girl," Tallis said. "We have a daughter." He beamed down at me.

Then a tiny bundle was placed in my arms. I had never seen a baby so small. Or so beautiful. She had blue eyes, the same shade as Osin's, the shade I always imagined Tallis's to be before they turned black.

I can only assume that Tallis sewed me up while I held our daughter, as I felt nothing and could not take my eyes off her to see what was going on around me.

All too soon she was taken away from me. "Drink this," Tallis said and more or less forced a strong liquid down my throat, almost making me choke. As soon as the cup was empty, it was replaced with another, containing something that tasted different.

"I am so proud of you," I heard him say once that cup, too, was empty. "Please don't leave me. I need you."

I tried to promise him that I wouldn't, but I couldn't speak. It was also a promise I couldn't keep. I closed my eyes and never opened them again.

Epilogue

My name is Adara Marie and I am dead. And I wouldn't have it any other way. Tallis made the right decision. He saved our daughter. Despite her small size, she lived. He named her Cyan Adara, after my mother and me.

She is now five years old and I have been there for every moment of her life, even though she doesn't know it. Tallis is doing a wonderful job bringing her up and is making sure she gets a proper education. Tephi and Cara help, treating her more like their daughter than their niece. Etain and Simion are also being more than just her uncles and she gets on well with all of her cousins. Osin and Tia visit regularly and she is a frequent guest at the palace in Sobek. She sees a lot of her grandparents as well.

Tallis has told me he has detected magic in her, though he has no idea what her discipline will be. He hopes she won't be a Sentinel. He's not the only one. He will remain in Amanet, working for Tephi, until she is old enough to join the academy, then he will move back to Sobek so he will always be close by if she needs him. Tia frequently reminds him that she needs a good Sentinel and it's about time he left Amanet so he can work for her.

He hasn't remarried or even shown any interest in any other woman. I want him to, but I know, deep down, that he won't. He still cries himself to sleep at night sometimes.

He talks to me a lot, even when he can't see me. He's trying to find a way for me to communicate with him. He wants to hear my voice again. Though I want the same thing, I wish he would stop. Concentrating on me is preventing him from living his life, but nobody has been able to persuade him to. Everyone has tried.

He didn't handle my death well. I think having a baby to look after is the only thing that stopped him going completely to pieces. It broke my heart seeing how much he was suffering. Is still suffering.

My funeral was a big event, bigger than even my father's for some reason. I wasn't in line to the throne, so I wasn't entitled to a formal state funeral, but Tephi insisted and nobody objected. I was stunned by the number of people who lined the streets to watch my coffin go by.

As is the tradition in Amanet, I was burned on a pyre. Tallis stayed until it had completely extinguished itself, holding our baby daughter in his arms. I couldn't understand why she was there until I overheard my two brothers talking a few hours later. They had forced Tallis to take Cyan with him as they were worried that he was planning on throwing himself on the pyre. I don't believe he ever would, but they were both concerned.

I worried about him for a long time, but not anymore. Though he still mourns me, his life has joy in it. His eyes light up whenever he sees our daughter and he spends as much time with her as he can. He talks to her a lot about me.

I didn't lead a long life, but it was a good one, especially the last year or so. And I have no regrets. Actually, that's not quite true. I do regret that it took me so long to realise how I felt about Tallis and now I can't understand why I saw him as a monster. He is the most kind, compassionate and honourable man I ever met and I count myself lucky that he chose me as his wife.

He still has to occasionally perform his duties as a Sentinel and he hates doing so as much now as he always did, though he doesn't let that stop him. What he does is cruel, but necessary and he saves many lives by using his powers.

Suddenly Cyan stops speaking to her father and looks over at me and I wonder, not for the first time, if she knows I am here. But no, she just heard something that caught her attention. She turns away from me and continues speaking to Tallis. She grabs his hand and leads him away. He stops, turns back to look at me and smiles. He always knows when I am near even if he can't see me; he always has, even when I was alive, and I think he always will.

My name is Adara Marie and this is my story, but it has not ended. It won't until death reunites me with the man I love.

From Trudie:

I hope that you enjoyed this book. Please help others have the same opportunity by leaving a review on your favourite platform.